# SUNSHINE STATE

*Also by James Miller*

Lost Boys

# SUNSHINE STATE

## JAMES MILLER

Little, Brown

LITTLE, BROWN

First published in Great Britain in 2010 by Little, Brown

A CIP catalogue record for this book
is available from the British Library.

ISBN 978-1-4087-0184-3

Typeset in Palatino by M Rules
Printed and bound in Great Britain by
Clays Ltd, St Ives plc

Papers used by Little, Brown are natural, renewable and
recyclable products sourced from well-managed forests and certified
in accordance with the rules of the Forest Stewardship Council.

**Mixed Sources**
Product group from well-managed
forests and other controlled sources
www.fsc.org  Cert no. SGS-COC-004081
© 1996 Forest Stewardship Council
FSC

Little, Brown
An imprint of
Little, Brown Book Group
100 Victoria Embankment
London EC4Y 0DY

An Hachette UK Company
www.hachette.co.uk

www.littlebrown.co.uk

For Hero, with love:
all the best ideas belong to her

Farewell happy fields
Where joy forever dwells: hail horrors, hail
Infernal world, and thou profoundest hell
Receive thy new possessor: one who brings
A mind not to be changed by place or time.
The mind is its own place, and in itself
Can make a heaven of hell, a hell of heaven.

MILTON, *PARADISE LOST*


The mind of man is capable of anything – because
everything is in it, all the past as well as all the future.

JOSEPH CONRAD, *HEART OF DARKNESS*

*The yacht tilted, rocking where it had washed up on the beach. Brittle grey light flooded the coastline, the dawn sky a fragile mask. Two nights of violent storms had stripped the vessel of its mainmast and worn and scrubbed the hull until it was left cast up and grimy as a shore-strewn pebble.*

*A figure appeared on the deck and then another. Unsteady, glad to be alive, seven women and four small children emerged. One after another they jumped into the sea, wading hand in hand towards the shore. Two remained on the boat, carefully passing the children to those standing thigh-deep in the water below. They began to salvage the vital equipment brought for their new life, the tents and medical supplies, bottled water and emergency rations, flares and a shotgun. The more able stumbled back and forth from yacht to beach while the rest stretched out on the sand, too exhausted to be ill any more, gazing apprehensively at the territory around them. The storm had sunk the two other yachts in their convoy and blown them miles off course. They were meant to meet people – allies, comrades who would protect them and give shelter. One of the women began to set up the satellite phone, frowning as she tried to hone in on the best signal. Another stood with the shotgun at the ready, anxiously scrutinising the shore. Beyond the beach, rising ominously above mangrove and palm, stood the fragile skeleton of a luxury hotel, the shorn balustrades and melancholy, moss-entwined gazebos fagged emblems of the former life of the resort: Palm Beach, once one of the most desirable locations in the United States, a closed paradise for the super-rich to frolic far from the concerns of the mundane world.*

*This was it, the virgin territory, the new-found world so long promised.*

*. . . Kalat . . .*

*. . . yes, and they heard it, his name whispered in the tropical wind and in the dark flickering across the midday sun . . .*

# LONDON

Mark Burrows was running through Kensington Gardens, his feet pounding the hard ground. Six weeks without rain had left the park parched. The summer had unfolded hot and slow, smothering London in layer upon layer of exhausting heat. He had watched trees and flowers wilt, grass turn yellow and the Serpentine contract into a muddy grey puddle. In two, maybe three weeks' time, he knew great storms would break, torrential wind and rain bringing fresh calamity from the sky.

All summer he had felt certain something was going to happen. Too much time had passed: enough time to become complacent, to grow lazy, to imagine that everything was over with, that he had done enough for them. And so every morning he ran, the same hard and steady pace, the same fixed expression, his tanned limbs glistening with sweat, his silhouette cutting along the path. He ran as if he did not have a choice. His limbs were toned and powerful, his physique the outcome of much discipline, much pain and persistence. A red cap was pulled low over his shaven head and mirrored sunglasses hid his eyes. Unlike most of the other joggers in the park, he never listened to music and his spartan appearance added to the sense of duty that surrounded the exercise. Each day the same routine: crossing from Exhibition Road into the park, treading the footpath that flanked the Long Water all the way up to the ornamental fountains opposite Lancaster Gate. There was no water in them any more, the white stone overgrown with the same scraggy brown weeds that were popping up everywhere. Another sign of how much everything had changed, the world warping and bending into unrecognisable shapes.

Mark was turning back on himself now, under the bridge and following the Serpentine's slow bulge before heading west once more along Rotten Row. He always finished at the place where he started, pushing himself on the final straight, summoning what energy remained to sprint as fast as possible, almost enjoying the glassy, floaty feeling that seemed to separate his mind from his aching limbs, as if such sensations could erase the memory of other, more keenly felt pains.

Today, as he entered the final stretch, such excesses were not forthcoming. He'd been nursing a stitch since the Serpentine Bridge and his pace slowed to a stagger before he finished up leaning against a tree, gasping and wiping the sheen of sweat from his face. Only seven o'clock in the morning and already the heat was intolerable.

'Hello Mark, I thought I'd find you here.'

Looking up, Mark saw a familiar man wearing a light-blue shirt and khaki trousers. Behind him, parked a little off the road, was a gleaming Jaguar saloon, the back doors open.

'Foxy,' he smiled. 'It's been a while.'

'Always later than you think and sooner than you hope, eh?'

'I'm getting used to it.'

'Look, you had better get in. Something has come up.'

'I'd rather not. I'll just sweat all over your beautiful leather seats.'

Foxy was not joking. 'Come on.'

Inside the car the air conditioning was so fierce that it was like stepping into a freezer. Mark's sweaty back slipped against the seats. Foxy nodded to the driver and they started off.

'Bad news, Mark.'

'Yeah? Do we ever get anything else?'

'We're in deep shit.' Foxy's mouth narrowed with concern. 'We need your help.'

'I thought I was past all this now.'

'I'm afraid we need you with us on this one.' Mark had known Foxy for more than ten years, first as an instructor and a mentor and then, most of all, as a friend. Shared secrets had forged tight bonds between the two men. Despite all the years of their acquaintance, Foxy didn't seem to age. Pickled by the strategies and secrets that had for so long shrouded his life, he had never lost his silvery wave of hair or his deep Tuscan tan.

The car swung round Hyde Park Corner towards Buckingham Palace. They swept through the military check-points, scanners instantly registering their government plates. Along the Mall hundreds of Union Jacks hung from the trees. Sprinklers swung back and forth, rainbow plumes keeping the grass green.

'Giving me the grand tour, are you? Reminding me of my patriotic duty?'

Foxy ignored the comment. 'What does the name "Kalat" mean to you?' he asked.

Mark thought for a moment. 'Nothing.'

'He has another name,' Foxy continued, looking not at Mark but through the window, the only sign of his agitation the faint tremor in his voice. 'Try Charles Ashe, his real name.'

Mark flinched, tried to suppress a gasp. *Charlie Ashe?* It couldn't be. *Charlie?*

'You served with him, didn't you?' Foxy pressed on.

'Of course we did,' Mark said. 'I always thought you were the one who put us together.'

'Charlie had rather more to do with it than you might think.'

'But he's dead, I mean . . . I don't understand . . . He's dead, isn't he? I thought he was dead.'

'We thought so too Mark – we told you he was dead, didn't we?'

He nodded.

'Well,' Foxy sighed. 'It's a right cock-up, it really is . . .'

Mark didn't know what else to say. He felt overwhelmed, a rush inside as if Foxy had just pushed him from a great height. 'Ashe was a good soldier,' he croaked, his throat tight. 'A survivor.'

'Quite.'

'He saved my life.'

Foxy nodded rapidly. He seemed a little annoyed by the remark. 'You see,' he went on, 'this is all rather awkward for us.'

'Awkward?'

'For a start, the chap is dead, or supposed to be. And then, well . . .' Again he broke off, as if it were all a bit much, at once too annoying and too distressing. A great one for protocol, Foxy, a great one for doing things the right way. 'We had intimations that something was up.'

'Intimations?'

'A few years ago we, ah, we intercepted a number of troubling communications.'

'I was never told.'

'Need to know, old boy, need to know. Anyway, it was nothing conclusive, just enough to seed a few doubts and raise a few eyebrows.'

'A few eyebrows?'

'Put it this way, we changed his official status.'

'You never found a body, did you?'

'This sort of thing,' he sighed. 'It's just not done.'

'What about my sister? Does she know that Charlie is alive?'

Foxy shifted, apparently discomfited. 'It's better for all of us, we think, if things remain just as they always were. From your sister's perspective as well, wouldn't you agree? We mustn't open old wounds. No need to cause any unnecessary upset.'

The car had stopped at a traffic light for what seemed an inordinately long period of time. 'Okay,' Mark said at last. 'So where is he?'

'That's part of the problem. It appears Charlie is hiding out in the Storm Zone.'

'Shit.'

'Quite.'

The car went through Trafalgar Square and turned towards the Thames. Buildings arose on the other side of the river drenched in the hot light like the glass and steel ziggurats of a forgotten, blood-soaked religion.

'What do you want me to do?'

Agitation crinkled Foxy's brow. 'There are a few things we do know. We know that he's not alone. We know that he is operating with a number of other individuals, many of whom are wanted by the authorities. His ranks are growing daily, with Americans, Europeans, Latin Americans and Africans. All sorts of people are travelling to the Zone, seeking him out. The Americans have made a number of attempts to dislodge him but they haven't exactly been what we would call, ah, successful. Encroachments on what he considers to be his territory have been fiercely repulsed. The fact is that Charlie – or Kalat as he is now known – is an open secret over there. Everybody seems to know of him but nobody will give us the information we need. It's only a matter of time before this thing gets too big to contain.'

'What about the media?'

'Not yet – thank God – but it won't be long. We do what we can at this end but the story will break sooner or later.'

'And so you think Charlie's a threat to us?'

'No, Mark, not Charlie. Ashe is gone. Our friend is gone. This is Kalat, and yes, Kalat is very much a danger. You know what Charlie was capable of.'

'He was the best.'

'That's right. And now he's no longer one of us. God only knows what he's been doing in those missing years, who he has seen, who he might have been talking to or what secrets he has divulged. Just think who he might have been training. It's a bloody shambles. We all know the Zone has long been a magnet for all sorts of undesirable elements. No one really knows what is going on over there.' The car stopped again at another set of lights. Two men swathed in blue robes moved among the traffic, begging bowls in hand. One paused, trying to peer through the reflective glass. Then the lights changed and they drove on. 'The Americans are very unhappy about all this, very unhappy indeed. They keep trying to get Kalat. Sooner or later they'll succeed. However, we'd rather deal with, ah, with our own dirty laundry. Needs must and all that. Besides, it's not like things are quite the same any more.'

Mark nodded. *Dirty laundry. A bloody shambles.* Hard to believe he was hearing Foxy use such words about Charlie, his old friend, the man his sister had married, the man who had chosen him for this work.

Foxy pursed his lips. 'The Yanks keep a lid on what goes on in the Zone. They pretend they still have sovereignty. The existence of Kalat proves otherwise.' His face was grave. 'There is a state within the state, Mark, a zone within the Zone. A circle of exception exists in the heart of control. It's all falling apart, Mark, the new world order, everything we have taken for granted over the last forty or fifty years is crumbling, evaporating in this damn heat. You know what we stand for. Order and control, remember that, the order necessary for stability, for progress and freedom. What happens over there will happen over here. It's only a matter of time. That's why we need you with us on this one. We can't just go in there guns blazing. That's not the way. We need someone more discreet. You knew Charlie as well as anyone. Try and make contact, talk to the man, find out just what the hell is going on.'

'And then?'

'We'll nip this in the bud.'

'I see. It's like that now, is it?'

'I'm sorry about all this,' Foxy shrugged. 'You do understand, don't you, this will be your last mission.'

Mark raised his eyebrows. He wanted to say, *I've heard that before*, but he kept his peace. Certain things just weren't done. Certain things could not be said.

'You're booked on a flight tomorrow morning. The necessary documents will be couriered over this afternoon.'

'Fine.'

The car pulled up outside his flat. 'Good luck, Mark, and thank you. I mean that. We all do.'

'Goodbye Foxy.'


'You're a little late,' said Alisha as he came in. She rose, resplendent in her purple chador, the silken robe emblazoned with sequinned lizards and dragons, her thighs and waist encircled with their filigree tails and wings. She had braided her short black hair with golden twine and adorned her ears and neck with bronze hoops. Alisha. There was the welcome brightness of her smile, her gleaming eyes punctuating the mahogany disc of her beautiful face. 'How was your run?'

'Not so good. I had a stitch.' He touched her belly through the soft folds of fabric, her warm skin tight with the slight four-and-a-half-month bulge.

'Mmm,' she sniffed at him. 'You're smelly.'

'Like a dog.'

She moved into the small kitchen. 'I just brewed some mint tea. Want some?'

'Please.' He listened to her bustling about. 'How are you this morning?' She never woke up as early as he did. Quite often she was still asleep when he returned from his morning exertions. He didn't mind this, found it comforting in fact, to think of her, safe at home, snug and cool between the sheets.

'I'm good,' she called.

'What about junior?'

'Junior's fine. You'll be pleased to know the Marmite craving seems to be diminishing.' She returned with a glass of tea.

'Thanks.' He took a sip.

She stood back, tilting her head and inspecting him. 'What's wrong?' she asked. 'Something happened, didn't it?'

He nodded. 'I saw Foxy.'

'What?' Pulling her chador tight around her, she went to the window. The power cut out, the ceiling fan stalling, the merciless heat closing in.

'I'm sorry,' he said, but the words sounded shrivelled and lame on his tongue.

'You promised,' she sighed. 'They promised.'

'It's Charlie.'

Her eyes darkened with confusion.

'Charlie Ashe – he's still alive.'

Her whole body seemed to shudder. Her mouth opened but nothing was said.

'He's in the Storm Zone,' he continued.

'What? Oh my God!' She spun round.

'He's . . . They think he's a threat, at any rate.'

'What do they expect you to do?'

'It's nothing really. I mean.' He tried to swallow, his throat dry. 'I need to see him, talk to him, something like that.'

She made a scoffing noise.

'I can't say anything else.'

'Oh no, of course you can't.'

'There will be a more thorough briefing when I get there,' he trailed off. Unsure what else to do he turned to peer through the shutters at the street below. He could see two women, head to toe in burqas to protect themselves from the sun, hurrying along, their black silhouettes cast against the white stucco. Another shudder and the power returned, fans spluttering back to life.

'I've got a good mind to phone Foxy myself,' Alisha kissed her teeth with disgust. 'They promised. You promised. Fuck them. Look at me!'

'I don't have a choice,' he faced her. 'They've done so much for us. They will take care of you, while I'm gone. You don't need to worry.' He didn't even know why he was saying some of these things. Frustration seethed inside and for a moment he was seized by another thought, more troubling than the last: that Alisha had already known this was going to happen, that she had been consulted by them and had given her opinion as to his readiness and suitability. They had used her this way before. She knew him better than anyone and was bound by the same ties. But no, he told himself, it couldn't be – the expression on her face, the flash of surprise, the white

13

jolt of fear – she didn't know. And she loved him. She loved him too much for anything like that.

Alisha shook her head, as if to rub away everything he had said. 'That man . . .'

He wanted to put his arms around her but it seemed far too late, a gesture rendered meaningless by circumstance.

'How soon?'

'Tomorrow morning.'

Somewhere in the city he could hear the peal of a siren. He felt as though they were a long way from anywhere.

For a while they said nothing. Alisha continued to look at him, her brown eyes brimming with hurt and accusation. He felt as if he had struck her, as if he had been forced to strike her.

Then she said, 'Does Susanna know he's alive?'

'No,' he replied. 'And we can't tell her. We mustn't tell her.' He looked at her hands as they cradled her belly, at the elegant fingers adorned with bronze rings. She had the hands of an artist or a princess, he had always thought so, too refined and beautiful for his world. 'You know I don't want this. I love you. I want to be with you.'

'Why do you say these things?'

'What else am I supposed to say? What do you want me to say?'

She turned away from him.

'Please,' he said again. 'It's not as if I have a choice.'

Nightfall brought a low cascade of heat, rumbles of dry thunder and brittle tremors of lightning flickering over the city. Mark went out alone, a purple scarf wrapped around his face, wandering through the Soho spice markets, moving amid the throng, women glinting past in striking psychedelic niqabs, burqas and hijabs, the men clad in long white thobes to reflect the light. Others in the crowd wore silken kurtas, brightly coloured turbans and head scarves, kimonos adorned with jewelled birds and cotton abayas in sunrise yellow and moonlight white or less exotic accoutrements such as baseball caps and sombreros. So much had changed since the days of his childhood, the winter wind in the high places, the cold twilight skies and the promise of snow. Inside he felt the terrible tug of a double loyalty: his obligations to Foxy, his responsibility to Alisha. All that and something else. He knew Alisha had seen it in his eyes and no matter what he might say, she knew it was there, an impatient, restless sort of curiosity, a dangerous pang triggered by a name, Charlie Ashe, alive again after all these years. He remembered the day Charlie married his sister Susanna in the church near the military base. A perfect spring morning, the trees in the graveyard resplendent with blossom. His mother, weak with illness but clutching at his arm with such happiness as the couple gave their vows. Back then, no more than a callow youth, edgy with resentments and drifting away from the stability sought by his older sister, he barely registered her love for this rather remote man. If not for Charlie's intervention, he had no idea where he might have ended up. Charlie had seen something in him no one else had. Had seen it or helped to create it, whatever the difference was. Either way the link was there, a noose that would tighten, hauling him back again and again. The heavy cord of duty, obedience and control.

He crossed Trafalgar Square for the second time that day. Men in fluorescent suits were sweeping up the red dust that had accumulated over the afternoon. High winds brought it across from Spain, scattering it over the city like so much fine confetti. Overhead a silver Zeppelin drifted past, transporting tourists to summer resorts in Greenland. Cameras swivelled and turned. Mark knew they had powerful lenses that could see through his clothes to detect weapons or explosives, and other sensors which would connect with the electronic chip on his ID card instantly communicating to whoever was watching just who was in the square. Well, that didn't matter so much. He had plenty of ID cards, many an alias, enough alter egos to see him through a lifetime of disguise and subterfuge. All in the service of the state.

He slept little that night. He pressed himself close to Alisha, conscious that it might be a long time before they could enjoy such intimacy again, one hand resting on her belly, savouring the faint cinnamon smell and the soft darkness of her skin. Awake and watching the grey light gradually fill the bedroom, illuminating the angles and slopes of her beautiful face, noticing the fluttering of her closed eyelids and feeling the overwhelming sadness of it all. He remembered Ashe and the things they spoke about during their mission in the desert, amid all the blood and the fire, the oil and smoke, the whispers under flickering stars.

Alisha said his name once as he prised himself from her sleepy embrace. 'See you soon, sweetheart,' he said, kissing her forehead.

Outside, a black car was waiting.

# SESSION #1

'Mark Burrows?'

'Yes?'

'Hi. My name is Dr Page – it's good to meet you.'

'Hi.'

'Well now, let me just explain the purpose of this meeting. Your superiors thought it might be helpful, while you are staying here – if we had a little chat or two.'

'Right.'

The doctor sits before him, attentive, her legs neatly crossed and her back straight, pen and paper at the ready, so prim and earnest she could almost be a secretary ready to receive dictation. Her almond eyes blink with intelligence at the slight man sitting across the table. He wears ill-fitting tracksuit bottoms and T-shirt, his skin pasty with confinement and illness, his expression neither shrewd nor absent but something in-between, a mixture of caution and reluctance. Not so much as if he suspects a trap, rather as though he knows the trap is inevitable and that it will close around him regardless of what he does or does not say. An awkward silence and he never quite looks at her. Her immediate impression is that he's not what she had been led to expect, but then she also knows that might be just the point. Legs and arms cross and then uncross. She clears her throat and tries to sneak a smile and for the first time he focuses his attention properly on the young doctor and sits up, consciously or otherwise mimicking her posture.

He speaks. 'Look, I just want to make something clear, okay, I didn't agree to any of this. I thought I was here for my arm. It's my arm that's fucked. I thought that was why they sent me here. I don't see why I should have to see you. There's nothing else wrong with me.'

'I appreciate that but—'

'Yes, yes.' He waves a hand at her. 'I know all about the normal fucking procedures. I don't need a lecture on protocol from the likes of you.'

'Mr Burrows, you must understand—'

'I'm sorry but I don't think you really do understand actually,' he cuts in quick. 'I mean, it's nothing personal, you look like a very nice person, I'm sure you are a nice person and everything, but that doesn't change anything.'

'I'm not here to change anything.'

'So? Are you meant to absolve my conscience, are you? A psychiatrist? Or are you a priest as well?'

'I have a report to submit.' She bites her lip after she says this, her skin flushing a shade darker as if the prospect were somehow distasteful.

'I just don't feel like it, okay?' he replies, shifting in his seat as he speaks. 'Why should I talk to you?'

'Whatever you say or don't say, I will submit my report in either case and they will read it in order to evaluate your suitability for further field work. I understand that your last operation was particularly traumatic and that it may have had psychological consequences. That's why I'm here. I'm here to talk to you.'

He makes a dismissive, blowing noise.

Her jaw clenches, a flex of muscle tightening beneath the skin. 'If it's any comfort, you should know I don't work for the government.' Her nails, he notices, are immaculate, as smooth and shiny as seawashed shells. 'My position is independent,' she continues, 'and my judgement is my own.' He glances at his own fingers, bitten ragged with anxiety. 'How your superiors will act on my report, I don't know. But I have no preconceptions. I don't really know anything about you or your history, what you've done, what has happened to you, anything.'

He shifts again.

'What I like to do is listen. I would like you to talk, to tell me about yourself. How you came to be here. That's all.' She taps her pen against the folder, waiting. A fly lands on the table between them.

'Is this what we do, then?' he responds eventually. 'We just sit here and you look at me with your pen in hand to write down anything of interest that I might say and then tell me it's all about my dead father or whatever? Can't we just agree that's what it's about and save us all a lot of time? I'm sure everything you need to know is in that folder anyway – they already know everything there is to know about me. There's nothing in here,' he taps the side of his head, 'that isn't already written down in there.'

'Mr Burrows, I think you misunderstand. You need not worry about the file. We all have the same interest – me, you, your supervisors – we all want you to get back to work.'

'Fine.' Another fly lands on the table. 'Can I go now?' he says at last. 'Or do I have to stay here for the full hour? I mean, what's the deal? I don't feel well.' He waves the fly away. 'I wish people would just leave me alone.' He makes as if to move but remains seated. Instead she gathers up the folder and, clasping it to her breast, she strides away.

# IRAQ

Mark worked with Ashe at a military base hidden deep in the Iraqi desert, part of Task Force 11, a murky counter-insurgency operation whose strategy had seemed obscure to all involved. He had spent months in training and preparation, an intensive, relentless period in which power had taken him, worked him, transformed him. In the desert, at last, they said he was ready. And for the first time in many months he met Ashe again and there he discovered things about the man even his sister did not know, secrets darker than anything she could imagine.

He remembered finding his brother-in-law reclining in a tent and wearing a traditional Arab dishdash, his head swathed in a keffiyeh. With his deep tan, his short moustache dyed black and an air of studied indifference, Ashe could have easily passed as the sheikh of some obscure tribe. 'Disguise,' Ashe had said – his first words on seeing Mark – 'I'm trying to follow your example.' Mark had been surprised at the lackadaisical manner of his superior, at Ashe's apparent indifference to camp protocols. His behaviour proved to be misleading. Once they entered the field, Ashe became something else altogether. Yes, there had been something relentless and elemental about the man, a barely restrained energy projected from his lean body and face.

Ashe specialised in sabotage. They called him a 'demolition man'. He blew things up. He made precise, nasty little bombs to put in suitcases and handbags or bombs to explode when the target opened a door or sat in a chair. He made devices to bring down buildings and bridges, wreck pipelines and runways, annihilate military convoys, breach fortresses, prison walls or the hull of a ship. Bombs to scatter shrapnel through a crowd or incinerate a roomful of evidence. Strategic bombs like mathematical equations that worked with neat efficiency and messy bombs, indiscriminate and terrifying, to spread horror and outrage like poison in a well.

He took Mark out into the desert. 'Here,' he said. 'Watch this.' His iron fingers set the charge. He hunched over the detonator, every ounce of his being devoted to the moment. Mark remembered the explosion, a blast of fire, ripples in the sand as shrapnel fell. 'That's what I mean,' Ashe said afterwards, his brown eyes shining with a feverish exhilaration. 'That's what it's all about.'

'Does Susanna know about any of this?' Mark once asked, as they camped in the chill night. Ashe shook his head, smiling at the secret intimacy between them. 'She knows I work for military intelligence. She thinks I write reports, manage files, that sort of thing. It's strange, how out of touch with truth women can be. Your sister – she lives in a world of her own. It is too beautiful altogether. That's why we're here. That's the world we have to protect.'

Mark and his sister had never been that close, age and circumstance conspiring to keep from them many of the confidences enjoyed by other siblings. Still he had always understood Susanna to be an intelligent woman, clear-sighted and strong. Sometime before – the precise order or memory was never entirely certain – the three of them had enjoyed dinner in a country pub not far from the Oxfordshire base. Susanna had spoken eloquently of the ideals they were safeguarding – democracy and freedom, the protection of human rights, the necessity of intervention in the face of tyranny and abuse. They had a duty to keep the torch burning in even the most afflicted regions of the planet. When she went to the bathroom, Ashe had winked at him. 'A true believer,' he had said. She spoke of their family tradition, the need to make their father proud, to reward his sacrifice. In these hushed moments of memory he saw his sister as an ardent priestess, a keeper of the flame, her faith indissoluble despite the travails that would assail it.

The agency trained Mark in stealth and disguise. They called him an 'invisible man'. Steeped in the dark arts of the inconspicuous, he knew how to move without being noticed. He had learned certain ways of walking and holding himself, of breathing and looking at others around him. There were ways to attract attention and ways to repel it, ways to make sure that even though people would see him, as he went past, they would fail to *notice* anything about him. Blending in was all about behaviour, about drawing a cloak of anonymity around himself and becoming swathed in the general manner.

On reflection he was clear about one thing only: Ashe saved his life.

He never saw who fired on them, one evening on the outskirts of a shabby, militia-controlled town. He remembered Ashe at the wheel, his foot down hard and the swerve of dust and squealing tyres, the metal thwack as bullets struck their pick-up, shattering windshield and dashboard. Then, as they escaped the immediate danger, the realisation that he'd been shot, the feeling of panic at the sight of his blood splattered on the interior.

Come nightfall and they had stopped somewhere in the desert. Dosed with morphine, Mark remembered lying on the ground as Ashe's strong fingers lashed a tourniquet around his shattered shoulder. He remembered the sky above, a cold wind blowing, the stars flickering like candles in the darkness. He tried to remember what it was they talked about during those long hours. He had the feeling it had been important but the memory was smothered by pain and the expanse of time. Ashe must have talked. Burrows had the memory of his voice – a taut whisper – the sound only, not so much the words, but a sound like the rattle of a metal fence in the desert wind. Sometimes he thought he still heard that voice, like a black edging to his dreams or the furthest ripple of a rock tossed into a great, still water. Sometimes he tried to tell them how he felt but it never did any good. By dawn they had been fighting again, their position rumbled by insurgents, shooting at shadows in the distance. Deliverance came as they were about to run out of ammunition, a dark metal angel dropping from the sky to sweep them from the battlefield.

'You don't work with a man like Charlie, you serve him. You don't talk to a man like him, you follow him. He does what he does and you try to be the best you possibly can.' The scene came back to him now, ten days after his evacuation, his arm stiff and swathed in plaster, enjoying a few days of R&R in Dubai before being shipped back home. He'd been chatting with a couple of operatives from the embassy, the three of them sat around the pool – rather awkwardly in his case – indulging in cocktails and cigars as the sun went down. Ashe had quite a reputation in the agency and so when confronted by the curiosity of his colleagues, Mark couldn't help but add to the legend. All the time, as he'd sat drink in hand, watching the Russian prostitutes and Indian businessmen carousing around the pool, he'd felt guilty, ashamed to be there while Ashe was still in the field, the mission ongoing.

Later, they said he was dead, killed in action.

That was all they told him.

# SESSION #2

Mark sits in a shady corner of the hospital garden, his posture urgent, one leg twitching as he waits.

'I'm sorry about yesterday,' he starts. 'I think I'm in a better mood today. I do understand that it is in my interests to talk to you. I do understand. It is in my interests.' The repetition causes him to suppress a momentary shudder of disgust, the reflex happening so fast most people would never notice.

She does. She wonders what warnings were visited upon him after she left.

Licking his lips, he continues, 'You will see that everything leads up to this – to my being here. It's not paranoia – not that at all. It's the truth, it's my reality.' As he swallows, his Adam's apple bobs up and down like a submerged fist. 'So what do you want to know?'

'Let's start at the beginning, with your childhood.'

'My childhood? Okay, sure. I guess we can start there.' He flinches again, his hands clawing up and down his legs.

'Give me a happy memory, a happy memory from your childhood, something you look on with fondness.'

'If I was to tell you about my childhood, what I remember . . .' he trails off momentarily. 'Okay, well, it's hard for me. These things are hard for me to talk about. But of course that's why you ask, isn't it? I know . . . okay, I know you're not going to let me off so easy. Where to start? I have to go back.' His leg continues to twitch, as if he can pump memory from pure motion. 'I remember one winter, a few days before Christmas, when I was a small boy and it was really cold, like it used to be.' He runs his hand over the faint blue dust of stubble on his jaw. 'I was out in the fields high above the village. The sun was about to set, I remember that, turning the sky all these wonderful colours. It was one of those sunsets, you know, and I remember these thin black clouds stretched across the horizon like the flags of some undiscovered nation and it's difficult now, you see, because on reflection everything seems so fucking ominous . . . those darkening clouds and the way the woods beyond the field turned black in the dusk. I was out there on my own. I used to like to play in the fields by myself, my thoughts rushing like I was the sky and the earth and the cold wind carrying the black clouds, the trees dark and bare branches blue . . . and I was the first star of the night flickering silver. I was all these things, you see. It was easy to lose myself . . .' He shivers and looks away.

'Very good, Mr Burrows.'

'My sister came running up through the field.'

'Susanna?'

'That's right. You know about her, do you?'

'Not really. I just have some facts.'

'You know about Susanna and Charlie Ashe?' She shakes her head. 'The love and now the loss.' He sighs. 'It's hard for her, really it is . . . First our father and now Charlie. It was through her that I met him . . . Anyway, I guess we can come to that.'

'Take your time, Mr Burrows.'

'Okay, so Susanna is three years older than me and back then I guess she was about three inches taller than I was. She was twelve, twelve years to my nine. I remember she came running through the fields to tell me dinner was ready, her cheeks flushed from the cold and her scarf trailing behind her, a red tail in the wind. It was blowing so strong we could hardly speak and the cold cut all the way through our clothes. I used to like that feeling, when no amount of warm clothes could keep out the cold ... anyway ... I guess I could tell you about trekking through frozen fields towards the village, the slate rooftops like icy pools reflecting the sky, the crows calling to one another. It makes me happy, to think of these images, you see, grass shining with frost, ice on windows. I remember our mother in the kitchen preparing dinner. These things, the way the world used to be.'

'Is that what makes this a happy memory for you – the presence of your mother and your sister?'

He hesitates. 'Yes. Maybe it is that, or maybe it was just the cold. We don't often get weather like that any more, do we? I often dream of moving somewhere far, far north, where there is snow on hilltops and the sun is low on the horizon and the air is dry and filled with the sound of Canada geese calling to one another as they fly across the sky. You're smiling. Well. Okay, I'll tell you what I think. Our father was away, you see, he was in the Army, although I didn't really know where he was or what he was doing I thought he was coming back – we all thought he was coming back. That's why. We thought we would see him again and that everything would be okay and of course back then he was still alive and things were still okay. You understand? Of course it was all about to change. Now, I don't know how much of this I knew at the time and how much has come after.' He shakes his head. 'I've lived with it for so long.' His voice cuts out and he looks down. She remains for a few minutes, waiting to see what else he might say, intrigued by the moods that grace his face, the constant shift and flux of an uncertain identity, as if he is not so much a man, rather the reflection of one caught in a fractured mirror.

'How are you feeling now?' she asks.

He shrugs, his expression settling like ash from distant fires.

'I'm not sure ...'

'That's okay.'

'Is it?'

'We can stop now. Well, then, until tomorrow?' She gathers her folder and papers together. As she leaves, she notices his leg has ceased to twitch.

# FLIGHT

His reverie was broken as an air hostess moved down the aisle, serving non-alcoholic drinks. The 747 cruised high above the Atlantic. He took a cup of coffee and nodded blankly back at her perfect smile. In the seat beside him a corpulent, greying executive kept chuckling at the Disney movie he was watching. Some time had passed since Mark had been on a civilian flight. The huge reclining seat and personal entertainment system were a pleasant change from the usual hard benches in a military transport. He noticed the majority of other passengers were American businessmen. Few others could afford the fuel and climate taxes any more.

Mark sighed, anxious to suppress his doubts about the mission. The thought of targeting Ashe unsettled him profoundly. Not so much because of his sister – she had remarried and they did not have much contact these days anyway. No, she had moved on, her faith shaken but in its way still implacable. Her new husband was a bland, affable man called Tom, a solicitor based in Oxford. She had three children now. A full-time mum with two small daughters, his nieces Joanna and Catherine and her son, the eldest, Charles. His nephew was eleven. The poor boy had never known his father. A rather quiet, intense child, he shared the same steady gaze as his father, the same inner confidence and steely certainty. An elsewhere boy, a bit of a loner. Often gone for hours, disappearing across the fields and into the woods to do who knows what. At least that was what Susanna told Alisha. A long time had passed since he had heard her mention her first husband. There was a small picture of him on the mantelpiece above the fireplace, a modest memorial tastefully arranged with a display of fake white flowers. Mark's own situation felt less certain. He was used to going where he was told and doing as expected. He had always understood his actions to be part of something greater than himself, something more important than his own concerns. The agency had a plan. The agency had a strategy more complex than he could comprehend. He had thought it best to put his trust in the constellation of forces that controlled his destiny. The phrases they used to unfurl – *safeguarding democracy, preventing terrorism, promoting freedom* – those grand words and concepts had been something to believe in, to bow down before and make sacrifice to. Like his sister he used to hug those slogans close, let them smother the doubts.

The plane jolted several times, the seat-belt lights flashing. 'Just a little turbulence,' said the pilot over the intercom. 'Praise the Lord, it's nothing serious.'

Mark realised the palms of his hands were sweating. Four hours to go. He stared at the icon of the plane on the map, willing it to cross the great blue expanse. He wasn't normally like this. Years of training had taught him the virtue of patience, the pleasure in waiting, the necessity of calm. That was part of his skill. People sensed fear. If he appeared frightened, he would draw attention to himself. It was the same with everybody.

Another jolt, harder this time, the luggage knocking about in the overhead compartments.

He sighed and tried to unclench his fists. He knew he ought to try and distract himself by watching a movie but these days he struggled to relate to such entertainments. Media drifted across his vision like so much colourful chaff, a buzz of irritating unreality. He almost felt like ordering a drink, if they still served alcohol on flights – they didn't – and if doing so didn't violate the ascetic hammered into his existence: obedience and control, restraint at all times and in all things, except for the critical moment when action became necessity and violence had to be overwhelming.

Eventually the 747 began its descent. As the seat-belt lights came on so the individual seat-facing screens switched to the same film. 'Welcome to the USA' – the words loomed large before a fluttering Stars and Stripes and the opening bars of 'The Star-Spangled Banner'. The screen presented a happy domestic scene, a fit and tanned man in early middle age enjoying breakfast with his two children. The man turned and smiled a famous smile at the camera. Despite himself Mark felt a touch of the benevolence and reassurance that the forty-ninth President of the United States, the Reverend Samuel Parris, was able to project so effortlessly and naturally. He sat in his rustic-looking kitchen, his wife Betty, thrice voted America's favourite 'Mom', her blonde hair contained by a modest blue headscarf, stood next to him, buttering toast for the family. His twelve-year-old son Elijah and nine-year-old daughter Rebecca, both blonde, delightful-looking children, sat at either side of him. Rebecca wore the same sober attire as her mother. Sunlight shone over the family, bathing everything – wooden welcome table, piles of fruit and fresh bread, jugs of milk and juice, plates of waffles and syrup, eggs and ham – in a golden glow, a forgetful radiance that seemed to say, 'Was it not ever so' and 'Could it have ever been any different?'

'Howdy folks,' said the President. 'And welcome to

America, and if you're a fellow American' – he gave a cheerful, slightly cheeky wink – 'welcome home.' Now the President was standing on a neatly trimmed lawn. He wore a simple white shirt and dark trousers, his sleeves rolled up in a way that suggested both informality and industry. A bright white clapboard house, with a huge Stars and Stripes hanging from the porch, was visible in the background. Mark knew – everybody knew – this was Hopewell, the small town in rural Kentucky where the President hailed from and preferred to pass his time – sometimes still preaching a sermon at the modest church where he had served for years – a scene of humility so far removed from the normal trappings of power that his office seemed ever more a miracle, an exception divine, a destiny fulfilled. Still smiling, Parris started towards the camera. 'As President, I'd like to extend my personal greeting to all visitors in our blessed land. As you know, the United States today faces many challenges – the threats against our way of life have never been so serious – but I know that together, as one nation under God, we will prevail against the forces of evil. A new republic is rising from the ashes of the old, a land of freedom and goodness. Out of corruption we bring forth virtue, a new faith, strong family values and an upright, patriotic life. Truly we are the chosen nation. Let the light of freedom shine on us all. God bless America, and God bless you. Let your stay be righteous, safe and happy.' A final shot of the man, his family all around him, a Stars and Stripes on one side, a huge white cross on the other. The President was smiling. His wife waved. To the strains of 'The Star-Spangled Banner', the film faded out.

'We will shortly be landing at New Baptist International, Atlanta,' announced the pilot. The pitch of the engines changed as the 747 approached the runway. 'Oh dear Lord Jesus,' the pilot continued, 'please bless us and this aeroplane. Please banish Satan from the engines, from the controls and the computer, oh Jesus, banish Satan from the wings and the landing gear, banish Satan from the passengers and crew, oh Jesus, guide us and save us and protect us. Hallelujah, hallelujah.' Many of the passengers began shouting and praying at the same time. The air was filled with groans and cries of 'Jesus' and 'Praise be', people rocking and wailing and singing hymns. Mark felt the sweat gathering on his face and under his arms. This was bad, this was much worse than he had expected.

'Thank you, Jesus,' said the pilot. 'Praise the Lord, we are back in America. The local time in Atlanta is currently twenty-one hours ten, temperature eighty-five degrees Fahrenheit.'

'Hallelujah Jesus,' a woman began to shout. 'We call your name and you answer! Hallelujah! You have brought us back to the Promised Land. After darkness there is light. Hallelujah, thank you Jesus!'

'Remember now,' continued the pilot, 'if any of you folks are visiting and you consider yourself to be a Muslim, Jew, Hindu, Sikh, Buddhist, atheist, a practising homosexual or a New Yorker,' the latter comment provoking a round of chuckles from the passengers, 'you will be required to fill out the necessary registration form. On behalf of the crew I would like to thank you for choosing Alliance Airlines.'

They walked down a long tunnel towards passport control. A ten-foot-high statue of Jesus, with blue eyes and long blond hair, dominated the concourse, a Stars and Stripes wrapped around his shoulders. Taking out his passport, Mark moved forward. There was no turning back.

# SESSION #3

'Okay, Mr Burrows, well, we made some good progress yesterday. I'm pleased. Shall we continue?' Dr Page smiles — she didn't smile yesterday — and in his weakness he is swayed by her good looks, the flash of her fine white teeth and the elegance of her legs, neatly folded, her narrow ankles visible above black heels, her skin the colour of sweet cappuccino and her elegant fingers, tapering like candles. It has been a long time, he realises, since he was in the company of such an attractive woman.

'Okay, so I suppose I should tell you about what happened just after Christmas.' Another sigh and he rubs at his head. 'I remember this awkward man came to the door, that's the first thing. He stood there looking sort of embarrassed, like he didn't really understand what he was supposed to do and I recall it was all so incongruous, because my mother started shrieking and fell to the floor as though all this time she had been held up by a cord and now the cord had been cut and suddenly her legs wouldn't support her any more, and I just remember thinking what had this man — who looked so harmless — what had he done to my mother? I'd never seen her like this. I'd always thought she was as strong and certain as the sun and then all of a sudden I realised it must have been my father, something had happened to him. Or maybe it was Susanna who made me realise. I can't remember . . . I guess I remember running up to my room, trying to escape this awful

32

news but of course . . . it was everything. It was everything. It was every-where. Our father was dead, killed by a roadside bomb and that was that. Soon after there were far too many people in the house, that's the next thing I remember, my mother surrounded by a flotilla of women, all of them doing stuff for her.' He sighs, his hands fidgeting awkwardly. 'Fuck, look, I don't know . . . it's weird, there's sort of a haze over these memories.'

'You're doing fine.'

This morning he clings to her smiles. 'Our aunt Lucy, who we never saw, she came to stay. She took Susanna and me to McDonald's for dinner four nights in a row. It was supposed to be a treat but we both knew it was because of what had happened. I still can't . . . I mean, I never went to McDonald's again. I still can't see those golden arches without thinking about Susanna crying and my aunt with her arm on her shoulder saying something like it's a shame or what a shame and that we shouldn't be sad because our father had been such a brave man, some crap like that. Those days people were crying all the time. That's how it seems.'

'Very good, Mark. What else do you remember?'

He makes an empty sort of gesture, as if to seize and release a handful of air. 'I remember going up to sit in my parents' bedroom. It was supposed to be their bedroom, even though my father wasn't coming back any more and my mother had taken to sleeping next door with Susanna. Signs of my father were everywhere – his clothes still hanging in the wardrobe, his books and other things on his shelf – it was weird even to think of the side of the bed where he used to sleep. I remember sitting there and not knowing how I was supposed to feel about it. My father was not coming home.'

'And so your father . . . what do you remember about him? What sort of a man was he?'

'Do I remember him? Do I remember what he was like?' He pulls at the skin around his thumbnail. 'No, I don't remember much, not now. Talk about my father and I think of a white space – a hot white space, like the aftermath of a bomb going off, when your eyes burn and your ears ring and you still don't know just what has happened. That's what I think of, that's all I can think of.' He remains, squinting tight-lipped and sombre in the bright morning sun.

'I know it's hard.'

'It's not that . . .' His words wither and he looks away. She tries another smile but it falters at the edge of her lips. Enough. He has withdrawn, she understands. She will get no more from him today.

# ARRIVAL

Passport control presented few difficulties. Mark had perfected the look of the put-upon businessman and he assumed his most natural and benign expression as the official stamped his passport.

'Have a pleasant stay.'

'I will. Thank you.'

He collected his luggage and caught a cab. It was still raining as he left the terminal and the humid air pressed against his face like a hot flannel. The driver, an overweight African-American, didn't say anything as they drove along an enormous, empty highway. Peering through the window, Mark struggled to get some sense of the city but it remained hidden, only a few lights out there, floating away in the wet night.

Back in London they had given him a false passport with a new name, Stephen Sterns, ten thousand dollars cash and a satellite phone. They gave him business cards and a laptop. He was working for Langton Consultants, a made-up company of course, a front for intelligence operations in the southern states. There was even a fake presentation on the laptop, should he need to prove himself to the authorities. There were other, more useful programmes as well, encryption and decoding devices, a powerful wi-fi link-up and freshly streamed satellite images of the Storm Zone. Mark's own faith in technology was less concrete. Experience had taught him that there was very little he could rely on in the field beyond his own talents.

The driver turned off the highway. Several SUVs blocked the intersection ahead. White crosses and stars, painted on the sides of the vehicles, shone bright in the taxi headlights. Men stood in front. They wore long black coats and wide-brimmed hats. The taxi driver wound down his window as one of the men approached.

'Destination?' asked the officer, shining his torch into the car.

'Holiday Inn, suh, on Andrew Young Boulevard, suh,' said the driver.

'Hmmm.' Mark squinted as the officer shone the torch in his face. 'Where you from?'

'England.'

'Passport.' The man quickly perused the document and then handed it back. 'God be with you,' he said, waving them on.

'What was that?' Mark asked the driver.

'Witch Hunters, suh,' replied the driver. 'Righteous folks.'

'I see.' He refrained from asking any further questions. He knew about the Witch Hunters – the President's personal force of religious police – ruthless Puritans dedicated to the rooting out of corruption and ungodly behaviour. They had more power in the South where the authority of the Church had grown stronger in the aftermath of the storms and wars, the terrible epidemics and economic collapse.

They headed through deserted streets into the central business district. 'Curfew tonight, suh,' said the driver. 'From midnight till dawn. Don't let them fellahs back there catch you out late.'

The hotel was as quiet as everywhere else. After checking in, Mark went up to his room and sat on his bed. Nerves and jet-lag had left him feeling tired and disorientated. In the anonymous room, with its drab curtains and kitsch picture of Jesus above the bed, he felt none of the excitement he used to feel when going on a mission. He turned on the TV, flicking through the channels. Various glossy televangelists were proselytising, healing, exorcising and exhorting viewers to donate money. He watched with little interest, the saccharine blandishments and folksy homilies grating on his nerves. The weather channel reported the continuation of drought across Texas, Arkansas and Oklahoma, floods of blood-red rain in Nebraska and storms of hot hail in the Dakotas.

He set up the satellite phone and made a call.

'Hello?'

'Hi sweetie.'

'You arrived okay?'

'Yeah.'

'How is it?'

They spoke for a few minutes. He said very little. She knew the limits of what she was allowed to ask. Every call he made was monitored. It was necessary to be discreet at all times, discretion and care. He told her how much he loved her. She missed him, she said. He told her to be strong.

The hour was late and he felt tired but he wasn't sure if he could sleep. This was another worrying development. Sleep never used to be a problem. He used to be able to drop off anywhere – in a bus, a car, on a military transport – it didn't matter. There had been a place inside himself where he could withdraw to conserve his energies and calm his fears. These days he found it harder and harder to reach that place.

He turned off the light, lay still and tried not to think about tomorrow. There was nothing he could do. The air con made a faint droning noise. He pulled the sheet over himself, turned over, turned back again. After a little while he realised he was walking in a forest. He moved slowly through the green shade, small insects and butterflies circling in the shafts of sunlight that pierced the canopy. Alisha waved at him from the other side of a river. Swathed in a crimson kanga, she had never looked so beautiful. But the river ran fast, foaming around rocks where they broke the surface. A strong wind blew up. He tried to say something but couldn't – there were so many eyes on the walls. Eyes cut from magazines and newspapers – pairs of eyes and single eyes, eyes in all colours, eyes in black and white, eyes with glasses, eyes hidden by shades, eyes that could see him still. On the other side of a veil a man with cut-out paper eyes where his real eyes should be. 'Kalat,' whispered a voice, hot and close.

He woke like a man floundering underwater. The room was pitch dark and intensely hot. He tried to turn on the bedside light but nothing happened. Stumbling from his bed, he moved to the curtains and peered out. Atlanta was swathed in darkness. The air conditioning had stopped and the resulting silence unnerved him. Power cut, he thought, wiping the sweat from his face.

Pulling on some clothes, he left his room. Emergency lights in the corridor bathed everything in a lurid red glow. The lifts were not working so he walked down five flights of stairs to the lobby. The night receptionist was listening to something quietly on a portable radio. A security guard sat dozing by the open door, an M16 rifle slung over the back of his chair.

'What's with the power?'

The receptionist, a fleshy pyramid of a man, simply shrugged. 'Power often goes off late at night,' he drawled.

'Doesn't the hotel have a back-up generator?'

'Yessuh.'

'Well?'

'Ah'm real sorry, suh. You know how it goes.' The

38

receptionist wiped at his perspiring face. 'Be on again in a couple hours.'

'Okay. It's very hot in my room.'

'Sure is. Sure is hot just about everywhere. We feel the fires of hell before we knows the kingdom of heaven. Say, you not fixin' to go out before daybreak, is you?'

Mark turned back from the entrance. He'd been trying to get a glimpse of the street beyond. 'No, I was just looking.'

'Not safe out. There's a curfew.'

'So I gathered.'

'You don't want them Witch Hunters to catch you. Sweet Jesus, they'll have your ass on a poker before you can say Lord Almighty.'

'Don't worry.' He stood for a moment in the doorway. The rain had died to a sticky drizzle.

At that moment the power returned. 'Praise be,' smiled the receptionist, the air conditioning humming back into life.

'Thanks,' Mark said. 'I think I'll go back up now.'

In his room he opened the curtains, looking out. A bluish tinge touched the sky and he could just make out the silhouettes of numerous buildings. He lay on the bed, trying not to think, waiting for the morning to arrive.

# SESSION #4

'Okay, Mr Burrows, do you think we could pick up from where we left off yesterday?'

This morning her smile does not seem to work. 'I don't feel so good today,' he says. 'I don't really want to talk about those things. It doesn't help and it certainly doesn't change anything. I know they said I should talk to you because they seem to think . . . well, I don't really know . . .' He waves his hands. 'Maybe they feel as though my integrity has been compromised by all the shit that went down over there . . .'

She ignores his comments. 'Yesterday we touched on your father's death. Perhaps we should follow on from that.'

'You mean the funeral and all that?'

'If you like.'

A twitch and a shrug. 'Mostly I just remember my mother crying,' he starts. 'It was a sound like . . . I don't know. An awful sound.'

'Go on.'

'I'd never heard anyone make a sound like that, not then. I know that sound now though, the sound of grief, terrible and raw. I don't remember much else about the funeral. I suppose you'd say I've sup-pressed it. I don't think that's exactly the truth though, not entirely, because this memory is overlaid with other, more recent memories, worse memories in fact . . . much worse.' As he speaks he pulls the skin around his thumb, a tiny blossom of blood christening the cuticle. Realising what he

40

is doing he stops and shifts closer, leaning across the table towards her. His eyes bulge slightly, as if he were holding his breath. He is perspiring so heavily that she can smell him, cloying and masculine. 'We did things out there, in the desert, Charlie and I and all the other Scorpion Men, the other members of Task Force 11. I can't even tell you about these classified horrors. So when you ask me about the funeral and when I think of my mother's grief I see the grief of a hundred other mothers and the sounds they make after a bomb has gone off and they find their husband or their children blown to pieces or burned to death, mangled bits of their children mixed up with other bodies. That's what I think of. What a fucking carousel of horror, I tell you. I mean, what does it matter? My father blown to pieces, my mother's tears and no one was ever the same again, were they? I suppose you'll see all this, my behaviour, all that, you'll say it's some kind of revenge, won't you? To do to others as they did to me. Maybe that's it. Could it be so simple? Do you really think?'

'I'm not saying anything, Mr Burrows.'

'You think you know, you think it's in that folder?' He is standing now, beads of sweat falling from his face.

'Calm down please, Mr Burrows. I'm just asking you to talk.'

'Calm down? What? Am I being aggressive?' His throat feels tight, filled with hot stones he can't cough up. 'Do you find me intimidating? Is that it?'

'Stop it, Mr Burrows – this attitude does not impress me. Cut it out now.' It is her turn to shift in her chair, one hand warding him away.

Rage crumples from his face and he sits back, embarrassed. 'Okay, I'm sorry. I'll calm down.' With the sweat on his face and the rapid rise and fall of his chest, he resembles a runner who has just lost a race, momentarily overwhelmed and exhausted by efforts unrewarded.

'That's better,' she chides. 'I'm not your enemy. I understand these things are hard to talk about.'

'Well.'

'It's difficult, I understand.'

Now his words come more slowly, his voice subdued but certain. 'It's true, in a way, because I don't remember much about the funeral, just tears, people crying.' Another pause, then something occurs to him. 'I do remember these other men I'd never seen before. They weren't relations or anything and they came over, offering words of comfort we seemed to have no choice but to accept. Strange. One of them told me to make my father proud. He had a voice like earth falling on a coffin. Afterwards I remember sitting in my parents' bedroom.' He stops again and looks away. 'A card came from the Queen, another from the Prime Minister and the Defence Minister. Even the leader of the Opposition sent one. Can you imagine? My mother had them on the mantelpiece for a little while. Words in them like 'condolence' and 'sacrifice' and 'bravery', as though any of them knew what the fuck they were talking about. Jesus. For a long time just the thought of it made me so sick and angry.' He gives a ragged sigh, anger and hurt swirling round his face in torrid currents.

'What else?'

'It rained all the rest of the winter, I remember that as well. On the news they kept showing pictures of all the ice that was missing from the Arctic, all these black spaces where there should have been white. At the time I remember thinking my father was lost in one of those spaces and there was no way to get him back. It wasn't just me. The whole world was changing so fast. When I was alone I used to go out into the garden. I could be the grass or the leaves in the trees. I could be the sky or the clouds scudding across it. Already I was learning, you see?' He looks back at her. 'Already I was starting to adapt. You'll see what I mean.'

As she leaves she glances back at him sitting still and staring into the distance, patient as a lizard on a rock.

# MR BRADLEY
# MR MARTIN

Feeling the effects of jet-lag, Mark took a cab to Langton Consultants. Atlanta's streets were sluggish with rush-hour traffic, a choke of enormous SUVs, pick-up trucks and limousines, a glittering parade of dark glass and chrome. Humidity made the air sticky, wisps of milky cloud blocking the sun and blurring the summits of the downtown sky-scrapers. Mark kept glancing up to see if he could catch a glimpse of the Atlanta Eco-Dome. Three years ago President Parris had announced the Eco-Dome programme, proposing the construction of ten thousand vast domes, visionary struc-tures of glass, steel, fabric and silicon to shield major cities from an increasingly inhospitable environment. As the heat-waves, the floods and storms, the plagues of insects and contagion reinforced the popular belief that these were the last days and times, that the Rapture and the Second Coming of Christ were indeed imminent, so the President was com-pelled to protect his electorate – the 'congregation' as he preferred to call them – from the very apocalypse predicted by his campaign speeches and weekly sermons. Only a hand-ful of the smallest domes had been completed, however, and most non-aligned scientists disputed their viability. Mark knew there was no question that the billion-dollar contracts to build these Ozymandian structures were hugely lucrative. He thought he could see glimpses of support structures for the dome, shadowy ribs of steel arched beyond the gloomy sky, as though the city had been swallowed by the skeleton of some impossibly vast fossil, but he wasn't sure, he didn't entirely trust his own perceptions. The haze, the heat, his fatigue, the disconcerting cleanliness of the downtown streets conspired to create an overwhelming mood of insubstantiality and illusion.

He did notice large numbers of state troopers on street corners or sitting in camouflaged Humvees. He clocked their weapons, the strategic value of their positions. The actual soldiers appeared rather aimless, their indifferent postures suggesting participation in a mission they didn't really understand. Other than the troopers and a few African-American panhandlers, the streets were almost entirely void of pedestrians.

Langton Consultants occupied the top floors of a nondescript office block in the Peachtree Center. Mark was familiar with the set-up. He'd seen plenty of similar operations scattered around the globe masquerading as NGOs in Afghanistan, cultural centres in China or English-language schools in Moscow. The offices often fulfilled two functions at once, with the majority of employees having no idea what really went on. A CCTV camera and a pretty receptionist watched Mark as he waited in the lobby, flicking through a copy of *Christian America* left on the waiting table.

'Mark Burrows?'

'That's me.'

'Welcome. Will Corbett, area chief. It's good to see you. Please come in.' They shook hands. Corbett was a fresh-faced man in his mid thirties, dressed in white shirt and khaki trousers. He spoke with the typical English tones of an agency manager, all apologetic polish and no grit.

Corbett led him to a windowless meeting room. Two other men sat around a polished black table.

'Gentlemen, this is agent Mark Burrows. Mark, this is Mr Martin and Mr Bradley. They are overseeing this operation.' The two men nodded. They didn't stand up or shake his hand or give any further acknowledgement. They looked at him with the disdain of fishermen contemplating a particularly unfruitful catch.

Mark stared at them both. Mr Martin retrieved a tissue and dabbed at his nose. With his bleary, red eyes and pasty complexion he appeared to be suffering from a heavy cold. Mark was sure he'd never seen the man before. However, there was something about Mr Bradley, his ruthless, intense expression and the small scar that raised his upper lip by a fraction that stirred a tremor of recognition.

'Take a seat,' Corbett smiled. 'Coffee? Tea?'

'Coffee, thanks.'

Corbett mumbled into the intercom. Moments later a secretary came through with a tray of beverages. No one said anything until she left the room.

'Okay,' said Corbett. 'Now, the mission is codenamed "Casement". This is a category-A mission and I don't need to tell you gentlemen what that means.' He looked at Mark. 'It's like this,' he went on. 'I know you were told a few things back in London concerning a former agent, Charlie Ashe. You worked with him, did you not, in Iraq, right?'

Mark nodded impatiently. Such questions pissed him off.

'Now, you've been selected for this mission for two reasons. First, your primary asset – disguise and infiltration – should allow you to penetrate and move around the Storm Zone with some degree of efficacy. Just as important, however, is your prior relationship with Ashe. We think this should work in your favour.'

'Sure. He's my brother-in-law, right?'

'Right.' Corbett flushed slightly.

'So just what did happen to Charlie? What do you actually know?'

Corbett paused for a moment, rubbing his forehead. 'We all know that Ashe went missing ten years ago, after the Black Hawk he was travelling in got shot down on the Kurdish-Iranian border during Operation Righteous Justice. His body was never found and he was presumed dead, officially.' Corbett coughed. 'Unofficially, however, his file was kept open. For five years we had no evidence to suggest he was alive. Since then, as Foxy must have told you, we've had clear proof that he is still operational. We just don't know who he is working for any more.' Bradley sighed and shook his head as if disgusted by what he was hearing. Corbett glanced at his colleagues, his cheeks still pink. 'In the last five years we recorded apparent sightings in the following locations.' He glanced down at his report, 'Mosul, Baghdad, Damascus, Istanbul, Tangiers and Naples.' Corbett pressed a button and looked at the large plasma screen on the opposite wall. 'We should . . . oh, this damn PowerPoint doesn't seem to be working.' He fiddled with the computer for a moment. 'Never mind. Anyway, after these sightings Ashe dropped off the radar for eighteen months, finally resurfacing first in Haiti and then Jamaica. That was last year. Another agent, codename Augustus, was sent to Kingston to make contact. We were unable to discover whether he was successful or not. The agent's body was found on the outskirts of the city a few days later – he'd been shot in the head. His hotel room was ransacked and key pieces of kit – his laptop and satellite phone – were missing. Assuming Ashe was behind all this, he was able to access our communications, for a short while at least. That might explain how he disappeared again. Finally we have a positive ID in the Storm Zone. Now can I get this damn thing to work?' Corbett fiddled with a couple of buttons until the screen flickered into life. Mark saw a grainy photo, clearly magnified many times, of a man in a white cloak standing on a concrete forecourt. He wore sunglasses and was pointing to something off screen. An AK-47 was slung over one shoulder. Another individual, swathed in dark robes like a Saharan Touareg, stood next to him. 'Okay, so this picture was taken three months ago by a USAF spy drone. The CIA passed the image over to us. They believe Ashe is the leader of a guerrilla group operating within the Zone. At least that's what they are telling us. They claim his group is responsible for numerous offensive actions on their interests. These include the destruction of several pipelines, theft of military equipment and supplies and most serious of all, an attack that left thirty Marines dead, including a three-star general. From what we know of his assets, Ashe is more than capable of such actions.' Corbett coughed and glanced at his colleagues. 'We think, in fact we are almost positive, that there is more which the CIA is not telling us. It's very hard to get information from the Zone that hasn't been heavily filtered by Pentagon sources.'

Martin sneezed loudly. 'Sorry,' he sniffed, wiping the table in front of him with his tissue. 'Part of the problem,' he continued, rubbing his nose, 'is that we don't have anyone in there. We don't have any independent intelligence. Everything we have is second hand, whether from the Americans or the Cubans or other rogue players.'

'I assume this is partly why you want me there,' said Mark.

'That's right.'

'Why doesn't the CIA go after Ashe?'

'Oh, they most certainly are going after him – as you put it.' Corbett nodded. 'That's why we want you to get to him first. If the Americans take Ashe . . .' He shook his head.

Bradley continued. He spoke quickly, his high-pitched voice edgy as if the whole procedure irritated him beyond belief. 'As you know, Burrows, there are plenty of fringe groups operating within the Zone. Some of them are perfectly peaceful but plenty have good reason to attack the military and a few actually have the capability to do so. The American government has never had so many enemies. Quite frankly we're not so much bothered by Ashe's attacks. They're a concern but they're not our affair. But we want to know – who is Ashe working for? What is he doing in the Storm Zone? Are these offences a prelude to something else, something that might affect us more directly? We have a number of hypotheses. First, we think it possible he could be operating for a number of environmental insurgencies – the First Worlders, Green Earthers, Planet Warriors – you know the names, you know the threat these organisations pose to the continuing stability of our transnational systems and the sanctity of our institutions. Many of these groups have a presence in the Zone. He's also been connected to the Queer Liberation Army, although we're not sure of his relationship to the homosexual cause. We also know of several Black Muslim groups out there as well, although there is some debate about how dangerous they really are. Maybe Ashe has helped them become more dangerous.' He shrugged. 'Our intelligence is contradictory. We also know that more people are travelling to the Zone, despite all our checks and barriers and regardless of the hostile environment presented over there. This too is a source of great concern. We don't know what these people are doing, who they might be meeting, how long they stay or indeed when they might return here.'

'Contaminated with God only knows what sort of reactionary ideologies,' Martin added.

'Why the name? Kalat? When did this happen? It sounds kind of Muslim, doesn't it?' Mark asked.

'We're not entirely sure when he took on this new alias. Most likely when he was still in the Middle East, although our intercepts show he was still using other predetermined codenames, as well as his own name up until his arrival in the Zone, which we estimate was approximately twelve months ago,' said Bradley.

'Does it mean anything?'

Corbett shuffled through a pile of reports. 'Kalat was a mountainous principality in Asia. It was founded in the mid seventeenth century but now it's part of Pakistan, Balochistan to be exact. It's a tribal area. There is a Qalat in Afghanistan between Kandahar and Kabul. In Persian the word means "fortress" or "fortified place".'

'Did Ashe go to any of these places?' asked Mark.

'We don't think so. Of course it is possible that he converted to Islam during his sojourn in the Middle East and became radicalised. It is thought that representatives of al-Qaeda made contact with him in Mosul but again we have been unable to verify these reports. We just don't know and we don't like this, not knowing things.' Bradley looked at Mark as he spoke, his gaze as relentless and remorseless as a CCTV camera.

With a sniff, Martin followed. His tone was more subdued than his partner's, the result of his cold or a more general disenchantment with the whole enterprise, Mark could not tell. 'The fact is, Burrows, the special relationship is not what it was. We don't trust our American friends on this, at least not those in the present administration.'

'Joke is if the end of the world doesn't occur during Parris's term of office, he won't get re-elected. Except it's not a joke.' Bradley didn't look as though he laughed much.

'We need you to gather what intelligence you can from Ashe – infiltrate his group if possible – then report back to us and we'll decide what further measures to take,' Martin continued.

Mark shifted in his seat. He felt their eyes on him. 'Don't

you think,' he began, 'Ashe will be suspicious if I just turn up? He'll know why I'm there. You said the last agent ended up dead.'

Martin glanced at Bradley. Corbett coughed again.

Mark took another sip of his coffee.

'It is our assessment,' said Martin, 'that your prior acquaintance will reduce the likelihood of such an outcome. Obviously you must take the measures necessary to protect yourself.'

'My what?'

'Your prior acquaintance.'

'Jesus. Don't you guys ever listen to yourselves?'

'Burrows,' began Bradley.

'Prior acquaintance, necessary measures? Bloody hell, this is Charlie we're talking about. He married my sister. He's my brother-in-law. They had a child together.'

'Technically the marriage was annulled six years ago after—'

'I don't know about this.'

'Burrows,' warned Bradley.

'Look.' Martin pulled out a fresh tissue. 'We understand your anxiety.'

'Bullshit!'

'It's our assessment that—'

'Bullshit!'

'Because of your relationship you have a better chance of getting through to Ashe.'

'He won't kill me, you mean.'

'We see an opportunity for dialogue.'

'As you said, he is your brother-in-law.'

'You know the score, Burrows. We don't make these orders, they don't come from us. You know that. It's simply our job to deliver them,' Bradley snapped. 'And it's your job to carry them out. So stop fucking about. We appreciate the fact that you've drawn the short straw on this one.'

'Yeah?'

'But we also understand that your recompense will be considerable. This is your exit mission. How old are you? Thirty-three? This is the end for you. You'll be out, you'll be free. Don't you want that? A generous pension for the rest of your life and you'll be able to do anything you want. Your girlfriend, Alisha, she's pregnant, right? Think about her. Think about your child. Once this is over you won't have to worry.' Something close to envy flashed in Bradley's eyes. 'You'll be out,' he said again. 'I'm forty-nine. I've given twenty years to the cause. I've got another ten, maybe fifteen before they will let me go.'

'You're a lucky fucking bastard,' said Martin.

'Well.' Mark folded his arms and looked away. 'So? Is that it?'

'There is something else.' Bradley nodded at Corbett.

'We intercepted this transmission from deep within the Zone,' said Corbett. 'The voice you are about to hear is that of Kalat. You'll understand, I think, the extent of his transformation.' He pressed a button on the computer. For a moment nothing – and then a thick, dull, lo-fidelity vibration. 'The sound quality is not good,' Corbett added. 'We've done the best we can.'

They all sat forward to listen to the voice: *'It can be so hard . . . sometimes, to see clearly. Everything is . . . obscured. A veil lies thick and heavy over us all, over the land and in the hearts of men. Even the hearts of the suzerain are obscure to themselves. Masters and overlords of the earth watching with electronic eyes high in the celestial mechanism, even they move as if through a glass darkly, even they cannot see the totality . . .'* A gasping pause, a ragged, asthmatic breathing and then an awkward hiatus. How to describe such a voice? Could he say it was Ashe? Could he say it was even the voice of a man? *Kalat?* A voice whispering in the ether, scratching in the darkness, perhaps not so much a voice even as an echo or a reminder of some forgotten travail. The others watched him, their heads tilted and attentive, Bradley and Martin gaunt in the crepuscular radiance of the dim office light. *'God is here. God is in the smallest things. The indifferent love of God in the smallest particle of dust and the torrent of wind and fire.'* Such a weight behind that voice, such a burden. *'The pain of the indifferent universe . . . two forces locked in perpetuity. They are here. The most insignificant particle contains the whole. Every event contains its opposite. The indifferent love of God. Love. Yes, love.'* Another pause, long and solemn. *'What of love? What of the petty, possessive love of man? We think we can own everything – houses and cars, even each other – illusion, such illusion. Even the rivers and the minerals within the earth, even the oceans deep and the skies above have become a portion for our greed, subordinated before our need to control . . . Illusion. Man cannot own another man. We must see clearly. We must strive for clarity.'* Another pause, gasping lungs wheezing. *'I too have loved. I too have had my portion of that human inheritance.'* The voice changed slightly, a soft sort of crooning, the low keening of a heart that was more than broken. *'Chains of love. Yes, chains of love tied my heart to you . . . chains of love . . . oh, the chains of love that made me feel so blue . . . now I'm your prisoner, what are you going to do? The love of God cannot be of such a petty portion, jealous and exclusive. I reject the jealous God. I reject one heart bound to another. Love is freedom or love is nothing. Selfless love. Love without attachment. Is it possible? A state of grace perhaps, to surrender that portion absolutely to the other, to give and to expect nothing in return. Nothing . . . and yet the veil lies heavy in my soul. Darkness falls, even amidst the brightest of lights. Two forces in perpetuity, delight and obedience, the one forbidden by the rulers of the earth, marked out, packaged and sold and drained of all meaning and the other raised on high to be called "freedom". Man enslaves himself through abstraction. We worship the abstraction and not the truth itself. We follow illusion and neglect the true portion of the divine.'* He stopped and sighed. There was just the sound of the tape, a persistent low-frequency scratching.

'Patience,' said Martin. 'There is more. He takes his time.'

Sure enough the voice returned, a whisper so low Mark found himself leaning close to the machine. *'You know, I still remember, even after all these years . . . I remember the voice of the little girl in the hospital . . .'* The voice seemed to crack and split, like a glass filled with stone. *'Every night, she said, I dream the bad soldiers come and take my daddy away to a place where they hurt him and now all I can hear are my daddy's screams . . . Yes. What will it take for us to understand? That little girl spoke with the voice of God . . . That was the voice of God. It is this Western civilisation that has lost its values and its appeal. Our governments have taken us into this choking life, an unsupportable hell, so that they can keep on ruling with total control. How long will fear, killing, destruction, displacement, orphaning and widowing be the sole destiny of one portion of the world and security, stability and happiness the province of the rest? The time has come to settle accounts. The very matter of the earth has turned against that which infects it. One portion has consumed the whole. Once there was fullness but with our greed we have squandered the heart of the universe and for what? How much more can we take? And you ask what am I doing here? Such is the inheritance of our power.'* Gradually the voice faded, a great weight sinking into inky depths.

'Well?' said Martin.

'What do you think?' said Bradley.

'Do you think it's him?' asked Corbett.

'I don't know.' Mark shook his head. 'He doesn't sound the way I remember. He doesn't sound . . .' He paused, struggling with the words.

'We think he may have gone completely insane,' Corbett said with a dramatic relish.

'Insane, maybe, we don't know. We don't think these words

helpful.' Bradley shot Corbett an evil look. 'Either way Kalat is advancing a very dangerous, radical agenda. We don't like it. We can't tolerate it any longer.'

Martin sneezed again.

Bradley looked at him with disgust.

'I'm sorry,' Martin replied. 'I've got a cold. I can't help it.'

Bradley turned back to Mark. 'If this was just some fringe cult making broadcasts like this, well . . .' He made a flicking gesture. 'But this is Ashe. You understand the severity of this, Burrows, you know what he's capable of.'

'Bring Ashe back to the fold,' said Martin. 'If you can. Tell him we can make an offer he can't refuse.'

'And if he does refuse?'

'We will decide what measures to take, based on the information received. You don't need to worry about that. Just report back to us.'

'That's easy for you to say,' Mark shot back. 'This man saved my life. This man married my sister.'

'And look how he repaid you,' Martin countered. 'Look how he honoured his covenant with your sister. With this. He abandoned her. He betrayed our cause. Remember that if your conscience pricks you so.'

'As for the Americans,' added Bradley. 'You need to play a careful game. It may be that should it come to such measures, we will decide to pass details about Kalat on to them. But until we reach that point you must consider the Americans potential enemies. The CIA, or CIA-sponsored mercenaries and death squads, Klansmen and Witch Hunters, are also operating in the Zone. Many will be looking for Kalat. Should your paths cross it is your duty to do everything you can to hamper their operations. Understand?'

'We have a car ready for you, and a weapon,' said Corbett. 'It will be necessary to leave immediately, I'm afraid. We suspect that US intelligence is aware of your arrival. Our communications are not entirely secure. There are informants everywhere. We need you to drive here.' A map of Florida appeared on the plasma screen. 'This town, Wind City, a border settlement near Lake Agnes. It's a seedy sort of place, a popular crossing point and service provider for nearby military facilities. The town is notorious for its people smugglers. See this guy.' Corbett pressed another button. A tanned, middle-aged man appeared on the screen. He had short white hair, glassy blue eyes, a large, slightly bulbous nose and wide mouth. A small gold cross hung from his right ear. 'Remember that face. We believe his name is Thomas Abraham, although he has many alter egos. He is most commonly known as Johnny Midnight.'

'Right.'

'He's a people smuggler with connections to the Queer Liberation Army. Large numbers of homosexuals have fled to the Zone in recent months – it's that or a stint of electro and hormone therapy in a "deviancy and moral hygiene centre". Abraham is sympathetic. We suggest you pose as a homosexual.'

'Or as someone looking to make contact with a homosexual relative,' added Martin. 'Tell him you're looking for your long-lost brother, your poor, gay brother. It's not so far from the truth, is it?'

'And this guy operates in Wind City? I mean, you can trust this guy?' said Mark.

'Nothing is certain. But he does represent one plausible route for you to take,' Corbett continued. 'Here.' He gave Mark a plastic wallet containing an American passport and a number of other documents. 'We have another identity for you. You're an American. You were born in Boston but you've spent the last ten years living in London.' Mark flicked through the documents. Another name: John Jay. He'd had so many different identities in recent years. He was one person, he was another. Names hardly seemed to matter any more.

Corbett gave him a slip of paper printed with a sequence of numbers and letters. 'This is your pass code,' he said. 'Memorise it. You'll need to give these numbers when you call in.'

He nodded. All this was familiar.

'How's your American accent?' Corbett went on.

'Be an American for us, Burrows. Give us an accent,' said Bradley.

'How does this sound, sir?' he replied, immediately changing his voice. 'More Northern than Southern, I think. I'll get into it. I'm a little out of practice.'

'That'll pass,' nodded Bradley. 'That will do.'

'There is much more unofficial traffic between the Zone and the rest of Florida than the authorities admit,' said Corbett. 'But you have to be careful. The border is a good five hundred miles away. We need you to drive there as quickly as you can.'

Mark shrugged. 'Do you have any idea where Ashe, I mean, Kalat might be? The Storm Zone is a large area. You can't just expect me to wander around until I bump into the guy.'

'Indeed.' Martin pursed his lips tightly. 'Ask on the ground. People live in the Zone, people who know many things we do not. Abraham might know. He's the sort of man who makes it his business to know what's going on in the Zone – who goes in, who comes out.'

'Intelligence suggests Kalat is in Miami, or what's left of the city,' continued Corbett. 'It seems to be the main location for various fringe groups. It's easy to hide there and some parts of the city actually have a semblance of amenities. We're monitoring the situation and will feedback to you as and when.'

'We'd advise you to head to Miami,' said Bradley.

'That would be our professional opinion,' said Martin.

Mark sighed. *Miami.* He had heard nothing but bad things

about the metropolis. 'You can't fly me in? You can't drop me by boat on Miami Beach?'

No one answered.

'We admit, this is a very difficult mission,' Bradley said eventually. 'However, we are confident you are up to it. You won't disappoint us, will you, Burrows?'

'No.' He looked at the table. 'I won't let you down.'

'Very good. Your rewards will be well deserved, I'm sure,' Bradley smiled. 'Now, let's get going, shall we?'

# SESSION #5

Rain this morning so they meet in the conservatory. A man without legs sits in a wheelchair in one corner, headphones strapped across his shaven dome, his eyes closed and his body rocking to the memory of a motion now lost to him. Burrows stands to greet the doctor, perhaps to make amends for his outburst the day before. Her response is more guarded. He notices that she wears dark lipstick the colour of crushed berries and her hair is scraped back in a severe bun. Tight lines ironed in her blouse seem designed to ward off further impropriety.

'I know we are here to talk about me, Dr Page, but I don't even know your first name. What is it? Will you tell me?'

'Alisha.' She allows another smile, mildly amused by his boyish attempts to please.

He notices teardrop-shaped earrings the same shade as her lips and tells her to call him Mark. 'Alisha,' he continues. 'That's a nice name. A beautiful name – do you mind me saying so? It suits you.' Talking to her, he feels something good, a hot glow, like a fingerful of fine whisky that warms from inside out. 'I'm sorry if I'm speaking out of turn. I bet you get a lot of this, don't you, lots of fucked-up soldiers like me. No? Well, I don't believe you for a minute. Still, whatever you think about me, I mean, if you think I'm fucked you should have seen Charlie Ashe. When I think back, I mean . . . what do you call a man like that, who could do the things he did? He was an ice-cold killer, you know, a force of destruction. My God. And my sister married him!' He shakes his head in a pantomime of astonishment. 'Perhaps she's the one you should be analysing . . .'

'Why don't you tell me a little more about your childhood? What happened to you after your father died?'

'Okay . . .' He is more tentative now. 'The years after weren't so good, if that's what you mean. Our father had been like an anchor, keeping us together and without him we just seemed to be cut loose, drifting away in this downward spiral. What's the saying? Going from bad to worse, well that's it, you know, that's the story of the years after. My mother had to sell the house and each place we lived afterwards was worse than the one before. Between the ages of ten and eighteen I think twelve months was the longest we managed to stay anywhere. I lived in Taunton, Portsmouth, Redhill, Reading, Aylesbury, Northampton, Leicester, Oldham, Worcester.' He reels the names off on his fingers. 'All over the place. The only thing I can say is at least I saw some of the country, not that it made much of an impression. My mother seemed to think things would improve and that must have been what drove her on. I think that in a way she felt that if she stopped then the force of what had happened would hit her and she'd break apart. She was trying to keep the family together, trying to hold on to things but what happened had already left her so she could hardly keep a handle on herself let alone the rest of us. It's like . . . oh, I don't know . . . Each year she declined a little more . . .'

The doctor watches his face, emotions wavering in and out of focus. 'Go on.'

'It's only now, looking back, that I realise I was developing my skills, if you'd call them that. I was becoming something that they would know how to use . . .' He gives a deep sigh. 'There are only so many times you can start a new school and encounter the usual playground predators or sarcastic teachers fed up with you because you're the new boy unfamiliar with what the rest of the class have already been taught. And so of course I'd get beaten up, get teased and abused, you know, all that.' She nods, making rapid notes.

'I became sensitive to the mood or tone of a place. Everywhere has its own colour or texture . . . I don't really know how else to describe it, but schools have it, streets and towns, bits of countryside, houses, offices, all sorts of buildings. The world is like a tapestry or a mosaic and every space is different but affected by those around it, the way a very ugly place like a rubbish dump or a prison can blight a whole town. I don't really know how to put it into words, it's more like a smell or a vibe. It can change too, I learned that as well. Judging the mood of a place – at this stage usually just schools or the estate where we'd be living – I would do my best to adapt, to accommodate myself, to blend in and appear like the others. It was a question of learning how to move with the minimum friction to provoke the mini-mum attention. I could suss out the best place to sit in a classroom or the safest spot in a playground. That's another thing, everywhere has a blind spot or a neutral space where you can be . . . if not exactly safe then at least discreet . . . Again, what I'm saying, I mean . . . these words, they don't really get it but there is usually a hiding place in even the most hostile environment. It was all just about self-preservation. I was a real loner, you see, no friends, nothing like that. What was the point? As I said, we moved so often – three, four times a year sometimes. What was the point of making friends?'

'How do you feel about that?'

'How do I feel?' His face twists with contempt. 'Does it really matter?'

'It does to you, doesn't it?'

'Maybe . . . I don't know. What's the point anyway? I don't want to waste my time wallowing in self-pity. I move forward. We like to think we have choices but really we don't. Forces beyond our control condition the way we are, the things that happen to us. A little self-knowledge is the best we can achieve. Listen to me. I'm talkative today, don't you think, Alisha? What's that? Nothing to say?'

'Plenty. But you're the one who should be talking. Tell me more about this method of accommodation you said you learned. What did you call it?'

'I suppose it was an understanding of sorts but I began to turn it into a skill. At the time I didn't realise what I was doing, I didn't see it any specific way. It was just something I did. I would follow someone down the street, for example, and observe the way they walked, if they took big steps or small ones, if they were strolling slowly or moving with purpose, if they looked as if they knew where they were going or not. I'd scrutinise the way they held themselves, if their head was up or down, if they seemed aware of what was around them or if they were lost in their own thoughts, if they looked at other people or avoided eye contact. There are so many attributes you can pick up on. Generally speaking, if you see other people before they see you, they *won't* see you. Sometimes I'd choose a person and mimic them as I followed them down the street. I'd do it so carefully that sometimes I could almost imagine I was them. The more you act like the people around you, the less they notice you, that was another thing I discovered. I didn't want people to see me. I wanted to be everyone else. I didn't want to be myself.'

'You didn't want to be yourself?'

'Is that so surprising?'

'I guess not,' she shrugs. 'What else?'

His legs cross and uncross. Tentatively he touches his injured shoulder. 'I started to do other things too, petty, stupid things. Shoplifting mainly, minor misdemeanours like that. My talent made it easier because I'd worked out how to go around a shop in such a way that no one would pay me any attention. Or else I'd ride buses and trains without a ticket in order to see if I could bluff my way past the inspectors. It used to give me such a thrill, you know, to sit on a train as the guard came along, checking tickets and for him to ignore me completely, because I'd perfected the look necessary to make him think he'd already seen mine.' He snorts. 'I did all sorts of pathetic little tricks like that. Sometimes I'd deliberately take risks – let the alarms go off as I walked out of a store with a load of DVDs or computer games in my pocket – doing it just to see if the security guard would notice. Once I even stood there, alarms bleeping, a stolen CD in my hand and the security guard didn't even see. He ran right past and grabbed some other kid and I just strolled away. It didn't always work. I often had to run for it. I got caught too, ended up with a criminal record, so on and so forth.' He makes a dismissive gesture. 'It doesn't matter now. That was one advantage of the agency. They don't give a shit about things like that. It's all wiped clean. It's all forgotten because what we end up doing instead is so much worse, no matter how bad you've been on the outside, it's nothing, nothing at all … Jesus, Dr Page – Alisha – if you only knew what we did, what we were like, you wouldn't want to help me. You shouldn't.'

She raises a hand, halting his flow. He realises his face is flushed and he can feel the sweat under his arms and down his back. All at once confusion descends and he looks about, helpless and disorientated. Outside rain still falls but he's not sure if that's a good thing or not. She tells him, 'Tomorrow.' Lips like dark crushed berries. Her skirt makes a faint swish as she glides past. In the corner the legless man continues to rock back and forth.

# WINTHROP

Corbett took Mark down into the car park underneath the complex. A bright red Ford Vindicator was waiting for him, a chunky 4×4 SUV with enormous chrome grill and hubcaps. Corbett gave him a black shoulder bag containing the latest Heckler & Koch 45, two hundred rounds of ammunition, shoulder holster and legal permits. In the Storm Zone everyone had a weapon. Mark checked the firearm, loaded a magazine and put on the holster.

'How is it?'

'It's good, it feels good.'

'Well,' said Corbett, awkwardly looking this way and that. 'You've got a full tank of petrol and there's an emergency canister in the back as well. I hope that's okay. You won't have any problem driving this thing. The sat-nav will guide you all the way to Wind City, although it doesn't work within the Zone. You won't be able to take the vehicle beyond the border anyhow.'

'Sure.'

'We've installed a tracker in the vehicle in case something happens. Call us when you reach Wind City. Someone will be down to collect it in a few days.'

'Okay.'

'Well . . .'

'Yes?'

'Good luck. I'm sure you'll be fine.'

'Yeah?'

'We will be in touch.'

'Right.'

They shook hands. Corbett continued to look at him with a curious mixture of embarrassment and envy. He gave a half-hearted wave goodbye as Mark set off.

Driving was easy, the car as comfortable as an armchair, the sat-nav guiding him out of the city and onto the freeway. Traffic was heavy, sixteen lanes in either direction: bulbous Pitbulls and Broncos, dark-tinted Stallions and Mustangs, gleaming Escalades, Vindicators, Superiors, Navigators and Protectors, a sluggish sea of swollen metal and blinding chrome. The air was hazy with exhaust fumes and Mark was soon snarled in the midst of a huge convoy of juggernauts that loomed higher than houses. Fifty miles or so beyond the Atlanta sprawl and the traffic began to thin out, the damp, grey pall that had swallowed the city giving way to gloriously blue skies.

As he drove he flicked through the radio stations. Most of those he could find were dominated by religious programmes, preachers and Holy-Jockeys giving on-air sermons or else banal chat shows and phone-ins on such topics as the best way to pray or how to encourage your neighbours to attend church. The music was a mixture of portentous Christian metal, power riffs and apocalyptic lyrics crudely lifted from the Book of Revelation, or else saccharine pop about waiting for the right man. Driving deeper into Georgia, he eventually found an oldies station playing African-American spirituals and gospel from the last century: *'When Israel was in Egypt's land, let my people go, oppressed so hard they could not stand, let my people go . . .'* The solemn beauty of the music, the voices tracing a heightened, abandoned ecstasy, helped to take the edge off his anxiety. Certainly he found it a welcome antidote to the territory he drove through, a landscape marred by the oppressive demands of a fierce devotion, gaudy mega-churches dropped like shopping malls into the wilderness, vast structures surrounded by acres of parking and huge neon signs adorned with pithy references from the Bible, or else small churches rendered harsh rather than humble with their austere appearance – unappealing metal sheds and windowless single-storey blocks wedged beneath the pine woods, bare as abandoned petrol stations.

As he drove he saw plenty of pictures of the President beaming across the Promised Land from giant billboards and hoardings. Parris in full presidential attire, resplendent against a backdrop of the Stars and Stripes or Parris with his children at a dinner table laden with fruits; Parris in his religious mantle, his eyes closed, a transport of religious ecstasy on his face and a Bible clasped to his breast; Parris the New Testament shepherd, crook in hand gazing benevolently over his flock; Parris at Golgotha, praying beneath a crucified Christ, the saviour rendered as a blond he-man, red blood running over a muscular torso and onto the President's outstretched hands; Parris the resolute warrior in desert camouflage, an M16 assault rifle in his hands, a mosque burning in the background.

*'Let them come out with Egypt's spoil, let my people go . . .'*

The deeper into the country he went so the traffic on the freeway began to change. There were fewer cars, more pickups and trucks. Dead armadillos and black twists of shredded tyre scattered across the tarmac. He overtook slow-moving supply convoys, a hundred vehicles long. Armed guards in SUVs flanked the trucks, assault rifles poking from open windows, country and western music blaring out. The guards would watch as Mark cautiously overtook them, sometimes flipping a bored finger as he went by.

For miles he saw nothing but huge Stars and Stripes, planted at regular intervals along the road, the vast flags fluttering from fifty-foot poles, hundreds of flags, maybe thousands of them. The flags, interspersed with advertising hoardings, towered over the pine trees that flanked the freeway. Nature made a splendid resurgence with mile after mile of dense forest as if the road were pulling him back to the earliest beginnings of the world. Swathes of glorious Georgia pine broken by expansive grassy fields punctuated by the occasional abandoned farm or derelict water tower. But there was little joy in the green brilliance and in such moments snatches of his past came back to him: *how much are you willing to give for your country? Will you serve? Will you devote your life?* All he had ever wanted was a higher purpose, something to give meaning and direction to the empty ebb and flow of his existence. That was all he wanted. He remembered the cold eyes watching him in the dark room, the clock chiming the quarter-hour, the file of papers they shuffled and shifted. He remembered the knock at the door and Ashe coming to greet him, an inscrutable smile on his face.

Here and there he drove past half-finished towns, acres of pastel-bright houses in rustic styles complete with garages and driveways so pristine they might have been built overnight. The odd flag flying from a backyard or front porch was the only sign that anyone actually lived in such developments. He frequently passed more primitive dwellings, trailers and shotgun-shacks with corrugated-iron roofs strung out on dirty yards set back from the road, faintly sinister abodes surrounded by weed and pine, properties smaller and lower than the pick-ups and jeeps parked outside.

Past the outskirts of one town and a portion of the highway was blocked by state troopers. Mark slowed to a crawl, keeping his papers ready for inspection. An overweight African-American preacher stood between the troopers, his round face gleaming with sweat like a polished door knob. 'Bless you, my child, bless you,' he shouted, waving his hands in benediction. Acres of sprawl followed: interchangeable arrangements of fast-food outlets, burger shacks, motels and garages, anonymous retail outlets, slip roads, vacant lots and abandoned construction sites.

He kept driving.

Mark thought about Hurricane Winthrop and the great catastrophe that had brought this embattled new world into being. In retrospect there had been plenty of warnings, Katrina, Dean, Wilma, Felix, Ike and all the other distressing symptoms of a planet in delirium. All his life scientists had been making doomy forecasts about global warming and climate change until the signs were undeniable to all: the annual rise in global temperatures, the degradation of Arctic ice, the retreating glaciers, the floods and droughts, deforestation and desertification, the heatwaves and inexplicable cold snaps. Despite it all no one had taken the necessary initiative, those in power worrying more about economic stimulation than planetary survival, the authority of global organisations crumbling as resource shortages produced an unseemly scramble for strategic control. War had spread like a fever between nations, an ever-growing arc of instability as one country after another collapsed under the pressures of the overheated climate. A catalogue of horrors but no one predicted anything like Winthrop. No one had even imagined it. Now the meteorologists and climate scientists looked back on the storm as a threshold event, a radical break, the moment everyone realised the planet had reached a critical stage. The storm hit America a decade ago, the same summer Mark had been sent into the field with Ashe. He recalled how he had been resting in his Dubai hotel room, recovering from his injury and watching on TV as the catastrophe unfolded. He remembered the satellite images of the storm, an immense white amoeba of wind and rain engulfing the precarious peninsula. No one who saw could forget the final satellite transmissions of a doomed news crew broadcasting from Miami Beach: the pitch-black sky at noon, the wind flinging palm trees like matchsticks, the wall of water racing to the shore, the dark tide engulfing seafront hotels and condominiums, the city dragged to watery oblivion. One of those iconic images of horror and destruction, like the World Trade going down or the mushroom cloud over Tehran, a moment forever seared into the global conscious-ness. After Winthrop the brutal hurricane season continued, multiple storms lashing the United States like the whip of a hysterical penitent. There was no chance for regions to return to normal, the damage was too great and the costs of trying to repair infrastructure each year too high. By the time it was all over, Florida, the United States and in many ways the entire world was left a very different place.

Weakened by years of recession, the federal government lacked the resources for reconstruction. The global economy nosedived, a period of fiscal adjustment to what meteorolo-gists and economists called 'climate shock'. Florida – once the fifteenth largest economy in the world – was now bankrupt and a steady exodus began as millions spurned the Sunshine State in search of a better life elsewhere. Five years after Winthrop the federal government mandated direct control of Florida. A new border was established as the entire area south of Interstate Four, running west to east from Tampa Bay through Lakeland, Orlando and up to Daytona Beach, itself separated from the mainland by massive military defences, was redesignated the Storm Zone, a depopulated and devas-tated landscape officially controlled by the Pentagon and used for purposes of research and training.

The years that followed saw storm after storm rage across the Atlantic, great sky-stalking tarantulas of destruction. Not only were the hurricanes stronger but the season began to expand, with devastating storms possible any time from early June to late November. Scientists began to speculate that the earth might even develop a permanent storm zone, rather like Jupiter's red eye, an area of perpetual instability, sky and sea, fire and wind brought together in continuous conflict. Mark remembered watching footage of Parris, then President Elect, his authority curiously bolstered by the government's seeming inability to cope, standing before Congress to proclaim that God had cast his vengeance on a sinful America. His prayers for forgiveness echoed across the continent.

According to Mark's intelligence briefings, five military camps were established in the Zone, at Orlando, Fort Lauderdale, Naples, Okeechobee and Sarasota, together catering for an estimated hundred thousand personnel. The rest of Florida still existed – Tallahassee remained the capital – although the population of the state had plunged from eighteen million to little more than two million. Even major cities outside the Zone – such as Jacksonville – were ghosts of their former selves, further diminished (like much of the South) by the annual battering of a carbon-charged climate. At first the authorities had assumed few civilians would remain in the Zone. Most settlements, at least those which had not been totally obliterated by Winthrop, were evacuated, while the federal government maintained a number of strategically situated towns, inhabited mainly by private contractors, for their own purposes. Populations became increasingly seasonal, with the majority leaving the area during the summer or else riding out the storms by hiding in underground bunkers.

Mark also knew that the construction of the Zone had other, unintended consequences. Just as hundreds of thousands of Americans fled the ravaged state so others moved in. Like the Wild West of old, there were fortunes to be made in this new frontier. Unregulated by the usual laws, the Zone attracted all sorts of adventurers and fortune seekers. The intelligence he'd been shown mentioned numerous competing groups, many building self-sufficient communities where they would grow their own food and sit out the storms in their own shelters. Some of these groups were tolerated by the military or even existed alongside the bases. But more sinister elements had also been sucked into the Zone's strange field: white supremacists and black nationalists, militant gay rights organisations, exiled Cuban terrorists, narco-traffickers from Mexico, Colombia and Jamaica, cells of Islamic extremists and environmental insurgents. Precise detail was scanty. There were rumours of all sorts of low-intensity conflict: narco-wars for control of lucrative supply routes, bitter ideological battles between fringe syndicates, sporadic flare-ups when the military launched operations on renegade settlements, the constant threat of banditry and pillage by roaming criminal mobs and lone fugitives. Journalists were banned from travelling around the Zone unless embedded in a military unit or under the protection of heavily armed security contractors. The few reporters who defied these rules were not seen again. All the intelligence he'd read and all the satellite projections he had studied on the flight over shed little light. The Zone itself loomed in his mind, inscrutable and implacable, an immensity of mystery that seemed encapsulated somehow by the voice he had heard on the sound file, the ghost of Ashe, the realm of Kalat, presiding over all, whispering to the darkness like a lonely God.

Mark stopped the car on a side road off the freeway.

Late afternoon, the sun low in the sky. He stretched his arms and breathed deep the scent of dusky pine. The air throbbed with the drone of insects and the chirp of birds. For a moment everything seemed good with the world. He savoured the feeling. It wouldn't last.

# SESSION #6

The sun is hot this morning and they sit partially shaded under a large elm tree some distance from the hospital.

'Tell me some more about Charlie. You served with him on your last mission — isn't that right?'

He nods. From this vantage point, if he does not look too hard, he can pretend the hospital is what it was before, a fine Edwardian mansion and that he and the gentle doctor are just friends reminiscing about old times.

'But you first met Charlie a couple of years before? When he and your sister—'

He nods rapidly. 'Susanna had been seeing Charlie for some time before I met him. I knew that she had this serious boyfriend and that he'd been in the Army and was now working for the government in some capacity. My mother told me. She was living quietly in Bournemouth by then. She was . . . she was very ill. But she was happy for my sister, though. At the time . . . I didn't really care. I don't know . . . I was dealing with my own shit . . . None of it is exactly clear in my mind, okay? This was a difficult period for me. I was eighteen, nineteen . . . Looking back I think what a dick I was.' He gives a bashful smile. 'I understand now that I was having what you doctors would probably call an identity crisis. You like that, don't you? Look at you, nodding up and down. Identity crisis.' He scoffs and she writes something. 'I guess what

I mean to say is that I was drifting. I was sloppy and unfocused and I had no idea what to do with myself or who I was or anything like that.' He gives a more thoughtful pause. 'I had no idea of the forces circulating around me.'

She watches a perplexity of emotion traverse his face — fear and guilt, sorrow and anger — such a complex commingling, as if he melts and reforms before her very eyes. Was it really the case, what they had told her about Burrows, that he was a man who could steal upon her and stand so close his breath would touch her face and she would neither notice nor remember?

'What about Charlie?' she starts. 'When did you first meet him?'

He shifts in his seat. 'It was ... um, I think, at a family get-together.'

'And? Did you speak with him?'

'No. Well ... not much.' He shrugs. 'There was no real reason why. I mean, he was twelve years older than me.'

'What was your first impression?'

'Confidence. He had a great deal of confidence. He had this aura of assurance about him. He always did. What I mean is that, you know, he struck me as a real man and I was still a young fuck-up. I remember thinking how strong he seemed — that's one thing — even though he's not particularly big, he's strong, you know. Is. Was.' He checks himself. 'I guess I could tell that Susanna must have felt safe, being with him. He had ...' His hands twitch as if something moves through them. 'His hair was still cut in this short military way and he had very piercing eyes. He seemed to look all the way into me ... me who was so used to being invisible. Of course there was that inevitable awkwardness and I knew Susanna wanted me to like him and what was more astonishing, I remember thinking, was that he really did seem to love her. He wasn't anything like the jerks she usually went with. I don't know what else to say about it really. It was our first meeting so I suppose I should dredge up some deeper significance or meaning but it isn't there. I drank too much at the party and then slipped off and went somewhere else, I can't even remember.' He shudders in contemplation of the person he once was. 'About a year later they were engaged. I didn't see them at all.'

'Why not?'

'I was doing other things and they lived far from me. Charlie was always away, that was one thing I remember hearing. I used to get this from my mother. I never used to talk directly to Susanna about it, we didn't have that sort of relationship. I mean, she'd never confide in me about her fiancé. But he was always away apparently, being sent abroad. It was due to his job.' Another smile as his lips flit with all the ambiguities contained by the word. 'Well . . . I would see him again . . . I would, but the circumstances were very different. I know what you people say about paranoia and that sort of stuff but just you wait, Dr Page – Alisha – when I saw him again, all this talk of power and the forces that shape our destiny and make us who we are, it's not just talk. It's not just talk.' He slouches back, his spirit expiring in a drain of sweat. 'Maybe you know all this . . . in your file.' He is defeated now, and her comforting smile passes unnoticed.

'It upsets you, doesn't it?' she says. 'To talk about Charlie.'

He narrows his eyes at her. 'Sometimes it just gets so . . .' He jabs at his head. 'Up here, you know?' Empty gestures. 'I've had enough now, thank you. Enough.' He gets up abruptly and starts back to the hospital, his walk bent slightly by the bullet that blasted his shoulder, his skinny frame casting an insubstantial shadow across the lawn.

# FLORIDA

The sky grew ominously dark as Mark approached the border. 'Welcome to Florida: the Sunshine State' announced the roadside sign. Barbed-wire fences and bollards narrowed the freeway, reducing traffic to a single lane. On the far side he saw a hoarding covered with a vast mural of the Rapture, the images painted in gaudy, hallucinogenic colours, like a kitsch Hieronymus Bosch. Upwards soared saved souls in a silver cascade to a shining heaven while those left behind tore each other apart against a backdrop of tornadoes and hellish flame. In heaven, swathed in white, Parris beamed down upon them all, a benevolent grandfather with a twinkle in his smile.

Mark worried that the Vindicator's Georgia plates might lead the authorities to question his movements. Traffic was being channelled towards a checkpoint, signs warning drivers to stop. He halted behind a heavily laden pick-up truck and watched as a lone state trooper exchanged words with the driver before waving the vehicle through. A mud-splattered patrol car sat in the side lane. Looking around, Mark couldn't see any other officers. Nonchalant, the trooper wandered over.

Winding down the window, Mark was surprised by the shambolic state of the trooper. A weary-looking man in a faded uniform, he must have been at least sixty years old, with glasses, a greying moustache and a heavy paunch.

'Evenin', sir.' The trooper leaned awkwardly against the door.

'Hi.' Mark eased his face into his most forgettable expression.

'You lookin' to come through?'

'Indeed.' He passed a fifty-dollar bill to the trooper. 'Thanks for your cooperation.'

'Not at all.' The trooper pocketed the note. 'Have a nice evenin', y'all.'

Entering Florida and the damage from the hurricanes became much more evident. Mark drove through an interminable area of forest broken by patches of wasteland and punctuated by trees stark and petrified like stone columns. A grey, powdery sort of dust filled the air and the quality of the highway declined sharply. The Vindicator shook and rattled over gashes and cavities in the tarmac. A secondary highway, fresh and gleaming like an oily black snake, veered off from the first but vivid signs and watchful cameras warned him away. The new road was for military use only.

After an hour or so fatigue took hold. Jet-lag and a lack of sleep lay heavy over his eyes. With few street lights or warning reflectors on the highway the beams of approaching vehicles seemed to sweep and dive towards him. Mark found himself yawning and shaking his head. He took the next exit and turned on to an adjacent strip lined with garages, fast-food restaurants and cheap motels.

He stopped at the first motel he saw, took a room and dumped his bags on the bed. He ran some water over his face and turned on the air conditioning. He lay on the bed and felt the road running through him still. He took out the satellite phone and entered the pass code. He told the voice at the other end where he was. They had no further instructions, no additional information. He toyed with the idea of calling Alisha. He felt the need to hear her voice and whisper words of love to her. But no. He put the phone away. With some effort he went outside, walking back and forth, stretching his limbs. The night sizzled with the pop of vaporised mosquitoes sucked into the lethal blue flicker of a bug-buster. Now and then the rumble of a passing juggernaut on the freeway broke the hush. Other than his Vindicator and a battered pickup the motel lot was empty. The owner was a young Hispanic who sat outside on a plastic chair smoking a cigarette. He raised a hand in weary greeting. Behind the man a silent TV replayed a real-life car chase from the on-board camera of a pursuing patrol car. Round the back was an empty swimming pool, weeds poking through cracked blue tiles. Across the overgrown lawn he saw a children's playground, swings rusting in the hot damp.

Hungry, he crossed the road, heading towards the cluster of fast-food restaurants on the other side. He could feel the heat of the day radiating off the simmering tarmac. He went into a Taco Bell. A Hispanic security guard sat at a table chatting to three older women, each with a small child on her lap.

As he sat down with his meal, Mark noticed a teenage girl lodged in a niche in the corner. He realised that he must be tired to have failed to spot her at once. The girl was not eating and had the look of someone who had been waiting for a long time, slumped forlorn on an uncomfortable plastic seat, a large rucksack occupying the space beside her. Realising that she was being scrutinised, she tensed up, a hand reaching protectively for her bag. Embarrassed and not wanting to scare her further, Mark kept his eyes on his food.

Back in his room he fell asleep moments after undressing.
open and shut
*I'm cold*

flicker

       the wind

             the eyes

Mr Martin and Mr Bradley. Two of them but they kept merging into the same person. They held up a newspaper and then a magazine and then another newspaper, certain words and numbers underlined for attention.

his name

       so many names

in the clinic there was a garden where they let them sit out on a sunny morning

       the wind

*I said I'm cold*

Mark was sweating and breathing hard. Weak light filled the room. He'd fallen asleep with the curtains open. According to his watch, it was a little after six. He sat for a moment, trying to work out what was wrong. His nerves were haywire. Experience had taught him to trust his instincts. Outside he could hear voices raised in dispute.

Peering out, he saw a white SUV on the motel forecourt, engine running.

Across from the SUV three men were standing over the same young woman he'd seen last night in the Taco Bell. Two of them wore baseball caps and denim jackets and the third the pressed white shirt and black-brimmed hat of a Witch Hunter. In his hand a long black stick. The girl was cowering on the floor as one of the men rummaged through her rucksack, tossing out items of clothing.

Quickly he pulled on yesterday's clothes and tucked his pistol into the back of his trousers before striding across the forecourt towards the altercation.

The girl saw him. 'Hey,' she shouted. 'There he is, hey, over here!'

Her tormentors turned round.

All three opponents were in poor shape, overweight and sluggish. The one on Mark's left, with his hands in the girl's rucksack, was very fat, his paunch flopping over his pants. Nonetheless, they were all big men and it would take several good hard blows to bring them down. Other than the Witch Hunter's baton he couldn't see any obvious sign of weapons, but he was sure they must have firearms somewhere. 'What's going on here?' He felt himself tense. 'I've been looking for her,' he started. 'She's my—'

'He's my uncle,' said the girl. Her brown eyes, wide with fear, met his with a silent appeal he struggled to interpret.

'Yes, I'm her uncle.' Mark nodded, trying to grasp her signals. 'I'm sorry if she's been causing a nuisance.' His lips struggled to form his finest WASP accent.

'She been hangin' around here all night,' said the Witch Hunter. 'It ain't allowed. We've had complaints. This a good clean town.'

'Gentlemen, I do apologise,' he dissembled. 'My niece had a row with my brother and she ran away. They don't get along so well. It's always happening. I've been looking for her for the last couple days.' What if they asked him the girl's name? He had to act fast. 'Come now, Jenny, leave these gentlemen alone. What do you keep doing this for? Your father is so upset.'

'Accordin' to her identity papers, her name is Mary Walton,' said the fattest of the three.

'I know.'

'You jus' said her name wuz Jenny.'

'No, I didn't. I said her name was Mary. You must have misheard me. She's my niece after all. I should know.' He fixed the men with his blandest and most inoffensive smile. 'I'm very sorry for the inconvenience.' Out came the wallet and he peeled off three hundred-dollar bills. 'I'll take her back home, don't you worry. As the good Reverend says, the father's law comes first, does it not?'

'And he's a blessed father to us all,' said the Witch Hunter, eyes gleaming as he pocketed the money.

'Don't let us see you here again,' said another, dropping the girl's rucksack.

The Witch Hunter put his face uncomfortably close to Mark. 'Train up a child in the way she should go,' he whispered, 'an' when she is old she will not depart from it.'

'Amen, brother, Amen,' he replied, keeping an eye on the trio as they got into the SUV. He turned to the girl, who was hurriedly stuffing clothes back into her rucksack.

'Let me help you,' he said, picking up a T-shirt. 'They're still watching us.'

'Who are you?' she said, snatching the garment from his hands. 'What you want?'

'I don't want anything. But you don't want to be left here, do you? With them? I'll drop you off down the road if you prefer. Come on.' He took her rucksack and she followed him to the Vindicator. He waved at the tinted windows of the Witch Hunter's SUV. 'Come on,' he said, putting the girl's rucksack in the back and opening the door.

'Ah don' believe this shit,' she said.

'Just get in. Don't make me regret this.' He opened the side door for the girl, trying to keep his movements cool and calm. Leaving the girl in his vehicle, he hurried back into his room, quickly collected his belongings and ran back. He half-expected to find the girl gone but she was still inside, watching him warily. He reversed out of the car park, gave another friendly wave at the SUV and turned on to the slip road. The SUV started after them, following at a distance.

'Motherfuckers,' the girl snarled. 'You'da think they would have sumthin' better to do.' She looked back. 'They followin' us?'

'Yeah.'

'Shit.'

'What did they want with you?'

'Ah dunno.' She squirmed in her seat. 'Shit. Guess ah'd end up in one of them correctional camps for sinful women, if ah was lucky. Somethin' like that anyhow.' She glanced back again and then she said, 'Who the fuck you supposed to be then? My guardian angel? Ah saw you last night. Ah saw you watchin' me.'

'Yeah, I noticed you in the Taco Bell. That's not the same as watching you.'

'Whatever.'

'What did you do last night? You didn't spend the whole night in the restaurant did you?'

'Look, mister, ah don' know who y'are or nothin.'

'That's true. I don't know you either.' He glanced in the rear-view mirror. 'I'm going south, I hope that's okay,' he said, gradually increasing their speed.

'Ah guess.' She squirmed in the vastness of the leather seat. 'How far you goin'?'

'All the way.'

She turned, facing him directly. 'That right? All the way?'

'That's what I said.'

'Hey,' she turned to him again. 'Don' you start thinkin' ah owe you somethin' for this – if you do, ah'll just get out now, right here. Ah don't owe you shit. It was your call, steppin' in like that. Ah sure do appreciate it an such but don't you get no ideas.' She gave a bitter little laugh. 'Don' try nothin', ah'm warnin' you.'

'It's okay. I thought you looked like you were in trouble.'

'Well, you was right about that one.' She made a sniffing noise. She was just a slip of a girl, her small hands dirty after days on the road, a well-travelled smell about her, the dull funk of unwashed clothes, sleepless nights and sweaty days. Dust covered her faded jeans and her lumpy woollen jacket which must have been far too warm for the climate. She also looked exhausted, great shadows under her eyes, her ashen face like snow on a beach. Despite her evident state, she was animated, fidgeting like a young princess dwarfed by a throne. The girl untied her hair, letting the mousy strands escape and drift around her face before wrapping it back up again, tighter and neater than before. She turned one way and another in her seat, constantly glancing behind at the white SUV which continued to follow. Mark also watched the vehicle. After a few more miles the SUV fell behind.

At such an early hour the freeway was largely empty of traffic. They passed a junction and then the SUV must have turned off because Mark couldn't see it following any more. The morning was hazy, milky clouds pressed against the sun like sheets of paper wrapped against a lamp. The glare made everything look flat and sapped of colour, road and wilderness drenched in the same dusty grey. A few more miles and he said, 'They've gone. They must have given up.'

'All right, good, you can drop me here.'

'What?'

'Look. Just drop me here, okay?'

'Are you crazy?'

'No, ah'm not fuckin' crazy,' she shot back at him. 'Drop me here or ah'll get out anyhow.'

'Okay, fine.' He pulled up at the side of the freeway. There was nothing around them, just a monotonous landscape of scrubby bushes. A lone juggernaut sped past, rocking the Vindicator in its wake. 'Are you sure you'll be okay?' he asked but she was already out of the vehicle and slamming the door. She stood by the verge, defiant. 'Fine.' He started off alone.

It was stupid to have picked her up, a major transgression of protocol. What did he think he was trying to achieve? He was jeopardising the entire mission. Why did he even care? He certainly wasn't saving her – indeed, as he tried to tell himself, he was putting her in grave danger. She was at risk simply by being near him. The whole thing was ridiculous and preposterous and he didn't need it, the abrasive smart of an unwanted conscience, as if he could atone for everything that he had done before. Anyway, he thought, it wasn't like he was abandoning her – she had asked to be left there. What else could he have done?

A mile or so down the road Mark pulled over.

*Fuck it.*

He couldn't shake the image of her by the roadside, surrounded by nothing, just waiting until God knew what.

He turned the Vindicator across the dividing verge and started back. There was no traffic and he soon saw her again, only a few feet from where she had been left, sitting on her rucksack and smoking. He stopped and got out.

'Hey.'

'You again.' She remained seated, watchful as a nomad, a trail of smoke punctuating the pale coma of her open face. 'What you want this time?'

'Look, I'm heading south okay. I'm going all the way to the border with the Storm Zone,' he shouted across. 'Maybe I can drop you somewhere. It's not safe, leaving you here. Why don't you come with me?'

'You think ah should trust you?'

He jogged across and stood in the grassy reservation that divided the north- from the southbound lanes. 'You've got nothing to fear, not from me anyway.'

She flicked her cigarette butt in his direction

'Well?'

She turned away, gazing at the horizon as if willing some manifestation of deliverance to appear.

'It's nice and cool in the car,' he added. 'What you going to do out here?'

'When you say the border, what you mean? Orlando?'

He shrugged. 'Thereabouts. I'm going to Wind City.'

'Really?'

'I can drop you somewhere else if you like but I've got to get there soon.'

'You ever bin there?'

He shook his head.

'Me neither. It ain't a good place. That's what ah heard.' She looked at him again, her hazel eyes steely with an experience that belied her years.

'Yeah . . . well,' he sighed. 'I don't care about that.'

'Okay,' she stood up. 'Wind City is good for me too.'

'We're on then?'

'S'pose.'

'Do you want me to get your bag?'

'It's okay.' She crossed the road towards him.

'You didn't really want to be left out here, did you?' he said, trying to smile at her as they approached the Vindicator.

'Ah ain't sayin' that ah trust you,' she glared, getting back inside.

Mark started up and they turned back across the reservation.

'It was gettin' kinda hot out there,' she admitted, dabbing her face and turning up the air con.

'No shit.'

The girl gave a weary sigh, as though the day had been too much already and then, leaning towards him, she asked, 'So what's your name?'

'I'm . . . John. Call me John.' If nothing else, he thought, he had an opportunity to practise his accent. 'And you're Mary.'

'Nice to meet you, John, ah guess ah should thank you.'

'Don't worry about it.'

'That was a good trick you pulled back there, with the

name,' she began. 'Ah thought they'd busted us.'

Mark found himself smiling. 'It's all about presentation, persuasion, tone of voice. You can make people believe anything if you say it right and look at them the right way.'

She didn't seem to pay much attention to what he said. 'Ah thought ah was never goin' to get outta that shithole. Hey, can ah smoke?' She produced a cigarette.

'Go for it. Just open the window.'

'You don' smoke?'

'Not any more. Not for a long time.'

'D'you still wan' to?'

He shrugged. 'Sometimes.'

'Ah know ah shouldn't, ah really shouldn't. Actually, ah won't.' She put the packet away. 'Goddamn.' She put her feet up on the dashboard.

'Where are you from?' he asked after a little while.

'Just some shithole.' She made a dismissive gesture with her hand. 'Nowhere you'da heard of or want to visit.' She produced her cigarettes again. 'Actually ah'm goin' to have one a these. Don't worry ah'll open the window.' She smoked with a furious sort of intensity, as if gulping water. 'So what 'bout you? Where you live?'

'Boston.'

'Where'bouts?'

'Oh, you know,' he shrugged. 'Beacon Hill.'

She considered his answer. 'You don' sound like no American to me. You don' even look American.'

'Don't I?' He felt himself flush.

She gave a little laugh. 'Shit man, don' look so pissed. Ah'm jus teasin' you. What you goin' down south for? Why don' you stay up in Boston? Things ain't so bad there, that's what ah hear.'

'Well,' he shrugged again. 'Can't really say.'

She gave another little laugh and tossed her butt out of the

84

window. 'Ain't we just a right pair of mysterious motherfuck-ers.' She shook her head and made a whistling noise through her teeth. 'You married?' she asked after a little while.

He shook his head.

'You queer? That why you goin' south?'

He laughed. 'That's it, that's right.'

'You ain't queer.'

'No? How do you know?'

'Ah just reckon.'

'How old are you, Mary?'

'That's none of your business, Mr John, or whatever you want to call yuhself.'

'Seventeen, eighteen?'

'Fuck off!'

'Okay, how old do you think I am?'

'Older than me, that's for sure.'

He smiled again. 'So,' he asked, after a short while, 'Wind City, why do you want to go there? What are you even doing out on the road like this?'

'It's a story. That's all ah can say. That's all ah'm goin' t' say. Ah don' even know you. Anyway ah don' care. The road ain't no more dangerous than back home.' She took out another cigarette. 'Ain't no different, not as far as I'm concerned.'

'What about your parents? Aren't they worried about you?'

She shook her head in disgust. 'Ain't no one back home but my daddy an' he can go to hell.' She lit up.

'You running away from home, that it?'

'Not exactly.' She shrugged.

'Why Wind City? I mean, why not California or somewhere like that?'

She made a shucking noise. 'Man, you sure are naive.'

'Yeah? Can't remember the last time anyone called me naive. Especially not a seventeen-year-old.'

'There's somethin' ah need down there. That's all ah can say.' She turned away, gazing studiously out the window and smoking hard. Then, apparently thinking of something, she asked, 'So you jus' plannin' on goin' to Wind City or you crossin' into the Zone?'

'Why would I want to do that?'

'Dunno. Ah thought 'bout doin' it.'

'No shit.'

'F'real. Loads of people cross over.'

'You know anyone?'

'Ah got friends that done it.'

'I heard it was very dangerous.'

'True.' She tensed her lips. 'But it's dangerous jus' 'bout everywhere. My friends, they live in this small village in the Zone an' they say it's real nice. They grow jus' bout everything they need. They ain't got to worry 'bout police or Witch Hunters or Church tithes. Nuthin' like that to bother them.'

'Nothing eh?'

'That's what I hear.'

The miles went by. They lapsed into a companionable if not entirely comfortable silence. Mark did his best to put the girl's concerns from his mind and concentrate on driving. His actions had left him feeling perplexed. It made no sense, picking up this stray. What was he trying to prove – that something good could be salvaged from the mission? That he could save life as well as take it? Did he just want someone to talk to? Even that was a strange feeling. He could go days, even weeks, back in England without having a proper conversation with anyone apart from Alisha, although she had told him many times it was unhealthy. Withdrawn, that was what she said. He was too withdrawn, too cut off from everything. He didn't know about that. Most of the time it made no sense to reach out to anyone anyway.

The highway deteriorated, clouds of dust and gravel

blown up from the broken surface forcing Mark to slow to twenty miles an hour and steer carefully to avoid the larger potholes. A procession of wretched people appeared out of the murk, most of them dressed in torn robes and cowls and others naked apart from loincloths and sandals. He saw some bent double beneath the weight of the huge crosses they carried on their backs, their skin burned by the fierce sun and others lashing themselves with leather whips and metal chains, their backs bloody and raw. He slowed right down, steering carefully. Some were crawling along the hard ground, dragging their bodies over the stones while others went wandering with eyes bound with strips of cloth or faces covered by leather masks, shuffling forward hands on shoulders one after the other in a macabre cancan. Amid the forlorn group he saw infants strapped to the backs of weary mothers or trailing behind parents, their limbs tanned and dirty, their hair matted with grime. Oblivious to the passing traffic, the wanderers seemed set on some path unknowable.

'Apocalyptics,' Mary said, shaking her head. 'Headin' for the next storm. They love it. They can't wait.'

Mark was surprised at how much the spectacle had shocked him. He had seen similar scenes of despair in the blasted and broken reaches of the globe but it was deeply unnerving to be confronted by a faith so degraded and fanatical in the United States. He almost said something about it to Mary but she appeared insulated by the indifference of youth, humming a quiet tune to herself as she gazed out of the window.

Deeper into Florida and Mark couldn't help but notice how most of the traffic they saw was heading north, out of the state. For miles they drove through a vague nothingness, a desert of neglected fields and unclaimed scrub, a non-place that seemed neither part of nature nor man. Dotting the land-scape, like the misplaced punctuation marks of civilisation, the odd abandoned motel or garage or else isolated water towers like antique alien craft frozen in fields of wavering grass, their bulbous summits sometimes marked with the names of forgotten settlements, and then isolated strip malls with frazzled neon signs, churches like bomb shelters surrounded by ugly clusters of single-storey shacks bent by the burning sun, and then once more the great nothingness. They never saw any people.

Around noon, feeling hungry, he pulled in at a brand-new service area, the place a gleaming beacon in the wilderness. A hugely fat woman pushed a mop over the shiny floor of the empty restaurant. A saccharine voice warbled a familiar hymn through speakers in the ceiling. 'Come on,' he said to the girl. 'We ought to eat something.' He ordered hamburgers and fries for them both. Mary ate avidly, gulping at an enormous vat of sweet tea.

'Are you looking for anyone in particular in Wind City?' he asked, pushing his food to one side.

'A doctor,' she said, still eating.

'They don't have doctors where you're from?'

'Mmm,' she swallowed. 'Not the sort ah need.' She blinked at him.

'I'm sorry.'

'Don' be. Ain't your fault.' She chewed thoughtfully. 'You can't get no condoms or shit like that no more. Maybe in Boston but not down here.' She swallowed and shrugged. Her eyes flashed. 'Hey – you goin' to eat that?'

'Be my guest.' He smiled and passed her the tray. He felt another twinge of concern for the girl. Part of him wanted to tell her about Alisha, about the baby they were expecting, but then he thought such a topic hardly appropriate under the circumstances. Better to say nothing.

'Do you believe in dreams?' she asked when they were back in the Vindicator.

'It's not a question of belief, is it? I mean, dreams exist.'

She rolled her eyes. 'Jeez, are you always such a dork? Do you think your dreams predict things that are goin' to happen?'

'Like what?'

'Ain't you never had no dream that came true?'

'I don't dream.'

'Bullshit! Everyone dreams.'

'I don't remember them. I don't think about these things.'

'Jeez. You ain't much fun.'

'Guess not.' Mark considered her words for a little while and then he asked, 'So you in the habit of having dreams come true?'

'Not exactly.' She shifted in her seat. 'But ah'll tell you one thing, ah've been having the same dream for weeks. Ah keep dreamin' bout this man locked away in a high tower. An' all around him is water and sunken buildings an' fire on the water an' this old man in the tower, he's like God.'

'He's God?'

'*Like* God. Not God but like God, just like dreams ain't real but at the same time they still sorta real, y'know?'

'Not really.'

'Jeez.' She shook her head, evidently exasperated. 'Hey?'

'What?'

'Can ah say something?'

'Go ahead.'

'You believe in God?'

'No.'

'Why not?'

'I don't believe in anything.'

'That's sad.'

Mark shrugged. 'I guess I believe in friendship and loyalty. I believe in keeping my word. I believe in doing what I've promised to do.'

She considered his words for a minute. 'That's more than most, I suppose.'

'Maybe.' He shrugged. 'What about you? You believe in the Right Reverend and his crew?'

'Get outta here,' she smirked. 'No one believes in that fraud.'

'I think plenty do. You know plenty do.'

'Fuck them. I tell you who I believe in.'

'Yeah.'

'The man in the high tower. That's who.'

He glanced at her, uncertain what else to add. She gave a weak smile, perhaps aware that she had revealed something a little too private and peculiar.

Late afternoon and the sky grew dark again, great clouds of dust and grit shutting down the heavens. It was easy to imagine things, in such conditions. Mary tried the radio a few times but apart from the federal weather channel, a sexless voice intoning information about dropping pressure and storm clouds off the Jamaican coast, there was nothing else, just a blank static hiss, an ominous sonic counterpoint to the conditions outside.

Mark thought it might rain but nothing came, just brooding skies bringing murky oblivion. They were getting closer to Orlando, the city of lakes and amusement parks, now a ravaged border zone dominated by massive military bases. Apart from a convoy of supply vehicles heading north, the highway was devoid of traffic and the surrounding countryside, from what they could see, was ghastly in its emptiness. Signs had been removed and if it wasn't for the sat-nav gently counting down the remaining miles, Mark thought he would have long since lost faith that such a road could ever lead anywhere.

A sign appeared through the gloom: 'Wind City 2 miles' and an arrow, highlighted in bright neon, pointed to a road off the highway. A cluster of other, amateur signs surrounded the arrow, advertising motels, bars, restaurants and shops. The turn-off was a huge, loping cloverleaf, multiple lanes designed for the days when this part of Florida was the holiday destination for millions. They turned along the slip road and then came to an abrupt halt. The way ahead was blocked by a wall of barbed wire and sandbags.

Mark pulled up. 'According to the sat-nav, we're almost here,' he said to Mary. 'What do you think?'

'I don't think Wind City exists on no sat-nav.'

'I think you must be right.'

'There.' Mary pointed to a faded board with 'Wind City' painted across it. A dirt track cut back underneath and away from the junction. 'That's the way,' she said. 'Looks like we made it after all.'

# SESSION #7

She feels apprehensive this morning, aware of how far they have come and worried about what else he might say. The restless stew of thoughts kept her awake long into the night and now she feels fragile, less sure of herself than usual. Entering the garden, she fails to see him, just a number of patients and convalescents sitting around, men with injuries visible and otherwise, men damaged and healing in saggy regulation clothing while nurses in white and blue wipe-clean suits patrol the area. Then – there he is. He gives her a little wave and she flushes, realising what he has done. She sits, retrieves her files and her pen. 'Blind spot eh?' He seems to move while remaining motionless, the way a lizard can spin three hundred and sixty degrees on a wall or a hot rock too swift for the human eye to follow. He studies her. Gaunt, as if she has also slept badly. She has a question primed to start the session but he goes in first. 'You probably already know what I'm going to tell you. You probably know all about this.'

She shakes out a no.

'No?'

Again.

He tries a smile. 'Look at you, sitting there like some inscrutable sphinx, watching me like that.' She remains still, determined to leave it up to him to say whatever he wants. 'I wish you'd let me look at that file of yours, let me see what they've written in there about me. All my dirty secrets, all the evil things that I've done . . . my badness.' She resists the provocation. 'Okay.' He stops himself. 'I'm sorry.' He sips some water.

'Shall we continue from where we left off yesterday? Hmm?'

He breathes in and nods at her. 'Okay, so shortly after I first met Charlie my life began to change. Not directly, let me be clear, none of this is direct and the only people who might know are dead or would never tell. Anyway, I became involved with people who asked me to do certain things. A coincidence? I didn't make a connection then, why would I? I was kind of fucked up. I was, oh, I don't know. How did all this come about?' He seems momentarily bemused, astonished by contemplation of everything that has befallen him. 'This man, he asked me to courier things out of the country – hi-tech items, like laptops, bits of weird computer hardware that I didn't understand, that sort of shit. It wasn't a normal sort of job, it wasn't advertised, it wasn't anything like that. I was introduced to this guy – his name was Mike although I guess it could have been anything . . . I met him, I mean, he knew, he seemed to know . . . I was involved with these other people, at the time, not good people.' He falters. 'I guess you could say what has changed? None of them ever killed anyone, right?' He bites at his bottom lip.

'What were they like, these people – you say they weren't good?'

'Oh, they were petty criminals mixed up in all sorts of scams – credit card fraud and benefit cheats, dodgy prescriptions for codeine and valium, crap like that, you know, handling stolen goods, mainly low-grade stuff . . . it wasn't even a gang, not really.' He gives another shrug. 'They used me because I could pull it off, the necessary deceptions, see? I could use a fake credit card or hand over a dodgy prescription and no one would suspect anything because of what I'd learned. No one would notice me, they wouldn't even look twice. If there is one thing I can be grateful for, it's that Charlie saved me, in his way. He turned me from being a punk, a pathetic gangster, into something else.'

'Something better?'

'Maybe.' His head tilts as though to avoid a punch. 'It would be nice to think so.'

'Tell me more about what you were doing with these criminals.'

'The operation was run by this alcoholic called Alan. He was a nice guy actually, sort of like a disreputable uncle, kindly, generous, not what you'd think, not at all. He used to call me his "shadow man". When he got drunk – which was most evenings – he'd claim to have been in the Army, said he got fucked up in Operation Iraqi Freedom. He had these scars on his leg he claimed were shrapnel wounds from an RPG.' He shrugs. 'I didn't exactly believe him then and I'm pretty sure I don't believe him now . . . but still it hardly matters.' He shakes his head. 'One night in the pub Alan introduces me to this guy – Mike. You probably know him too. He's probably in your file, Mike, Alan, all of them. Set up from the start. Susanna, my mother, everyone's in on it, aren't they?' That dangerous light enters his eyes again and his face seems even more taut, his jaw clenched, a single vein throbbing in his temple like a blue snake sliding beneath the surface of a scorched plain. She is ready to say something but he stops her. 'Okay. Calm, yes, calm at all times. I'm sorry. Just give me a moment.' He swallows and blinks several times, his complexion glassy with sweat.

'Are you all right?'

He waves away her concern. 'Fine. Sometimes I just get a little . . .'

'Sure.'

'It's just so hot and these pills they give me make me feel so weird sometimes, the dreams and everything, it all comes back to me in snatches, like this, whizzing images and colours and shit.'

'That's okay, Mark. Take a moment if you need it.'

He doesn't pause. 'Okay, so I'm in the pub and we've been drinking, Alan and me and some of the other lads – I can hardly remember their faces let alone their names any more but this other guy has joined us – Mike – Alan introduces me, this is Mike, he says, and it's odd 'cause Mike is definitely not the sort of person we usually hung out with. He was terribly well spoken, all very rah rah rah, a public-school type with this smart suit and clean shirt like he'd just come straight from the bank. Normally I'd just have thought, Fuck off you twat, you know, but actually he seemed really genuine, very affable and generous. He kept buying us all drinks. He was on the level. He didn't look it but … well, that was the impression he gave. A little bit condescending maybe … I mean, now I think about it he must have been a spook because he had one of those faces that was hard to remember, that sort of erased itself even as you looked at it.' The irony of his words causes his lips to twist into something that is not exactly a smile but more an expression of indecision, a faltering uncertainty about the events disclosed. She makes a note. 'I guess he was one of those people who could crop up all the time, in different disguises, in different places. He could have been a banker or a civil servant but he could also have been a doctor or a journalist or someone who might just start talking to you on a train and you wouldn't know why but before you knew it you'd have told them half your life story. Well. This I do remember. At some point in the evening we seemed to be talking alone and I felt kind of flattered; you see, not that many people had really shown me that much attention and he was buying drinks and I couldn't really see why he was being so nice and he kept saying that Alan spoke highly of me and I remember trying to ask him how he knew Alan but he was always vague about that, saying something about how they used to be in the same regiment. I thought it was all a bit odd but then he was telling me he had this job, said he wanted to try me out, and if I did well it could be a new opening, could be lots of money, a step up, all that. I remember he leaned close and there was something charming about him and he was saying did I want to keep doing this for ever – cheap scams and that – was that all I wanted, all that sort of blah. Of course I thought there must be a catch but what he said, it sounded fairly kosher. I just had to deliver these things, like I told you, and okay, so I knew it wasn't exactly legit, but it didn't sound any more risky than what I was doing already and from what he said it was going to be a load more cash and so I found myself agreeing. I wasn't fully myself at the time – as I said – drinking too much, doing drugs, sometimes I'd wake up in my room and I wouldn't know who I was or what I was doing or anything. It was like something was inhabiting my brain, controlling me.' The vein throbs and he taps his skull. 'At the time I didn't hardly speak to my mum or Susanna, I had nothing to lose, that was the way I saw it. My whole life seemed to be on this precipice, like I said, I already had a record and whatever this Mike guy was offering, well, it didn't seem any different. I was desperate, that's the short of it, and I was close to doing something really stupid.' She waits, wondering if he will elaborate. He takes a sip of water, swallows hard and sits back, rubbing his injured shoulder and stretching his back. 'Okay, so maybe the items they asked me to transport were stolen or secret, maybe it was all some kind of industrial espionage. I figured if I didn't ask it couldn't hurt. I didn't know then and I'm still not sure. Perhaps it was all part of my initiation, my training for what was to follow. I know it sounds paranoid but you'll see . . . You're nodding, Alisha, like you know all this already? Is that it?'

Her lips press tight. 'I've already told you, Mark – I don't know anything.'

'You'll write your report, won't you? I need to get out of this place.'

'Don't worry about that. Tell me what it was Mike had you do.'

He inhales deeply. 'Mike didn't waste time. That was sure. The job came two days later. I was emailed a set of instructions and two tickets, one for a safety deposit box and the other for a business-class flight to Vienna, a morning flight, with the return booked for that evening. Real early, about four a.m., a car came to collect me, just a local minicab, and took me to an industrial estate near Heathrow, a storage depot. I used the ticket to open this box and inside was a totally normal-looking laptop. Then we drove on to the airport. As instructed I was wearing a suit and tie. I didn't look any different from any other young business executive. I caught the flight and everything just happened normally, the way it should. I'd been given the address of a hotel near Vienna airport. I got a taxi there and waited in the lobby. After a short while a man greeted me. He knew my name. I don't know how he recognised me or anything but this was all as I'd been told to expect.'

'In the email?'

'Yeah. And so this guy, he spoke English with a German or an Austrian accent, ridiculously formal and polite. He sort of ushered me into the bar and we both had a beer and made weird small talk about the flight or the weather or something. After a bit of this bullshit he came to the point. Mike had said the contact would give me a newspaper with certain words underlined in red. It turned out to be the *Financial Times*. The whole thing was very cloak and dagger but in a funny sort of way. So he gave me the paper and I gave him the computer and went back to the airport to catch my flight back home. I wasn't allowed to go anywhere else, Mike had made that clear as well – no sightseeing.'

'Did you enjoy it?'

'I guess I did. It was easy and exciting at the same time.'

'You weren't scared?'

'I was nervous until I saw that it really was just a newspaper that I had to take back. The whole job was quite strange.'

'What was in the paper?'

'A few words and share prices had been ringed with red pen. I thought that maybe it was just some weird insider-dealing shit, I don't know, I never understood any of that crap. At least I wasn't being asked to smuggle drugs, that was all I'd really been worried about.'

'What happened when you got back?'

'A driver was waiting for me holding a sign with my name, all like I was a proper businessman. When we got to the car Mike was inside. He took the paper from me and I remember he seemed quite tense until he'd had a look and then he lightened up. As we drove back to London he told me I'd done well and that he'd use me again. He had a bag with him. There was money inside, rumpled twenty-pound notes, a thousand pounds. I'd never seen so much cash before.'

'How did you feel? Were you pleased?'

'I don't know how I felt.' He watches as she makes another note. 'They drove me all the way back to my flat. I was living in this horrid bedsit in Hackney. Mike made this big deal about where I lived, saying things like, nice street, or, isn't that your window up there? He made it clear that he knew exactly where I lived. Before I got out he touched my arm and looked at me in this funny sort of way that was friendly and menacing at the same time and said I'd better not see Alan or any of the guys again, said I had to stop doing all the old things I used to do. He told me to wait but that he'd be in touch again in a week or two. That was it.' He sits back, arms folded. 'Don't you see, Alisha, it had already started? I just didn't know it. Of course, idiot that I was, I did call Alan a couple of nights later when I'd been thinking about what had happened and started to freak out. I wanted to ask him where he'd really met Mike and what the fuck was going on. And get this, okay, when Alan answered the phone and realised it was me he sounded scared – at first I thought he was taking the piss – but he said we couldn't speak, that I mustn't call him and then he hung up. I mean, fuck! Already the wheels were turning and forces were working, shaping me to their ends, using me in ways I'd never imagine.'

'What do you mean by forces? You felt as though you weren't in control?'

'Damn right.'

'But you continued to work for this man – Mike?'

He nods.

'Why was that? Were you frightened of him?'

'It wasn't really fear . . .'

'Money?'

'That had a lot to do with it, yes.'

'So?'

'For a couple of weeks afterwards I just sat about at home. I can't really remember what I did, just the usual I suppose, smoking and drinking, getting stoned, going for walks by myself, going to bars and failing to pick up girls or talk to anyone or anything. I would think about being other people, the crowds of shoppers on Oxford Street, the nameless hordes gathered outside pubs on a Friday afternoon . . . I would think about the sun and the white clouds, the way the light shone from certain buildings or the patterns made by birds as they flew across the sky.'

'Why?'

'I didn't have a shape . . . I was looking for something.' He stops and looks away. 'We all want a purpose, don't we? You can put that in your report. A purpose.'

'Maybe I will.' She gives him a cold look. 'And so Mike called again, or?'

'No, he didn't call. I never spoke to him again. The instructions always came via an email with a ticket.'

'Did you have to reply to the email?'

'I simply had to send a reply saying yes, to show I'd received everything. I could have replied no but I never did and I don't know what would have happened had I done so. The routine was always the same. A minicab would come and drive me to a storage depot where I'd pick up the product before being taken to the airport. Sometimes it would be Heathrow, sometimes Gatwick or Stansted, and I'd fly to Frankfurt or Zurich or Brussels or Madrid, someplace like that. I did so many trips it all seemed the same after a while. I'd always meet the contact in a hotel near the airport or the main railway station, you know, and we'd sit in the lobby or the cafe or even the bar and it was always a man, usually about my age, smartly dressed, speaking English with a foreign accent, and I'd give them the product and they would give me a paper or a magazine, always with words or sentences or numbers underlined or highlighted. That was the most interesting part after a while, that was the bit that started to intrigue me. Sometimes it would be the *Financial Times* or *The Economist* or the *Guardian* but it could just as easily be the *Herald International Tribune* or *El Pais* or *Le Monde* or even something like *Vogue* or *Elle* or *Men's Health*. Once it was *Playboy*! Weird, huh? I started trying to figure out what the message was, you know, what it meant. On the flight back I'd write out the words and numbers that had been highlighted, try to put them in some kind of order. The thing was, I could often construct sentences that seemed to make sense, but still what did it mean? It didn't make things any clearer. I had no idea if this was the meaning that was supposed to be there or if I was just inventing my own silly meanings. I still had no proper understanding of what I was doing or who I was working for. It would drive me half crazy sometimes. I knew there must be some risk, the amount of money they paid showed me that. Sometimes I'd get as much as five grand. Five grand cash waiting in the car in twenty- and fifty-pound notes. Can you believe?'

99

'It must have been quite extraordinary.'

'To start with, yeah. But after a while I began ... I mean, it just seemed like something I had to do.'

'You had to do?'

'It was better not to think too much about it. As I said, the money helped.'

'And you never saw Mike again?'

'Never.'

'How long did you keep doing this for?'

'All summer. Do you remember that summer? There was that record heatwave across Europe. Tens of thousands of people died – the very old and the very young, the sick and the poor. Week after week of blazing heat and I spent my time flying to and fro, swapping computers for newspapers in the air-conditioned lobbies of hotels.'

'Nothing lasts for ever, does it?'

'Yeah, it all fucked up in the end. It was always bound to. Probably you know this too, probably you know what happened next. I met Charlie again. That's one thing. I met him again and then everything really started, everything that has brought me here, to this hospital, to you – Alisha – to us, sitting here in the garden, to me, talking on.' He rocks back in his seat.

'That was good, Mark, very good.'

'We're stopping now?' A smudge of disappointment marks his brow.

'Tomorrow.'

'Well, I'll be here, don't you worry, I won't be anywhere else.'

As she walks away she can feel him watching her. She glances back and he already seems to have gone, to have merged into his surroundings, just one of half a dozen patients taking the morning air. Suddenly frightened, she hurries away.

# WIND CITY

Down the dirt track they went, bumping and splashing through puddles and potholes as trees, wild creepers and huge, distorted palms loomed out of the gloom. Here and there reflective signs hung from branches or broken telegraph poles advertising bars or hotels in the city. They passed a clapboard church in a clearing, its steeple sheared off and NO GOD IN WIND CITY sprayed in black letters on the side of the structure. Moments later a dozen motorbikes overtook them, roaring past, red rear lights rapidly advancing into the muggy dark. Mark felt himself tense, readying himself for what was to come. Mary was also silent, blue shadows gliding like ghosts over her face. Jungle turned to town and they passed a cluster of overgrown lots and an abandoned bus incongruously painted in psychedelic swirls. Before Winthrop, Wind City had been a different town with a different name, an ordinary subdivision of tract housing in the Orlando sprawl. Since then a strange metamorphosis had taken place.

Ahead the street surged with people spinning like motes of dust. Mark slowed to a crawl as the crowd pushed past, mostly young soldiers drunk, excited and very much off-duty, streaming in and out of the bars and clubs that lined the road, faces glowing in the neon light of signs advertising cheap drinks, cheap food, lap-dancing, pole-dancing and XXX shows. Catching sight of Mary, some pressed their faces against the window, leering at her and making kissing noises, tongues lolling as they called out obscene compliments.

Mark turned off the main drag and drove down a quieter, darker sidestreet. Although it was only early evening, the stygian gloom and drunken crowds magnified his feelings of severance from the normal course of things. 'Here we are,' he said to Mary. Arrival had sharpened his sense of the mission and he found himself suddenly impatient to dispense with the young woman. 'Is there anywhere you want me to drop you?'

'Freaky place,' she mumbled. The crowds seemed to have diminished her earlier bravado.

'I've seen worse.' He stopped the car. 'Do you know anyone here? Will you be all right?'

Mary nodded. 'Ah got an address,' she spoke softly. 'Someone gave me a name.' For a moment she appeared quite stricken and then she took a deep breath, her face solemn. 'Okay, well, that was fun.' She opened the door.

'Wait,' he touched her arm.

'What?'

He wanted to tell her something but the words wouldn't come. 'How much do you need?'

'Ah no, you caint . . .' she said, hesitating.

'I can. How much?' He produced a wedge of dollars from his belt.

'Well . . .' She bit her lip, awkward. 'Ah guess three hundred ought to do it.'

'Take five.' He pressed the notes into her hand.

'Thank you.' She gave him a weak smile. 'You're a sweet guy.' She bent forward, quickly kissing his cheek.

'Good luck.'

She shut the door behind her. A group of women dressed in scanty outfits stood under a shelter on the other side of the road. He watched her walk towards them, so small under her heavy rucksack, the sight provoking a swirl of feelings he struggled to define. *A sweet guy!* That was a first. His hands clenched the steering wheel. Starting the engine, he drove away.

Most of the hotels were concentrated two blocks from the main strip. Dozens of new buildings were rising from the swamp, a confusion of half-constructed two- and three-storey structures awaiting further floors and finished roofs. Diggers and cement mixers and piles of scaffolding filled the vacant lots, the ready industry seizing on the town's festive atmosphere. Taller, older buildings loomed beyond this chaos of new development, silhouettes of former condos and hotel towers now dark and craggy as medieval castles.

Mark stopped at the Pink Triangle hotel. In the bright glow of its neon hoardings he could just make out a Spanish-styled structure beneath the scaffolding. The receptionist was a skinny Asian man with bleached blond hair and gold-capped teeth.

'Can I help you?'

'A room.'

'Fifty dollars a night, payable in advance.'

'Here.'

'Can I see some ID?'

'Why?'

'For the book.' He turned round a ledger.

Mark passed him the fake passport.

In the corner a muscular security guard sat watching him, bare-breasted and macho, a gold medallion nestling in a jungle of hair, Uzi machine pistol by his side. Smoking incense sticks surrounded the small statue of a laughing Buddha beside the counter. 'You here for some fun, darling, or are you crossing over?' the receptionist lisped.

Mark gave him a stony look. 'Strictly business,' he replied.

'Oh? Buying or selling?'

'A bit of both.' He kept his tone neutral. None of this made him entirely comfortable. These questions. He was used to blending in. Receptionists, doormen, security guards, cashiers, shopkeepers, these people were meant to forget him the second after they spoke to him. He was supposed to leave no trace in the minds of those he had encountered.

The room was damp and smelt of marijuana. A single fan sluggishly churned the humid air. Decoration was sparse, a cracked mirror above the bed, a framed black and white photograph of teenage boys slouching against the wreckage of an American tank on the wall opposite. They stared at Mark with indolent eyes, their hands languidly gripping grenade launchers, heavy machine guns resting against skinny torsos. There was no television. The attached bathroom was clad in stained blue tiles. A cockroach ran out of the shower. The walls were sweating in the humidity.

Mark took out his phone. The weak signal took a while to connect. He gave the pass code. 'This is Operation Casement. I've reached the first objective.'

'Affirmative,' said the voice at the end. 'We have your co-ordinates.'

'What now?'

'Make contact. Go to a place called the Hive. Intelligence suggests that Abraham uses a bar called the Angry Crocodile as a pick-up point.'

'Understood.'

Afterwards he called Alisha, his heart beating a little faster. They spoke briefly. She sounded much further away, the signal intercut with static. She had been dreaming about him, she said. She thought she had felt Junior give a little kick but she wasn't sure.

'Do you miss me?' she said.

'Sure I do.'

'Are you sure?'

'Yes,' he said.

Faint rain was falling like a claggy mist. Somewhere people were letting off fireworks. The loud bangs made Mark flinch, his hand twitching instinctively for the pistol strapped underneath his sweat-soaked shirt. Explosions bloomed through the haze like pink and green flowers, smells of gunpowder and trails of smoke thickening the soupy atmosphere. Gangs of drunken soldiers were milling around outside bars and fast-food shacks. He recognised the insignia of many different corps – Airborne, Rangers, Marines and Navy. On a corner a squad of military police stood guard, batons and machine guns glinting in the sheen of reflected lights.

He ate tacos and beans in a small restaurant served by a sullen Haitian boy with a scar on his cheek. A rhesus monkey sat in a cage, watching him crossly. A Mexican soap opera played silently on a wall-mounted TV. Everyone ignored it. He could still hear the fireworks, one bang after another and the whoop of excited young men relishing an evening of freedom.

Afterwards he wandered along the main drag, heading for the Hive. Among the bars, strip joints and restaurants he saw numerous clinics and medical walk-ups. Neon signs flashed advertisements for mood lifters and libido jackers, VD cures and womb cleansers, methadone and opiate substitutes. He wondered if he might see Mary again, darting furtively into some upstairs operating theatre. It was stupid of him to have picked her up. There was no way of knowing whom she might talk to. He was very foolish, compromising the mission in such a way – and for what? Since when did this desire to atone take hold? Since when did he think he could help anybody? The voice in his head went on like this, round and round. He had hoped talking to Alisha might help but the thought of her so far away made things only worse. Something else was also troubling him. Why did Ashe never contact Susanna? His brother-in-law had spoken so often of his love for his sister. Why then the silence? What had happened to him and why had he let her go? It was hard to reconcile certain forces, Mark understood that much, the intensity of the field with the oblivion of home. Love and danger, violence and kindness, how to tread a delicate path between incompatible worlds? He knew there was no easy answer, no clear way. He could only hope that it was true – what Foxy and the others had promised him – that this really was the end, his exit mission, his final foray into the field and that he could go home, a lover and a father, a man restored to himself, all dues paid.

The Hive was a disaster relief depot originally used for storing food and medical supplies after Winthrop. Although a faded FEMA logo was still visible on the side of the shed, the structure, like the town around it, had undergone a significant transformation. Crowds thronged the huge doorway. Flamboyantly dressed transvestites and prostitutes flanked the entrance like gaudy statues, accosting the crowd with crimson lips and wrists dripping with cheap jewellery. 'Come here, darlin'', 'Lookin' for fun, sweetie pie?' Among them spaced-out flower children drifted with starry, empty faces and he saw stumbling alcoholics and migrant labourers in stained overalls and wild-boy runaways with seductive smiles and truck drivers and private contractors swollen with the joy of hefty expense accounts and wives at home far away. Gliding through the throng, hustlers and hipsters like sharks in a coral reef, their faces obscured by baseball caps, their bodies sheathed in coats too warm for the climate. 'What yuh wan' man? You wan' pussy? Li'l girls, virgin pussy, boys, anythin' man, anythin' you fuckin' want.' Mark ignored them all.

The structure was vast, the depot subdivided by partitions into dozens of smaller cubicles. Ladders and staircases led to upper-level walkways and platforms. Flags and banners hung from the rafters, the Union and Confederate flags, colours for Mexico and Jamaica, Cuba and Honduras and other places that he did not recognise: red stars and black pentagrams, an eye in a pyramid, a crescent moon, a blue handprint on a white background. The place resounded to the throb of air-conditioning units and fans, shouting and laughter, the pulse of a dozen different styles of music. Pungent odours filled the air, grilled beef and fried chicken, sizzling Asian woks and deep-fat fryers. He walked past stalls selling plasma screens and mobile phones, laptops and computer parts, alcohol and cigarettes, stacks of ready-to-eat meals that must have been looted from military bases or relief centres, medical equipment, tents, survival suits, watercraft, sports gear, mountains of Nike and Converse trainers, NBA- and American football-branded clothes. One section, protected by Peruvian security guards in black uniforms brandishing metal detectors, was devoted to firearms, racks stacked with shotguns and assault rifles, machine guns and rocket launchers, boxes of ammunition, knives and crossbows.

He asked a stall owner for the Angry Crocodile and was directed up a staircase and onto a large platform suspended across the main expanse of the Hive. The venue had a tacky swamp theme. A stuffed crocodile hung in a cage over the bar while fish tanks, rubber plants, fake palms and green lights added to the kitsch mood.

He couldn't see anyone inside who looked like Johnny Midnight. The place was busy, but not unduly so. All the customers were male. A boisterous group of Marines sat in one corner chugging Budweiser. Most of the others sat alone or in twos and threes. Everyone was drinking.

'Get me a beer.'

He sat on a stool, drinking slowly, doing nothing, waiting. As intended no one paid him the slightest attention. The joint lacked the brashness of some of the bars on the main street but it certainly didn't seem queer. The Marines in the corner were very young and getting very drunk, bragging loudly about some kind of sporting rivalry. Most of the other men were his age or above, with the steady, slightly depressive air of regulars. A retro jukebox in the corner was playing an old Willie Nelson record.

When he realised the barman had forgotten about him, Mark ordered a second beer. Being invisible was almost too easy sometimes. The more he drank, the more he got drunk, the more they would notice him. A little later someone sat on the stool beside his, a light-skinned African-American wearing a smart white shirt and a fedora which he put beside him on the counter. The man ordered bourbon. He caught Mark's eye and gave a nod. His face looked quite youthful but traces of white dusted the thin hair around his temples. The man took a drink. Mark took a drink. After a little while the man looked at him again. Mark knew the type. There were some who would always notice things. Mark waited a bit and then shifted slightly on his stool so that he deliberately caught the man's eye. The man winked. 'What's up, bro'? I ain't seen you here before? You new in town?'

Mark shrugged. He let the man talk on a little, waiting to see where his conversation would lead them. His name was Lance, he said, and he was local. 'You in service?' he asked.

Mark shook his head. 'No, I'm not a military guy.'

'I did my time.' He rolled up his sleeve, showing a large tattoo on his forearm. 'Fifty-first Airborne, the righteous fire, I was a warrior for Christ.' He gave a laugh. 'We sure gave the infidel hell.' He gave an edgy, slightly unnerving smile. 'I got the scars where they hit me. I got the scars. I ain't gonna show you them, though.' He went on, 'You ain't from here, that's for sure. You come just for a little diversion or sumthin' more?'

Mark decided to throw the guy a line. 'I'm looking for someone.'

'You think you find him here?'

'In Wind City. No.'

'Who you lookin' for?'

'My brother.'

'You think he's in the Zone?'

'Could be?'

'That a fact?' Lance leaned closer.

'Do you think?' he began.

'What?'

'Sometimes . . .' he paused. 'I don't know. Maybe it's hopeless.'

'Nothin's totally hopeless.'

'You see . . . I've been living in England for the last decade.'

'England? I ain't never been there.'

'I had to come back because our mother is gravely ill. She's dying. I need to find my brother.'

'And you think he's crossed over?'

Mark lowered his voice to a whisper, 'I don't know for sure but . . . My brother never had a girlfriend.' He glanced around. 'But he always had a lot of close male friends if you get my drift.'

'Oh sure,' Lance nodded solemnly. 'There's a lot like that, on the other side.'

109

'Maybe you can help me.'

'Maybe I can.'

'You live here?'

Lance shrugged. 'You might put it that way.'

'But you know people, right?'

Lance contemplated his drink. 'Depends.'

'I'm looking for a guy called Johnny Midnight. I was told he might be able to help.'

Lance smiled. 'We all know Johnny Midnight. Everyone knows Johnny.'

'Could he help?'

'Maybe.'

'Could you get him to see me?'

Lance swallowed the last of his drink. 'Johnny is a busy man.'

'I can pay. I can pay everyone. Dollars, euros, whatever.' He touched Lance on the shoulder. 'My mother is dying. She's got no more than a couple of months left. She wants to see my brother – Charlie – my older brother, one last time. She hasn't seen him for five years. He doesn't even know . . .' he broke off. 'I'm desperate. You understand?'

Lance nodded. 'What's your name, buddy?'

'John. John Jay.'

Lance contemplated his empty glass. 'Meet me outside Ricky's Hot Tamale shack in one hour. It's on the main street, opposite a lap-dancing place, Magnetic Chicks. You'll find it. Be there in an hour. Bring some ID. Johnny's a cautious brother, you dig? I ain't promisin' nothin', mind.' Lance slipped from his stool and made for the exit.

Mark finished his beer and sat for a while. He looked around but no one paid him any attention. Leaving a few dollars on the counter, he headed out.

# SESSION #8

This morning he appears even more agitated than before, twisting his hands in a thrum of anxiety. No sooner does she sit than he starts: 'I suppose we've come to the part where I have to talk about the rest, haven't we?'

'Well, Mark, that's up to you.'

'It is okay, you see, I like you, Alisha, I realised that for sure yesterday. It struck me that I was almost looking forward to our session, regardless of what I have to tell you. Of course, let me be clear, all the stuff you told me about your impartiality and such, I don't believe that, I'm sure everything we say goes back to the agency but I understand. You say you're here to help and maybe you are helping me, but it's only because I decided I like you that I'm talking about these things, that's the reason. And I guess it's pleasant out here, in the garden, under the trees, with the dappled sunlight, the nurses in the background, the fact that we can all pretend that I could just leave if I wanted to, just stroll down the gravel driveway and through the gates and go gambolling off through the Surrey countryside, la-di-fucking-da, like I'm a sparrow, a rabbit, a field of corn fluttering in the hot wind, like everything is fine and normal . . .'

She cuts him off with a daggered look.

'Sorry.'

'I thought we'd agreed you wouldn't behave like that any more.'

111

He takes a deep breath. 'I know. I promise I'll keep my voice down. It's just that what I have to talk about, it's not easy. Look at me, I'm sweating like . . .' He dabs at his forehead.

'Why do you find this so hard?' she asks.

'It's Charlie. He did this to me. He did it. You know, I keep thinking I'll see him again. They say he's dead but sometimes I find it hard to believe a man like that can die. I have dreams about him, strange dreams.' He shudders and covers his face with hard-bitten hands.

'Just take your time.' She resists the impulse to reach across and touch him, to offer just a little comfort.

'It's difficult,' he starts. 'The words, I mean, they don't always . . . to put it into words . . . how can I convey what happened or what it meant? You sit confident with your certainties, like this means that and these things are secure, reasonably secure at least.' He bangs the table. 'But for me it's different. The world melts and the earth evaporates into the sky and maybe nothing is solid or real any more and things I would never have believed turn out to be true.'

'Try not to get upset.' There – she's done it, her hand resting for one brief moment on his, the clammy feel of his skin. He does not flinch. From the files she has seen she knows he does not have a wife, nor a girlfriend, but she does not know how long it has been since a woman made love to him. Then it's her turn to flush. She doesn't know where these thoughts come from. 'Okay,' and she smiles in momentary relief. 'Let's just get back to where we were yesterday.'

Another deep breath and he nods. 'Like I said, I was delivering these items around Europe. By this stage I'd been doing it for about six months. I must have done twenty or more drops, I was making tons of cash and it all seemed so easy.'

'And nothing had gone wrong?'

'Not yet.'

'You didn't have any doubts or?'

'Sure, sometimes when we were flying back home I'd have this weird feeling like I was being watched or followed but it was never anything certain. It was more like a sensation, like someone brushing the back of my neck with their fingers. As I said, places have their own moods but airports and aeroplanes are always hard to judge, a little like hospitals, I suppose.' He gives a dull shrug. 'The spaces themselves are too anonymous and interchangeable for a start, and then they are too emotional, so many different people united only by the fact that they are all going somewhere, and some will be scared of flying and some will be indifferent and some will be sad because they're leaving loved ones behind and others will be happy because they are going on holiday – you get the picture – so the mood is always mixed-up. And sometimes on the flight back, when I'd be trying to decode the messages, I'd get these weird sentences coming out, shit like 'Presidential death train 36' or 'Global Armageddon index contracts third quarter'. I'm misremembering, but that's the gist, it was that sort of thing, and I never really had any way of knowing if these were the codes or if I was just inventing meanings and anyway there were codes within the code, I was sure of that too, you know. The word "president" didn't just mean president and numbers referred to other numbers, I'm sure of it.'

'Did you ever write down any of the code words? Did you keep a record?'

He cuts her question with a hard look, deflective, impenetrable and disapproving, once again the agent, the secret-bearer. His expression leaves her feeling foolish, out of her depth, momentarily embarrassed at her naivety.

He continues, 'Towards the end of that summer I was stopped at security leaving Stansted airport. I was meant to catch a flight to Berlin.' His mouth tightens. 'We'd had a different arrangement that morning. Normally, like I said, I'd go to a depot to pick up the product but this time it was already in the back of the taxi. I remember the driver said something like "There it is" and he seemed different as well. He didn't look like the usual minicab driver but then – you know – what does that mean? I remember looking at this machine and wondering what the fuck it was – like, it was the size and shape of a laptop, made of silvery metal, but it was heavy and I couldn't open it. There was nothing

I could do except put it in my hand luggage and go on as usual. The airport was packed and I queued for ages to get through security. I thought the crowds could be used to my advantage as there were more than enough people to blend in and the security muppets were busy. When I came to the scanner I put the machine in a plastic tray with my keys and phone, the usual procedure. Of course my senses were going crazy, I knew something was wrong.'

'Why did you go through with it?'

'I was frightened of what would happen if I didn't complete the mission.'

'You were frightened?'

'I suppose so.'

'You were even more frightened of Mike – these people you didn't even know – than the law, the police?'

'If you put it that way, yeah, I was.' She nods and writes something down. 'I went through the metal detector and waited to get my stuff back. Trouble was, they stopped the scanner and I could see the guy who watched the monitor call over one of his colleagues and they were looking at the screen and I knew it was the machine. Now, you know, with my training I could have probably bluffed my way through. Believe me, in Iraq Charlie and I could brazen our way through militia and army checkpoints in a truck packed with explosives. I could have smiled and dissembled and pulled all the tricks and they would have let me pass without even knowing why. Not then. It was a set-up – don't you see? That was the point. It was a test.' He presses his finger hard on the table. 'One I was never meant to pass.' He swallows and wipes the sweat from his face. 'I tried to run for it, to barge my way back through the crowds and I remember thinking that if I could just make it through departures I could jump in a cab and get the hell out. In the main concourse I tripped over a baggage trolley and went sprawling across the floor. Police were coming after me. They were blocking the exits, everything. I was totally fucked. They cornered me in a WHSmith's. I ended up throwing paperbacks at them and screaming things and they shot me with a Taser. Blam! It was like all the lights went on and off in one go. The next thing I knew I'd been cuffed and was being dragged down a long corridor. I could see the strip lights flickering past above and I had this weird sensation like I wasn't wholly in my own body. They took me to a room and told me to wait.' He touches his face, one finger pressed against his forehead. 'That was when it started. That was when it all started. That's why I'm here. That was the moment. That was how it began.' He wipes his face again and shudders. 'This is where the story starts.'

A voice calls his name. The chief consultant and another man arrive. As they lead Mark away he gives her a parting look that she remembers for a long time but can never quite decipher.

The next morning when she arrives as usual the chief consultant takes her to his office and tells her that the decision was made that night to release Burrows. He gives no further reason. She submits her report as authorised.

# JOHNNY MIDNIGHT

Ricky's Hot Tamale shack was a small outlet at the far end of the main drag. As Lance had said, the stall was opposite a lap-dancing club. Ignoring the bouncer on duty, Mark sat himself on a concrete step sheltered by an overhanging sign. Rain had driven most people inside and he waited, watching puddles grow in the cracks in the street. He couldn't see anyone else lurking outside, no obvious sign of ambush or subterfuge. Normally his senses were primed for such a possibility but he felt nothing, only a twitch of anticipation, a texture as murky as the weather.

He crossed the road and went over to the counter. An elderly black man regarded him with something close to indifference.

'Lance sent me.'

The old man turned and shouted something to someone behind him. Moments later a small boy, eleven or twelve years old, appeared from round the side quickly pulling on a waterproof.

'See the boy?' said the old man. 'Follow the boy.'

The boy made a coaxing gesture and led Mark down a muddy back alley piled high with trash and through to a wider avenue of abandoned suburban houses, driveways gated and barred, windows boarded up, gardens rampant with greenery. At the end of the road a barbed-wire fence formed a barrier around a new compound. The entrance was marked by a guard-post painted with the Darkwater logo, a Stars and Stripes bent in the shape of a shield. Darkwater were one of the main private contractors operating in the Zone, providing everything from bodyguards to road building. However, there was no sign of anyone on duty. The boy led him into the compound, a collection of mobile homes, each attached to a small windmill and solar panel. The place was dark and Mark kept stumbling and splashing in muddy holes in the ground. Rain ran down his face, soaking his shirt and pants. His leather shoulder holster chafed against his wet skin. The boy, clearly familiar with the route, hurried to a cluster of mobile homes at the far corner of the camp. As they approached, a security light flipped on, dazzling him. Blinking against the light, Mark saw a number of trailers had been knocked together to create a much larger, interlocking structure. The boy ran up to the front door and banged on it with his fist. Then he turned, dashing back into the night.

Mark hesitated, unsure what to do.

The door opened.

Several men were standing in the trailer.

'Yes?'

'I'm here to see Johnny.'

'Okay.'

He stepped inside.

Someone moved behind him, closing the door and pressing a cold metal object to the back of his head.

He spun round, his right hand going up and knocking the weapon away, his left hand grasping his opponent by the neck and driving him back, hard and fast, smashing him against the wall, his knee going into the man's groin. His opponent made a noise like a deflating football. Keeping his left hand tight around the man's neck, Mark reached for his automatic, drawing the gun and releasing his opponent. 'Stop! Stop.' As the injured man slumped downwards he turned, gun ready, only to face a pump-action shotgun and a snub-nosed pistol.

'Drop the gun,' someone was shouting.

Mark let his automatic fall to the floor and slowly raised his hands. One of the men darted forward, picking up his weapon.

'I got his gun, Johnny.'

'Search the punk.'

Hands ran up his legs and down his arms, removing his wallet, phone and passport.

'That's all.'

The man Mark had disarmed was getting up, rubbing his neck and crotch. 'Asshole!'

'You're lucky I didn't kill you,' Mark said. He looked at the men surrounding him, trying to calculate his odds.

'I knew you were in the military.' There was Lance, pointing the shotgun.

'Everyone put your weapons down and chill.' A heavily tanned man with bright white hair stood at the back of the room. 'We don't want no one to get hurt. We won't shoot you as long as you don't hurt nobody.'

'Okay.' Mark lowered his arms.

'I'm Johnny Midnight.' Unlike the others, the man seemed completely relaxed. 'You must be John Jay,' he said, ushering him forward with the confidence of a game show host introducing a new contestant. 'Lance, Steve, put down your guns, it's cool, everyone be cool.' Johnny smiled. He was better looking than the picture had suggested. With his coppery tan, bright blue eyes and gleaming white smile, he looked more like the captain of an exclusive yacht, the sort of lothario Mark would have expected to find frequenting the casinos and marinas of the English Riviera or the upmarket Baltic resorts. He wore a white, short-sleeved shirt unbuttoned to reveal a crop of greying chest hair and a muscular torso. He thumbed Mark's passport. 'So you're John Jay.'

'Looks like it.'

'Sorry about all this.' He gestured at the men around him. 'But we have to be careful. Come through. Let's hang out a while. Lance tells me you're looking for your brother. We should talk. Follow me.'

'Can I have my things back?'

'Sure.'

'And the gun,' he added, pocketing his documents and phone.

Johnny nodded at his lackeys.

One of the others returned the automatic to Mark, who slipped it back into his shoulder holster.

'Lance, come with us. The rest of you, amuse yourselves.' Mark followed Johnny from the first trailer and into a second, adjoining structure. The walls were covered with pictures of country and western singers and steroid-pumped body-builders, a weird parade of cowboy hats and rippled pectorals. More men sat around a small table piled with chips and cards. The air smelled of cigarettes and aftershave. They seemed to be waiting for something. 'This way,' said Johnny, opening a trapdoor in the floor.

Mark followed him down the ladder and into an under-ground shelter roughly the same size as the trailer above but with a much lower ceiling. The three men had to stoop slightly. Walls and floor were covered in concrete slabs but some attempt had been made to furnish the den. A small lamp gave off a dull light and there were rugs on the floor, a large sofa and several plastic fold-out chairs. A plasma screen was mounted on one wall, maps of Florida and the United States on another. Despite these domestic flourishes, the air was damp and unwholesome. Mark could feel the weight of swampy earth pressing around them.

'Welcome to my lair.' Johnny beamed. 'We've sat out many a category-five down here, kicking back with some beers, a few DVDs, all the comforts of home, ain't that right, Lance?'

'Sure is, Johnny.'

'I got to tell you though, chemical toilets sure start to stink after a couple days. Not to mention,' he tapped the ceiling, 'the crick in your neck you get after bending down so long. Anyway, take a seat.' He gestured to the sofa. 'You want anything?'

Mark declined. He still felt a little muddled after the beers at the bar. His reactions had been slower than normal. He didn't like the advantage Johnny had achieved.

Johnny continued, 'We got a kitchen through there, a couple of digs – this shelter can sleep twelve – a store room, showers, back-up generator, the works.'

'You seem well prepared.'

'This is America, man, you gotta take care of yourself these days. Ain't no one else gonna help you.'

Lance brought a six-pack and took a seat opposite them.

Johnny cracked open a can. 'Lance tells me you're looking for your brother, something like that?'

'That's right. Our mother is dying. She wants to see him again . . . one last time.'

Johnny nodded vigorously. 'That's sad, man, that's real sad. What makes you think your brother is on the other side?'

'I'll be blunt. My brother is gay. He couldn't take it any more.' Mark knew certain techniques that made telling lies seem like the perfect truth. It was all down to the story he told and the way he told it. Certain details had to be clear in his mind, as concrete and definite as if they had really happened. There was no need to say too much. 'He told me he was going into the Zone.' He paused, pretending to endure some burden of disclosure. 'I haven't really heard from him since.'

'Haven't, or haven't really?'

'I've had a couple of messages. Not much. It's my understanding that . . . what I mean is, I think he's joined the Queer Liberation Army.' There was a moment's silence. He was sitting very close to Johnny and he could sense the man weighing up certain possibilities. 'Can you get me through?'

'I can.'

'How much?'

'That depends.'

'On what?'

'If I want to, for a start.'

'What do I need to do to convince you?'

Johnny sighed, rubbing a large hand over his face. He wore gold rings on several fingers.

'Please,' Mark continued. 'My brother. I can go myself, I'll go anyway, I don't care. But you've come highly recommended.'

'Who told me about you?'

'I can't say. Someone who shares a common concern. They're still in the closet, still in the States. You understand.'

'Okay.' Johnny nodded slowly. 'If you really want to cross over with me it will cost two thousand dollars for basic costs and expenses. You can bring that when we go. But I need two thousand euros on top of that advance.'

'Euros?'

'The dollar ain't worth shit no more. I want a real currency.'

'I don't have euros.'

'I don't want cash, man, Jesus!' He rolled his eyes theatrically. 'We'll give you details of an offshore account to transfer funds to. Can you do that?'

Mark nodded.

'That's just the basic. I can do you a tailor-made package if you prefer. Once we're over there you'll be put in touch with certain people who know certain people, if you catch my drift. Costs are variable.' He scratched his lip.

Mark shifted. 'I don't know . . . I'm not sure if I need that.'

'It's a funny sort of place, the Zone,' Johnny went on. 'Wouldn't you say, Lance?'

'Sure. Real bundle of laughs.'

'In a sense it's the real America, the home of the brave and land of the free.' He touched Mark's knee, his blue eyes promising further disclosures. 'Some people love it over there, some people hate it. You won't believe it when you get out there.'

'Looks like the end of the world,' said Lance.

'The end or the beginning. You should see the swamps and the forests – mile after mile without people, no roads, no houses, no cars, no electricity wires, no sewers, nothing. It's like heaven and hell rolled into one.'

'Don't forget about the military,' added Lance.

'You got to remember, there are three elements to the Zone.' Johnny was clearly in his element. 'The grid, the white and the red. The grid is the military. The bases are connected and there are some fortified towns between them where the service workers and contractors hang out. These places got good roads, got shelters, got McDonald's and Burger King and Witch Hunters and born-again evangelicals waiting for the Rapture to whisk them to heaven, all the usual crappy Americana you get everywhere. Avoid those places. You'll need a pass for a start. I can get you a fake if you want but it'll cost, and what's the point? Your brother won't be there. Now the white – that's the swamp, the forests, the empty coastline – nature in its essence. And then the red, that's the rest.'

'Miami,' said Lance.

'Miami,' Johnny echoed his friend. 'Miami is red, Fort Lauderdale is red, most of Orlando, just over yonder, that's red and Palm Beach – or what's left of it – is red too. There's people in the red. There's houses, in places there's electricity, community, of sorts, and guns and drugs and gangs, strange tribes, weird religions, devil cults, all sorts of fucked-up shit you wouldn't even imagine.'

'Not so different from the rest of the States then?' Mark smiled.

'I dig you, man.' Johnny smiled back. 'Some would say the Zone is better than the rest of the States. You can be free out there. Of course there's danger, there's risk. Some prefer that. Not your average American.'

'I'm not your average American, nor is my brother.'

Johnny nodded. 'I think we understand each other.' He touched Mark's knee. 'I got to warn you. There are plenty of conflicts down there. The military stays out of it most of the time but now and then they'll launch an operation, crack down on some narco-traffickers or environmental insurgents, maybe send an expedition into Miami, looking for suspects, terrorists, whatever. Why do you think they have the Zone for training? It ain't just for exploding new bombs in the swamp.'

'Righteous anger. Warriors for God. Divine vengeance. Christ the tiger. Fire from heaven.' Lance slapped his hands together. 'They say a new army is rising in the west, Witch Hunters and Klansmen, Christian warriors to fight a new Holy War.'

'Unless you want to hire your own platoon of Darkwater guards, nothing can be guaranteed. Certainly I can't guarantee your safety. I can't guarantee nothing.' Johnny smiled again. 'But with one of my packages I can make things easier. You won't get jacked the moment we leave you. We can get you transport, connections, all those things.'

'What do you reckon, buddy?' said Lance. 'People get mur-dered out there all the time. No one knows. No one even gives a shit. You think you tough now with all that badass shit you pulled but you just one man, what can you do?'

He could see that they had a point. It was in his interest to utilise local intelligence, to garner what support he could. Clearly these people knew far more about what was going on in the Zone than Foxy and all the others back at headquarters. Satellite imaging, remote viewing, communications inter-cepts: none of it could replace eyes and feet on the ground. Besides, it was clear that the agency had dealt him a bad card. He needed more help. He sat for a moment, considering their words. It was very quiet and warm in the bunker and his damp clothes were clinging to his skin. 'My brother's name,' he said at last, 'is Ashe, Charlie Ashe. We had different fathers. Do you know that name?' He watched Johnny carefully. The man's eyes closed a fraction, a shadow briefly creasing his face.

'Ashe, Ashe, Ashe.' He seemed to be testing the name on his tongue. 'Lance, you know anyone by that name over there?'

'I don't know nobody. Lots of people in the Zone.'

'Lots of people in the Zone,' Johnny went on. 'I don't know, I don't know about that.'

'Recently though, I've heard he is using a different name – a new name.'

'Oh yeah?'

'Kalat. Ring any bells?'

'Kalat? What kind of shitty name is that? That ain't no American name.'

'That's right.'

'Kalat. Well I'll be. Kalat. What you think of that, Lance?'

'Sounds like our friend here is stirring some bad shit, that's what I think.'

'I'm not stirring anything. I'm just looking for my brother. I heard everyone knows about Kalat over there. Are you sure you don't know that name?'

'Well now.' Johnny shifted, looking abruptly uncomfortable. 'It might be that I could put you in touch with someone who knows a little more than me. No promises mind, no promises.' He crossed his legs. 'It would be expensive, you see what you've told me changes things a little . . .'

'How much?'

'Oh, I don't know – Lance, what do you think?'

Lance shrugged. 'I'd say double the usual.'

'Double the usual, indeed . . .'

'My mother is dying. I don't care how much.'

'His mother is dying of course, sad, sad and touching, a son's devotion. We love our mothers, don't we, Lance?'

'My mother's dead.'

'And mine's in a care home in Dallas. An expensive care home, mind.'

'The money doesn't matter.'

'Ten thousand euros.'

'Fine. Give me the account details and I'll make a transfer.'

Lance made a whistling noise. 'The brother is serious, Johnny, real serious.'

Johnny gave Mark an affectionate squeeze. 'I don't know how you heard about me, son, but I'm sure glad you did.'

'When will we go? How?'

Johnny pursed his lips. 'Can't say for sure, not just yet. Normally we like to wait for a storm. Nothing too dangerous but hopefully strong enough to reduce surveillance capacity a little. For the package we arrange a proper delivery, get you across in a vehicle, that sort of thing.'

'Will you come with me?'

'Well now, it depends . . .'

'For ten thousand euros you can go over with me.'

Johnny cocked his head, weighing up something. 'I can't be sure. We will have to see. There are some other individuals booked to cross.' He waved his hand. 'We share the same interests.'

'I should think so.' Mark leaned forward, this time putting his hand on Johnny's thigh. He gave the man a friendly squeeze. 'Don't fuck me on this, Johnny.' He squeezed tighter, pressing Johnny's flesh between his fingers. 'Let's be clear from the outset.' He let go of Johnny's leg.

Johnny made a whistling noise and tried to laugh. 'Our Mr Jay is a bad boy, you see that, Lance?'

'I see it all right.'

He rubbed his leg. 'I like this man, Lance. You like him?'

'I don't have no opinions.'

'Don't you worry, Mr Jay, for ten thousand euros everything going to be real lovely. All you got to do is wait a little, just a couple of days. I can't rightly say exactly when we'll cross over, not now. We have to wait for certain conditions.'

'I'm not going to transfer the money in one go. I need a guarantee.'

'Sure you do. Transfer half as soon as you can and half when we're about to cross. You can do that?'

'I guess I'll have to.'

'Where you staying?'

'Should I tell you?'

Johnny shrugged. 'I know this town. Take me about ten minutes to find out.'

'The Pink Triangle.'

'Good choice, very good choice. I know those people, lovely people. You just relax, Mr Jay, you enjoy yourself in Wind City. It won't be long now, I promise.' His smile opened bright, white and as wide as the grille of a Cadillac. They shook hands.

. . .

cold wind
stars flickering like candles
behind the veil the voice in the darkness

. . .

# WIND CITY

Mark sat up, wiping sweat from his face. The bedside fan fluttered ineffectually against the heat. Opening the metal shutter that covered the window, he flinched as sunshine came flooding in. The light was so bright he had to put on his sunglasses before looking out. Last night's rain had left the sky a ferocious, relentless blue. He yawned and rubbed his face. In the hotel car park he could see the Vindicator parked alongside an assortment of mud-splattered vehicles. Above, large birds circled languidly on hot vapours. He splashed some water on his face and made a call on the satellite phone. He explained the situation and made arrangements for funds to be transferred. The signal was weak, static slicing the conversation into snatched strands.

In daylight the sober Wind City looked even uglier. The place felt like the edge of the world, a bedsore of broken antennae and palm trees torpid against an empty sky. The ennui of green lizards sunning themselves on shattered concrete, beer bottles and cigarette butts ground into the cracked red earth, vultures pecking through mounds of festering garbage. Dilapidated shacks, prefab sheds and trailers painfully insubstantial, flimsy props on the verge of sinking back into the alligator swamp. The town was eerily deserted, its inhabitants hiding away as if ashamed. Stray dogs roamed the streets fighting over gutter scraps. He saw the odd alcoholic or junkie stumbling about seemingly oblivious to the incredible heat and others, groups of beggars even more desperate, filthy outcasts rummaging through overflowing bins and skips piled with glass bottles, tin cans and soggy plastic bags. The afterbirth of civilisation. By eleven it was too hot to go out at all and Mark lay on his bed, naked and drenched in sweat.

Memories came back in the heavy heat: sitting in the pickup as cars and trucks sped past filled with terrified people fleeing the smoke rising from the town, Ashe at his side, patient as a reptile, his glazed eyes hardly blinking as the second bomb went off just as planned, twenty minutes after the first, a ball of fire incinerating the retreating traffic, engulfing ambulances and police cars, flames ballooning into the sky, the shockwave rippling through the street. The slight, sly smile playing across Ashe's lips . . . red stones rising out of the sand . . . Scorpion Men . . . Task Force 11 . . . cold wind at night in the depths of the desert and distant stars far above, the two of them wrapped in blankets shivering in the midnight chill listening to the details coming through on the short-wave radio . . . the electric shift and shiver of conspiracy and counter-claim.

'Sometimes we have to do bad things. Sometimes the way of good is mired in evil. Ignore the judgements of those who stand far away. For those of us who have to act there are always complications, always consequences.' Foxy spoke in such soothing tones as they sat in the back of a car heading out of London into the green security of the Home Counties. His voice was like the wet afternoon, the dull skies throbbing in time to the pain in Mark's shoulder. They said it was to do with his injury, with impaired motor function, although he thought he felt fine. A slight stiffness but nothing much really – *It just aches now and then*, he tried to explain – that and the small white scar left behind, a crescent moon hanging in the skin above his arm. 'I'm so proud of you,' said Foxy with a smile. They let him sit in the sunshine, his head soupy with everything, the trees heavy with pollen and the scent of medication. Nurses gliding past silently, false eyes painted over their eyelids, the ground melting like sand and the red rocks beneath. *A messy business . . .* the physiotherapist to rub the pain in his shoulder, the beautiful psychotherapist to ease the pain in his head and the man behind the mirror to tell him about the chopper going down. 'Ashe was a good agent.' He smiled as he spoke. 'Ashe was one of the best.'

Mark tried to answer their questions, but it wasn't easy. When he thought about Ashe it wasn't so much that he thought of a man. He thought of Hurricane Winthrop and all the other great storms, the swirl on the satellite, towers of cloud and wind whirring white and black, engulfing the territory. In the afternoon heat it was all too indistinct: Ashe's face and voice like old film over-exposed and projected against a white wall in bright daylight. He saw the red and white pattern of the keffiyeh swathed around the man's head and he recalled his eyes squinting in the Arabian light, his strong hands twisting the copper wire and setting the charge. Aftermath of yet another bomb, images working over and over: the bodies of pilgrims scattered about the highway, a bus consumed by fire, people with their clothes blasted off and their skin peeling from them like raw snakes, outstretched hands and dazed eyes dark with panic, the strange silence over the awful scene like a great shroud in an empty square. Sometimes it was so hard to dislodge the memories, choked up inside like an avalanche about to fall, so hard to know what to say or how to say it. Up there, waiting, memories of the future, a ton of rock about to fall.

For a long time afterwards he was sent only on category-C missions, dull affairs for the most, his time spent staking out dubious mosques in shabby northern cities, following itinerant clerics, rogue travel agents and disseminators of extremist literature. None of it ever amounted to much. Sometimes arrests were made and vague plans thwarted yet most suspects were innocent in all but attitude. Then they sent him to China where he spent his time escorting men to meetings in skyscrapers in smoggy mega-cities. He planted bugs in washrooms, under desks and in underground car parks. Easy work. Easy to bluff his way into an office disguised with a suit, a briefcase and a bona fide cover story. Easy when all he had to do was eavesdrop on industrial secrets, facilitate illicit exchanges of information, circulate bogus rumours about share prices and market confidence. He didn't have to kill anybody.

Months spent in training, learning new skills, perfecting old ones. He rehearsed all his usual routines: entering luxury hotels without being challenged, bluffing ticket inspectors when he didn't have a ticket, getting to the head of a queue without anyone really noticing, slipping in and out of cinemas, posh restaurants and exclusive nightclubs. Walking the streets, an invisible man, a mirror reflecting those around him.

He lost touch with Alisha and lived with a woman. She wasn't beautiful but his feelings for her were complex and anxious. All the same, civilian life began to rub, the dull monotony of it, the pointless rituals of Friday night, the tedium of a Sunday afternoon. He found it hard, the burden of having to be the same person, day after day. After a while he didn't know what to say to her, couldn't engage with discussions about her family or her friends or her job. Eventually the woman asked him to leave. 'Emotionally distant,' she said. 'Secretive,' she said.

Nigeria was his next category-A, shortly after the Islamic junta seized power and nationalised the oil fields. Sent in with a cadre of agents to rescue British oil workers taken hostage deep in the delta, but the mission was fucked, events moving faster than anticipated, women and children released without harm but the headless bodies of two dozen Shell executives found in the swamps. He remembered Lagos, not so much a city as a great combustion, hyenas in the streets eating the remains of drug dealers and alcohol pedlars, ominous crowds massing outside embassy buildings, sharia law and endless slums. Shortly afterwards the bombings started.

During this time he made contact with Alisha again. He had not forgotten her and had in fact thought often of her smile and her dark eyes so sympathetic and understanding. Nonetheless it was hard to know whom to trust any more. He would tell her to wait on the crowded concourse of Victoria Station or outside the Natural History Museum or among the fashionable crowds in Spitalfields Market, always a location charged by the press and thrust of the city and there she would be until he appeared – as if from nowhere – like a ghost, a manifestation, suddenly by her side, whispering 'Hello' in her ear and looking boyishly pleased with himself, delighted by his sneakiness, and afterwards she would wonder how long he had spent watching before making his approach, checking she hadn't been followed, moving only when he felt certain and then they would start down busy shopping streets or into the relative quiet of the park and then when he was confident that no one could listen in, they would talk. 'They can hear us from far away,' he would say. 'From across a busy street they can do it. They have powerful microphones. They can filter out the other noise. You wouldn't believe it, not until you see. Then you'd realise.'

Sometimes he went further, insisting on checking her handbag or the pockets of her overcoat. 'It's not that I don't trust you,' he would say. 'But they might plant something on you. You'd never realise. Someone bumps into you and sticks a tiny bug on your coat and then they can hear everything.' He'd turn pale at the sight of unmarked white vans parked by the roadside and slow-cruising people-carriers with dark-tinted windows. 'This is central London,' she would argue. 'White vans are everywhere. Those people-carriers, they're just minicabs.' 'Maybe,' he'd say, pensive and distracted, glancing one way and another. 'Maybe.' Anything could be a sign. She knew it was hard for him. His paranoia had become a magnetic force drawing everything into it. Sometimes he would break mid-sentence and hurry away, spooked by fears beyond explanation. On other occasions he was calm and they talked for hours. Gentle moments when he would take her hand, their feelings growing fragile and tentative, a golden curl, a spur of light between the clouds, the dappled pattern of sunshine playing across leaves gently swaying in the dry trees of the park. Sometimes weeks went by and she would hear nothing and wonder if he had been sent away again. Sometimes her phone would ring very late at night, her heart racing as she answered, 'Yes? Yes? Yes?' but no, it was never his voice that she heard. She told him all this much later when they were together, with the blessing of Foxy and the tacit approval of the agency.

Come sundown and huge thunderheads blossomed in the sky, cathedrals of heat and water, cloud towers churning crimson in the evening sun. 'Storm coming,' said the receptionist. 'Nothing too heavy though, a category-three at best.' Catching his expression, the receptionist continued, 'Are you sure I can't get you something? You look all-in.' He lowered his voice. 'Need any weed? We got the chronic, straight from plantations on the other side.'

At sunset the military transporters arrived, disgorging an

eager army of young men from nearby bases. Like a lush after the first drink, the town came spluttering back to life. Restless, Mark cast himself into the crowd, drifting from bar to bar. He had always liked the company of fighting men, admired their values, the spirit of discipline and sacrifice, dedication to the higher cause. But he felt little solidarity with these youngsters, pugnacious with freshly shaven heads and new tattoos. There was something forced about their delirious, drunken amusement, the patriotic and regimental chants brimming with bravado. There was a hot space in his mind, a polished, stinging brightness to blot out. Later he saw the girls cavorting in the disco flash, long legs raised on improbable heels, bending and twisting to show off hardened, gleaming bodies. He threw money at their seductive, gyrating silhouettes . . . the world glazed with sweat, a blurred haze of heat and alcohol. What was left? Light in his eyes, a polished space in his mind, the room spinning . . . He made it to the bathroom and lay afterwards on the cool tiles, water running over his face.

The following morning there came a knock at the door of his hotel room.

He blinked at the blond receptionist.

'Rough night, sweetie? I've got a message from Johnny.' The man smiled. 'He says, "Tomorrow night. Make sure you're ready."'

. . .

. . . flicker
Behind the veil the voice . . .

. . .

# THE RED

Two hours before dawn. A large truck was waiting in a small clearing on the outskirts of Wind City, headlamps illuminating the damp grass. It had obviously been appropriated from another of the private contractors that serviced the Zone, the side adorned with the DynoCorp logo, an eagle perched over a tilted globe, a cross grasped in one yellow talon, a lightning bolt in the other. Three other men stood by the truck. They were much younger than Mark. With their large rucksacks and shared expressions of nervous apprehension they resembled a bunch of students about to embark on an adventurous gap year. Mark was wearing khaki trousers, boots and a linen shirt baggy enough to help disguise his firearm, strapped under his arm in the shoulder holster. In his rucksack he carried his laptop, satellite phone, ammunition and a change of clothes. His money was strapped to a belt wrapped around his waist. The waiting was over. He was going back into the field.

'Gentlemen,' began Johnny. 'I will spare you introductions. Until you get across it is better that you know nothing about each other. You share a common cause, that's all I'll say for now.' He wore a black DynoCorp cap and waterproof jacket. There was another man with him whom Mark did not recognise. 'Everything is in order and we should pass into the Zone without hindrance.'

'And if we do get stopped?' Mark asked.

Johnny frowned. 'We won't. I've done this many times. Don't worry.' He led them to the truck. Hidden deep inside, surrounded by ready-to-eat meal-packs, was a small compartment. The three others got in.

'I hope you're appreciating the personal service,' Johnny said.

'We'll see,' Mark replied. 'You got the first instalment of the money?'

'You wouldn't be here if I hadn't.'

'And we're going to be met at the other side? You've had confirmation from the Queer Liberation Army?'

'Sure. Relax.' Johnny dispensed a friendly slap on the back. The gesture struck Mark as slightly forced, as though Johnny were feigning a confidence he didn't entirely feel. But there was nothing else for it now. Johnny had told him that members of the insurgent force would meet them on the other side, offering a degree of protection and most likely information about the whereabouts of Kalat.

He followed the others into the compartment. Even sitting down the low metal ceiling was uncomfortably close with no room for anyone to stretch their legs. They waited in the darkness as more meal-packs were loaded on board. Soon they were thoroughly boxed in. One of the men turned on his torch, playing the light over the faces of the others. 'Cosy, isn't it?' He giggled nervously.

'What's your name?' someone asked.

'Better wait until we get over, like Johnny said,' said Mark sternly.

After a while the engine started, the air conditioning needed to chill the ready meals bringing some relief. The truck started moving.

'The crossing is only ten miles away,' said one of the young men, whispering as if someone might overhear them. 'It won't be long and then we'll be free.'

Mark kept silent. He shut his eyes, trying to focus on the pulse of the road and his own steady breathing.

After a long and uncomfortable half-hour they came to a stop. No one said anything. Mark put a hand inside his jacket, resting his fingers on the handgun. It was hard to breathe. Sweat ran down his back and his legs felt stiff and cramped. He felt a sharp wave of anxiety, sensing border guards outside with their sniffer dogs and infrared scanners. *Dammit!* He should have never put such trust in unknown elements to enable the mission. He was irrevocably compromised. He should have raised more objections in Atlanta, should have insisted that they drop him on some remote stretch of Florida coastline no matter what they said about budgetary and manpower constraints or the need for on-the-ground intelligence accumulation. *Fuck them!* Still, he told himself, too late now. He had to remain calm, there was no point dwelling on anything but the present situation. He knew that he'd been through worse. He'd been conditioned to expect such things: the hole and the box, the sharp wall and the screaming light, the wrap-up and the knock-down, false flag, Mutt and Jeff, all the nasty tricks needed to dismantle a man, to break him into component parts and extract the necessary essences. He remembered the hours and days in the cell, sweltering in a heat that seemed to come from everywhere, wall, floor and ceiling, bright neon lights visible even with eyes closed, his arms tied high behind his back, his body weak from thirty-six hours without sleep, forty-eight hours without sleep – *wake up, you cunt* – fifty-six hours without sleep, just a dreadful twilight world where nightmares bled into the real, sixty-two hours without sleep, the walls melting, eyes in the walls and a man without eyes telling him to sign the document and then it would be over, the man who said he was his friend and the man who was anything but, the plastic bag they put over his face, holding him down with the wet cloth and the running tap – *you're in the shit now, you cunt* – screaming at him through megaphones, dogs with their fangs drawn snarling and soldiers with guns cocked.

The truck started its engine. They were moving again.

'Thank God,' one of the men exhaled.

Now that they seemed to have made it safely into the Zone the other men began to relax a little and started talking. All were homosexuals, fleeing the repression in the United States to join the Queer Liberation Army and the Rainbow Love Faction. Excited, they spoke about the promise of the Zone, of communities where they could live without persecution. They said every week hundreds crossed over. They carried letters of recommendation, testimonials from lovers prepared for them by fixers working in American cities for the queer underground, a nebulous network moving people, weapons and funds back and forth in the fight for sexual rights.

A little later the truck came to another halt. After a short moment the rear doors opened and the ready meals were cleared away. 'We're here,' Johnny was shouting. 'Come out guys.'

One by one they scrambled from the truck. The warm dawn air tasted fresh and Mark was gratified to see the sky above, purple with the dawn. They had stopped by the side of a wide road, grass growing through the tarmac. Tall trees draped with moody swathes of Spanish moss loomed around them and the undergrowth vibrated to the trill of unseen insects. It was impossible to tell where they were and Mark wondered if they had actually crossed into the Zone or if Johnny had simply driven around the outskirts of Wind City for the last hour.

He wasn't the only suspicious one. 'Where's the contact?' one of the men asked.

'I'm not sure,' answered Johnny. 'They should be here. Maybe they've been delayed.' He took out a satellite phone. 'I guess I could give them a call . . .'

That moment Mark sensed something, a tremulous disturbance, a faint tremor gleaming like shards of vaporised metal. 'I think—' he began.

'Perhaps it's them,' said one of the others.

A little red dot of light was dancing across the front of Johnny's shirt. Red threads stretching back into the bushes. There was a strange expression on Abraham's face, a sort of amused disdain. 'What is that?' said someone.

Mark moved fast as a dull *phut-phut-phut* noise erupted from the darkness of the forest, running round the back of the truck where he saw one of the men who had been with him in the compartment zipping his fly and looking at him with confusion.

Mark grabbed the man by the hand, pulling him towards the undergrowth, bullets zinging past, something slamming into his rucksack and causing him to stumble as they rushed onwards, hurrying deeper until his rucksack snagged on a briar and yanked him over. 'Shit, shit, shit.' Quickly, with agitated voices behind shouting orders, he jerked himself free. 'Come on,' he said, urging his companion deeper into the jungle, flinching as branches and twigs lashed at their hands and faces. A path of sorts emerged along a muddy stream, water glinting in the faint light like purple velvet, their feet splashing loudly. A hundred metres further and Mark grabbed his ally and pulled him behind a large tree. The man started to say something but Mark placed a hand over his mouth. Gun in hand, he glanced back. The forest was very dark, the chinks of light appearing through the canopy only magnifying the gloom below. Their attackers were certain to have night-vision and he knew the two of them would be lit up like torches.

With a cry of panic the other man leaped to his feet and ran out from under cover. Red lights darted through the trees and the man went down.

Mark pressed close to the damp ground. He could hear someone advancing. A figure emerged clad in dark fatigues. He was almost on top of him. Mark rose up, grabbing his opponent's machine gun with his left hand and pushing it away. He drove his handgun into the assailant's stomach and squeezed the trigger once, the man shaking as he was shot, the blast muffled by such close contact. Shoving him against a tree, Mark fired a second time before releasing him, lifeless, to the ground.

Mark picked up the weapon. It was a customised Colt M4A1 with silencer and infrared laser pointer, the sort of firearm favoured by special forces, but he figured these gunmen must be private contractors, sloppy-shot mercenaries with poor reactions. Had they been special forces he knew that he would be dead by now. Looking through the infrared sight, he saw the greenish outline of another rapidly approaching figure. His opponent crouched down and raised his weapon. Mark ducked back behind a tree, the undergrowth rippling and whistling as shots whisked past. Then he leaped out, aimed at the man's head and fired twice. His enemy spun round and went down. He checked again, looking for other approaching figures. Nothing.

Mark could hear his companion moaning in pain where he'd fallen. He hurried over. 'Can you move?' he said.

'I don't know.'

'We've got to get out of here. I'm going to help you up, okay?'

'Okay.'

'And then we run. Ready?'

Grabbing the man's arm, Mark pulled him up. He squirmed in pain but managed to stand. 'Come on.' Mark pulled forward, the man limping behind.

Moments later and the undergrowth changed, thinning slightly and Mark was startled to see a number of evenly placed concrete supports leading up to tracks that ran about twenty feet above them, cleaving a high path through the jungle. He followed them until the canopy dropped away and they ran into an open expanse of shattered concrete. Grass grew waist-high through the untended expanse, wheel-less cars rusted in the undergrowth along the verge. Across the precinct half-submerged by creepers and coated by a thick tapestry of moss stood a huge building, the structure rising from a web of vines like the stricken hulk of a sunken cruise-liner.

The two men ran inside. Wreckage everywhere, a chaos of exposed pipes and wires hanging down in twisted ruination. They hurried through the entrance hall, splashing through a toxic mix of stagnant water, slippery moss and broken glass. The ceiling had fallen in, fragments of tiles and blocks in great heaps, dirty water dripping through the splits and cracks above as if they had entered a cave, a deep hole filled with concrete stalagmites and drooping nooses of electric cable and copper wire. Ahead Mark saw a silver escalator. The two men scrambled over the rubble and up it into a much larger chamber, a looming interior, faded walls rising to thick green creepers which hung like mossy stalactites from the ceiling. Huge bats, disturbed by their arrival, flapped about in the hazy miasma, stifled particles of dust making things seem larger and further away, the far wall adorned with strange designs, traces of a faded mosaic, a fragmentary cascade of colour, burnished textures in red, gold and bronze like frescoes in a Byzantine church or the unearthed paintings of an unknown prehistoric tribe. Across the concourse and above them Mark saw that the twin tracks which they had followed through the undergrowth ran on into the building. More astonishing still, he saw a monorail train stalled on the tracks, as though the line had been seized during a huge storm and slammed into the building in a fit of climatic violence.

But there was no time to absorb such sights. 'We have to find a vantage point,' he said to the wounded man. 'Can you keep moving?'

The man's shirt was dark with blood. His eyes rolled white like waves in a distressed ocean. 'Stay with me,' Mark shouted. Rooms led off the lobby, external corridors stacked upwards inside the rising pyramid vault of the structure. He chose a room on the left which he thought would allow him to survey the jungle and should, if more men came out in pursuit, give a good vantage point from which to open fire. Pale wallpaper was peeling from the walls like flayed skin and a sodden mattress furry with fungus was dumped in one corner. All the glass had been knocked out of the huge window at the far end and a single curtain, stained green by the elements, lolled languid in the gaping space. Of course! He saw it now – they were in the remains of a hotel. He let the injured man slump to the floor and then collapsed next to him gasping for breath.

He forced himself to sit up and check the SMG, sliding the magazine out. Eight rounds left. He slid it back into the weapon. He took off his rucksack. Something about it felt wrong. A bullet had torn through the back shattering the laptop. Bits of plastic and wiring fell on to the floor. *Shit shit shit*. Quickly he pulled out his things. The satellite phone was still intact. Watery waves of relief washed through him. The injured man rolled on to his stomach moaning in pain.

Mark went over to the window, looking first at the open space they had traversed. No sign of anyone coming after them. Dawn light stained the sky a luminous golden pink and transformed the forest into a wonderland of emerald and viridian. A flock of birds broke from the canopy calling as they flew upwards. Following their flight Mark gazed across the landscape. He saw a number of structures rising from the sea of green: a blasted tower, a looming dome glinting white like a monstrous egg and then, most incredible of all, an ethereal castle, immensely tall, with battlements, delicate turrets and a mighty golden spire gleaming in the soft dawn. The building seemed to float above the forest, a mirage of pink and pale blue, too beautiful to be real.

'What the fuck?' he exclaimed, as astonished as an explorer who had just glimpsed a lost city in the depths of a rainforest.

A dark shape, like a huge metal insect, rose out of the jungle, the roar of rotor blades breaking the morning calm. Mark pressed his face to the dirty floor as the Apache helicopter buzzed their ruin, the broken curtains flapping frantically in the mechanical breeze. The roar of engines increased, the craft hovering menacingly close, the building shaking with vibrations. The wounded man cried out, his moans lost in the metallic grind. Mark knew the Apache would be scanning the building with heat sensors and spectral cameras. For a minute it seemed as if the helicopter were going to land on top of them and then abruptly the pitch of the engine changed and the curtain stopped flapping. The Apache flew over the building, circled once and then headed away. As the sound gradually receded he crawled over to the injured man.

'What's going on?' the man gasped, his face slick with sweat.

'You've been shot.' Mark squatted over him. 'I'm going to roll you over. I need to see where the bullet went in.'

'It hurts.'

Mark nodded. 'My name is John.' He gripped the man's hand, squeezing hard. 'What's your name?'

'Richard.' His voice was tight and high, like a balloon about to burst. 'Richard Sheridan.'

'Good to meet you, Richard. We're in deep shit, I'm afraid. Now this will hurt, I'm sorry.' Taking his arm and ignoring his cry, Mark rolled him over as gently as he could. There was a small, neat hole in the left shoulder oozing bright red blood. He couldn't see any sign of an exit wound.

'It's bad, isn't it? Oh God, it's bad.' Richard started to sob. 'I've been shot. I don't fucking believe it. I've been shot.' He wasn't very old, Mark thought, no more than twenty-one, twenty-two, and his blood was everywhere. The man was dying. Mark took a first-aid kit from his rucksack and sprayed the wound with an antiseptic painkiller. Then he took out a medi-pad and slapped it over the man's bloody shoulder. It was like trying to halt a flood with a sandbag. A sickening sense of futility overwhelmed him. Dirty hands clawed the hot air. 'I've got a number,' Richard gasped. 'On my phone . . . by my pocket . . . is it there?'

'Yes.' Mark unclipped the mobile from the man's belt.

'We were meant to meet . . .' He coughed weakly. 'Johnny arranged it . . . Where's Johnny?'

'He's dead.'

Panic and horror rushed through Richard's eyes.

'We were ambushed,' Mark said.

'The number . . .' Richard started again, his hands twitching at Mark. 'Captain Stone. The QLA. They were meant to meet us . . . you could . . . you could call him.'

'Do you have the number?'

'It's there . . . the first number.'

Mark pressed the call register. 'That one?' he said, holding the phone for Richard to see.

Richard nodded. 'They were expecting us,' he mumbled. 'Johnny said . . . We were supposed to meet . . .'

Mark considered the odds. Without medical attention

Richard would soon die. If he used the phone there was a danger that the people who had attacked them might detect the signal. He wiped sweat from his face. His predicament was far from positive. He didn't even have any water. He went to the window. No sign of anyone else. The rising sun was melting the sky, turning it from tender pink to shocking blue. A few clouds gathered on the horizon. He had another look at the fairytale castle. The earlier illusion of pristine beauty was fading with the changing light. A large crack ran through the middle of the structure and one of the towers leaned precariously, on the verge of collapse, while the wind had snapped off another turret. Beyond he saw more structures, a strange skyline of ruined resorts and amusement rides poking up like the rigging of wrecked ships from a tide of rude undergrowth. He looked at Richard's phone. The signal was weak but it was there. He dialled the number.

It rang several times. Then, 'Yes.' A cautious voice. 'Richard, is that you?'

'It's not Richard,' said Mark. 'But Richard is with me. He's hurt bad. We need help. We were ambushed. Everyone else was killed, Johnny, everybody.'

'Who is this?'

'You don't know me. My name is John Jay.' He spoke quickly, keeping his voice calm and direct. 'I was crossing with Johnny and others. We were attacked. We were expecting to meet you but we were ambushed. I managed to escape with Richard but he's been shot. We are hiding in a hotel in DisneyWorld. Can you help us?'

'Who attacked you?'

'I don't know. Mercenaries. Darkwater forces. I've no idea. They had an Apache helicopter but they've gone now, I think. I killed two of them. If you don't help us, we're fucked.' He lowered his voice. 'Richard won't live long.'

'Hold on. We'll call you back.'

Feeling dazed, Mark waited, one hand anxious on the phone, watching as Richard lapsed out of consciousness, his breath ebbing in erratic, ragged gasps. A few minutes later the call was returned. Mark gave the best description he could of their location and was told to wait outside for a helicopter.

'Do you think Richard will last that long?' said the voice.

'I'll do my best.'

Richard came whimpering back to consciousness. 'Help is coming,' Mark told him, squeezing his hand. 'Hold on.' He rummaged through the man's trouser pockets. In Richard's wallet he found $2000 in hundred-dollar bills and a number of false IDs, a DynoCorp contractor card, a driving licence with a picture of Richard but a different name, a Retina-Card which may or may not have been genuine, a picture of Richard in a bar somewhere and a SIM card. The room felt glutinous with heat and moisture. Rousing himself Mark gathered together his things. He hefted Richard on to his shoulder in a fireman's lift. Slinging the SMG over one arm and holding his rucksack with his free hand, he started back down.

– I'm cold.

*Flicker*

  – I said . . .

*Flicker*

  – I'm hurt. I'm hurt bad, aren't I?

Yes, yes you are.

  – Am I going to die?

. . .

  – I am, aren't I? I'm dying.

# QUEER LIBERATION

Pausing on the dead escalator, gasping for breath with Richard draped as heavy and unwieldy as a carpet over his shoulder, Mark had reason to regret their upwards flight. Richard was in shock, sporadically shaken from his state by Mark's jolting steps. Struggling back outside, he lowered Richard to the ground and slumped beside him on the forecourt of the former hotel. Nasty little black flies swarmed in the yellowish air. Dazed with heat, thirst and shock Mark lost consciousness. He was woken by a vibration in his pocket. Richard's phone.

'We're five minutes away. Coming from the south. Pay attention.'

Moments later another helicopter dropped down from the sky, an old Black Hawk with zebra stripes and a rainbow flag emblazoned on its tail. Mark crouched, shielding himself against the blown air. Four men jumped out of the chopper, two of them carrying a stretcher. All wore unfamiliar camouflage uniforms with horizontal green and brown stripes and customised American football helmets sprayed dark green. Mark raised his hands, keeping the SMG on the floor, anxious to avoid provoking his saviours. One of them walked straight up to him. 'John Jay?' he shouted over the roar of the helicopter.

Mark nodded. The man's face was partly hidden by a scarf and mirrored shades. Three stars were painted on his helmet. 'I'm Captain Stone. I'll need to take all your firearms, I'm afraid. It's that or stay here. We won't wait.'

Mark handed over the SMG and his pistol. The captain gestured at another trooper, who quickly frisked Mark before taking his rucksack.

'Come on.' They clambered on to the helicopter. The stretcher bearers secured Richard and rigged him up to a drip. The captain passed Mark a bottle of water and he drank eagerly. Moments later they rose up over the hotel and banked hard, tilting downwards. They flew low, just above the tree-tops, circling Cinderella's castle and heading south over what was left of DisneyWorld.

Mark stared at the landscape, what Johnny had called 'the white', watching the shadow of the helicopter as they crossed a large lake, the shore dotted with pillaged resorts. Weird storm forces and warped tides had drained most of the water, leaving behind vast circles of swampy brown land, brackish pools and stagnant hollows slithering and thrashing with alligators and snakes. Here and there, breaking the dense terrain, he saw the fractured spine-ways and concrete conflagrations of the old highway system, a faded grid of suburban subdivisions, motels and retail centres, and in the distance the charred geometry of a petrochemical complex. Was this the real America, he wondered, this postmodern wilderness, this catastrophic landscape conjured forth from a sun-glazed utopia of retirement communities, golf courses, themed shopping centres and genetically enhanced orchards? It was hard to conceive of such sights. After all, he had sat in many helicopters, had flown over many a savage landscape, but those had been the faraway places, the failed states, the swarm lands of a dark fanaticism. And yet . . . he could see it now . . . those places had also been this place. Here he was at the end point, the terminal beach of Western civilisation.

He glanced at the troops from the Queer Liberation Army. Two were tending to Richard with saline and bandages. Captain Stone sat opposite, shouting into a radio words unheard over the roar of rotors. A fourth crew member manned a swivel-mounted machine gun, scanning the ground for threats. Familiar postures, as if everyone were trapped in a pastiche of all the American wars gone by, Korea and Vietnam, Iraq and Afghanistan, Somalia and Iran. But this was still America, he told himself, this was America.

Stone leaned forward. 'Okay, now you can tell me what the hell is going on.'

'I was being smuggled into the Zone by Johnny Midnight. We were supposed to meet with you guys,' he shouted back. 'We were ambushed. I don't know who they were. Everyone else was killed, I'm pretty sure. I managed to escape with Richard. I shot two of them. That's all I know.'

'And you're John Jay?'

'That's right. Johnny said you guys could help me.'

Stone held up a hand and spoke into the radio. The chopper banked hard, engine grinding and creaking, metal plates struggling with the stress. Mark held on tight, his stomach plunging as the horizon tilted precariously, their pilot either highly skilled or extremely reckless. They flew over a large flat clearing, possibly the former car park of a huge out-of-town mall, now dense with grass. To his astonishment he saw a dozen men on horses charging across the furze, riders wearing colourful, feathered headdresses, their skin decorated with strange designs, their mounts adorned with brightly coloured blankets. The riders reared their steeds, waving spears and rifles at the helicopter.

Stone pointed at the horsemen. 'You see that? Seminole tribesmen, they have a claim to the area. Watch out, they take pot shots at anything they see.'

Mark looked again but already the riders were gone, sucked back into the wilderness.

'Your name checked out,' Stone continued.

'What?'

'Your name,' Stone said again. 'It checked out. You were expected.'

'Right.'

'The thing is,' he went on. 'We have a bit of a situation.'

'What do you mean?'

But Stone was on the radio again. Mark tried to make out what was being said but it was difficult, with the noise, the crazed velocity of their flight and the medical team beside them frantically trying to patch up Richard. They had strapped an oxygen mask to the wounded man's face and one of the team was injecting him with something, the other trying to balance plastic sacks filled with necessary fluids. It was obvious that they knew what they were doing and Mark had to admit to himself that with the helicopter, the uniforms and equipment everything appeared very professional. He was impressed. He had heard numerous rumours about the Queer Liberation Army but precise, verifiable intelligence was hard to come by. He knew that the group had emerged after the San Francisco rampages which followed the Thirty-Fifth Constitutional Amendment. First notice of the QLA came after they claimed responsibility for the bombing of a Kentucky mega-church closely affiliated to Reverend Samuel Parris, a terror-spectacular which killed more than a hundred of the righteous. Since then the group had waged a steady campaign of bombings and assassinations across the United States, responding to the random lynching, the correctional incarceration and chemical castration of homosexuals by attacking religious and political targets. For several years intelligence had been rife with reports of training camps and bases being established in the Zone, with evidence that the organisation was entering a new phase and moving from discrete splinter cells to more organised, interconnected networks. Mainstream media had sought to demonise the army, claiming they were in league with Colombian and Mexican drug cartels, even asserting that Hezbollah and Hamas had provided training and weapons despite glaring ideological incompatibilities. Mark had always understood such reports as part of a tactic perpetuated by Fox and the various Christian TV networks intended to conflate the disparate opponents of Parris's regime into a single demoniacal block, evading both the differences between these groups and the reasons for their defiance. More credible was evidence that the group gained funds through a combination of extortion, blackmail and a secretive subscription system funded by wealthy European and Canadian homosexuals. Whatever the truth, the group appeared much more professional and better equipped than he had expected.

Abruptly the helicopter started to circle the canopy, rising a little, engine grinding and shaking violently before dropping to land in a narrow space between the trees.

Additional troops, some wearing the same striped uniform and others dressed more casually, ran forward pulling a huge swathe of camouflaged webbing. The space above them was quickly covered, all sight of the helicopter hidden from anything flying above. They had landed in some sort of a base, activity all around, men hurrying between tents sprung among the trees. A fresh squad of heavily armed troops moved towards them while others brought up a small fuel tanker, preparing the chopper for the next flight. Richard was rushed away on a stretcher.

Stone waved his hand and the squad surrounded Mark, rifles raised. 'Relax.' Stone pulled an automatic from his belt and gestured at Mark. 'Just put up your hands.'

'You really don't need to do this.'

'Shut the fuck up, spy!' One of the troops struck the back of his leg and he went down. Hands pinned him to the floor and someone lashed a binding wire around his wrists. Then they yanked him up and frogmarched him forward, keeping his head down. He was led into a tent and shoved into a chair.

'Why are you doing this?'

Stone slapped him across the face and put an automatic to the side of his head. 'No more lies. Who are you?'

Mark took a deep breath, flinching against the press of the hard barrel. He had anticipated something like this. 'I'm John Jay. My name is on the list, you said.'

'With a big fucking question mark beside it!'

'How should I know what that means?'

'Your identity wasn't verified through the approved channels.'

'Johnny Midnight—'

'Midnight didn't know who the fuck you were and Midnight's dead. Everyone else is dead.'

'I told you, we were ambushed.'

'John Jay isn't your real name, is it?'

'Of course not. Do I look fucking stupid? No one enters the Zone using their real name. Listen, I've already killed two men this morning, two of the men who killed Johnny and the others. I'm here because I wanted to save someone and because I need your help. Understand? I need your help.'

Stone took a step back, holstering his pistol. He removed his sunglasses and rubbed his face. He was younger than Mark had expected, in his late twenties at best, tanned and fit with the all-American good looks of a fitness instructor or lifeguard. A taut sheen of stress marred his handsome countenance. 'Okay, let's start again. We don't have much time. What's your real name?'

'My real name is Burrows. Mark Burrows. That's not the

name on my passport or anything else but that's my real name. I'm a security consultant. You can call me a spy if you like but I'm certainly not your enemy. I'm English. I'm looking for someone. I told Johnny all of this. I'm looking for my brother-in-law, he's in the Zone and I've reason to believe he's joined the QLA.'

Stone didn't blink. 'Your brother's name?'

Mark stared at the captain. 'He goes by a number of names. His real name is Charlie Ashe but I suspect you know him by another – Kalat.'

Stone took a step back. He seemed about to say something only to hesitate, as if unwilling to reveal himself at that moment. The name Kalat had sparked something though, Mark saw it pass among the soldiers, a quiver of recognition. Another soldier entered the tent and whispered to the captain.

'Okay. You two keep watch on him,' Stone addressed his men. 'The rest of you follow me.' And with that the squad hurried out.

Ignoring his guards, Mark slumped back and closed his eyes. This was all a bit much, rather more than anticipated. At the same time though, he could not deny the thrill he felt to be in such a place amid all this action. Almost like the old days. In such moments he found his thoughts turning against the paltry comforts of home, the dreary responsibilities of the domestic. As far as he knew no one from the agency had ever been to a QLA camp before. Foxy and the others would be pleased. Now it was just a question of calculating how much to reveal to Stone, how far honesty would enable his mission and how much he needed to keep back. He was reasonably sure he could turn the situation to his advantage but he could also tell that Stone and his men were scared and he knew scared people sometimes acted rashly. Certainly he knew no reason why they couldn't help each other. The agency had no argument with the QLA. The persecution of homosexuals under Parris was one of the President's many divinely inspired and biblically authorised policies that had caused rifts with the British government. In public, declarations of support were still given but privately he knew matters were rather different.

Stone hurried back into the tent, his expression more pensive than before. He went straight up to Mark. 'Okay, who are you working for?'

Mark shrugged. 'I thought I made it clear,' he said quite calmly. 'I'm not working for anyone.'

'What do you want with Kalat?'

'So you do know him.'

'Stop shitting us, Burrows – if that is your name. We know you're CIA or British intelligence.' He sneered. 'You're not one of us, that's for sure.'

Mark kept his voice calm and steady. 'I'm looking for Kalat or rather I'm looking for Charlie Ashe. The man he was. He really is my brother-in-law. He married my sister Susanna fifteen years ago in a church in Oxfordshire, on May twelfth to be exact. It was a warm spring day. They had a child, my nephew, also called Charlie. He's eleven now. Ashe is supposed to be dead. He was supposed to have died ten years ago. He was a soldier, part of British special forces. He was supposed to have been killed in an operation during the Iran wars. That was what we were told. Then I get information that he's operating out here, in the Zone. I need to find him. My sister needs to contact him. It's a purely private matter. Will you help me?'

'Who do you work for?'

Mark did his best to maintain his composure. The wires binding his wrists were starting to smart. 'I'm not the CIA. I think you know that. Look, who is in charge of you? Who is your commanding officer? Let me speak to them.'

'Don't think for a moment I'll tell you.'

'Come on, how about a little quid pro quo? I'll be straight with you if you'll be straight with me.'

'Very funny.'

'I don't have anything else to say.'

'You survived the ambush.'

'I was just lucky.' He looked at the captain. 'I also saved the life of that boy back there. Look, you have some sort of situation here. They have an Apache gunship. If one of those hits the camp, you'll all be fucked. I'm prepared to help you guys. I know how to handle a gun. I'm on your side. I just need to know where I can find Kalat. That's all I'm asking.'

Stone waited a moment, considering his words. 'Kalat has a lot of support in the Zone.'

'Does he support your cause?'

'No.' Stone rubbed his face. 'I don't think he has any particular interest in our fight but he respects our existence. He shares our understanding of this territory as a place for the persecuted, the oppressed and the outcast. What you don't realise is that we're the real Americans now. We're fighting for true American values, the Declaration of Independence, the Constitution, the separation of Church and state. It was there once. It can exist again. The government fears a space like this. They don't understand. They mistake it for a vacuum, for chaos and anarchy.'

'What is it, then?'

'A space where imagination can take over,' he said boldly. 'A space where people can be themselves, a space wrenched free of history.'

'Yeah? I thought we brought our history with us? There are no exceptions. There never have been.'

'Of course you say that.'

'What?'

'You are one of them, after all.'

'I don't know what you mean.'

157

'Your government labelled us a terrorist organisation.'

'My government?'

'The British government.'

'I don't know what you're talking about. Anyway, as I said, you shouldn't assume I represent any government or anyone but myself and my own desire to see Kalat. I have an obligation, a family obligation. Look, whoever Ashe has become, Kalat, whatever, he will remember me. He will see me.' Outside they could hear further commotion, people shouting and the sound of engines revving and vehicles moving away. 'If you won't let me help you at least let me go. I paid Johnny Midnight a lot of money to get over here.'

'You might reveal our location.'

'Don't be ridiculous. You're busy dismantling this base even as we speak, aren't you? Either we help each other or let me go. My concern is with Kalat. You're welcome to your struggle. I've nothing against you or your cause. A man's sexuality is his own business. You're right to fight for it.'

Stone sat down opposite him. 'Why should I believe you?'

'What is there to lose? The same people who are trying to kill you are trying to kill me. These attackers, I doubt they like Kalat much either. My guess is they won't stop here, with you guys. They'll press on. I need to reach him.' He looked earnestly at the captain. 'Help me and I'll help you or else just let me go.'

'Like that? You wouldn't last long.'

'That's my problem.' Mark hesitated for a moment, unsure whether to the push the point. He went for it. 'Stone, there are people who support my being here. They can help you. You shouldn't think everyone in the UK favours the way things are going in the United States. Money, weapons, intelligence, we can provide these things. I'm not your enemy.'

The captain looked at Mark for what seemed a long time. Then with a sigh of reluctance or recognition – Mark could not tell – Stone reached forward and untied his hands.

'Thank you.' He rubbed at his chaffed wrists. 'So do you mind telling me what's going on?'

'We've had reports that a nearby settlement has been attacked,' Stone said. 'A community sympathetic to us. We're not sure who it is but we think they must be Witch Hunters or Klansmen. Mercenaries perhaps, we don't know. Of course we've also lost contact with the party that was supposed to meet your group this morning. You should have been escorted to a secure location hours ago.'

'I told you what happened. We were wiped out.'

Stone cracked his knuckles. 'There are many of us. We occupy many locations. No matter what they do, we fight on.'

'What about Richard? I hope my efforts weren't totally in vain.'

'He's in surgery. He might just make it. If he does pull through, it's thanks to you.'

'You have a hospital here?'

Stone ignored the question. 'I'm awaiting a report from one of my scouts. Anyway, you're right, we're in the process of evacuating this base and I'm assembling a squad to see what is going on in the settlement.'

'Captain, let me be clear. You're under attack. Give me back my equipment and let me join this squad. Let's get these motherfuckers.' Mark gave a grim smile.

'You're sure?'

'I'll prove it to you. Then perhaps you can help me.'

'Okay.' Stone nodded severely. 'All right. Welcome, Mark. You've just joined the liberation.'

. . .


–  We're in danger, aren't we?
            We're not safe. We need to be quiet.
–  They're out there?
            Yes. But it's okay. We can fight.


    *the wind*

. . .

# FREETOWN

Thirty minutes later three customised Chevrolet Suburbans left the camp. The vehicles charged forward along a narrow muddy trail, plumes of dust billowing in their wake, branches and boughs brushing against the windows. Front and rear vehicles had been adapted, their roofs cut away to allow for a swivel-mounted heavy machine gun. All three were fitted with bull grilles and extra headlights and painted in tiger-stripe camouflage, while metal plates had been bolted on to side panels and doors to reinforce the bodywork and shield the tires. A large rainbow flag, emblazoned with the letters 'QLA', flew from the machine gun on the first vehicle. Metal grilles covered the side windows, slots cut into them just big enough to accommodate the barrel of an M16 rifle. Antennae rose out of the back, jammers and heat detectors designed to thwart guided missiles or disrupt timed bombs.

Mark sat in the middle vehicle, wedged on the front bench between the driver and Stone. He would have preferred to be near the door to facilitate a faster escape if the Suburban were disabled but he knew he was in no position to choose. Stone had returned his money and equipment along with his pistol and an M16A4 assault rifle with a 40mm grenade launcher attached to the barrel. The stock of the rifle had been painted in rainbow colours but otherwise the weapon was in good condition. He was carrying four hundred rounds of ammunition and five grenades. They'd also found him a flak jacket with QLA camouflage and an ill-fitting combat helmet. Four more troops sat in the back of the Suburban. Between the three vehicles a total of twenty members of the QLA were on the offensive. A wave of excitement washed through him. Less than eight hours in the Zone and already he was rushing to battle with the QLA.

They burst out into a clearing, passing houses sunken and rotten as hulks dredged from the ocean and washed onto a grassy shore. Mark glimpsed voracious gardens overgrown with enormous magnolia and gnarly trees devoured by the debris of exploded supermarkets.

Then they swerved on to a freshly laid road, the tarmac a gleaming glossy black tongue. 'Okay soldiers,' Stone said over the CB radio. 'We're on the DynoCorp road to Freetown now. Stay alert. We might encounter problems at any moment.'

Faster, they sped past tall palm trees leaning to the sky, slender wind-ripped trunks like the long necks of strange sea-creatures and overgrown plantations of cane, sharp green leaves drenched in the sticky fullness of the afternoon sun.

The CB radio crackled into life. 'This is Alpha Car, unidentified vehicle approaching, over.'

'Roger that. Status?' said Stone.

'Civilian, it's signalling to us, over,' replied the front Suburban.

'All cars slow down, full defensive, I repeat, full defensive, over,' Stone ordered.

'We have recognition,' said Alpha Car. 'They're from Freetown, over.'

They pulled up beside the vehicle. Mark could see several

men inside, faces white with shock. Bullet holes had punctured the rear window and frosted the glass. 'They attacked us.' The driver was hysterical. 'We just got away. They're right behind us. We've got a man hurt bad.'

'Who are they?' Stone shouted across Mark.

'I don't know, they came without warning.'

'How many?'

'At least thirty. Maybe more. We're going to Fortress. We need a hospital.' With a screech the car sped away.

Stone spoke frantically over the radio to a scout who was observing the situation up the road and then made another announcement to the rest of the convoy. 'I've got confirmation,' he said. 'They're in Freetown, burning the place up. We are three miles from contact. Head to the abandoned Shell garage on the outskirts. Be vigilant, over.'

'Freetown?' Mark asked.

'It's an unofficial settlement,' Stone answered. 'There are a lot of them in the Zone, all part of the red. They've got a store and a petrol station, a basic clinic, a brothel, a bar and a couple of storm shelters. It's meant to be neutral territory. Everyone uses it – other off-grid settlements for basic supplies, Darkwater and DynoCorp operatives for a bit of fun. You'll even see the military there now and then, when they want something they can't get on base.' He shook his head. 'I'm shocked it has been attacked. There are unwritten rules. These settlements, they are tolerated places, they serve everyone's interests.'

The road curved slightly, trees flanking either side, thick and close. They passed the carcass of a long-abandoned truck, its stripped-down metal frame rusted with orange blooms.

'Ahead, ahead,' the CB crackled from the lead vehicle. 'Approaching, evasive action, evasive action!' The lead Suburban swerved, brake lights flashing. Their driver spun the wheel towards the right but he was too late – Mark saw a motorbike approaching very fast – then the sudden shock as it glanced off the side of their vehicle, the impact knocking them forward and back. They started to skid. The rear Suburban halted in front of them. It took a moment before he realised they'd spun all the way round and were facing the opposite way. Wreckage lay scattered across the road. He looked in vain for signs of the rider. Stone was shouting into the CB. Engine roaring, wheels screaming, the driver yanked their vehicle into reverse. Pulling hard on the wheel, he turned them back the right way.

'Keep going,' Stone yelled. 'Keep going.'

The lead Suburban started forward. They drove parallel, the two vehicles dominating the road, the third behind, hogging the line.

Another motorbike appeared out of some trees and cut into the road before speeding away from them.

'Nix it!' Stone was shouting into the radio.

The heavy machine gun roared. Tracers ripped forward. The motorbike's fuel tank burst into flames. The rider, clad in a long white cloak, was blasted into the foliage. Their vehicle shook as they ploughed over the wreckage.

Ahead a black bar of smoke divided the sky. To the left Mark saw a ruined petrol station, the Shell symbol just visible on a faded hoarding. A third motorbike went tearing across the forecourt and into the road. Bullets exploded around the bike but he drove too fast, weaving from side to side and moving rapidly away from them.

'Prepare to engage,' Stone shouted. 'They've spotted us. Hit the town. Go, go, go!'

The Suburban picked up speed. Another SUV was blocking the road ahead. It had been shot up, shattered windows splattered with blood, a door hanging open. The alpha car took it on the left side and they swerved past on the right, shaking as they hit the verge, clouds of dust erupting around them.

They drove into the settlement. Mark saw several buildings, customised trailers and prefabricated shacks forming a rough strip along the new road. One structure was engulfed in flames, greasy black smoke obscuring the way ahead. They swerved to a halt next to the lead vehicle. Something came whizzing out of a building and ricocheted off the alpha car. An explosion behind them and their Suburban rocked with the reverberation. The machine gunner retaliated with a blast of gunfire.

'Let's go.' Doors were flung open. Mark flipped the safety off his M16 and followed Stone out, racing behind him towards the nearest building. The structure consisted of three trailers stacked on top of each other, each part connected by external walkways and a spiral staircase which ran up the side. A neon sign said 'Lucky's Girls'. He crouched beside Stone, the four other troops from their car at the rear. They kept their heads down, lying close on the ground. Meanwhile their Suburban reversed out of the line of fire and the third vehicle moved forward, stopping parallel to the first. Both heavy machine guns let off several intense bursts of gunfire, the sound like a chainsaw chopping apart the air. Keeping low, Mark moved close to the building. A door was open to one of the rooms. A black-haired girl in her underwear was screaming at them in Spanish. Mark gestured at her to get back. One of the Suburbans drove forward about ten metres, the gunner firing all the time. Acrid black smoke hung in the air. Mark could hear the *pat-pat* of bullets hitting the Suburban and the loud *kack-kack-kack* as the heavy machine gun returned fire. Then the heavy machine gun stopped. The turret swivelled back and forth but nothing happened. The Suburban started to reverse. Mark could see the gunner crouching low as bullets struck the armour-plated turret. A grenade exploded next to the vehicle. Something went whistling past Mark's head. Shots peppered the wall above them. 'They've got our bearing,' he shouted at Stone. The Suburban stopped reversing. It had lost a wheel and orange flames were licking up from the engine. The gunner jumped from his turret. The driver opened his door and the two men sprinted away. Bullets cut through the air. Mark pressed his face to the dirty floor and tried to make his body as small as possible. One of the QLA troops behind screamed in pain. He looked back. The trooper was clutching his leg. His comrade dragged him into the brothel. Shots rang out. He touched Stone on the shoulder and pointed to the next building along. Stone nodded. 'Cover us,' he shouted at the two men behind. He glanced at Stone and the two of them started running. A pandemonium of gunfire. Something whizzed past his face. They reached the next building. Thick smoke made it hard to see the enemy. They lay flat by the building, the prefab structure punctured with holes. Mark fired several short bursts to where he guessed the enemy must be hiding. A momentary pause. No shooting, nothing, just the smell of gun smoke and the crackle of flames. Stone was shouting into his radio. Then the gunfire started up again. Stone grabbed Mark by the shoulder and pressed his face to his ear. 'The scout says they're bringing up reinforcements.'

'Load your grenade launcher,' he shouted back, sliding a projectile into the chamber.

A white pick-up truck came out of the smoke, half a dozen men gathered in the back. The pick-up slowed down, no more than twenty metres away. Stone and Mark fired at once. One grenade hit the front of the vehicle and the second struck the back, explosions throwing men into the air. The shockwave knocked Mark on to the floor. His ears were ringing and he couldn't see anything. He sat up, struggling to catch his breath. His helmet had fallen off. Stone was next to him, his face stained with smoke. He was saying something but the words sounded far away. Flames had engulfed the pick-up. A bloody, twitching body lay beside them. Shots were echoing around the street. Shaking himself, Mark got up, put his helmet back on and moved round the burning pick-up. Bodies everywhere. He didn't look too close. Ahead the road opened up, a number of parking bays forming a small square in front of a three-storey brick building that must have predated the storms. Keeping low the two men ran over. A ghost-like figure appeared in the doorway of the building, white cloak and hood billowing. Mark fired from the waist, blossoms of blood erupting across the white gown, the man spinning round and tumbling down. He reached the side of the building and pressed his back to the wall. Stone was behind him. He looked around. Everything hazy in the smoke. His heart pounding, his ears ringing with concussion. He thought he saw something on the other side of the road but looking again, no, no one was there. He turned to Stone. His eyes shone out against his sooty face. Mark grinned at him. Somewhere, above the gunfire, someone was screaming. 'We must take this building,' he said. 'Get them to bring up the other vehicle.'

While Stone gave the order on his radio Mark slammed another grenade into the chamber. He darted to the front of the building. Stepping over the man he'd shot, he fired the grenade into the interior, ducking as the blast blew out shards of wood and glass. He stood up, spraying bullets inside. Then he was out of ammunition. He ducked again, loading a fresh magazine into the rifle. Stone was behind him, firing shots at targets on the other side of the street. He scrambled into the building. The floor was a mess of shattered glass and broken furniture. Acrid smoke filled the room, causing his eyes to smart. Judging by the remains of the bar at the back, the place must have been a saloon. Stone fired at something and Mark saw a man collapsed in a doorway. Outside the Suburban had arrived and two more QLA troops ran into the bar.

'Up, up,' he shouted at them.

He took the stairs, hurrying on to the first floor. A body lay on the landing face down in a pool of thick blood. In front a closed door. 'Ready?' he shouted at the QLA soldier with him. He kicked the door open and ducked back. Inside he saw upturned tables, broken glass scattered everywhere.

A wall of heat and smoke rose up around him, the explosion knocking him over. Someone fell on top of him. He pushed the body away. The QLA trooper had taken the full force of the blast. The air thick with dust, plaster and bits of wood falling. He saw Stone, shooting up the stairs. He loaded another grenade into the chamber and aimed in the same direction. The blast sent a fresh deluge of dust and grit tumbling over them. Stone was shouting something. He shook the man off and ran up. The explosions had badly damaged the staircase and he stumbled near the top as the wood gave way. Keeping a tight grip of his rifle, he pulled himself up. He wasn't thinking very clearly. Everything had taken on a deranged texture. A grey man was lying in the corner of the corridor. Mark realised he was a Klansman covered with dust. Part of his left foot was missing, fresh blood pooling around him. He still held a machine pistol. Mark kicked the weapon away and then kicked the man in the face. He stumbled along the corridor and into an upstairs room. He could hear shooting outside. A bedroom, the place a mess, sheets scattered across the floor. A pillow had been punctured and small feathers floated about in the air. A middle-aged woman lay on a bed so wet with blood that at first he thought she was sleeping on a red blanket. He went to the window and looked outside. The Suburban was still defending the front of the bar. He couldn't see anyone else. He heard another burst of gunfire but couldn't tell where it came from. He went back to the wounded Witch Hunter. The man lay still, looking at him with numb, yellow eyes. He grabbed the man by his collar and hauled him over his shoulder in a fireman's lift.

'Stone!' he shouted. 'You there? I've got a prisoner.' He started down the broken stairs, only to stumble, the wounded man falling over his shoulders. The pair of them tumbled to the floor below. The Witch Hunter screamed in pain. Stone and another QLA trooper were tending to their injured colleague. Carefully Mark rose to his feet. He felt dizzy and sick. He didn't think he could hear any more shooting outside. He turned to the Witch Hunter crumpled at the bottom of the stairs. Blood seemed to be everywhere. Mark put his foot lightly on the man's leg, just above the wound, and pointed his rifle at him. 'How many more of you are there? Talk or I'll kill you. How many more?' He pressed harder, the Witch Hunter squirming with pain.

'Why should I tell you?' The man's eyes were two stones cast into a dark well. 'You are scum, effluent of the Devil. Why should I forsake my place among the chosen? Let me tell you.' With some effort he pushed himself up on his elbows. 'We are coming and we will run you down – you deviants, you filth, you heathen trash – we will cut you out like the cancer you are, burn you from your holes. You can't hide from the wrath of God!' He spat out a bloody glob of mucus, half of it sticking to his chin and collar.

Mark turned away. The shooting stopped. He went over to the window. He saw a white horse galloping down the road. Terrified by the burning vehicles and blazing building, the unfortunate creature baulked, rearing its head and shaking itself. It dragged behind it a corpse caught up in the stirrups. The horse turned and galloped off behind the shacks on the opposite side of the road. Mark watched the space it had vacated for a moment, as though some fresh spectacle might appear, conjured into being by the strange grace of the Storm Zone. Aftershocks continued to echo in his ears. Behind him he could hear Stone tending to his dying colleague. In his mouth the strong tang of cordite and blood.

He turned to the captain. 'We should get out of here.'

Stone shook his head. 'I need to help this man.'

He looked at the wounded QLA trooper. His eyes were closed and his body had been bent horribly by the blast. Dark streaks of blood stained his uniform.

'Take him or leave him,' said Mark. 'Either way we need to get the hell out.'

'Okay, I'll call the scout.'

Mark went back to the window. Several QLA troops had taken up defensive positions outside. The other Suburban, the one that he'd been travelling in, had also manoeuvred into the square. One of the other wounded troops lay next to it, having his leg bandaged. They were too exposed. He didn't like it. In the corner the wounded Witch Hunter was still trying to harangue them in a croaky, dried-out voice.

Stone put down his phone. 'I can't reach him,' he said, wiping at his face.

'What do you mean?'

'What I said. Look I don't know. He isn't answering.'

'Filth. Scum of Sodom. Holy war! A holy war! God will strike you down!'

'We need to get out of here. We need to get out fast.'

Stone saw something in Mark's face. 'Are you sure?'

Then they heard it: a low, dull throb, like an ache in the heavens, the dread vibration of metal slicing fast and low through the atmosphere. Both men ran to the window.

'I don't see anything,' said Stone.

'Tell your men to get the fuck out of here,' Mark shouted.

'The wrath of God,' jabbered the Witch Hunter. 'Sodomites, filth, scum.'

At that moment the Apache appeared, cleaving apart the sky, swooping so low Mark could see the white cross painted on its base like a huge tattoo on the stomach of a renegade priest.

'Back!' Mark pulled the captain away from the window.

The building shook, cannon fire pulverising brick, sheet metal and concrete. Mark clung to the floor. He heard the whoosh of a rocket and the world shook again, mighty explosions turning everything red and white, the super-heated atmosphere rippling with the flex and twist of shock and aftershock and then, a swamped, concussive echo, stench of burning oil and ruptured metal, his bones rattling, air sucked out of his lungs by the heat-blast and he felt as though he were being flung up and down and then pressed hard against the floor by a giant hot fist.

Gaping silence, and the Klansman started to sing a lisping hymn in a faraway voice, everything trembling and shaking. The front of the saloon had collapsed and the two soldiers struggled over a mound of pulverised brick and carbonised wood. One of the Suburbans lay on its side, burning fiercely. The ground wept smoky hot tears into the fractured heavens. Bits of men were everywhere, charred hunks of flesh and twists of gut, smears of blood and tattered fragments of uniform and weaponry. Stone fell to his knees and threw up. Mark shook his head. He wanted to say, 'I told you so,' but his mouth didn't work.

Leaving the captain, Mark hobbled slow and suddenly weak through the remains of the settlement. A little way from the main stretch he passed two more corpses lying in the grass. An adolescent girl and an older man both shot in the back. Black flies buzzed around the bodies. He wiped the sweat and dirt from his face, dizzy and shaken by the aftermath of battle. He sat down, momentarily sickened, trying to regulate his breathing. Slow, deep breaths. Everything wobbly and filled with a nauseous wonderment. He'd felt this way before in the aftermath of battle: a gushy, woozy sort of euphoria, an almost horny feeling, spasms and twitches of desire pulsing through his body. In Iraq the weird sexual urges that would seize him after a bombing, compulsively jacking off in the back of the pick-up or the silent desert night. Desire inflamed by the proximity of death. He moved on, wiping at the sweat running down his face. So fucking hot . . . drenched in sweat, saturated by sweat, pissing sweat . . . keep going . . . Jesus . . .

A number of reinforced cabins and trailers set further back from the road had been left relatively unscathed by the fighting. He moved among them, peering through grilled windows, looking at unmade beds and rudimentary living quarters, evidence of hasty flight all around. A little further away was a much larger block, windowless and made of reinforced concrete. The structure was much more robust than the others. A door to the bunker was open. Venturing inside he realised this was what he had been looking for – a store room, packed with supplies. He walked between boxes of equipment, sacks of rice, corn and pasta, barrels of cooking oil, tanks of filtered water and several vehicles surrounded by maintenance equipment. Rummaging around he found a survival kit and rucksack. The kit contained a waterproof sleeping bag with mosquito net, a medical set with bandages, powerful antibiotics, painkillers, blood boosters and water-purifying capsules. He found a large water bottle and filled it with filtered water from the huge tank in the corner. He splashed water over his face and drank several mouthfuls. He found a box of Ready Rations and quickly ate a couple of power bars. The surge of sugars and nutrients immediately made him feel better. Further exploration uncovered a stash of Pentagon maps of the Zone. The detail was impressive, military bases clearly marked, large white spaces linked by new roads outlined in black. He could see the official settlements, places like Bunker and Fortress, Ironside and Deluge, Cloudtown, New

Zion, New Canaan, A-town and Babel, situated strategically along new roads and within the shadows of military bases. Other areas were shaded red to signify danger, abandoned towns crossed out and marked with skull and crossbones, the disused highways and turnpikes printed in a faded ink. Other areas were distinguished by more ambiguous signs: question marks, toxic hazards, symbols for pollution and contamination, images of wild beasts and reptiles.

Folding the map he went to look at the vehicles. A Swamp-Hummer, a couple of buggies with sturdy 4×4 tyres, a battered Ford estate. At the other end of the bunker was a large garage door. He opened it. Jungle loomed everywhere. Back to the vehicles. He thought about taking the Swamp-Hummer and then decided against it. He wanted something smaller and more inconspicuous but still speedy and hardy enough to traverse the Zone. It was necessary to get moving, and fast. He went over to one of the buggies. Keys in the ignition. He filled it up with extra petrol and lashed his supplies to the back with thick cables, adding a fresh cask of petrol and another large bottle of water. He checked his watch. Quarter past four. About three hours of daylight left. He started the buggy and drove back to the main square.

Four QLA troops were waiting with the captain, one of them had his arm and head in bandages. Beside them sat three traumatised women and a couple of battle-shocked men.

'I found some survivors,' said Stone. 'Lucky's Girls had the best storm shelter in the settlement.'

'I need to get going,' said Mark. 'Can you tell me where to find Kalat? I've done what I can for you for the time being. If I get out of this, I'll do more, I guarantee. You promised me information in return.'

'I did.' Stone nodded. 'We do our best to be honourable but you may find you are already too late.'

173

'What do you mean?'

'We heard that he was hurt – injured or sick. I'm not sure what. We sent a doctor to look at him but the doctor never made it. We just don't know. All I can say is that he's in Miami, if he's still alive. I'm pretty sure of that.' The captain gave a weary sigh. 'You may find your brother-in-law much changed. Everything changes out here . . . He won't be the man you remember.'

'Have you heard him?' said one of the soldiers. 'Have you heard his voice?'

'He talks to us,' Stone went on. 'He broadcasts messages across the swamps. Strange messages full of poetry. Some say he is a prophet or a hierophant, one who holds the key to great secrets. Some claim he predicts the future. Others don't believe he even exists. They say he is some kind of myth, a force for freedom, pure and untouched, uncontaminated by any cause or ideology. Some say the voice in the broadcasts is generated by computer, amalgamated from a thousand different sermons and speeches pulled from the net, cut up, sampled and reformulated. Some even claim he's a creation of the government, a means of channelling revolutionary forces and bending them into the service of the state. Who knows?' Battle had left the captain haggard, with weary rings darkening his eyes. He took Mark's arm. 'Listen – this is important. The way ahead is dangerous. Stick to the old roads – that way you are most likely to avoid the military and Darkwater patrols.'

'I found this map. Show me.'

The captain traced out a route for him along the abandoned Florida turnpike. 'There is a town – here.' He pointed to an empty space on the map. 'Ashbury. It's a nice place. It has official protection although no one will admit it exists. The people there are decent. You can trust them, more or less. They will look after you. You won't make it tonight but maybe tomorrow evening if you are lucky. The road runs out after Ashbury. You will have to travel by water through the Everglades. The people in Ashbury will be able to arrange transport. Near Miami things change. You will see signs and wonders. Be warned, Kalat's people don't care so much for white skin.'

'His people?'

'You'll see what I mean. They are devoted to him. They worship him. He seems to inspire devotion. At least this is what others have told me. But if he is dead . . .' He made a vague and faintly ominous gesture.

'Thank you.'

The two men shook hands and then embraced. Nodding at the other survivors, Mark got on to the buggy. Without a backward glance he started off, deeper into the unknown.

. . .

At dawn, after driving all night, he reached the suburbs of hell. Vacant lots and weapons-testing ranges. Moments like this, he could almost believe what had happened was a dream, an unreal phantasm pieced together from news reports and scientific surveys, government programmes and cult novels and dry academic books from university libraries about American literature, crimes against humanity and the sexual perversions of adolescents . . . cut up, mixed and sliced and rearranged and punched into his head . . . Spectral cameras and psychopathic X-ray flicker. The manifold amnesia of history a tingling burning sensation like shingles under his skin, his flayed nerves prone . . . electrified torture victims and circuit boards.

At dawn, after driving all night . . .

Alone in the garden as he waited to see her he could almost believe that none of it was real and that nothing had happened. Almost imagine he was still a boy again running with his sister happy in the cold wind through the high field under crisp December skies.

Almost.

. . .

# NEW AFRIKA

With the late afternoon sun hard against his eyes Mark travelled along the old Highway 27, a route marked as redundant on the Pentagon map. The vehicle was top-heavy and with his rucksack and all the excess equipment lashed to the back he had to drive carefully to reduce the risk of overturning. Slow and steady he went, the road ripped with twists of vine and yellow weeds like the rotten rigging of a floral armada. Twice overwhelmed by the post-combat shakes he had to stop, pacing the verge mumbling to himself and running sweaty hands over his sweaty face. Then it would pass and he resumed his journey, a slow passage through the detritus of modernity: abandoned strip malls and retail parks strung out and rotting, morbid acres of tract housing and condo developments, twisted webs of telegraph wires and the lonely shadow of water towers and forsaken churches and mile after mile of industrial units resplendent with lurid growths of mould.

Once he stopped where the old highway intersected with a new DynoCorp road, the two strips entwining in a concrete nexus. He hid inside the rotten shell of a McDonald's drive-thru, watching a passing military convoy. The rumble of hundred-ton supply trucks shook the ground and sent forth a great spray of hot white dust. He counted fifty juggernauts, like a school of great green whales, their summits brushing the blue horizon. In their wake a flotilla of armed Humvees, heavy metal music audible over the diesel drone, the relaxed soldiers lolling in machine-gun mounts as though hanging out at a frat-boy pool party, a parallel universe of order and discipline stamping like a great boot through the jungle. The sound of their passing lingered long in the stillness of the Zone.

Several miles of further slow travel through the lush ravages of the landscape and he came upon a jeep crashed in the middle of the road. Huge holes were blasted in the back of the vehicle and both front doors hung wide open where the occupants had rapidly fled. Moments later he saw what was left of them, the body of a woman, her legs and lower torso missing and slightly further away the pulverised cartilage and carbonised bones of a second victim, little more than a red and black smear on the macadam. More burned holes punctured the road. Beyond them another blasted vehicle, a twist of scorched metal and a pool of dark oil. Devastation cognate with an airborne attack, he thought, the rapid fire of an Apache chain gun or Hydra rockets. Further ahead fresh plumes trailed across a sky turning ominous with rain clouds. According to the map he was approaching an informal commune, 'New Afrika', identified as a black nationalist settlement.

A razor-wire fence marked the perimeter of the community and the road wove on through a pair of iron gates which had been blown apart. The settlement occupied a former development of retirement condos set around a lake. A faded sign said, 'Eldorado Court', half swamped by rampant orange trees. The idyllic lake had burst its bounds and a large portion of the built area was submerged. The rest, set on slightly higher ground, was still intact. Mark approached the three-storey weave of blocks, each painted white and topped with the faux-Spanish vernacular of red tiles and fake chimneys. Lashed to a high tree a hoarding presented a large black man swathed in white robes, one finger raised authoritatively. On Mark's left a golf course had been recultivated as a paddy field. On the other side the car park was now filled with green crops. But signs of violence were everywhere. Many of the condos were pockmarked with bullet holes and grenade blasts. Bodies lay scattered outside the buildings, black men, women and a few children, their robes stained with blood. His approach startled several vultures from their feasting, the scavengers too gorged to do more than raise their gory beaks.

Mark cut the engine and dismounted, rifle in hand. Two skinny dogs, either strays or former pets from the settlement, hung around watching, too frightened to bark or growl. The sky was growing dark, the evening hush broken by the ripple of distant thunder, the air thick and hot with the promise of rain. The nearest building was gutted by fire, spires of black smoke drifting from open windows. He moved into the second, advancing through rudimentary living quarters, a prayer room with mats and sayings from the Koran hanging from the walls. Next some kind of dormitory, neat white beds laid out in rows and a classroom, desks and chairs upturned in flight, pictures of Africa, religious and political leaders, Marcus Garvey, Haile Selassie, Malcolm X, Martin Luther King, Nelson Mandela, Barack Obama and others decorating the walls.

He found a kitchen designed to cater for a large number of people. The place was untouched by fighting and after rummaging around a little he found some canned goods and dried pasta. He ate quickly and mechanically, with little taste or appetite. An ambience of outrage continued to linger but instinct told him the place was deserted and if anyone had been left alive they were now long gone.

He went back outside and moved the buggy into the lobby of the next block. He closed the door to make sure there was no evidence of his presence visible from outside. Raindrops the size of light bulbs began to fall from the sky. He went inside, walking through another prayer room. The place had been vandalised, torn copies of the Koran scattered about, a turd left to fester in the corner. Abusive words and slogans had been daubed over the walls. In another room he found three dead children, the youngest no more than a baby. Laid out in a row by a bed, each shot in the head. The smell of dead flesh. Someone had pinned a picture of Jesus to the wall. The saviour resembled some sort of rock star sporting long golden locks and wearing the stigmata like a fashionable tattoo. He held an M16 assault rifle and stood before a huge Stars and Stripes. 'One God, One Church, One America' was written below. Sickened, Mark tore the poster from the wall. What had these people done? he wondered. Stamped out and in the name of what – religion? Power? Truth? How could these children have been a threat?

On the top floor he found a pristine room with a comfortable sofa and thick rugs on the floor. Down the corridor was a bathroom. The toilet flushed and lukewarm water came out of the shower. Setting up his halogen torch, Mark refreshed himself and then returned to the room, using a chair to barricade the door. Amid the rumble of thunder he could hear dogs howling.

He thought again of the dead children, their little bodies slowly starting to rot in the room below, and with that thought a slow slab of dread went rolling through his body. Reluctantly he took out the satellite phone and turned it on.

'Yes.'

'This is Casement.' He was surprised at how weak his voice sounded.

'Yes,' said the voice.

He gave the pass code.

'Yes,' said the voice.

'I've entered the Zone. I'm staying in an abandoned settlement approximately fifty kilometres south of Orlando. Plans have been disrupted. I lost much of my equipment.' He gave a brief report, informing Control about the QLA and the nature of their engagement with the Witch Hunters. As always he spoke quickly, sticking to the facts, doing his best to avoid emotion and ignore the disquiet within.

After the call he sat still, staring at a slogan from the Koran hung on the white wall opposite. He couldn't remember enough Arabic to read it. He felt lonely and abandoned, stranded deep in this strange territory. Alisha . . . He looked at the phone but he knew he couldn't call her. His feelings were too twisted, too bottled up for words. So often he hardly knew what he really felt any more. He took a deep breath and tried to force down such anxieties. This was what he was trained to do. His self-reliance had to be absolute. There was supposed to be freedom in duty, a sense of liberation to be found in the burden of the mission. Out here he could do everything that was necessary. That was what the agency had always taught him. That was what Ashe had shown him, out in the desert, with all the smoke, the blood on the sand. Dead children should not matter. Ravaged homes should not matter. The aims of the mission were supposed to be above all of that, his goal more important. But now, as he stretched out on a sofa, the M16 close beside him on the floor, his pistol a comforting weight in his shoulder holster, he was far from sure about anything. Exhausted but still on edge, his thoughts turning compulsively back to those dead children. One day soon he too would be a father. Had he done anything, he wondered, to make the world better for his unborn child? Intermittent cracks of thunder rattled the windows, flashes of lightning illuminating the room through locked shutters. Outside, almost in imitation of his troubled thoughts, he could hear things knocking and banging in the storm.

. . .

Behind the veil the voice in the darkness.

    –   I remember how dizzy we were.

Love?

    –   Yes love.

                   *. . . the wind*

    –   We lay in the grass, her arms around me, the stars bright above, a warm summer night and everything hushed and the gentle weight of her body was a joy indescribable . . .

# ZONE

The night's cloudburst brought no freshness and when Mark went outside the morning was already engulfed in a sticky heat. Dogs, picking among the corpses, formed a melancholy audience for his departure.

He had travelled only a few miles before the environment began to take its toll. Like an alcoholic reviewing the humiliations of the last night, images of the men he killed went flashing through his mind. Their bodies, all those bodies and again, incessant, the dead children, laid out on the bed. He had taken care to avoid passing through those charnel rooms when he left. Perhaps it was his imagination but he thought he could smell them, ripe and rotting in the heat. How many men had he killed over the years? How many women and children had died as a result of their bombs, their intelligence, their noble intentions? He would never know. Loathing seized him, an intense self-hatred. He had never wanted to do these things. He had never wanted to hurt anybody. He knew these thoughts were no good. Foxy would never tolerate such doubts. 'Weakness,' he would say. 'The unwarranted pangs of an unnecessary conscience.' He would talk about the big picture, the wider strategic ends. According to Foxy there was always something to eclipse the collaterals. But this morning, amid the disorientation of the Zone, Mark was unable to see it.

After a while he noticed freshly laid barbed-wire fencing marking off the fields on one side of the turnpike. Amid the wire warning signs promised lethal force against trespass. In the distance he saw a number of fortified homesteads, the low structures resembling weapons silos or maximum-security prisons rather than actual residencies; water towers and eccentric windmills with shiny silver rotors and blacked stacks of solar panels rising up above electric fences and defensive ditches. He saw no sign of life but the structures added to his sense of disquiet. Were these compounds home to hardened survivalists or did they serve a more sinister purpose? Anything seemed possible. They could be farms for cocaine production, the dormitories of a new apocalypse cult or worse, he thought, CIA rendition camps and interrogation centres, film studios for snuff movies and child porn.

Eventually though, the fencing gave way and the wilderness was restored. He drove for a long time. Now and then he would pass an object utterly severed from any comprehensible context. A lone refrigerator upright in the middle of the road; a deflated bouncy castle caught in the branches of a tree like a stranded hot-air balloon; a hoarding of the President, his face peeled away to reveal the plastic smile of a female model; an inverted TV helicopter driven head-first into the ground; a series of cheap garden statuary, tacky cherubs, defiled nymphs and a cut-rate Venus de Milo scattered around the roadside; a giant plastic hamburger surely ripped from a roadside restaurant and plonked in a tangle of saw grass – unless the sign was all that remained and it was the restaurant itself that had been scattered; the sudden blizzard of shredded newspapers that started to fall around him, the inky deluge tumbling inexplicably from a sky as empty as the terrain below.

Later he took shelter from the intense sunshine in a ruined mansion set off from the turnpike by a shield of trees. A recent construction, no more than thirty years old, brash and adorned with spurious ornamentation. The property was intact and Mark could tell the owner must have evacuated only a few months ago. He wandered the cool empty rooms for a while, noting the dusty spaces where once had been a sofa, an armchair, a dining table. Upstairs he hoped he might find a bed and lie down for a little while but everything was gone, the few stray objects that remained possessed an uncanny meaning: a headless doll, a mobile phone charger, a set of fine bone china, a spy thriller published to great success a couple of years ago, a series of strange plastic objects suggestive of sex toys or anatomical equipment. All the same the rooms were dry, the windows held and the doors could be locked. There was nothing to prevent him from stopping here, from moving in, if he wanted to. He could use the gun to hunt game, he could try and grow vegetables and eke out a precarious, hermetic self-sufficiency. The agency would assume he had died, killed in some mysterious manner and Alisha would mourn him, bring up their child, get on with her life. Gradually the pain of these past attachments would fade and a true freedom might come to him.

For a few hours he dithered in the mansion, resting and toying with fantasies of reinvention and escape. But as the sun dropped a little, the heat diminishing by a fraction, he found himself back on the buggy, taking his bearings, checking the map as best he could and driving on.

Some distance ahead and his thoughts were broken by a sudden crash. Four F-40 fighter jets fell from the sun like angelic shards, engines booming with supersonic vengeance. Cleaving across the heavens, the jets powered forward and then rose upwards at an incredible speed. A dozen explosions erupted from a far-off glade, a ball of fire blooming, a shockwave flexing across the terrain. The fire rose, smells of sulphur and gasoline, trees burning like tapers. No further sign of the jets and amid the immensity of earth, sky and water the fires were soon diminished. He had no idea what targets the fighters had blasted to oblivion, whether this was a sign of further conflict or merely a rehearsal for other, undeclared wars.

He drove on.

Mark had to admit it, he was lost. For all the detail on the map, he was no longer sure of his location. For several hours he had driven slowly along the old turnpike and although he was sure he could match the road with the route marked on the map, his precise position was far from clear. When he stopped the immensity of the Floridian wastes loomed around him. Anonymous wilderness of heat-soaked palm and dripping fern, a plantation of swampy growth so dense he could almost imagine himself in aeons prehistoric, as if the jungle might erupt to the crash of grazing Brontosaurus or the deadly trample of a blood-thirsty Tyrannosaur. Shadows glazed the sky, twilight unravelling a fresh shroud of heat across the teeming jungle. Once again he took his bearings with his compass. He was off track a little, deviating by several degrees from the direction indicated by Stone, but then the road allowed him no other option. He began to regret not staying at the mansion for the night and determined to stop at the next feasible shelter. Eventually he came across an old motel, a typical single-storey L-shape, one wing crushed by fallen trees. The remaining side seemed reasonably intact and a sign still stood by the roadside, dead neon letters promising midweek deals. He pulled up and drove in, skirting a swimming pool clogged with algae. Parking out of sight of the road, he dismounted and stood for a moment, listening to the low thrum, click and trip of countless insects chattering in the jungle dark. Treacherous scrubs of grass poked through the tarmac, sharp green clumps as thick as his arm. Above bats flapped around twilight tree summits.

Mark unslung his rifle and wandered about the ruin. Most of the rooms were like cells, foul with sodden fabrics, crusted with mould and slime. Finally he found one at the far end that seemed to have been spared most of the ravages of the weather and settled in, making a rough bed on the hard floor, eating a power bar and gulping warm water to try and stave off pangs of hunger and dehydration.

Overwhelming darkness, a night as pitch as any that had fallen in antediluvian ages and impossible, almost, to imagine that there had ever been a time when unnatural light had illuminated man's way. Down he lay, trying hard to sleep, his ears acute to each and every scamper of rodent, wild pig, errant cat or reptile moving through the bush, each snap of twig and crush of bracken pricking him back to cautionary wakefulness.

Eventually the thoughts came, drifting steady as castaways washed on velvety shores . . . Ashe missing in action and no body to recover, no remains to bring back, none of the usual pomp or ceremony, no coffin swathed in the Union Jack to lower into wet earth, just a dry memorial service in a small chapel in the Oxfordshire military base. He remembered how his arm continued to ache from the bullet taken, while Susanna sat by his side, dry-eyed and brittle with grief, her tight-wound body swaying through the platitudes and perorations, the baby grizzling in her lap. In the toilets he had swallowed more tranquilisers and anti-depressants, anything to try and block the reverberations of guilt that echoed within like the plash of stones dropped into a deep well. None of the grey men had been there, the grey men in dark suits with voices like spades cutting earth, like dirt falling on a coffin, none of them. He remembered talking to Alisha about it weeks later, during dusty walks through autumnal woods of sombre red and faded gold. These walks he remembered but not so much the discussion. He remembered the touch of her hand, her smile and the warmth of her soft lips on his cold cheek.

*Kalat . . .*

He opened his eyes.

He scratched his face and legs, feeling things, many things, crawling over him. Fumbling in the dark for his pocket torch. There. Playing the light round the room. A column of ants moved with militant purpose across the floor. He brushed them from his clothes, skin and hair, standing and shaking himself and scratching. Cursing them and stamping on them. He pushed open the door and went outside. The night enveloped him like an amniotic sac. No sign of the dawn, just the steady sizzle of insects. He squatted down and rubbed his face, unwilling to turn on the torch again or give any sign of his presence. Squatting like a sweaty acolyte, he waited with steady patience, seeking first light or else enlightenment, whichever came first.

Gradually the sky turned, the dawn stealing in greenish and luminous. A low breeze rippled palm, mangrove and moody overhang of moss, almost cool, or as near to cool as was possible in such a torrid zone. As soon as it was light enough to make out the road without using his headlights, Mark resumed his journey, the daybreak weighty with doleful clouds.

He entered a substantial town. The turnpike was flanked by the tawdry sprawl of fast-food joints and drive-thru units typical of American mono-culture but better preserved than most he had seen so far, structures largely intact, walls, flat roofs, windows and hoardings present, albeit cloaked under a slimy layer of swamp grease and storm rot. Cars and trucks were scattered about, mashed up in metal heaps or rotting in grassy lots, the whole random universe of the industrial age broken into cryptic fragments and merged with a terrible-grown nature. He stopped and checked his map certain such a large town must be marked. No good. The place could be one of several, each with its name crossed out, storm oblivion signalled by these authoritative strokes. The surrounding area was blank, blank, blank – blank also the space where Ashbury was supposed to be, somewhere in the void ahead, a desert of white space to hide the darkness overwhelming.

Driving towards the downtown, he looked in vain for some artefact of the lost Florida to situate his course. He passed single- and two-storey shopfronts and offices with blackened façades, evidence of fires extinguished and floods receded, the road engorged with mounds of rubble, heaps of plastic and rain-polished cans. Suspended from an old stoplight at a junction was a corpse. Most of the flesh had fallen away, the leathery strips that remained giving glimpses of bone and cartilage. Man or woman, he could not tell, its head patched with scrubs of rank black hair, eyes sucked from their sockets by scavenging beaks, withered flesh yanked across a grisly visage, the mouth pulled back to reveal an endless grimace of smiling yellow teeth. Plastic cables were wrapped around its wrists and torso, the whole macabre contraption having fallen slightly so that the spectacle hung but three feet from the ground, a human scarecrow to warn away strangers.

He stopped and scanned the surrounding buildings.

Badness clung to the air, a palpable malaise. He felt the hairs on his neck and arms prickle, a creepy background feel-ing like an itch he couldn't scratch. He withdrew his pistol, keeping it in his right hand and then restarted the buggy, the engine so loud in the dead town. Cautious, he drove left-handed round the corpse. Some impulse – he wasn't sure what – caused him to veer off the main street and turn east at the junction.

He drove through a once pleasant neighbourhood of ranch-style houses set behind hedges and lawns. After ten years of abandonment the properties appeared swamp-born and sunken, gothic shells with prone walls and gaping windows, dwelling places for cannibals or troglodytes. He pulled up at the verge and turned off the engine. Here, as everywhere, the tarmac was shredded with scrubby grass but at the same time – and perhaps it was just his heat-fagged, nerve-shredded imagination – the grass seemed less abundant than elsewhere, more pressed down and muddy, as if someone had recently gone trampling through, and these streets were in use by unknown others. He stood and listened to the empty sigh of the wilderness, a silence so total he thought he could almost hear the faint slip and twitch of plants curling and unfolding around him, their leaves bending and tilting to the wet air, snakes and worms and unmentionable insects churning through the dense loam, all around the pressure of vengeful nature prising the world from the ruinous fist of man. Then something else – a faint banging noise like a door being slammed shut – the sound shaking him from his reverie.

Mark clambered off the buggy, holstering the pistol and taking out the assault rifle instead. His ears strained against the surrounding silence and again he had that feeling, his skin itching unbearably.

He waited.

He thought he could hear something else – scrunching sounds – like someone running along a gravel path.

Most of the houses on the street were fronted by gravel driveways.

He snapped into action, running towards the nearest, low and fast.

The front door was missing, the hall littered with broken glass and shrivelled palm leaves. To his right the living room, the parquet floor stained black with water marks.

He peered in.

Someone was sitting on a sofa.

He almost opened fire, or screamed, or did something, but then he saw it wasn't a person, it was a mannequin, the sort used to display clothes in a shop window.

The figure was naked and someone had applied make-up to its features, adding a crude clown's face. It sat facing a huge plasma TV, the screen a black pit cut into the wall. A large mirror hung above the TV and Mark jumped again when he saw himself, a wild and grimy castaway, shocked by the savage light inhabiting his eyes and the thick stubble that coated a face drawn with fatigue.

Beyond the lounge was a ransacked kitchen, the floor and surfaces rancid with fungus. The wall had been ripped away to give a clear view of the garden. Another mannequin, this time a blonde wearing a red bikini, reclined on a lounger beside a swimming pool scummy with storm water.

Several things were apparent but Mark's weary mind struggled to process the implications. As he stood there, staring at the sunbathing mannequin, he thought again that he could hear the faint scrunch of someone running over gravel and something else, like laughter, the giggle of a child spying on him from afar. A flock of birds burst upwards, wings clacking into the sweaty sky and he jumped as if a bomb had gone off.

He was still trying to pull himself together when he heard another sound, more definite this time, a high-pitched metallic whine. Several sounds together in fact, the roar of engines pitched full throttle  vehicles  several vehicles travelling fast and getting louder. He ran back into the house, sprinting upstairs to the front bedroom. He half-expected to see another mannequin, or maybe two, a couple engaged in some parody of congress on the bed but the room was bare, burn marks on the floor and a mattress stained blue with mould pressed up against the window. The sound of engines was getting louder. He moved the mattress aside a little and peered out. From here he had quite a good view of the street. He could even see his buggy parked up against the verge.

*Shit.*

He went charging back downstairs, the rifle slung awkwardly over his back, running out and grabbing the buggy by the handlebars and quickly tugging the machine up the path towards the house, the sound of the vehicles steadily encroaching as he pushed the buggy into the spacious hallway, struggling with the cumbersome bottles of water and petrol strapped to the rear, shoving it out of immediate sight as the vehicles went speeding past, one after another – but he turned too late to see anything – witness only to the sound of their passing, to the tyres screeching and gears grinding, as if the crazed drivers had turned the neighbourhood into a race track. Swearing and shaking, he manoeuvred the buggy back round so that it was facing the doorway. All the time the sound of high-powered cars continued to reverberate around the streets, engines rising then suddenly fading as though he were being encircled by a pack of combustion-driven wolves, their carbon-fuelled radiators scenting the air for living man. Back upstairs, trembling and panicked, he quickly checked the other bedrooms before returning to his vantage point, rifle ready.

For a long time he lay still, waiting, his ears acute to the faintest sound, queasy exhaustion and fear battling within. After a while a wind started, the palms outside beginning to lisp and bend. He continued to hear the engines ebbing and throbbing in the air until they became not so much the sound of individual vehicles but something more mysterious, the rasp of a thousand metal wings, as though a swarm of locusts patrolled the fallen heavens. He waited. He ate another power bar, his aching body not entirely his own. Time passed, slow and horrible, the wind blowing, the grimy house rustling and quivering and he struggled to know whether he could still hear the vehicles or if it were all just his imagination and he hid from sounds of his own invention. He was losing track, getting sloppy. How could he have been so stupid as to leave the buggy out in plain view of the road? What was he even doing cowering in this forsaken place? Thoughts came in waves, like nausea, like vomit clogged in his mind. Shadows poking sharp in a hole, bitter rusty waves of frustration crawling over his skin and burrowing through his veins. If only he wasn't so lost, if only he wasn't alone in this place, and why – Ashe, always Ashe – the dead man resurrected, *Kalat*, his brother-in-law, his fellow agent, his nemesis, if it wasn't for him none of this would have happened, none of this would be happening – the heat and the Zone and the murdered children laid out in a row and the sound of engines strange outside roaring – if it wasn't for him he would have ended up . . . it didn't matter, he wouldn't be here, he wouldn't have to go through all this . . . Ashe was supposed to be dead, had been dead for so long, so why now, why here? Ever since they gave him that strange metal object to take through Stansted and the scanners went off and he tried to run and they shot him with the Taser and locked him in a room until the man from Special Branch took him somewhere else, to rooms far from the light and then the other men came who didn't say exactly who they were or who they worked for but talked about detention orders and threats to national security and put a hood over his face far from the light and had files, bulging files of information about him, and photographs and transcripts of conversations he'd forgotten ever having made or emails sent and we've been watching you for a long time, they said, keeping a very close eye and he had always thought he was invisible and so it went on, questions, questions, questions, his arms yanked back and tied to a chair in just such a way that it hurt like his sockets would pop and the questions went on and on, a hand on the back of his neck pushing his face on to the table and he thought so this is what really happens but that was just the start, the hours, the days, the weeks, and sometimes they let him sleep and sometimes they woke him with bright lights and the sound of babies crying or people screaming, sometimes they made him watch tapes of women being raped by men with death masks and other men with hands bound being decapitated by men with scarves and hidden faces and they said this is what we are up against, they said this is the enemy, they said you work for these people and sometimes they took him out-side into a concrete yard that stank of shit and fear and he was in the shit, they said, and then they would make him stand in awkward positions until his legs turned to jelly and he collapsed or they would make him run, back and forth or do push-ups until his arms didn't work any more, screaming at him you're in the shit, and when he couldn't do what they said any more or pissed himself or lashed out at them they would seem pleased and then more would come, a dozen of them sometimes, with riot helmets, shields and body armour chanting army songs, somehow ridiculous, urging him to fight them and he never could and they would drag him back to the cell until the questions started again and sometimes it was the man who said he was his 'friend' but whatever he was, he wasn't his friend, and sometimes it was the man who said they would break him down and build him up anew and sometimes it was the man older than the others but also somehow ageless, a man who had been old for ever with his deep Tuscan tan and wave of silver hair and he would look at him with something like tenderness and say, 'My name is Lucius but everyone calls me "Foxy".' 'Foxy?' 'That's right, and I'm going to be looking after you from now on. I know we'll be great friends', and sometimes it was none of those men, *Kalat*, and now as he fumbled with the satellite phone grimy with sweat and dirt, trying to call them, still them, those men secure in their castles of fire and light and he remained in the shit, and nothing had changed, he saw it now, his mind a black hole scraped by knives – and the number, what was the fucking number? But his fingers knew it, even if his mind was too busy, thoughts surging like an avalanche, like a deck of cards flicking fast, too fast, and he was trying to get a signal but nothing, the sky blocked it all out and still the sound of engines sometimes getting closer, so close and loud he thought they must be upon him only to turn away at the last moment. Still the phone would not work. It wasn't like the movies, he knew that, where the agent always had some hi-tech miracle gadget to link him instantly with the control room, this Hollywood dream-world where communications flash effortlessly across the globe. No, never like that. Most of the equipment they gave him never worked properly. Budget cuts, systems failures, program bugs, lack of manpower, failures of investment, whatever it was, it always fucked up. He swore at the phone and flung it across the room, so angry now he could have smashed it to pieces. No. He had to be calm and controlled. Had to. He realised his hands were shaking, his whole body shuddering and trembling. He put his hands to his face and they came away wet. Jesus. He was crying. He was tired and hungry and lost and now he was crying. Murdered babies laid out in a row. He forced his emotions back into the hole. *Fucking pussy.* He'd been through worse than this. *Fucking wimp.* What would Ashe think, he told himself, to see him like this, sobbing like a lost boy?

Gradually weariness began to envelop him, his thoughts spinning out into constellations cold and distant and he saw himself through a satellite or spectral camera, alone in his cell with darkness all around and somewhere, out there, in the distance, Kalat, a giant stalking the forest, hazy as a sky-scraper glimpsed on the horizon. Rain joined the wind and the steady drum of drops on the roof offered some comfort. With the rain came a breeze and he let it waft over him, imagining he was not really hiding in a wrecked house but floating on a gentle cloud . . .

*flicker*

          I think I fell in love with Susanna the moment I saw her

the moment I laid eyes on her

      they ask a lot of us, don't they?

      when we left for Iraq I had an ominous feeling I didn't tell anyone

An explosion jolted Mark awake, his eyes opening into the darkness. Another boom rocked the night white, lightning illuminating a split-second scene of rain-lashed palm and water dripping through slits in the ceiling and forming small pools in the gaps and cracks where he lay curled on the raw floor.

        I had an ominous feeling

             she comes to me in dreams, darling

Susanna, and

  I keep saying goodbye, over and over again I say goodbye but there's never enough time to say all the goodbyes we want

             they ask a lot of us, don't they?

He opened his eyes to a world filled with brightness and heat. With a groan he prised himself up, stood and stretched. Peering out he saw white steam rising from the wet ground, a gauze of vapour that enveloped the street in a ghostly, insubstantial haze. Past ten in the morning. He must have slept for hours. He drank some water and ate another power bar. The satellite phone was where he had left it in the corner. He tried again but the signal was so weak he could have been stranded on a distant planet. The battery was getting low so he switched it off.

He started the buggy and drove out of the house and up the street. Further up the road he saw three individuals, two of them pulling and one pushing a U-Haul trailer loaded with scrap. The scavengers – two men and a woman – were threadbare and weary. All of them had rifles slung over their shoulders and four dogs, equally ragged and mangy, skirted around their feet. The two parties stopped and gazed at each other.

Keeping one hand close to his pistol, Mark called to them. 'I'm looking for the road to Ashbury. Can you help?'

The party stared at him, mute with incomprehension. The woman, tanned and weather-beaten, her face hidden by lank black hair, her body clad in a filthy blue dress, spat on the floor and said, 'Jes' git back to th' ole turnpike an' keep goin' south. Ya'll see th' signs. Ya can' miss 'em.'

Mark nodded thanks. 'Can you tell me the name of this place?' he added.

There was no answer from the trio. One of the men turned to his friends. 'Cum on nah, ain't got n' time t' stan' roun' jawin'.' The group resumed their journey, paying Mark no more attention.

After a couple of wrong turns he rejoined the turnpike. The area around the junction had been scorched, the burned ground muddy after the night's rain. Hanging from the rafters of a charred Shell garage he saw the remains of another body, just a torso, head and a single wire-lashed arm dangling above the stumps of petrol pumps. Black birds hovered overhead on hot thermals. Stealing himself, he continued forward.

. . .

behind the veil the voice in the darkness
–        I had an ominous feeling

at dawn
after driving all night
at the gates of the hospital
on the outskirts of hell
        almost
        he could almost believe

. . .

# DARKWATER

A pale rider in the brightness of morning, his sunglasses reflecting the glare, his low-pulled cap and khaki trousers flaring in the breeze of his transport, Mark felt glad to be moving again. Penetrating further into the wilderness and the landscape became more waterlogged, streams and stagnant pools sprouting weeds, grasses and bulrushes, the opaque surfaces reflecting the brutish tinge of the sky. Occasionally the upper floors of flooded buildings would appear, glimmering and mirage-like on the meniscus horizon, visions of a shabby, tropical Venice beached upon a lagoon of unpredictable and impossible vastness.

At times the salty flow and drag of the fractured tide reclaimed the road and he had to drive carefully, turgid water washing over his knees. Twice the buggy stalled and he was forced to dismount and push, slow-going in such conditions, amid the heat, the mulch and mud. Further on the flood diminished as the undergrowth thickened and he drove into a forest of melaleuca trees, their pale trunks stretching upwards like the elongated corpses of plague victims. Under the canopy he found some relief from the intensity of scorching sun and shimmering water. The battered strip led him through wild plantations and woodland

200

entanglements silent apart from the cry of unfamiliar birds.

Around midday, just as his surroundings had lulled him into a pleasant sense of oblivion, Mark found himself passing through an informal settlement, a series of squalid shacks raised on wooden stilts and people slouched on steps and ladders or attending to rusted vehicles. By the roadside women were carrying plastic buckets of water on their heads, naked children trailing behind. The track turned and passed through a clearing where a number of men stood in uneasy assembly. They wore dirty overalls and broad-brimmed cowboy hats and some held shotguns and rifles. In the middle chained together on a wooden stage were a dozen young black men and women, naked and bent by their situation. A corner of the clearing was dominated by a huge wooden crucifix, a Confederate flag suspended between the boughs of an ancient tree. No one moved and nothing was said. Squinting eyes did not flinch at his passage. He accelerated away, passing further shacks, structures so rudimentary it seemed impossible that anyone could live in them and then the forest died away and he drove onwards into the watery vastness of the Zone.

Across a plain of powdery sand and dried grass littered with the skeletons of dead animals he saw orange flames licking skywards from huge pyres, blazing as if to defy the afternoon heat. Shambolic crowds were gathered around the mighty bonfires, their arms raised, seemingly transfixed. The side of the road was jammed with mud-splattered 4×4s and SUVs, dented pick-ups and a rusting Greyhound bus, motorbikes and buggies of all description, even horses tethered to carriages fashioned from scrap metal and driftwood. He drove quickly, anxious to distance himself from the solemn spectacle.

By mid afternoon the temperature was boiling. Huge

clouds, generated by the heat, filled the sky. A low and distant rumbling cupped the far view and now and then a slovenly wind sent a languid ripple through the palms. He took shelter in a shady grove. There he stripped to his boots and pants and hung his sweat-sodden clothes on the surrounding branches. Parts of his face and shoulders smote from sunburn. He applied soothing cream from the medical kit and sat for a while on his jacket. The drinking water in his supplies was hot and his back and arms ached after hours spent in control of the buggy. He rested for some time. What a strange world, he thought, this vast swampscape of empty possibility.

Checking the satellite phone, he saw that the agency had attempted to contact him. For a while he looked at the phone, contemplating a call-back. But he did nothing. So humid and still no rain. Clouds began to disassemble, wispy particles defeated by the afternoon blue. Flocks of birds went swooping upwards in shuddering, sudden rhythms. Recovered a little, he continued his journey, the heat melting the way ahead and casting so many mirages across the throbbing road it seemed as though the whole world had turned to water.

Mark had been travelling steadily for some miles when he saw two chunky black Jeeps gunning rapidly along a side road about to intersect with the turnpike. There was no doubt they had seen him and he knew there was no way he could outrun them. Nor in the flat landscape was there anywhere to hide. Instead he stopped and waited. The two Jeeps pulled up on either side, boxing him in. Both vehicles were jet black, splattered and stained with mud and dust, menacing bull-bars at the front bulky with halogen lights and tow ropes, windows tinted like obsidian mirrors reflecting back the muted glare of the sky. Distinctive Darkwater logos decorated the doors.

'Turn off your engine and step away from the buggy. Keep your hands up,' shouted a voice through a microphone. Mark did as told. Darkwater patrols operated throughout the Zone, protecting authorised settlements or escorting contractors between various bases. Occasionally they would be used to supplement military operations or guard VIPs but Mark knew their rules of engagement were supposed to be very strict. In theory they were not allowed to open fire unless under immediate threat and were prohibited from taking offensive actions against any rogue elements.

He stood quite still, watching the two vehicles. A door opened and two men emerged. They wore black flak jackets and wraparound shades, guns and ammunition strapped to thighs and arms.

'What's going on, buddy?' asked the first. He was a very tall, muscular man, his hair buzzed into an aggressive crewcut, a sub-machine gun hanging from his vest.

'Not much, buddy. What's up with you?'

'Where you going?'

Mark shrugged. He allowed his face to fall into a neutral expression, neither innocent nor guilty, simply natural, as if he were supposed to be here, doing this, and everything were fine. It was important not to appear frightened or aggressive or do anything to spoil the appearance of being a normal, ordinary part of the environment. 'I'm heading to Ashbury,' he said, quite simply.

The Darkwater trooper sniffed and looked him up and down, taking in his dishevelled state. 'Where you come from?'

'New Canaan.' Mark named one of the nearby settlements he had seen on the map.

'That right?'

'That's what I said.'

'Why you out here then?'

Mark gave a slight smile and looked at the floor. 'Well, it's complicated and not all that interesting.'

'Yeah?'

'Women, you know.'

'Right.'

'The one in New Canaan found out about the one in Ashbury. She chucked me out. What can I do?'

The trooper remained impassive, apparently indifferent or unconvinced by Mark's explanation. 'You got any ID?'

Mark produced his passport. 'That okay?'

The Darkwater trooper scarcely glanced at the document. 'That's fine.' He spat and gazed at the horizon. 'Hot as a motherfucker, ain't it?'

'Want to give me a lift?'

'Often like this.' The trooper wiped his face. 'So fucking hot.' He called out to his companion, 'Yo homes, you see anything?' The second guard was snooping around the buggy.

'Nothin' Jim.'

'I got a way to go, if that's all right with you.' He walked back to the buggy. The troopers were already losing interest. All of this was very familiar to Mark, a consequence of his asset. The patrol would leave with a faint memory of having stopped someone – as they were supposed to – but if pressed all the details about him would be hopelessly vague.

'Wait a minute!' The trooper suddenly turned and grabbed Mark's arm. 'You want to watch out.'

'What is it?' Mark tensed up.

'On the way.' He licked his lips. 'I don't know. It's mainly just rumours.'

'What?'

'Made me think, what you said, about woman trouble.'

'Uh-huh.'

'Out that way, in the swamps.' He pointed off across the flat terrain. 'Over there.' He lowered his voice. 'Feminists.'

Mark tried to suppress a laugh. He looked again at the speaker but the trooper wasn't joking. 'A gang of them. They hate men. They deny God. You better watch out. If they get you . . .' He made a chopping gesture. With that he signalled to his crew and returned to the Jeep. The patrol started up and sped away.

Mark watched them go.

. . . behind the veil

         the voice

            the eyes . . .

. . .

# ASHBURY

He began to see signs for Ashbury. The first had been painted crudely at the bottom of a highway sign giving directions to Miami and Fort Lauderdale. Ashbury, the sign declared, was only thirty miles away. Further on, as he passed through the remains of a small town, he saw a second sign proudly raised in a garage forecourt. A giant arrow pointing left, the same direction as a smaller road. Mark hesitated, referring again to the Pentagon map and his compass and then looking about him. The way ahead was open, the pocked and pitted turn-pike stretching onwards. In the distance an upturned juggernaut was caught in twisted congress with a warped electricity pylon. On his left behind a barbed-wire fence was a modest bungalow. A woman sat on the front porch in a rock-ing chair. Around her a number of feral children were playing on the ground. The woman herself was blob-like in a shape-less pink dress, a floppy yellow sun hat obscuring her face. Mark got off the buggy, leaving the M16 with the vehicle. Keeping one hand close to his pistol, he advanced slowly towards the fence.

'Hello there,' he called out.

The woman didn't respond.

'Listen,' he said. 'I want to go to Ashbury. Is that the way?

Do you know what it's like?' Still no response. 'Is it a nice place?' The three small children had stopped playing and gazed up at him, open-mouthed. The woman remained silent. 'Okay then, thanks.'

Mark decided to follow the direction indicated by the sign. The side road was in a better state than he had anticipated, cavities filled with fresh mounds of gravel. The road ran through an interminable area of suburban devastation, a once perfectly planned community of colonial-style villas neatly arranged around cul-de-sacs and crescents with waterways criss-crossing the streets in some long-gone planner's attempt to create an aquatic paradise. All now blighted, the majority of villas stripped bare by the wind, the canals overripe with poisonous weeds, the waters violated by abandoned vehicles. Then these traces of the old Florida ended abruptly and the swamp took over.

For another ten miles he followed the patchy route through the thick green undergrowth. A huge Stars and Stripes, reminiscent of the sort that had lined the highway from Atlanta, but faded by the elements – an anaemic red, a watery blue – hung almost shamefully from overreaching branches and then a new metal sign, 'This is still America' in bold white letters against a blue background, a skeletal Uncle Sam below. 'Peace and Love', said another, decorated with a peace sign and faded portraits of JFK, Clinton and Obama and then, 'Ashbury Loves You, Approach With Caution', and after that, 'Peace: We Don't Want To Shoot' and 'God Bless America', all painted in the same bright white letters.

Moments later he pulled to a halt before the settlement

The undergrowth in front had been cut back and his approach was blocked by a stretch of canal and beyond that a fifty-foot-high concrete blast wall. Together they formed a barrier as formidable as the moat and buttresses of a medieval castle. 'ASHBURY' was painted in bright colours on the

208

blocks, along with a psychedelic montage of rainbows, water-falls, a smiling sun and groups of people holding hands and dancing. The bold designs and naive decorations made him think the mural was for a classroom or community centre. The effect was disconcerted further by the lashings of razor wire set in front of the canal and on top of the wall. The road led to a metal gate with a metal drawbridge. A much larger gateway, tall enough to accommodate a freight truck, was cut into the blast wall. Built into the wall stood a watchtower bristling with antennae, cameras and spotlights. An American flag fluttered from the top of the tower. Feeling like a foolish knight on a doomed errand, Mark drove forward.

There was an intercom by the gate. He pressed the buzzer.

'Identify yourself.'

He saw little point in lying. 'Mark Burrows.'

There was a pause. 'You're not on the list, dude. Do you have business here?'

Dude? 'I'm a traveller. I'm just looking to spend the night.'

'Not business?'

'I can pay for accommodation. I just need shelter.'

With a buzz the gate opened and the drawbridge dropped down with a loud clang. A smaller portion of the gateway was open and he drove into an antechamber, boxed in by concrete walls. From the top two men were looking down with interest. He sat tight. There was nothing else he could do now. He had to trust that Stone had been honest about the temperament of the place.

One of the men shouted out, 'Hey, we don't know you, do we?'

'That's correct,' he shouted back. 'You don't know me.'

'Okay, that's cool. Listen man, we're going to ask you to leave everything there and walk through the door on the other side.'

'Why should I leave my equipment?'

'You'll get it back. You don't have anything we'd want anyway.'

'If that's not cool with you then you're free to leave,' said the other guard. 'We'll let you back out.'

Mark did as he was told, leaving the weapons by the buggy. He kept his cash and the satellite phone in his rucksack, which he held outstretched, careful to avoid any sudden movements. He walked through an open doorway and into an extended metal cage. The two men were waiting for him. They wore baseball caps, mirrored shades and blue T-shirts that said 'GUARD JOE' and 'GUARD ED'. To his surprise neither appeared armed.

'We're going to open the cage in a moment, okay?' said Joe.

'Good.'

'Just a couple of ground rules first. This is Ashbury. Now we don't know what you've heard or what you expect but let's be clear. This is our place, our home. Don't make no mess, don't make no fuss. If you want to do some business that can be arranged, and if you want shelter and provision then we are happy to oblige.'

'I'm heading south.'

'Someone will be able to help you,' said Ed.

'What I said stands,' added Joe. 'Be respectful and we will be respectful to you. We have protection, you should remember that.'

'The last thing I want is trouble.'

They opened the cage. Joe ran a scanner over Mark's body and bag. 'Okay buddy, you're clear.'

'You look like you've come a long way,' said Ed, assessing his filthy condition.

'Yeah.'

'What are you, man? Some kind of easy rider?'

'I'm going to Miami.'

'No shit.'

'Believe it.'

Ed stuck a sticker saying 'Visitor' to Mark's front. 'Remember, dude, this is Ashbury. It's still America, only better.'

They gave him directions to a guest house in the centre of the settlement. Leaving the fortifications behind, Mark quickly found himself walking into a perfect little world. The gently curving street had been freshly laid with glistening black tarmac turning squishy in the heat. Pretty trees, boughs heavy with fruit, lined neatly trimmed verges. Well-tended flowerbeds radiated sweet perfume and sprinklers hissed back and forth, showering the flora with graceful rainbows of moisture. Somewhere he heard the soothing drone of a lawn-mower. The road continued to curve round past neat clapboard houses with porches and window shutters painted in pastel shades of blue, white and pink, vines curling grace-fully over walls and garage doors. Gleaming SUVs and 4×4 trucks sat proud on tiled forecourts and driveways. American flags and peace banners hung side by side from newly painted doors, a sight impossible elsewhere in the States. Two small children cycled past laughing. A man washing a car gave Mark a friendly wave. 'You must be looking for the Hodgkin's guest house,' he called out.

'That's right.'

'Just keep going. It's on your left. You'll see the sign.'

'Thanks.'

'Have a nice day.' The man went back to scrubbing his vehicle.

The Hodgkin's guest house was just where he was told it would be. A homely middle-aged woman wearing a white apron and a floral dress was waiting on the porch. 'You must be Mr Burrows,' she beamed. 'Do come in. I was told to expect you. You can call me Sue. I've just baked some cookies, if you're hungry.' Her long white hair was woven with blue flowers and the wrinkles around her lips and eyes traced the lines of her former beauty. She led him into a cool parlour where he signed the guest book before passing over three hundred dollars. 'Honey, you look all out,' she smiled. 'Don't worry, we'll get you fixed up in no time.'

Ten minutes later he lay freshly showered on a crisp double bed with clean white sheets, an air-conditioning unit blowing fresh air over his naked body, a plate of cookies and a glass of cold milk on the bedside table. His room was furnished with antiques and it was difficult to tell how old anything was, if the settlement pre-dated Winthrop or if the houses had been designed to look older. Indeed he struggled to know what to think about the town at all, such a pristine bauble when compared to the destruction elsewhere. Lying there, cool and comfortable, he almost felt like a boy again, safe for the moment but about to embark on a great adventure. He could almost imagine that none of it had happened, that the last twenty years had been nothing but a brief nightmare, that he had fallen back through time to a point when there was still hope for the earth, to the moment before certain thresholds were breached and certain forces unleashed. Easy to let his thoughts slide with the fading light, the evening bringing a heavy, tropical calm. Images passed through his mind, the frosted fields and cold blown clouds above the village, the faint light of home gleaming through the darkening forest and he was the grass, the frost, the evening swallows circling the trees, his sister running towards him, her cheeks so pink and her red scarf trailing. Hard to believe how the cold went all the way through his clothes. Hard to believe how much had changed in this greenhouse world, everything festering and rotten in the endless heat. So hard to believe.

As he charged the satellite phone, Mark knew that he

should call the agency back and give an update on his progress. Failure to maintain communication was a major breach of mission protocol. They might have important information to give him. They might even want to abort the mission and send him back home for reasons that would not be made clear. The agency was like that. They never had to explain themselves. Ashe would remain locked in his past, the secret of Kalat forever shrouded in the Zone. And so Mark did nothing. Out here the thread of loyalty felt very thin indeed.

An hour later he sat at the dinner table, his plate piled high with roast chicken, potatoes, fresh vegetables and gravy. He ate avidly and drank glasses of cool water and fresh lemonade. Afterwards Sue appeared from the kitchen with cherry pie and cream. He ate that as well. The dining room could not have been more wholesome, with blue china, perfect white tablecloths and sturdy wooden furniture. The walls were decorated with all sorts of cheery knick-knacks, pictures of wild horses and handsome Native Americans, watercolours of flowers and sun-dappled cottages. A side table was adorned with silver-framed family photographs, smiling children on a beach, a graduation ceremony, a young couple at their wedding.

'Are those your children?'

'Why yes. That's my son Brock with his wife Dee. They live in Seattle now. She's in real estate and he does something with computers.'

'That's far away.'

'Very far.'

'They didn't want to live here?'

'No, no they didn't. Oh, and there's my daughter Megan.' She touched a portrait of a teenage girl giving a geeky smile through her braces. 'She's much older now of course. She used to live here.' There was another pause, almost long enough to be awkward and then she said, 'You look tired.'

'I am.'

'I guess you must find it a little strange, a place like this, in the Zone.'

He nodded.

'A lot of people think that. For many the hurricanes were a disaster. But for us they were an opportunity. You see,' she went on, 'here we have the chance to create the sort of America we always wanted. The sort of America that could have been, before everything was ruined.' She sighed. 'Of course it's not quite the same and behind the walls there are a lot of bad things but here we are quite safe.'

'And the storms? I mean, these houses don't seem very strong.'

'Oh my goodness!' She waved at him with a dishcloth. 'These houses are much tougher than they look. And we have the best shelters you've ever seen.' Noting his expression, she continued, 'Sure, sometimes we lose a few tiles, and the odd palm tree gets blown over, but in all honesty we don't even get that many hurricanes, not in this part of the Zone. I wouldn't believe everything you see on the television. A lot of it is exaggerated.'

'Really?'

'The great tidal waves and two-hundred-mile-an-hour winds. All that baloney.'

'But outside . . . it's a mess.'

She flinched as if he'd said something rude and glanced out of the window. 'Appearances can be deceptive. Anyhow, we're still Americans, you know,' she said. 'Still citizens. We still have our passports. Just because we live out here . . .' There was a long pause and then she asked, 'Did you enjoy your dinner?'

'Very much, it was delicious,' he replied. 'As you can see

there's nothing left.' He smiled. 'So,' he added, 'how long have you been here?'

'Oh well, since the beginning.'

'The beginning?'

'My husband, Bob, you'll meet him soon, he was one of the founders.'

'Founders?'

'That's right.'

'So was the place founded after Winthrop or—'

'Naturally,' she trilled, cutting him off. 'We're not from around here originally. I'm from Baltimore, my sister still lives there and Bob, he's from San Francisco. Where did you say you were from?'

'Oh. Boston. But I've been living in England for a long time, that's why, my accent . . .' He smiled apologetically.

'England. How lovely. I'd love to visit. It must be marvellous.' She fixed him with a spotlight-bright smile. 'So you'll be travelling on tomorrow, will you? I was told so.'

'I'm going south.'

'Miami?'

'Maybe.'

'Oh dear, no, I wouldn't go there if I were you.'

'I've no choice. I'm looking for someone. My brother-in-law.' He looked down at his empty plate. 'I've had information that suggests he is in Miami.'

'Have you heard from him?'

'Not exactly. He's supposed to be dead.'

'I see. Gosh.' Sue looked embarrassed, wringing her hands in her apron. 'You get a lot like that, out here, people hiding. That sort of thing . . . I'm sorry. I don't mean to pry.'

'Not at all. Actually I was wondering if you might know of him.'

'Oh dear me, Mr Burrows, I shouldn't think so. I never go out past Ashbury, really, I don't know a soul!'

'He's an Englishman. Or he was. His name was Ashe. Charlie Ashe.'

'I see. Well, I have to tell you, hon, they say a lot of people are coming to the Zone. Coming from all over the world. English people too. I mean, we always thought the situation was better in Europe but . . .'

He cut her off. 'He calls himself something quite different now.'

'Really?'

'He calls himself Kalat. Do you know the name?'

'I . . . no . . .' She flushed.

'Please,' he pressed his case. 'You might be able to help me. I know it's dangerous out there.' He dropped his voice to a nervous whisper. 'I need to find him.'

'It's just a rumour really,' she stammered. 'Rumour and conjecture. I don't like to listen to such things.'

'What sort of things?'

She flushed again. 'They say . . . well . . .'

'Go on.'

'I wouldn't know. Maybe you should ask my husband.'

'I will.'

She turned back to go into the kitchen and then hesitated again. 'They say he's the Devil, do you know that? They say he's no longer a man.'

'The Devil?' He frowned.

'Or an angel, a fallen angel. I don't know. That's what they say.'

'Who says this?'

'People. Some of the men out here.'

'What do they say?'

'A lot of the men here have travelled all over the Zone. They know it well. Some of them claim to have seen him. One or two say they served him.'

'How?'

'In his army. At least that's what they say.'

'His army?'

'Mr Burrows,' she flustered. 'It's not for me to comment. I mean,' she continued. 'Sometimes we have to fight to preserve what we have here. There are people who would destroy it. Isn't that always true of Americans? We've always had to fight to defend our way of life, our freedom.' She gave a little laugh. 'Like when we got rid of the British. You know.'

'Does Kalat threaten you?'

'Us? No, no. Goodness me, no.' Her expression changed again. 'Actually he protects us.' And she twisted a large gold ring on her finger.

'Against who?'

'Others. You know. If you got this far, you've seen them.'

'The government? The Witch Hunters?'

She shook her head. 'Well, hon, anyway, that's a shame, that you're going to Miami, that's a real shame, that's all I can say. I certainly wouldn't advise it. It's a real pity you can't stay, a strong young man such as yourself. A real pity. There's good work to be done here. We need people like you. There's nothing south of here, that's for sure. There are no roads any more. You'll need to go by water.'

Mark nodded. He could see that the woman was too anxious to give him any more credible information. 'Is it possible to arrange transport?'

'I'll speak to my husband about it. Ashbury has a small river port. That's how we make our livelihood.' Sue retreated back to the kitchen. 'Just make yourself comfortable,' she called. 'Help yourself to lemonade. Bob will be back soon.'

She was right. Bob arrived a few minutes later. A stout man with a thick grey beard, he came in mumbling something about an aphid infestation and mopping at his bald head with a cloth.

'You must be Mr Burrows,' he said, lighting on Mark. 'Pleased to make your acquaintance.'

'Likewise.'

'We're delighted to have you here. I hope Sue has been looking after you.'

Bob already seemed to know all about his travel plans and after some small talk the two men set out into the sticky evening, Bob spraying the air around them with mosquito repellent. 'Darn critters will drive you crazy.'

'This heat . . .' Mark began, wiping at his face.

'Yeah. Well, you can get used to anything, I figure,' Bob answered, although his face ran with sweat. He gave a brief commentary as they strolled along, pointing to various houses and giving snippets of gossip about some of the residents. 'It's a broad community, Ashbury,' he went on. 'We take all sorts. Democrats and Republicans. Jews and homosexuals. We got some blacks, a nice Mexican family, some Chinese. A lovely Cuban couple live over there, Carlos and Maria Sanchez. Lovely people. It don't really matter where you from. Over thataways is the school, the leisure centre, a few shops.' He pointed to a side road lined with more suburban houses.

'You got a church?'

'Hah, well now, like I said, we take all sorts.' He gave a wry smile.

The area of suburban villas was smaller than Mark had first thought, the residential neighbourhood blocked off by another fortified wall. A guard sat on duty at the gateway, smoking a cigarette and listening to an iPod, a twelve-gauge shotgun resting between his legs.

'Evenin' Bob.'

'Evenin' Rick. Hot, ain't it?'

'Ain't it ever.'

The area beyond was marked by a series of concrete warehouses. 'This is where we keep everything of importance,' said Bob. 'Forgive me if I ain't more forthcoming.' Floodlights, attracting a blizzard of insects, illuminated dozens of workers' bodies glistening with sweat, loading green bales into the warehouse. They walked in silence for a few minutes. A sweet, sharp smell filled the air. 'Behold.' Bob pointed to a plantation on the other side of the road. Mark saw hundreds of tall green plants, with five-pointed leaves, growing in neat rows. 'Best-quality sativa this side of the Rocky Mountains.'

'You grow marijuana?'

'That's right. Don't look so surprised, dude! Ashbury's security and wealth depends on it. We sell to all-comers.' For the first time Mark noticed a reddish, glassy quality to Bob's eyes.

'What about the military? Don't they—'

'Sure they do. They love it. Keeps the grunts happy.'

'I see.'

'This is still America. Never mind the President, never mind the Pentagon, never mind the Church, never mind all that Illuminati bullshit. This is still America. We just don't believe in quite the same things. You know what I'm talking about?'

Mark hesitated, unsure how to respond.

Bob didn't seem to notice. 'I'm talking about Jerry Garcia and Timothy Leary, you know? Hunter S. Thompson, Ken Kesey and Neal Cassady, Jimi Hendrix and Jim Morrison, all those dudes, they were true pioneers, explorers of the final frontier. The mind, you get me, man?' He tapped the side of his head. 'Here we explore the inner realm. We keep one dream of America alive. You dig?'

'The sixties were a long time ago.'

'Time's just relative, man. Time's what you make of it.'

'Yeah? I don't see us getting any younger.'

Bob ignored him and they stood in silence for a few minutes, contemplating the green rows fading into the gloom.

'Ain't that just a beautiful sight,' Bob said eventually. When Mark didn't respond he continued, 'I understand you looking for a way to Miami. That right?'

'I'm looking for someone, my brother-in-law, Charles Ashe. Except now he calls himself Kalat. Your wife seemed to have heard of him. I believe he's hiding out down there.'

Bob reached for his arm. 'Don't be foolish. You look like a good guy. Shit. *Kalat*. He fucks with your head. They say he's the man behind the Man, you know?'

Mark moved his hand away. 'No.' He lowered his voice. 'The Man sent me. You dig?'

Bob faltered for a moment. Then he smiled. 'Dude, you shit me, you really do.' He tried to laugh. 'Brother-in-law, my ass.'

'Your wife says Kalat protects you. What did she mean by that? Does he control you?'

'No, dude, your thinking is all wrong.'

'Yeah?'

'You're thinking like them, out there. It's not like Kalat allows or does not allow anything. I'd call him an enabler. He makes certain things permissible. He's no ruler. He ain't the Pentagon or the CIA. He's more like a disruptor. He's anti, you follow? A negation. Kalat sanctions us. His words enable us. His very being makes us possible.'

'I don't think I understand.'

'Of course you don't understand.'

Mark frowned at him.

'Maybe if you make it to see him, maybe then things will have changed for you. Maybe then you'll see things a little more clearly. You've got to let his voice in. You've got to get it inside you. It's like a little tinkle that gets louder and louder. The doors of perception, man. The Zone might look like hell if you can only see one way. But if you shed your preconceptions, your expectations, if you purge your mind of all that bullshit out there, then you'll realise something else.'

'Yeah?'

'Even in the worst of times a new possibility can emerge. There are still things we can hope for. The dream hasn't died. It hasn't even gone away. It's had to change its shape, like everything else. It might not look quite the same, not at first glance, but it's still here. I hope you'll make it and maybe, just maybe, he'll let you talk to him. Maybe he'll grant you that honour. Kalat will teach you to see. And then . . . then you'll realise.'

'Just help me find a boat going out of here. I'll worry about the rest, okay?'

Later Mark lay in his room, exhausted but too anxious to sleep. Bob had taken him to a small waterfront piled high with bundles of harvested marijuana and guarded by stoned hippies with tie-dyed camouflage shirts and M16s painted with peace signs. There Bob introduced him to the pilot of a riverboat due to leave at dawn. The pilot didn't venture his name and asked only if Mark could handle a gun. Mark handed over a number of bills and was told his weapons and equipment would be delivered direct to the boat. He told Bob he'd donate the buggy to Ashbury.

Now, with everything set, the night seemed to drag around him, his thoughts mapped out by the steady drone of the air-conditioning unit. Once he thought he heard things in the street outside, voices raised in argument, but it was too indistinct to be sure. Several times he heard Bob get up and amble awkwardly down the corridor, floorboards creaking and then a flush from the bathroom. He could still picture the stoned fool, tapping his head and jabbering about 'the mind'. The door was locked and he'd jammed a chair against the handle, just to be sure. Not that it would make much difference. They had his firearms. If they wanted to get him, it would be easy. He felt awkward and exposed. If they gleaned his true purpose, these people might do anything. Stone had said he would be safe here but it was hard to match promise with reality. He tried to conjure Alisha, the warmth of her smile and the wisdom of her counsel, but the very thought of her seemed remote, as though heat had corrupted memory, his remembrance growing faint like old prints in a photo album. Bleached by the sunlight, everything seemed far away.

. . .

    –   I'm cold
*Flicker*


. . .

# ZONE

An hour before dawn Mark was back at the harbour side. The pilot greeted him with a brief handshake and led him on board. The boat was an ex-military tug, painted black with a raised cockpit and an open stern upon which two deckhands, tanned, blond teenage twins from Texas, were loading shrink-wrapped bales of marijuana. A fourth crew member, a caramel-skinned African-American, sat high on a swivel-mounted machine gun at the rear of the craft. Topless, his torso gleaming in the wet morning gloom, a cigarette burning between tight lips, he regarded Mark with cautious disdain. A fifth crew member shuffled around in the cockpit, a huge man, lumbering and fleshy like a melting pink snowman.

'That's my son,' said the pilot, his accent as thick and slow as the Mississippi. 'Bo. He ain't exactly right.' He tapped the side of his head with a pudgy finger. 'But he don' do no harm. Don' mind him.'

Bo moved onto the deck, his vacant blue eyes regarding Mark with slack disinterest. A ream of dribble trickled from his lips.

Mark sat down at the back of the boat, watching the pilot supervise loading the rest of the crop. Lack of sleep had left him feeling groggy and fragile and he watched everything through a slow stupor.

After a few minutes they set off under the soupy sky. 'We're gonna fallah the waterways to Miami,' the pilot explained. 'Or what's left of 'em. We got business there an' you can get off, if you're sure you wanna.'

A thick white mist rose up from the salty waters, suffocating as steam from a locked bathroom. Vague shapes appeared through the haze and then a blast wall painted with a huge smiley face and a sign, 'You Are Now Leaving Ashbury', and then another, 'Don't Fear The Reaper', painted above a large mural of a skull and bones with a spliff blazing between bony jaws. They cruised past a final guard tower which rose from the Everglades like an immense fist. A flare went whooshing upwards, an explosion of purple light illuminating the stygian scene.

'Hey motherfuckers,' a man shouted from the top of the tower. He dropped his pants, jiving his body at them, his erect penis jerking up and down like a broken aerial.

'Stick it, asshole,' the pilot shouted, flipping a finger back at the crazed guard. Bo moaned and shook his head from side to side, his eyes rolling like two discarded marbles.

'Here.' The African-American thrust a cup of coffee into Mark's hand. 'This will sort you.'

'Thanks.'

'I'm Steve,' he said.

'Mark Burrows.'

'Pleased to make your acquaintance.' He gestured at the pilot. 'Chuck tells me you've got military training.'

'That's right.' Mark sipped at the hot liquid. 'I was in the forces for a long time.'

'Good. Things can get quite treacherous out here, in the red.'

'Well, as long as I'm on board, I've got your back.'

225

Steve nodded, his gaze shifting from side to side. 'You been out in these parts before?'

Mark shook his head.

'We've done this trip enough times. You never really know what to expect though, never really know what might happen . . .' He shrugged, his words trailing off. Mark sipped his coffee. 'So,' Steve continued, 'forgive me for asking, but do you want to tell me why you're heading out with us?'

'I'm not paying you all this money to tell you anything.'

Steve pursed his lips and nodded. 'We all have our secrets, I suppose.'

'And you guys.' Mark gestured at the weed. 'You sell dope. You going to tell me about that?'

Steve shrugged. 'Sure.' A brief smile. 'That's no secret. We trade with various groups deeper in the Zone. Marijuana thrives in this climate. It's a valuable commodity. We use it to acquire other items, sometimes even cash. Much of what we pick up we sell back to Ashbury. It suits everyone.' He looked around them. 'There's a lot of money to be made out here, if you know what you're doing.' The misty haze was brighter now, like a radiant fabric wrapped around the ship, the approach of the sun signalled by a growing luminosity. 'All these hurricanes have done some weird shit to the Everglades,' Steve continued. 'Waterways come and go, the sawgrass marshes are swamped then dry out and turn to desert. Lake Okeechobee expands and explodes its banks and then contracts into no more than a stagnant puddle. Each new storm brings its own strange changes.' Steve pointed at the pilot. 'Thankfully Chuck's an experienced navigator. He fucks up sometimes but he knows these waters better than almost anyone. Hell, the military won't even come out here, not even the Marines.' He spat. 'All they do is buzz past in their choppers, taking pictures, trying to make new maps. They're scared to touch the ground.'

'And do you get much trouble?'

Steve pointed at the heavy machine gun. 'Ole faithful up there has got us out of enough scrapes. I guess it depends what you mean by trouble. In some ways it ain't so different from anywhere else. Just depends where you're from, you know, and what you're used to.' He went silent and seemed to withdraw. There was something about the man, Mark thought, something he couldn't quite put his finger on, a sort of slipperiness. Even though Steve was present before him, the man's voice was indistinct and his face unmemorable. To describe him, after just one meeting, would be a struggle. Then Mark realised: Steve was like him, another invisible man, a walker in the crowd. He would have to be careful.

The day settled into a steady monotony. They chugged through an unnatural nature, a labyrinth of mangrove trees forming a dense cage around the boat, dripping foliage hanging out of the brown water, branches twisted like the broken limbs of flood victims. Sometimes the water churned muddy brown or a menacing deep red. Sometimes it was flecked with submerged flickers of blue and silvery grey or else foamed with toxic swirls and tangles of unmentionable waste. Mark gazed upon his surroundings with a sense of bewildered, oppressed wonder. They would pass traces of the old world, a broken road bridge, the slimy supports like the chthonian dolmens of a barbarous civilisation, huge shopping centres or penal colonies, the grey shells given over to unknowable uses, wrecked golf courses and retirement communities, structures consumed by the undergrowth, walls and depressed rooftops fused into weird combustions.

At noon, sheltering from the sun under a canvas canopy strung over the back of the craft, they ate soggy power bars and a spicy rehydrated vitamin soup cooked up by the twins. Everyone stripped down to their shorts, wilting in the incredible humidity. Mark was itching from dozens of mosquito bites peppering his back, neck and arms, the red welts like love-bites given by some insatiable amour. One of the twins – distinguished from the other by a white scar above his left eye – applied a cooling cream. 'Dunno what's worse,' he said. 'Mosquitoes or the no-see-ums. No matter what you do, they get you sooner or later.'

The afternoon dragged on, slow and horrible. He felt a faint touch of fever, a glassy, shaky quiver running through his body. Shuddering he watched the others crapping and pissing over the side of the boat. Bo pulled off his clothes and paced back and forth like a tethered bear, fat thighs and arse quivering with each heavy step. Sporadically he seized his penis in one meaty fist and let out a long, low moan, an almost mute gasp of anguish and frustration.

They passed alligators gliding like leathery logs through the leaden waters. One of the twins produced a shotgun and blasted at the reptiles, shrieking with delight as the stricken creatures sank back beneath the surface. The heat seemed to thicken the haze and several times Mark was sure he saw bat-like shapes fluttering through the gloom, their sharp-edged shadows hinting at the presence of other, more unfathomable beings.

Later the boat stalled. The water was thick with monstrous jellyfish, thousands and thousands of them, white and puffy, churning the water like rancid milk. Suffocated fish were caught amid their slimy tendrils and clouds of black flies swarmed above. The stench made Mark want to retch and he clung to the side, paralysed until the pilot managed to restart the engine, the propeller ripping through clotted masses of poisonous membrane.

To keep calm, to maintain control, to keep back the nausea that shifted through his body, Mark clung to his old routines. He dismantled the M16 rifle, intending to clean and reassemble it, to check the components and make sure he could rely on the weapon in a firefight. But once it was in pieces he felt suddenly confused, his fingers slippery with grease and sweat, unable to work out what to do. Eventually he managed to reassemble the gun but the task took much longer than it should have. Head spinning, he yearned for some respite, a cool shade or a fresh breeze. He found himself leaning over the side of the boat, bile heaving from his lips.

'Here.' One of the twins touched his shoulder. 'Reckon you got a touch of swamp sickness.'

'Yeah?' he spat.

'Take a drag on this, buddy.' The twin passed Mark a joint.

Mark looked at the young man in astonishment. What the hell. Exhaling smoke through his nose, he passed the joint back and started coughing. 'Been a while since I done anything like that,' he spluttered.

'That's the shit, man,' laughed the Texan, patting his back.

A pleasant lightness came over him and with something approaching detachment he sat back and observed the passing swamp, suddenly fascinated by each mazy twist and reach of low branch, bough and fern-cloaked tree. Bo crouched in front of him, watching his face with an empty sort of intensity. He began to bellow, slobber frothing his lips, tears running down flabby cheeks. Steve took over the wheel so the pilot could cradle his son's gargantuan head in his arms and whisper soothing words to him. Slumped against a bale of densely packed weed, Mark looked on with incomprehension as the father rocked his son to the slow sway of the boat.

Darkness came suddenly, bringing rain warm and constant. The pilot stopped the boat, turning a spotlight on to the back of the craft. The crew stripped off and began washing themselves. Mark joined them, taking soap offered by one of the twins and scrubbing vigorously. The warm rain fell, water gushing out of drain holes on the deck. Afterwards, as the rain continued, they moved into the cockpit, brewing fresh coffee and tucking into more rations.

Steve fiddled with the boat's radio, tuning through layers of static.

'Is he there?' asked one of the twins.

'It's about time,' he replied.

'Not that shit again,' the pilot sighed, turning away and rubbing his wet torso with a towel.

The others ignored him.

'There,' said Steve.

The voice came drifting across the static ether, no more than a whisper and yet so very loud: '*So it has come to pass, my children of the swamps . . . my dancers at the end of time . . . the last of the great American pioneers . . . This is where we have ended . . . all the promise of the West squandered in the storms of a dying planet . . . in the rage of the impotent . . .*' The voice faded slightly, sending a shiver slithering across Mark's skin. There he was. Kalat. '*What has happened and what is left?*' Mark looked at the crew huddled close around the radio as if waiting for the revelation of some mighty truth. '*Once I was a white man, a European, an Englishman . . . whatever label you wish to use. All of Europe contributed to the making of me. All that European history, all that American confidence . . . Twin fists of Western power . . . Yes . . . I was the perfect tool, an instrument of the Gods, exalted and terrible, an avenging angel in bondage to my enlightened masters and the lofty concepts with which they disguised their will to power . . .*' Kalat paused and there was a long sigh. The crew sat transfixed, a joint passing between the twins. Mark strained forward, trying to discern in that intonation some spark of the man he had once known. '*I am no longer an Englishman,*' the voice continued. '*I am no longer a European, no longer a white man. I am no longer a child of the West. These old identities, these past selves, have been burned away. Cooling fires have soothed my soul with the balm of the dispossessed.*

230

*The sorrows of this sad world lie heavy on my shoulders, like wings of iron and chains of lead. None of us are the same as we once were . . .'* Another long pause, everyone waiting, even Bo perfectly still, his eyes closed as though in a deep meditation. Only the pilot appeared distracted, flicking restlessly through an old map of Florida like a sceptic at a séance. *'There is always a first time . . .'* A deep sigh. *'And so there is always a last time.'* Another pause. *'I remember . . . the first time I saw the woman who became my wife. Such is the texture of our lives . . . the fickle treasure of remembrance. I remember the first time we kissed and the first time we walked, hand in hand, through the park in the soft rain . . . what comfort in such distant memories?'* The sudden mention of his sister sent a shudder through Mark's body. He remembered other conversations, such a long time ago now, the two of them alone in the desert, fingers and eyes soiled with the grime of a dozen bombings, and Ashe's voice waxing rhapsodic about Susanna, gentle sermons of love as if she had become for him a symbol of everything that still had value in the world. *'I remember the last time. The last night we ever spent together. The last time we ever kissed. I did not realise it was the last. I did not realise the direction forces would take me. Had I known . . . no . . .'* He sighed deeply. *'Some things are too painful. We have only a little knowledge . . .'* Another pause. *'I left early in the morning, easing myself from our warm bed and her embrace. She stirred and mumbled my name. I told her not to worry. She never saw me again.'* Another much longer pause and the rain fell steady and the air in the small cockpit turned thick with marijuana smoke. Mark sat, scratching at the bites on his back and arms, unsure just what to think. *'This is a time for last things, my dear friends, a time of endings. Love endures, yes, long after sorrow fades like a spring flower in the heat of summer. But such flowers have deep roots and they nourish even the most parched emotions . . . This is a time of last things, a time of endings . . . Such waste and stupidity. What is left? We have torn ourselves asunder to feed our greed, our waste and our fear. We have violated earth and sky to suck up the frozen power of the sun and with this we have propelled ourselves forward, faster and further, and yet for what? For this? This is what remains.'* A spitting noise fizzed through the tape. *'Here is our home, this Zone at the edge of civilisation, and now I ask you, my children, what best can aid us and render this hell more tolerable?'*

The pilot got up with a start. 'I ain't listening to this fucking shit no more.'

'Chuck!' Steve admonished.

'Always the same ungodly bullshit.' He went outside.

The others glanced without approval at his departure and turned back to the radio. *'I have sought for us all some small deliverance through all the coasts of dark destruction. We are not one side nor are we the other. I have served the cross and the eagle and I have served the crescent and the man in the mountain and all proved false. The war is a false war. Conflict unreal, division begat by greed and the abstraction of that which was pure and present into that which is absent and corrupted . . . Between the eagle and the crescent, the lion and the star . . . A pyramid of power controls both sides but the masters have put out their eyes so now tormented clouds obscure the light of heaven. All are enslaved to systems without meaning or reason. The deepest ocean, the most remote mountain top – despoiled. The domains of the true Gods are vanquished and we have usurped divinity with degraded symbols and meaningless abstraction. Our desire for mastery has made us all slaves. We are the slaves of systems . . . the cross and the crescent, the one and the zero . . . What now is left I ask you? Who are the pure of heart? Who can see clearly and who has been purged? I tell you, all that remains to cherish is the memory of love, the comfort of another, the small truths disclosed in intimate moments . . . But what of I? My skin is hard and my soul is barren . . . What is left of me but these sighs of woe in this region of sorrow? Doleful shades where peace and rest never dwell and where hope never comes . . . Such is the texture of my soul . . . As I look out at the drowned city, in the depths of my misery I can but ask and I can but dream of what a world this might have been . . . Such a place of wonderment and beauty . . . Such fullness . . . Can we learn to see with eyes pure and new? Can we seize from the swamps an alternative to our predicament? Can we slip the noose of our history? Can we break the cycles of conquest and submission? Can we dare to hope that the watchers with instruments celestial and the controllers with their mechanism infernal will allow us the autonomy we crave? And if fight we must, what then the toll and what the consequence of yet more blood? What forgiveness is left from dead hands, dead tongues and dead eyes?'* The voice began to fade, intercut with strange electric clicks, pops and cuts and then another voice took over, brashly American and Southern and much clearer. 'Yessir, you can be proud that together you've helped liberate thirty thousand Christians from the torment of slavery and helped them survive in the merciless land where suffering is multiplied by the jihad perpetuated by a ruthless Islamic regime and its terrorist thugs. Faithful, God-loving Christian people, behold their smiling faces and behold their devotion and this despite a genocide carried out against them. Let me testify, I've witnessed mothers and children fighting over food, refugees forced to leave their homes. Go to your phone, dial the toll-free number, go to the website, send your gift, let us help a family to live and not die.'

'Turn it off,' sneered one of the twins.

Silence returned to the cabin.

'You know who that was?' said Mark. 'The first voice, that person you were listening to. You know?'

'We know,' nodded Steve.

Mark hesitated, their faces turned to him, eyes like dark discs in the dingy cabin. 'That's the one I seek,' he said.

For a minute no one spoke and then Steve replied, 'How can you seek one who has dominion over us all?'

'Kalat? He's no God.'

'That's right,' added the pilot. 'He's a lunatic. All that bull-shit he spouts, ah can't stand it.'

'Chuck . . .' Steve admonished. 'You shouldn't speak like that.'

'Why not? Fuck you. Ah don't need none of his bullshit, nor none of yours.'

'He's the exalted one, the protector,' started one of the twins.

'And you're just a no good cowpoke dopehead. What the fuck you know 'bout shit? Don't listen to these idiots.' He turned to Mark. 'This crew of jokers, they just a bunch of superstitious shit stirrers. Money, that's what we're here for. Nutin' else. Let's turn in. Long day tomorrah.' His pallet was in the corner of the cockpit, his authority signalled by the privilege of a fan set beside it. 'Go on, all a you git the fuck out, ah'm sleepin' here. Steve, for makin' me listen to that shit, you take first watch. You,' he pointed at one of the twins, 'cowpoke, you take the second. Fall asleep 'cause you too stoned an' you swimmin' back to San Antonio.'

Mark got up and followed the others back into the humid night. The twins unrolled a tarpaulin over the back of the boat. Mosquito netting was unravelled around him. He lay down on a sleeping mat on the damp deck amid the bales of marijuana.

When he opened his eyes someone was crouching over him.

Steve.

The two men gazed at each other.

'You come to tuck me in?' he said. 'Give me a goodnight kiss?'

'What do you want with Kalat?'

'You don't need to worry about that.'

'You can't hurt him.'

'He's just a man.'

'You don't understand.'

'He's just a man.'

'He's more than that.'

'Not to me he isn't. He's my brother-in-law. He married my sister, get it? That was my sister he was talking about.'

Steve gave a contemptuous snort. 'You don't know him any more.'

'We'll see.'

'You can't kill what he represents.'

'What do you think he represents? What do you really know about him?'

'He has something.'

'I don't want to kill him. I know him. I know him better than any of you.'

'Not any more,' Steve said again. 'You think you know him but you don't.' He moved away, taking his seat on the swivel-mounted machine gun.

Mark remained lying on his mat, one hand on the pistol, his heart pounding, waiting for what sleep might come.

. . .

stars flicker like candles

Behind the veil the voice in the darkness, the ripple and shock as the car bomb explodes silently in the hospital garden under the trees in the dappled sunlight . . .

'Ignore the judgements of those who stand far away.' The reassuring tones of Foxy as they sat in the car travelling through the grey English countryside.

'I've done bad things,' he tried to say to the beautiful doctor who came each morning to soothe the ache in his mind. 'I've done bad things,' he tried to say but the words would not come.

Sometimes he would meet her on the station concourse or the stone steps outside the museum. Sometimes they watched him too closely and he would break away before it was too late for her.

His thoughts were confused during this period.

He could almost . . .

He watched live coverage of Hurricane Winthrop on the television in his room on the sixty eighth floor of the empty Dubai hotel. When he tired of the destruction he looked out of the window at the desert. Soon the sand would consume the city, hot wind creating dunes thousands of feet high and hundreds of miles long. It was said that religious leaders emerged from such places, visionaries and mystics, men of God, but as he watched the satellite images of the vortex rampaging through Florida, he was no longer sure.

Later they told him Ashe was missing. There was talk of a helicopter crash on the border with Iran.

The pain in his shoulder kept him awake night after night.

. . .

# ZONE

Early light grey and low as the tug stopped to make its first trade. They pulled into a narrow inlet overhung with moss-drenched mangroves. A speedboat was waiting with three men on board. Mark watched as the pilot exchanged a bale of marijuana for two small crates stamped, 'Fragile'. The pilot took the crates into the cockpit and spent some time checking the contents. Steve, the twins and Bo remained on deck. One of the men on the speedboat unwrapped a corner of the bale and sniffed at the contents while the other two stood back, watching them. Despite all the firearms on display the mood seemed relaxed enough, Mark thought, a sense of routine familiarity underpinning the proceedings

The pilot emerged from the cockpit. '¿Esta buena?' he called across to the speedboat.

'Si, esta aconojante.'

'Vale. Parece estar. Nos vemos por ahi.'

'Vale claro. Hasta luego.'

'Hasta luego, tio.'

The speedboat took off, quickly disappearing back into the swamps.

After a minute or two the pilot restarted the craft and they continued to head south, deeper into the Everglades, travelling through ever more constricted passageways, watery tunnels girded with webs of creeper so thick that the craft became caught and the twins would plunge into the waters with axes to hack at the undergrowth. Clambering back on to deck, they burned leaches from their limbs and lit huge joints. Fetid odours of salt and soggy decay filled the air, the cloying whiffs of heavy wet weeds and the festering smell of dead fish upturned in stagnant waters as if all were rotten and they journeyed through a great realm of corruption and disease.

Dazed and sweat-drenched, Mark kept thinking about the words Ashe had spoken last night. Despite the heat the anguish in that voice left him feeling chilled and he couldn't help but think with dread wonder at what Ashe must have suffered to speak in such a way. *Kalat*. Was that why the others listened with such rapt attention? Did that fractured voice touch some deep yearning inside those around him? Had Ashe broken free, prying himself from the hands of his masters, sundering control and overleaping all bounds in his disobedience and defiance? Could he be a free man, a man beholden to no other, remade in the prickly power of his new name? What had happened, he wondered, to transform the soldier he had once known into this ghostly voice of the storms?

The sultry afternoon slunk towards the simmering evening, the bloody sun soaking the water a deep red. Come nightfall they drifted into a new settlement, the pilot signalling their arrival with several loud blasts on the boat's horn. Their approach was answered by a chorus of fireworks that went shooting upwards from the shore, the sparking lights and sudden blasts illuminating a striking assembly. The bank was crowded with men, ghoulish smiling faces and swirling eyes painted on to their swollen bellies. Some wore headdresses of feather and ribbon, in imitation of the tribes that had once inhabited the region while others had shaven heads painted in bold swathes of colour. The women had gathered their hair into elaborate turbans, their necks and arms ringed and looped with all sorts of bangles and beads, witchy charms and amulets. Their breasts were bare and they wore sandals and brightly coloured sarongs made of animal hide and belts of plastic, rubber and snakeskin. Excited children ran around, astonished and delighted at the jubilation triggered by the boat's arrival. Some in the assembly carried baseball bats and golf clubs but they held the items awkwardly as though they had forgotten just what to do with such relics. Flaming torches bathed proceedings in a glow, orange light glimmering off limbs and torsos. On one side a motley group of musicians were banging snare and bass drums and clashing cymbals, a demented serenade blaring forth on rusty trumpets and saxophones, the ensemble like a deranged jazz band dredged from the ruined barrios of New Orleans. More fireworks went screaming upwards, the fresh barrage seeding smoky flashes of pink and blue and luminous green in the stagnant waterway.

One man stepped forward. 'Hi there,' he shouted. His muscular body was emblazoned with swirling tattoos and jagged designs as though he had been sown together from multiple fabrics. Around his shoulders he wore a leopard skin, his face peering out from the jaws of the wild cat. He raised a staff decorated with animal skulls, teeth and claws, bits of shiny metal, bright feathers and wisps of fabric, all of it glittering in the gloomy firelight. In his other hand he held a long chain which led to two metal yokes, each fitted around the neck of a teenage girl. The two supplicants cowered at his feet, their slender, naked bodies painted with tiger stripes and leopard spots. 'We were wondering when you'd get here,' he continued. Despite his appearance he had the laid-back, cultured Southern accent of a management consultant from Atlanta or Charlotte.

'Hail mighty Chief Jeff,' the pilot answered. 'King of the River, Lord of the Green Jungle, Master of the Salty Marsh. We bring the healin' of the nation, the holy herb to cleanse your mind an' soothe that which ails you.' The tug was secured by guide ropes lashed to landing posts set in the riverbank. 'Y'all stay on board,' the pilot said to them. Taking Steve, he disembarked and followed the leader into the settlement.

With the end of the arrival ceremony the majority of the tribe retreated back into the gloom. A few children remained on the bank watching the boat in case it might reveal some fresh marvel. Mark gazed after them, struggling to believe that they were – or had been – ordinary Americans, former citizens habituated to refrigerators and air conditioning, soft beds and cable TV, the same Americans he had seen all over the great nation, eating burgers, listening to iPods and driving SUVs. It was hard to know what to think. He had encountered primitive people on missions in Afghanistan, Nigeria and elsewhere but this was something of a wholly different order, the wilful abandonment of one society for another, more visceral existence. These people had chosen to howl and leap and spin, to adorn their bodies and make horrid faces, as if such deliberate primitivism could assuage the wounds of their past identities. He almost envied them.

The night wore on. Seeking refuge from the constant mosquitoes, Mark followed the twins into the cockpit. The sound of drumming, relentless and erratic, drifted across from the village. The absence of a steady rhythm was unsettling, the beat a jagged, atonal pulse. Occasionally he heard ghastly yelps, shrieks and other sounds that were even harder to decipher. Indifferent to such disturbances, the twins sat smoking and fiddling with the radio.

'The man is silent tonight.'

'Silent tonight.'

'Silent night!' They broke into stoned giggles.

'You boys mind me joining you?' he asked.

'Do want you want, buddy.'

'So is it true,' the first twin asked, 'that you be hunting Kalat?'

Mark nodded. 'I'm looking for him, that's right. What is it about him, those broadcasts and such? Why do you listen?'

'Everyone else just tells you what to think but Kalat, he tells you *how* to think,' said the first twin.

'Yeah?'

'For sure.'

'One of the ole boys back in Ashbury,' the first twin continued, 'he served Kalat. He worked for Kalat back when he first came to the Zone.'

'What did this man say?'

'He say Kalat appeared on a beach after a great storm – one of the biggest since Winthrop – a storm so violent most of the military bases were evacuated. He say they were on the beach looking for salvage when they saw this man, walking naked and pure like Adam himself through the new white sand. He say that Kalat ain't like other men. He say Kalat is what them call an archon. You know that?'

'Sounds like a mighty big word for a farm boy.'

'Don't shit me, buddy. An archon is one blessed with supreme insight.'

'He's a ruler,' the second joined in, drawing hard on his spliff. 'One who can legislate between worlds.'

'I don't even know what that means. That doesn't sound like anything to me.'

'This world,' continued the first. 'The world of man and the rest of the universe. Creation. The glory of nature. I've heard them say an archon is an angel, or a demon, someone what talks direct to God.'

'I don't believe in God.'

'You think we put our faith in Jesus?' The first spoke with sudden passion. 'You think we believe their lies? Fuck that,' he said. 'We've seen this country go to the dogs, everythin' we dreamed about destroyed. The droughts. Believe. No rain for ten years. If you see our daddy's farm, then you'll understand. The Texas dust bowl. Shit. You'll see. We ain't stupid, this ain't nuttin' to do with God – this is man, all man, man, man.' He took a deep draw on the joint. 'We're out of balance. We've gone too far the wrong way. Someone like Kalat – he's the correction. You got Parris an' all his preachermen spoutin' the Gospel and sayin' put our faith in Jesus while everythin' goes to shit an' they get rich an' live safe and well. They don' give a fuck 'bout the likes of us. We just want to be left alone to do what's best for ourselves with none of this other fucking bullshit.'

'We're all niggers now,' added the other. 'We're all niggers an' Kalat's the ju-ju king.'

'You think?'

'Look around. Open your eyes. Fuck Jesus. Look. These people here, will you look at these people.'

'They're Americans, man,' said the first twin. 'Beautiful Americans doin' their own fucking thing. They don't need no government tellin' what they can or can't do. Fuck. I'd rather be free out here than a slave back home. These here the runaway slaves, it's them back home that are in chains.'

'Let me get this,' Mark interrupted. 'Kalat is a symbol of freedom for you. Is that it?'

'Nah man, that ain't it at all,' the first said. 'He speaks in a higher tongue. He has purified his words and thrown the stars down to earth.'

'You going to tell me what you mean by that?'

'You think you know him so well, you tell us.' The twin touched the side of his head. 'You find him, then you know.

He'll open your eyes. If you can't see already, you will, sure enough.' Like a two-headed beast in the gloom, the twins nodded in unison. 'The Storm Zone ain't just a place. It's also an idea. You got to learn to see it right. You heard Kalat speak. You think you know someone like that?' He made a fleeting, fearful gesture, pointing to some mysterious object just beyond the field of vision. 'You know what they say? The Pentagon sent a force of Marines to smoke Kalat from his hole. A thousand Marines, battle-hardened warriors fresh from the Middle East. And you know what?'

Mark shrugged. 'Tell me.'

'They couldn't get him. Some of the brothers in Ashbury were fighting with Kalat. Them say on the third day of the battle, with the sky yellow with smoke and fire, Kalat appeared like an angel of death. Them say a hundred Marines turned their guns on themselves and the others – those who escaped – went loony, driven mad by what happened.'

'They say that?'

'For real.'

'Kalat's a soldier. I know that much. I served with him. I fought alongside him.'

'You think he could whip that many Marines?'

Mark shrugged. 'Could be. He's a ruthless killer. Or he was.' His face was sharp in the dark light. 'You would not want to see what we did, back there.'

For a while neither twin responded. There was a faint fizzing noise as the joint was passed between the brothers. 'What you think you gonna do,' asked the second, smoke pluming around his face, 'when you find him?'

'I don't know,' Mark faltered. 'I just have to talk to him.'

'Yeah?'

'And then we'll see.'

'That's right.' The first twin nodded, squinting with narrow red eyes. 'Then you will see.'

Mark went back outside. Drumming continued to reverberate through the trees. He felt it as well, in that demented rhythm, the perverse yearning to abandon the mission, to shed his obligations and his ingrained loyalties, to adorn himself in a savage mantle and join those others on the other side of the river, dancing and screaming in the night, beating out all the frustration of his life in a frenzy of abandonment. And yet he did nothing, a deeper resolve holding him steady like a steel chain.

The pilot and Steve returned to the boat followed by half a dozen villagers. Mark watched as the remaining bales of marijuana were removed. The Chief waited by the riverside, overseeing the proceedings. A chorus of women stood beside him, rocking back and forth, ululating in grief or joy – Mark could not tell – images of white snakes and reptiles tattooed to their pendulous breasts and heavy thighs. On the deck Bo gave answer to their wailing, his voice pitched in perfect response, his naked body swaying like a metronome.

After the marijuana had been offloaded three more villagers appeared. Unlike the others they wore pointed hoods and long capes that made Mark think of the Klan but their robes were dyed blood red and marked with strange black crosses. Crocodile heads hung from their necks on silver chains. They climbed on to the boat, each carrying a small metal box. The women's wailing rose in pitch and intensity, some tugging at their hair and hammering their breasts, one even falling to her knees, clawing desperately at the ground in an extravagant pantomime of emotion. Bo's moans also grew louder and he tilted back his head, his knuckles white as he gripped the side of the boat, his body shaking violently.

As the red-hooded men disembarked leaving the boxes on-deck, the women's wailing turned more doleful and low-key. Bo slumped to his knees, apparently exhausted. One by one the women slunk away until all that was left was the faint

245

keening of their mournful voices. The drumming also stopped, the steady hum of insects reclaiming the night. Only the Chief remained, standing watch on the bank.

'Until next time.' The pilot made a saluting gesture while the twins untied the guide ropes.

'Until next time,' the Chief shouted back. 'May the Gods give you safe passage, fresh blood, new eyes, strong hearts and pure lungs.'

The pilot sounded the horn and they pulled away. Soon all Mark could hear was the drone of the engine. He moved over to one of the units, putting his hand on the cold metal box. 'Better not touch that,' said Steve. He took the box from Mark and opened a storage unit on the deck. Despite a few moans from the twins, the three men began to load the boxes. Watching, Mark felt a keen desire to know what was inside them but he also sensed such a question would not be welcome.

Leaving the others to their tasks, he moved to the relative privacy of the mounted machine gun and set up the satellite phone. He dialled a number. The phone was answered almost immediately.

'Hello?'

'It's me.'

'Jesus! I've been so worried. What's happening?'

'It's okay. I'm sorry. Conditions out here have been difficult.'

'Foxy came to see me yesterday.' He didn't answer. 'Why haven't you called them? They've been trying to contact you. We were starting to fear the worst.'

'What did he want from you?'

'He needed to know if you'd been trying to contact me. He wasn't happy.'

Mark knew that the agency would be listening in to his call.

'Is everything all right?' she asked.

'The mission is proceeding as planned,' he said, choosing his words as much for Foxy's benefit.

'Mark, you need to call them. Why haven't you called?'

'It's complicated.'

'You know what they'll do.'

'I know.'

'That's the last thing we want. Please just call them.'

'Alisha, I love you.' The words tasted dead on his tongue.

'Call them,' she said again. 'And then make sure you come home.'

Rain started again, flashes of lightning illuminating brief scenes from the passing wilderness, wild curls and tangles of undergrowth, glimpses of a ruined town, a gas depot, its storage domes glinting like Byzantine monuments, acres of wind-flattened trees and upturned bushes, mournful expanses of dull nothingness. They travelled through the night, the pilot attentive in the cockpit, infrared goggles strapped to his eyes. Mark sat out, shunning the others, letting the rain soak him. It was a wet world, a dark world, a drowned world, a sun-scorched world. 'Someone has to get their hands dirty so the people back home stay safe.' This was the voice he remembered. 'The people we love. Your sister. My wife. The life we have. Sometimes a little darkness is necessary for there to be light.' He wanted to ask him. He wanted to say. In the desert. He wanted to say, when did it start? And why me? He remembered the days in the room far from the light. Thirty-six hours without sleep. The shouting. Forty-eight hours without sleep. The knock down. Fifty-six hours without sleep. 'We're not in England any more,' said the man who promised to break him. 'We can do what we want with you here.' He told them so many things he no longer knew what he said or who he was. No one left to trust, no one left to believe. The door opened and there was Ashe. 'Old friend,' he said with a smile. 'You've done very well, even better than I anticipated.' Hands were shaken and papers signed. Ashe led him through long corridors and past thick metal doors. When they emerged into the outside the fresh air hit him like a fist. 'Well done,' Ashe said again. They were in an industrial estate in Hounslow. 'You'll be hearing from us soon,' he said, leading Mark to the waiting taxi. 'Send my love to Susanna.'

A hand shook his shoulder. He opened his eyes, blinking at the weak grey sky. Steve stood over him. 'You've been sleeping.'

Mark looked around. It was almost dawn and the boat had pulled up against a concrete wall slithery with green slime. Seagulls circled above, tracing patterns against the sour sky. They had sailed across a wide bay choked with yellow weeds. A broken highway bridge stretched from one side to the other. On the horizon a handful of condo towers rose up like colonial outposts abandoned to dense jungle.

'This is as far as we go.'

'I see.'

'Back that way,' Steve gestured across the water, 'those towers and things you can see, that's Miami proper – you know, downtown, Little Havana, Coral Gables, the old airport, Dade County, mile after mile of storm-trashed fucked-up nightmare. Nothing but psychos, bandits, outlaws.'

'And Kalat.'

'Yeah, and Kalat.' He paused, wiping at his face. 'The pilot won't take you no closer. Too dangerous, he says, and I'm inclined to agree. Miami Beach though, especially South Beach, it's okay.' He gave a grim smile. 'Art deco hotels, hip clubs, lovely sand, all that shit. You'll love it.'

'I like an American with a sense of irony.' Mark saw that the pilot remained in the cockpit, scrutinising another map. Bo was curled up asleep under a mosquito net. One of the twins slumbered in a hammock strung across the deck. The other, the one with the scar, handed Mark a tube of soothing cream. 'Those critters have bitten you bad,' he said. 'You're gonna be itchin' like a dog with crabs soon.'

Nodding thanks, Mark took the cream.

'You might need these too,' Steve added, passing him several power bars and a bottle of water. He stuffed the rations into his bag and then, gathering his things together, he clambered on to the shore.

'Mark,' Steve called. 'Remember something. Whatever you think you know about Kalat, you're wrong. You don't know him. He is the overlord. He has a message to us all. You should leave him be.'

Mark looked at the man a final time. Then he turned away. He set off, scrambling over the concrete wall. He started to walk. A terrain as flat and dry as a desert, a barren stretch of pulverised concrete and vaporised sand, remains of villas and apartment blocks, buildings ground to dust by the elements. A faint, hot breeze stirred the salty air. After a while he realised he was no longer clear what Steve looked like, his memory of the man's face washed from his mind. He suspected that Steve would remember him still.

He walked towards a dark line, perfectly straight, that matched the horizon. It took a while before he realised it was the sea. Here the desolation was complete. There was no real beach any more, just dry white concrete and dust. The ocean was almost still, the sticky surface throbbing slightly. A web of plastic bags stretched the length of the shore, millions of bags and bottles and coils of webbing like the shed skin of a hundred thousand snakes. The smell of chlorine lingered in the air. Seagulls slashed down from the sky, white blades scavenging scraps of dead fish bobbing among the plastic. He saw many dead birds, their beaks, feet and wings ensnared in the detritus. He sat for a while, wondering what to do.

. . .

                   the wind

–   I'm cold. I'm hurt bad, aren't I?
         I'm cold

                  the eyes
                     the wind

. . .

# BEACH

Mark followed the dense tangle of rubbish along the shore, a vast sterile barrier reef of plastic in all colours and sizes. Ruined buildings dotted the expanse of the beach, their warped forms and gutted foundations giving the merest hint of the metropolis that stood before. Confronted with such destruction, he found it hard to believe that ten years ago Miami had been a thriving, cosmopolitan city of six million. Now only mocking traces remained. Shimmering on the horizon, a skyline of fragmentary towers, luxury condominiums and corroded hotel skyscrapers like stalagmites rising from the antediluvian plain. Above it all the sky was opaque, a cataract across the dark eye of heaven. Again he heard the voice of Kalat: *This is a time for last things. This is a time of endings*, his words whispered dry-mouthed as shards of glass.

Behind him he saw a plume of dust and then another. He hesitated, squinting through his sunglasses, the horizon iridescent like molten plastic. The swirls were getting closer. With nowhere to hide all he could do was lie flat on the ground, sheltering as much as possible behind his rucksack and tracking their approach through the scope on the assault rifle.

Three battered SUVs travelling at great speed. Impossible

to tell who was in them. He had to hope they were travelling too fast to see him. Sure enough the convoy whisked past, each vehicle loaded with men and women, faint whoops of wild delight carrying across the beach. The vehicles sped towards a seafront cluster of buildings. Some of the structures retained their façades, the old frontages like skinny ghosts with balustrades, spires and elegant twentieth-century curves, glassless windows and open doorways affording clear views of the void beyond. Backless, roofless, without walls, these frontages evoked the set of an art deco seaside Western.

Venturing closer Mark noticed further signs of activity: ashy remnants of campfires, scattered drinks cans and beer bottles, items of clothing and cigarette butts recently discarded. Approaching cautiously, darting between shorn walls and heaped mounds of rubble, he saw vaporous ladders of smoke rising into the bleached stillness of the sky. A dusty Vindicator and a customised Dodge pick-up truck were parked next to a bent wall. Now he could hear music – a regular electronic beat – and people calling to one another. More of the buildings had survived on this part of the beach, some standing three or four storeys tall, the boutique hotels and trendy apartment blocks gaunt as skeletons dipped in acid. A warm, dry breeze scattered the smoky towers and stirred up thin streams of fine white dust. A man and a woman came stumbling from the doorway of a gutted condominium, both of them laughing, clearly drunk and oblivious to his presence.

Mark walked on. More people were milling about the ruins, dazed, lost souls, seemingly uncertain of where they were or what they were doing. Many in the crowd were dressed for the beach, young men and women wearing swimming trunks, bathing costumes and brightly coloured T-shirts, although Mark struggled to imagine anyone sunbathing or swimming in such conditions. Others had a more harrowed appearance with pale skin and shaven heads, their eyes haunted and glittering like stones cast into water. They wore cowls of sackcloth and wandered barefoot over the hard ground, reminding Mark of the ragged procession he had seen driving into Florida. Apocalyptics, that was what Mary called them.

'What's going on?' he called out to a young man seated on a low wall, his head tilted towards the sea. The man glanced at Mark but didn't say anything. No trace of recognition in his empty face, his eyes focused on something far away, some abstraction or projection distant and vague.

Mark strolled along Collins Avenue past the husks of shops and restaurants worn by a decade of wind, relentless water and searing heat. Nature had been creative in its destruction, warping the environment into disturbing shapes, buildings bent into coral-like structures of calcified concrete and moss-engraved stucco. The faded architecture of catastrophe, buildings folded and inverted, tide marks like geological tracings staining walls in hues of ivory and damask, sienna and cobalt. He negotiated an area of rippled earth, the tarmac torn to shreds, gaping holes plunging down into murky saline pits. A strange realm, this aquatic desert, an isthmus of wet ruin and dry bones gleaming like precious metal in the white rock.

He came to an open area surrounded by broken-down three- and four-storey apartment blocks. Electronic music was pumping from a sound system and a dozen or so people were dancing slowly, their eyes closed and arms uplifted in a sort of exhausted ecstasy. A barbecue had been set up and Mark smelled burgers, onions and hotdogs. Further away, towards the open beach, a dozen or so crosses had been set on the ground. Mock crucifixions, devotees lashed to the crosses, bodies glistening with sweat, contorted faces twisted against the sun. He watched as a young man was cut down, falling exhausted to the floor, another standing ready to take his place. Men dressed like medieval monks assisted the process, some helping to strap the next devotee to the crucifix, others attending to the crucified with water and bandages. Apart from a few half-hearted glances no one paid Mark much attention, the mood somewhere between a religious service and a beach party. People were distracted enough for him to know that, with his asset, he could glide inconspicuously through their midst. As no one else seemed to be armed, he shouldered his assault rifle, adjusting his posture and expression as if he too were part of the strange proceedings.

He approached the barbecue. 'Hey there, soldier,' called a man busy turning sausages. 'You look hungry, you want to eat?'

'Yeah.'

'There you go. You want ketchup?'

'Got any mustard?'

'Praise the Lord, we got it all.'

'What's going on? What is this? A beach party?'

'You could call it that, sir, you could indeed. We're having a revival, a little festivity before the next storm.'

'When's that?'

The man, his eyes hidden by wraparound Oakleys, nodded at the sea. 'Not long, sir, couple of days. No more.' He flipped sizzling sausages.

'Will it be a big one?'

He shrugged. 'We hope so. We praying for one big enough to wipe away all our sins and carry us up to our Lord.'

'You're going to be here for that?'

'Not yet. Not this time. One day, though.' Perhaps Mark had gone too far with his questions, as the man turned his attention to the next customer.

Mark moved a little way from the festivities, sat down and ate quickly.

Further from the dancers and the music he saw a small congregation kneeling in the sand. An overweight man in pastor's robes was intoning passages from the Bible to them with a megaphone: 'And the waters prevailed exceedingly upon the earth, and all the high hills that were under the whole heaven were covered. Fifteen cubits upward did the waters prevail, and the mountains were covered and all flesh died that moved upon the earth, both of fowl and of cattle, and of beast, and of every creeping thing that creepeth upon the earth, and every man, all in whose nostrils was the breath of life, and of all that was in the dry land, died.' At the end of the service the pastor moved among his flock, touching his hand to their heads. Some wept, some kissed his dirty robes, some buried their faces in the dusty ground.

As the congregation broke away Mark saw a young woman walking in his direction. She was dangerously skinny, her frail body wrapped in little more than a filthy sheet and he could see scabs on her head where she'd caught herself as she cut off her hair.

'Excuse me, miss.' He waved at her.

For a moment she didn't seem to notice him. Then, after a second look, she stopped. 'Could you tell me what's going on?' he asked.

It took a while for the question to sink in. She had the vacant, withdrawn demeanour of a drug addict or psychotic. 'We're here,' she said at last. 'We've come for the Rapture.' Beads of sweat were running over her sunken cheekbones.

'What do you mean?'

'The Holy Rapture, the great storm that will sweep us all up to heaven.' She faltered, gesturing lamely at the sky. A rank odour emanated from her pasty skin. 'We are ready.'

'Where have you come from?'

She seemed to struggle to comprehend his question. 'Cleveland,' she said at last.

'How did you get here?'

Another pause. 'I walked,' she said. 'We all walked.'

'You walked all the way from Cleveland?'

She nodded. 'God was watching over us. The journey was not too hard.' She swayed slightly as she spoke.

'Why this place?'

Her eyes clouded with confusion. 'Well . . .' she began. 'There are devils in this city. But here the Lord watches over us.'

'I see.' Mark paused, wondering how he was supposed to get through to her. He tried again. 'When will God send you to heaven?'

Her face twitched slightly, pained by something. 'Flesh and blood cannot inherit the kingdom of God . . .'

'Are you all right?'

She didn't seem to understand what he was asking. 'I tell you a mystery.' She raised a finger. 'We shall be changed. The last trumpet will sound and the dead will be raised incorruptible and we shall be changed.' She turned her head to cough, spitting into the sand. 'The corruptible must put on incorruption,' she continued. 'The mortal must put on immortality and then shall be brought to pass the saying, "O Death, where is your sting?"' A strange smile crossed her face. 'It will be wonderful. God be with you.' She stumbled onwards.

Mark wondered what to do next. There must be someone here who was rational, he thought, someone with credible intelligence about Kalat or what was going on. He ate another burger and watched more vehicles arrive, each loaded with excited young people. Revellers sat around drinking beer and dancing. Couples slipped away to make love in the ruins. Preachers and pastors moved among the throng, reading from the Bible and taking prayers. He saw hands being laid on the sick and heard voices raised in exhortation. No one paid him much attention. He found it hard to discern the mood of the place, the weird mixture of masochistic piety and carefree party. Half of those in attendance were clearly fanatics, their grim demeanour testament to the harsh pilgrimage they had endured to get here. The other half seemed indifferent to the dangers of the place or the consequences of being caught in a storm, like they had simply drifted to the beach in search of a new thrill. He wondered if they were day trippers who had driven over from the official settlements in the Zone, off-duty Darkwater and DynoCorp operatives, or maybe military support staff, cooks, cleaners and technicians for the various bases. The alternative – that these people might have also crossed over illegally – was even harder to take. He didn't understand how they could have made it this far. The agency had briefed him about increasing numbers of people being drawn to the Zone, falling under the orbit of Kalat or other forms of archaic order. Perhaps these migrants sought the same. Or perhaps they simply clung to the memory of Miami past, their motions a desperate attempt to resurrect that sybaritic, hedonistic city. He wanted to ask someone but the mood of disconnection was too strong. Instead, as the relentless heat and lack of sleep took its toll, he found himself slumped in the foyer of a once beautiful art deco hotel.

'Hey soldier.' A young man wearing a dog collar smiled at him.

'Hi.'

'Come inside, rest. You look weary, pilgrim. We are all warriors for Christ.' The pastor led him into the building, a large silver cross set above the doorway. 'Here is shelter from the sun and cold water. This is the time of the Tribulation, my friend. Deliverance will come.' He touched Mark gently on the shoulder. More pilgrims were resting inside the building, stretched out on roll mats, some sleeping, others praying or reading intently from the Bible. He sat down in a shady corner, accepting the bottle of water the young pastor gave him.

'Do you know the best way to get across the bay, to downtown?' he asked.

'My son, are you crazy?' The pastor blinked with bewilderment. 'Don't even think about it. First you've got the Marines, then you've got the bandits and then you've got the heathen terrorists. You don't stand a chance. We're much safer here on the beach. Once this was a fallen place, full of sodomy and idolatry, but the wrath of God has purified it for the righteous. God is watching over us.'

'I'm looking for someone.'

'We are all searching, my friend. Are you willing to accept Christ as your saviour? Let God into your heart and you will find the answers you seek.' The pastor was so earnest and likeable that Mark almost wanted to go along with him.

'No . . . Not God. I'm looking for someone called Kalat,' he replied. 'Apparently he's the true lord of this place. Do you know of him?'

The pastor flinched. 'The Devil has many guises, brother. Don't fall into Satan's snare.'

Mark waited for the worst of the afternoon heat to pass. He knew there was no point venturing across the bay into the city until the following morning. Outside he could still hear the sound of music and people shouting and laughing. He found himself thinking about Mary, wondering what had happened to her, if she had ever left Wind City. Perhaps he should have never left her alone, such a young girl, so vulnerable in such a savage place. He tried to work out why he was thinking these things, what it meant, this sensation that had embraced his nerves and hung heavy as a pendulum in his heart. The agency had always told him he wasn't responsible for the things they made him do. He was just a means, they said. There was a chain of command, they said, a network of orders and instructions feeding back into the web of control. Foxy, Mr Bradley and Mr Martin and those other grey men were not responsible either. But he also knew that the men at the very top, the public face of the organisation, the directors and the ministers they were accountable to, had no real idea of what was being done in their name. The system was designed to stop the consequences of what happened from folding back to hurt those in command. The agency was like a sponge, able to absorb and diffuse each action. Still, he thought, someone, somewhere, had to accept something. Things didn't happen without reason. Maybe that was what Ashe had chosen to do, he thought. Maybe he had finally assumed responsibility. Perhaps that was the condition of his freedom, to have accepted the consequences, to have borne within himself the weight of so much death and confusion. Unless the opposite had occurred and by giving himself a new name and a location remote from previous connections Ashe had sought a final reinvention. After all the training, the years of subterfuge and deceit, Ashe had taken his knowledge to the ultimate end – distancing himself once and for all from everything he had done – his opposition now explicit. It could be that he had become a force of pure anarchy, an incarnation of the terrible storm that had created the Sunshine State, antithesis of all reason, meaning and control. Without boundaries, what restraint? Without order, what hope for man? And yet, when he thought back, Mark wondered if they had not always been the agents of chaos, tools bent to the service of a terrible power. Considering all they had done together, despite the noble words supposed to underpin their mission, the enlightened ends outlined in Parliament for the benefit of the public, their part had always been the more terrible. A litany of death and destruction for what? Dead babies laid in a row? Iraq, Afghanistan, Somalia, Nigeria, Iran . . . each intervention had ended in atrocity. Mark couldn't deny the truth of his experience. Seeking to remake the world in their own image, they had defiled everything they were supposed to stand for.

Later in the afternoon he took out the satellite phone and checked the battery. Power was low but it was still working. He climbed up to the top of the hotel and went out on to the flat roof. Tall palms rose like distressed arms above a shattered cityscape of gutted balconies, peeling concrete, gaping windows and sagging towers. Molten city, in the heat of evening, atmosphere stagnant with the stench of chlorine and bleach wafting across from the dying sea. The sky growing dark under the burden of swollen clouds, summits tinged with green and yellow shades. Looking west he saw an unmarked black Apache scuttling fast and low over Biscayne Bay. The setting sun turned the towers at the far south of Miami Beach into black tombstones, their ragged silhouettes looming over a torpid Gomorrah.

He dialled the number they had given him.

With the weak signal it took several attempts to connect. 'Identify yourself.'

'Is Foxy there? I need to speak to Foxy.'

'Identify yourself.'

He gave the pass code. 'Casement. This is Casement.' The usual rituals.

'We've been waiting for you to call.'

'I'm in Miami Beach. Can I speak to Foxy?'

'Foxy is not available.'

'I need to speak to him.'

'You're speaking to Control. You don't need to speak to Foxy.' Mark hesitated, unsure how to answer. The voice continued: 'Attention, Casement. We've isolated the location of some of Ashe's broadcasts. They are coming from downtown Miami. He broadcasts from a number of skyscrapers around Bricknell Avenue. His HQ is in this area, we are certain.' The voice gave a series of coordinates.

Mark paused, feeling weirdly disconnected from their commands. 'Are you saying I should try and reach this place?'

'Affirmative.'

'Conditions on the ground are not easy.'

'You have your orders.'

'I've heard a storm is coming. Can you confirm?'

'We don't have any data about that.'

'What do you mean?'

'You heard us.'

'Listen, about Ashe . . .' He paused, rubbing his face. 'Everyone seems to know about him out here. They say he's very powerful. They say he repelled a Marine assault on Miami. If he did that, I mean . . . what can I really do?'

'Your orders are to proceed to downtown and make contact. Understand?'

He couldn't think of anything to say. He put the phone down for a moment. London seemed very far away from this place, the expectations they had of him almost irrelevant. 'Look,' he started.

'Don't question us.'

'I don't think you understand.'

'No, you don't understand! Remember the operation. The bigger picture is not your immediate concern.'

'But I'm here!'

'Other things are at stake. Don't forget that.'

'What?'

'Think about your girlfriend. Think about Alisha Page. The good doctor. Think about the child she is carrying. Your child. Understand?'

He swallowed. 'Leave her out of this.'

'That's up to you. That's up to what you do. Make contact with Ashe. Then call us. Understand?'

'Affirmative.'

The line went dead. Mark swore and put the phone down and rubbed his face. He had never dared to question the agency before. He thought of Alisha, pregnant and alone. He thought of a black car pulling up outside their apartment, Foxy and his men sitting inside. There was nothing they wouldn't do. He realised his hands were shaking. He sat down, trying to pull himself together. Finally he stood up. Turning back he saw another man on the roof, watching him.

. . .

*the wind*

Are you there?

    –   Yes

Not fading out on me, are you?

    –   No . . . no it hurts too much for that.

Good. You need to hold on to the pain, it will keep you alive as long as you can feel it.

    –   It really hurts, it's not good, is it?

You've been shot.


*the eyes*


    –   Love.

Yes

    –   Talk to me about love.


. . .

# HOLLOW

As soon as he saw the figure Mark spun round, swiftly unslinging his rifle, flicking off the safety and pointing it at him. The man was squatting on his haunches, regarding Mark with a calculated watchfulness, like a monkey about to spring for a scrap.

'No need for the gun, mate,' he said, raising his hands and standing up.

'You're English?'

'So are you.' His interlocutor was in his late thirties at most, tough looking with tight black curls of hair, a dark stubble and blue, perfectly round eyes – bright spheres that seemed to add a shade of youthful energy and glamour to an otherwise weather-beaten face. He wore tatty camouflage fatigues, a motley assemblage of faded colours that left him looking like a cross between a harlequin and a commando. His air of adventurous abandonment was enhanced by the two pistols hung cowboy-style in holsters on either side of his belt, as well as the strips of ammunition draped across his chest.

Mark did not lower his rifle. 'Yes,' he replied cautiously. 'That's true, I'm English too.' He wondered how much of the conversation the man had overheard. 'What do you want?'

'I think I can help you.' The man took a cautious step forward, keeping his palms outstretched as if Mark were a dangerous dog liable to spring at any moment. 'My name is Philip Priest,' he continued. 'That's my real name – the one my mother gave me and no one else.'

'Okay.'

'So . . . who are you?'

'Why should I tell you?'

Philip shrugged. 'Common courtesy?' There was a strange innocence about his smile and his bright eyes did not blink once. 'I used to be like you,' he continued.

'What does that mean?'

'I knew they'd send another. I knew it. Kalat said as much. He knew. He foretold it all.'

'You know Kalat?'

'Maybe.' He gave a coy, slightly skittish shrug. 'If one can really know someone like Kalat that is . . .' The man's words started to trail off and then he caught himself, tugged by an invisible string. 'They sent me to kill him,' he went on, nodding his head up and down. 'It's true. They did.' He closed his pronouncement with a solemn jerk of his head.

'What are you talking about?'

'You know just what I'm talking about. Admit it, they've sent you here for the very same reason.'

Mark lowered his rifle a little. Feelings of weariness surged over him and he felt himself drift, layers of fatigue ravelling and unravelling like the motions of a troubled ocean. What should he say? Looming clouds had bathed everything in an oppressive green light. A sluggish west wind came wafting in, salty with ocean chemicals. 'So you found Kalat,' he said after what seemed an age.

'No mate.' Philip shook his head. 'It's not like that.' He

pursed his lips. 'You don't find Kalat. How can I put this? He finds you. He found me. And in the end . . . in the end I was grateful.' As he spoke an expression of distress rippled across his features.

'Grateful?'

'Yes, you see?' He held up his hands. 'He saved me . . . in the end . . .'

Mark gazed at Philip. There was something so improbable about his being there. He wanted to ask how he had succeeded in getting so far, to have reached this place, this rotten outpost of the West. His very presence evoked disconcerting sensations of intangibility.

'They sent you to kill Kalat?'

'Something like that, although they never say the words, do they? They never exactly say what they mean. Still,' Philip licked his lips, 'when it came to it, I couldn't, you know?' He shook his head in some pantomime of confusion or disgust at his failure to find an expression appropriate to the feelings. 'He is more than they said he is.'

They were disturbed by shouting in the street below and the crack of gunshots. Both men leaned over the edge of the flat roof. Several revellers were arguing with each other in the street below, one of the men brandishing a pistol as the others jeered.

'Who are these people?'

'Oh, I'll tell you.' Philip grabbed his arm, eyes glittering like precious metal in a muddy stream. 'Here, we grope together and avoid speech – you know the poem, don't you? Here we are, gathered on the bank of the tumid river – you know the one? You know what it means? This is the place.' He shook his head with a feverish sort of intensity, as though such motions could conjure a truth greater than the words spoken. He seemed on the verge of great emotional excitement, a revelation of the nerves that kept him in a position of almost overwhelming apprehension. He let go and walked one way and then came back, mumbling something under his breath. More shouts came from below. Mark saw the crowd dispersing, several black SUVs moving with ominous purpose along the avenue. Philip held tight to Mark's arm. 'You knew Kalat didn't you?'

'I knew him by a different name.'

'His old name. That's right. They told me.'

'Charlie Ashe.'

'Yes. It's no good. He has renounced it now. He no longer answers to that name. He no longer recognises that person. We must all change our names. Ashes to ashes, you know, dust to dust.'

'We'll see who he answers to.'

'And why did they send you? Have you thought about that?'

'I served with him in Iraq.'

'Of course, of course . . .' He sighed and nodded. 'Well, I never had that privilege although he must . . . I mean . . . Perhaps he only had the seeds, back then.'

'What?'

'Of his greatness, I mean. He must be changed, you see?'

'I don't—'

'He must be greatly changed since then. Of course he himself said that the next one, the one after me, that is, you—' Again he squeezed Mark's arm, as if to reassure them both of certain realities. 'He said the next one would be one who knew him. You. He foretold it.'

'I don't know what you mean.'

Philip nodded vigorously, seeming to agree with his confusion. 'We have all gone a little too far, don't you think? When I was with him . . . Oh, how we talked. We talked of everything. I forgot about sleep. The night . . .' He fixed Mark with eyes open like blue spotlights. 'Everything! Of love, too . . .'

'He talked to you of love?'

Priest's head twitched up and down. Around them the thick wind stirred, a sudden scattering of raindrops shed from the almost black sky. Rumbles on the horizon. 'We had best go inside,' Philip said. 'These storms can come very sudden. It wouldn't do to be struck by lightning, would it?'

Below they passed through rooms filled with pilgrims pressed together, broken chambers reeking of unwashed bodies, sweaty armpits, dirty assholes, piss and sperm, the insomniac funk of a mindless devotion. A group in a corner sang hymns in hoarse voices. A gaunt young man hammered at a tom-tom. They found a corner by a window. A scrap of blue cloth used to cover the broken frame swelled in and out like an unhealthy lung. After a moment Philip started again. 'He cast me out, you see,' he said. 'He accused me of betraying him.' He shook all over as he spoke, quivering with a chilled passion. 'Even though we had fought together – I had fought for him, defending his city. But after that I wasn't safe there any more. His men are fiercely loyal and liable to do anything. He has a woman with him, a witch, a sorceress. She took a dislike to me. What can I say? It was not prudential to remain any longer. Listen, you know this – Kalat is a great man but he's sick, he's ever so sick. He's dying, I think. I don't think he has long left. A disease has swept through the city. A plague. It struck the Marines first but then it struck everybody. Some said Kalat brought forth the pestilence himself. But I don't think so.'

'You don't?'

'It's tempting but no. Sanitary conditions over there are woefully inadequate. All that dirty water . . . We mustn't lose sight of everything. We mustn't surrender to superstition and fear. Not like these around us.' He shook his head vigorously.

'You said something about the Marines.'

'They attacked. A veritable army. They came like us, like you and me, to kill the man. And they failed, just as I failed and just as you too will fail.' In his high-pitched, jabbering voice, he told Mark how he arrived in the Storm Zone some months ago on what the agency had told him was to be his exit mission. When Mark ventured that similar assurances had been made to him, the man broke into a jagged sort of laugh. 'Always the same shit,' he said. 'They tell us the same shit and they read from the same script, it don't matter who we are. We're nothing to them. We're interchangeable and replaceable. It's a set-up, it's a scam. They betrayed me the same way they betrayed Kalat and the same way they will betray you too.' Perhaps it was fatigue, a certain inevitable fraying of the emotions that he had learned to expect from such hardships, but Mark found himself struggling to process the man's words. A chasm of doubt opened within and he felt himself dangling precariously, a solitary climber clinging to a dangerously thin rope. There was a point at which all dangers became equivalent. He had come too far, he realised – he saw it now, if he were able to see anything – he could only go further.

When he came to talk more directly about Kalat, Philip became flustered and his sentences hung unfinished, the purpose of what he was trying to say fading like weak clouds against the sun. The centre of his experience seemed at once too great and too mysterious for his powers of expression. He continued to touch Mark on the arm or the leg as he talked, trying to make plain some unspoken intimacy, some common feeling given to them by their encounters with Kalat. Kalat, he said, had 'unshackled his mind' and 'opened his eyes'. Kalat had 'suffered much' and had 'shook himself free of the firmament'. He was a 'fallen star', he said, and a man much 'misunderstood', one who had 'overleapt all bounds' and had taken what he called 'the law' unto himself. They talked long into the night, Philip said. They talked of love and what it meant, love of another, love of one's country, love of one's duty. There was a great sadness to Kalat, he said, an aura of melancholy that surrounded and touched those around him, sorrow for past deeds, sorrow for all that had been lost. Philip's language grew obscure at just the moment when clarity was needed, something to cast a clear light over Kalat and what he meant for them all. The only thing that shone through such vagueness was the enchantment that must have befallen the agent, Kalat's glamour reflected by the passion that animated his opaque sentences and in the sudden twitches of his racked body, as though all his old loyalties had been sucked out of him, the vacuum filled by Kalat's power. He was, Mark could see, utterly smitten. His devotion to Kalat dominated him, consumed him, laid claim to every ounce of his being.

When Mark pressed him for more details about the Marine assault on Miami, Philip's account became sharper. The wilderness that had engulfed his soul had not entirely dampened years of military training and conditioning. He explained that the assault had taken place three weeks after he arrived at Kalat's base. Three hundred elite Marines had formed the core of the attack, landing at Biscayne Bay in high-powered attack boats, while two SuperCobra attack helicopters and an AC-130 Spooky gunship provided air cover. The Marines had been wearing state-of-the-art Chameleon battle-suits, launching a swift and decisive assault. Within an hour, he said, half of Kalat's men had been killed or otherwise disabled. The Marine advance was stalled by a number of well-placed IEDs – Kalat had honed his bomb-making skills – but by evening he had abandoned his main base and retreated to a secondary camp in Little Havana.

'We fought all night,' Philip went on. 'Keeping back the Marines. I personally killed four of them. I fought for Kalat.

The weather was changing – a storm blowing in – and that neutralised the Marines' air support. The storm that night was quick but terrible. We sat it out and we were high enough to avoid the subsequent tidal surge. The Marines were less well prepared. The following afternoon Kalat led a counter-attack while the Marines were still trying to regroup. He came to them with thunder and lightning and they had never seen anything quite like it – very terrible it was. He could be very terrible. You can't judge a man like Kalat, not as you would an ordinary man. He wanted to shoot me too one day – but I don't judge him – I can't judge him.' Philip wiped his face and gave a nervous, half-hearted laugh. The day after was strangely quiet, he explained, the Marines failing to muster their own counter-attack. Skirmishes continued sporadically over the next few days and then even those died down. They would hear helicopters and jet planes and spy drones circling the city, he said, but no air strikes followed. Instead a creeping swamp fever burned through the camp. He said the Marines must have been first afflicted and that this had thwarted the counter-offensive. But then Kalat was also struck down, he explained, and it seemed there was little anyone could do. 'He cast me out,' Philip went on. 'He blamed me for the attack. He said I had led the Marines to him. I told him this was not the case – I was innocent, I protested. But it wasn't enough. I wasn't so innocent. They had used me – don't you see? And when I didn't deliver Kalat to them . . .' Again he shook his head. 'The same will happen with you.' He lapsed into silence, some highly wrought motor of speech having finally wound itself out. A hot wet wind blew through the building bringing flourishes of rain and cracks of thunder. 'It's like this . . .' he continued. 'You must understand . . . Kalat knows. I know . . . It was foretold . . . sick . . . he's ever so sick . . . a great man . . . you can't judge him, you mustn't judge him . . . he has suffered much . . . his voice, when you

271

hear him . . . terrible and mighty . . . you must understand . . . we talked of love.' The man continued to twitch and shake with spasms of feeling.

After a while Mark spoke. 'What will you do?'

'I'm trying to leave. I've been stuck in South Beach for too long. I have to find the energy. Then I will go. There are still places where a man can be happy.'

'Can you escape the agency? Do you really think they will just let you leave?'

Philip shrugged. 'One day they will come for me. But I think – if I must wait, and wait rather than run, then the waiting should be comfortable – don't you agree? It doesn't matter any more anyway.' Mark didn't answer. 'And you – do you think you will kill him?'

'I don't know. He saved my life.'

'He saved your life. Of course.'

Mark swallowed and looked at his feet. 'I don't want to kill him. He married my sister, did you know that?'

A perverse smile touched Philip's lips. 'He married your sister – oh I see, I see. Susanna.'

'That's right.'

'Yes of course. We talked so often of her.'

'You did?'

'Such beautiful words, such a tribute of feeling to his wife. If you could have heard him . . . such tenderness, such gentle garlands to wreath around his loss. He is like a poet. He touched my soul with his love for your sister. Can you imagine? He touched my soul. How typical of them to make you confront such a choice. Have they no shame, no feeling at all? And they say Kalat is mad . . . I should warn you though, you can't reason with him any more. You won't win him over. He's far, far beyond all of that. You should come with me. Forget all this. Together we'd be stronger.'

Mark considered the suggestion. What was there to stop

him? He could discard the satellite phone and slip away. He could contact Alisha. Perhaps she could join them somewhere, if Foxy and the agency didn't get to her first. Perhaps it wasn't totally impossible . . . What else was there to hold him back, save the pull of ingrained loyalties, the fear of disobedience. True. All that and something more.

Philip sensed his indecision. 'Yes,' he hissed. 'You can hear the call, can't you? The tug of the man. You fear him – but you can't resist. He is a dark star, sucking others towards him. Who do you fear more? Kalat in his tower, a sick man wild with visions, or those back in London? What might he offer?' He squeezed Mark's arm. 'He has it, you know? There is a charm upon him, terrible and sublime, that reaches deep into the mind.' The wind blew hard, the ragged curtain flopping against them.

'I've come too far,' Mark said.

'You've heard him speak, haven't you? Whatever he was before – now, now he is much changed. Even in chaos there is logic and a pattern. It's just a question of vision.' Philip jabbed at his forehead with a grimy finger. 'It's no surprise that I met you, no coincidence. When you look back you will see that there are no coincidences. Deep assignments run through our lives. There are connections everywhere. Speak with him and you will see that the whole of life has form and meaning.'

'I don't know . . .'

'Yes, you do. You seek answers. You have come so far.'

Mark nodded, numb with the weight of memories pressed against his eyes like angry thumbs. After all the questions, after everything . . . Kalat, the desert wind tugging his scarf, his body bent attentive over the bomb. They drove all night. Men without eyes in the suburbs of hell.

Kalat.

'Listen to me.' Philip was still talking. 'The city is very

perilous. You must be careful. When you cross over to the downtown area, you'll see numerous skyscrapers on the waterfront, opposite the old freeway bridge. Bits of the bridge are still there. His men occupy the towers – I'm not sure which one he'll be in. But he's there.' Mark looked at the man, waiting for more. 'There's little else I can say. His people will kill you if they don't like you. Pray for mercy – or leave with me.'

Mark nodded. He was so tired that even the possibility of death seemed an abstraction, something to contemplate with indifference.

'Cross via the Venetian Islands,' Philip continued. 'You can still get over to the mainland that way. There is a small deployment of Marines on one of the islands – I don't know what they are still doing there, it's like they've lost touch with their commanders. They are desperate men. Tell them you have been sent to kill Kalat and they might let you through. They hate Kalat. I think they see it as their task to try and protect South Beach from the people on the mainland.'

'Are you sure?'

'Of course I'm not sure! They are just as likely to shoot you the moment they see you. Although, that said . . . they told me they were very low on ammunition. You can still reason with them. But approach with caution, at all times – caution!'

Flashes of lightning cut up the darkness, highlighting the Apocalyptics huddled in the ruins like refugees fleeing the Black Death. Philip was sitting beside him. When he opened his eyes again the agent was gone. Rain fell relentlessly, droplets dripping through the cracks in the ceiling and running over his face like tears.

. . .

    – I'm hurt. I'm hurt bad, aren't I?
Yes, yes you are.

    – Am I going to die?

. . .

    – I am, aren't I? I'm dying.

. . .

# OUTPOST

In the haze of early morning Mark roused himself from the hard floor. He felt pretty bad, limbs stiff from another uncomfortable night, throat rough with an incipient cold, skin burned raw by the sun and itching with scores of angry mosquito bites. His clothes were caked with dirt and his unwashed body reeked of sweat. Of course they had trained him to expect such conditions. They had taught him the discipline of deprivation and hardship, installed the need to keep going regardless, to hold tight against despair and weakness. But at this moment, with the threat from the agency upmost in his mind, he yearned to be at home with Alisha safe in his arms. He thought he would do almost anything to be back in England, to feel a cool breeze on his face, to know that she was free from all of this, and that everything was going to be okay. As he descended through the building he saw himself in a chipped mirror: his face drawn with marks of abnegation, his skin ravaged, shiny with sweat and greased with stubble, his bloodshot eyes squinting forth like twin suns through a veil of mist. These chinks in his defences were a worry. He had suffered worse on past missions but now he felt himself wavering, unsure if he could cope with much more. If he could no longer depend on himself, all was lost.

Some of the Apocalyptics were awake, whispering to one another in huddled groups. On the ground floor of the building two priests were handing out mugs of hot black coffee and bread to the pilgrims. The holy men offered him refreshment with a mixture of sympathy and trepidation. Taking the provisions, Mark sat in a corner, eating and drinking, trying to save some strength for the privations ahead. Outside the sky was overcast and a strong wind blew in from the sea. In England such conditions would have signalled a chilly morning but the air was charged with heat. The night's rain had done nothing to alleviate the humidity.

He started walking through South Beach. In places the city was remarkably well preserved, the layout of the streets and many of the modern condominiums and art deco blocks intact, if altered. Petrified palm trees lined the route, shorn of leaves, stumps stained ashy grey. He passed rusted SUVs and pick-up trucks consumed by growths of bright coral, negotiated a twisted tangle of fallen electricity cables, a frozen stoplight, street signs for Collins and Washington Avenues, the husks of once great American chain stores – McDonald's, 7-Eleven, Starbucks and Subway. The ruins of an abandoned cinema stood at one corner, faded billboards facing desolate streets. There were more people around than he might have anticipated. He saw a destitute African-American couple arguing as they pushed a shopping cart loaded with cans and bottles, a supply shop in the shell of an Armani boutique selling barrels of petrol and electricity generators, looted MREs, car tyres, candles, axes and flags. The proprietor sat outside, shotgun resting on his paunch. Two young men rode past on shiny bicycles. With their clean white tees and neatly pressed jeans, they appeared an uncanny apparition of South Beach past. Mark stared at them in astonishment, wondering if the metropolis had other, hidden resources he had not counted on.

Further ahead he saw someone had been busy spraying passages from the Bible around the city. On the pale skin of an empty advertising hoarding they had written, in flowery, wavering capital letters, *For I will take you from among the heathen and gather you out of all countries and bring you into your own land.* Across a battered sign to the airport he saw another, *The serpent cast out of his mouth water as a flood after the woman so he might cause her to be carried away of the flood* and then, scrawled over the balconies of an apartment block, *The earth helped the woman and the earth opened her mouth and swallowed up the flood which the dragon cast out of his mouth* and further on still, sprayed across the calcified battlements of a multi-storey car park, *Let the one who hears say come and let the one who is thirsty come, let the one who wishes take the water of life without cost.*

He stopped for a few minutes resting on a bench and mopping his face. All around he could see cars, trucks and even boats – luxury yachts once worth hundreds of thousands of dollars – slammed into buildings, upturned in yards, heaped on top of each other in eloquent testament to the fury of the storms. He reflected on the reports that had come from the city after Winthrop hit. The thousands drowned in their cars stuck in tailbacks on the freeway as they tried too late to flee the city; streets transformed into surging canals; ferocious tides sweeping away entire neighbourhoods; burning water as oil depots and gas lines exploded; gun battles in the aftermath as state troopers fought to reclaim the city from gangsters and looters. Two weeks later a second huge hurricane, not as great as Winthrop but still formidable, prompted another evacuation, wiping out many of the federal services originally sent in to save the stricken population. Scoured, battered and stripped of ornament by the elements, the raw streets of Miami brought back memories of Baghdad and Basra, the bleak precincts of Gaza and Kabul. Meteorological

278

catastrophe and political strife had collapsed the distance that separated First from Third World, north from south, East from West, rich from poor. In the end the planet had won, the elements applying a force far more radical than capitalism or democracy. Unnatural intensities, evangelical Christianity and radical Islam bloomed like poison algae in the stagnant waters of the new world order. People clung to what they could. He could see it now. Chaos, fear and stark necessity hand in hand with prejudice and bigotry, these were the only constants. Climate shock had brought the world to its knees.

Mark wandered until he reached the western edge of Miami Beach. A small bridge stretched across the water to the Venetian Islands, a series of once exclusive residential enclaves. The bridge was intact, the road partly blocked by rusted razor wire. He imagined the defence had been placed shortly before Winthrop hit, a last-ditch attempt to protect Miami's elite from the storm-panicked hordes they had imagined would rise up in the wake of the hurricane. He squeezed through the wire, advancing slow and low, his rifle at the ready. On his left, as he entered the first island, he saw a number of medium-rise apartment blocks, residences rotten and overrun with weeds, some with the upper floors torn off, the inner workings of the buildings pulled out. That prickly feeling again, the sense that someone was watching him – certainly those empty windows and grassy balconies offered ample places to hide – and he felt sure his approach was being tracked through the scope of a sniper rifle.

Despite the rash of anxiety that shadowed every footstep he crossed the small island without incident, moved over the next bridge and on to the second island. A faded sign read 'Rivo Alto'. He knew that the real Venice had been almost entirely submerged, the lagoon unable to contain the Mediterranean any longer. While that beautiful, sepulchral city had been sucked into a watery nemesis, these small islands had erupted into a tropical fiesta of rude life. Wild palms, Spanish moss and lush creepers overwhelmed the remains of million-dollar mansions. He hesitated, unable to see an easy way through. In the wind the palms made a rustling noise like a horde of locusts. He took a step forward and all at once some-one was shouting at him.

'Stop or we'll shoot!'

He froze.

'Put down your gun and your bag and then put up your hands. The pistol too. Do it!'

Two figures clad in camouflage darted out from the canopy, M16 carbines pointed at him. Mark did as he was told. 'Who the fuck are you?' one of them screamed. 'What are you doing here? What do you want?' The soldiers looked wild, their unshaven faces pinched with fatigue and smeared with dirt. Their uniforms were torn and filthy and they had palm leaves and strands of grass tied to their helmets and wrapped around their arms, shoulders and legs like cannibals, their savagery intensified by the isolation.

'Calm down.' Mark raised his hands and spoke forcefully. 'My name is Mark Burrows. I just want to cross over the island.' The two Marines looked at each other. 'I heard this way was safe,' he continued, glancing from one to the other. 'I just want to cross,' he said again.

'Why the fuck shouldn't I just shoot you?' yelled the first Marine.

'Why didn't you? You had your chance. You still can.' Mark answered. 'Get a grip, soldier – I'm on your side.' He kept his voice firm and measured. Exhausted as he was, he could see that he was in much better shape than the two Marines.

A third soldier, a sergeant, emerged from out of the under-growth, holding an automatic pistol. His face was almost entirely hidden by his helmet and the camouflage scarf wrapped tight around his mouth. Like his comrades he also wore a Chameleon battle-suit, although the camouflage patterns no longer responded to the environment, having settled into a dull, stagnant shade. Mark realised the soldiers must truly be cut off, lacking even power to recharge their equipment. 'What's going on?' asked the sergeant.

Mark reiterated his position. 'People in South Beach said you guys would let me through.'

'He might be a spy, from over there,' said the first Marine, gesturing behind them.

'I'm not from over there!' Mark pointed west. 'That's where I want to get to.'

'I say we just kill the fucker,' shouted the second, cocking his M16.

'Shut up, Jones, remember, you're a Marine.' The sergeant turned to Mark. 'Where you from?'

'England. Can't you tell by my accent?' The sergeant and his men seemed nonplussed. It was possible, Mark realised, that they had no idea what an English accent sounded like. 'I just need to get across,' he said again. 'I don't mean any harm to you guys, none at all.'

The first Marine whispered something to his sergeant and Mark thought he heard them say 'Kalat'.

'That's right.' Mark flushed. 'I'm going to see Kalat.' He knew there were some circumstances where his asset was little help. 'I've been sent to try and stop him.' He spoke fast, unsure of the effect the words would have.

The sergeant gestured at his men and one of them took Mark by the arm, the other seizing his bag and rifle. With the sergeant leading the way they escorted him along a narrow path through the undergrowth. Uncertain as he was of what might happen in their hands, Mark calculated that he was safer with these soldiers than out on his own. Circumstances had been hard on the Marines but their discipline held. If it came to the worst, he reckoned he could appeal to their militaristic sensibilities. He understood soldiers. He had worked with American forces before. A well-trained soldier had a mind like polished metal, clear and hard and bright. Aggression, loyalty and a fear of losing face in front of comrades were the main motivators for any group of Marines. Despite his depleted condition, he knew that he was still stronger than they were. And they admired strength, they understood leadership, they would respond to decisiveness.

They pushed through the island and came to another bridge. Much of it had collapsed and they walked carefully over a narrow metal support, a girder no more than a foot wide. Below, the water was clotted with mud and webby entanglements of noxious weed. 'Keep going.' The marine jabbed at him with the M16. The party walked on to the third and, it seemed, the largest of Miami's Venetian Islands. Exotic gardens once belonging to corporate financiers and football players, Cuban oligarchs and Latino rap stars had erupted in a discordance of colour, a labyrinth of scented petal and sharp bramble, overgrown hedges rising around lush lawns ostentatious with wild flowers. Poking through the jungle he saw relics of the former civilisation, the metal barriers of a driveway gate, the rusted husk of a luxury SUV, walls smothered in ivy, a Doric column, the cracked portico of a mansion.

They led him to a shallow zigzag trench cut between the foundations of wrecked buildings. The trench wove through wine cellars loaded with bottles of moulding vintage and media rooms with shattered plasma screens stuck to overgrown walls, an exposed underground garage blocked with the rusted sarcophagus of a sports car and a drained swimming pool slippery with mud. The Marines had established an austere camp in the centre of the island. Built around the skeleton of a vast Italianate mansion, the base was hidden from the sky with webbing strung from palm trees. Bits of kit, spent ammunition, rusty radios, sleeping bags, ration packs, stained bandages, old uniforms and a battle-shot Stars and Stripes were scattered about the place. A regimental flag hung between two tall palms. Pulsing in the wind, it struck Mark as a wry reminder of the order lost amid such chaos. Otherwise the place stank of shit and vomit, clouds of black flies feeding on the mood of abandonment and despair. A fourth Marine lay in the corner on a plastic sheet, wrapped in a filthy blanket. On their approach the soldier tried to sit up but it seemed too much effort and he slumped back down, a wretched cough hacking through his body.

The sergeant pointed to a pile of sandbags and gestured at Mark to sit down. Then with a groan he placed himself opposite, removing his helmet and scarf. A young Hispanic with a blood-stained bandage wrapped around his forehead, the sergeant was every bit as exhausted as his men. 'Check the bag.' He made a vague gesture with his hand and Mark watched as one of the Marines went through the rucksack, pulling out what remained of his belongings. The soldier retrieved his satellite phone and held it aloft like a magical grail.

'Does it work?' the sergeant asked him.

'Just about,' he replied.

'Call them, sarge,' said the first Marine.

'There's no need for this,' said Mark.

The sergeant pointed his gun at Mark's face. 'You, shut the fuck up, okay?' He put down his gun and with great care unfolded a sheet of paper. Then, reading from the sheet, he dialled a number and waited. The other Marines leaned forward, apparently more concerned about the call than anything Mark might do. Nothing happened. The sergeant sighed and tried again. 'Hello?' he began. 'Hello, this is Forward Five to Com 12. This is Sergeant Gomez, First Marine expeditionary force . . . no, no I don't have the clearance code. Did you? What? Operation Babylon Rock. I don't know the latest codes.

I said . . . Look, we're totally fubar here, we need assistance, we need orders, we've lost contact.' He wiped at his face. 'Just twelve of us left, sir, still defending the perimeter. We face threats from all sides.' He paused, nodding to something that was being said to him at the other end. 'Yes sir, I know, yes, I know our orders were to take down that motherfucker.' There was a long pause as Gomez sat listening, his chapped lips forming unfinished words. 'We have someone here,' he said at last. 'I'm using their phone. They claim to be English . . . What? I can't hear you. I see, but we're stuck, sir. We need supplies, we need munitions.' He stopped and looked at the phone. 'I lost them.' He started to cough, turning his face away and spitting.

'What did they say? What shall we do?' asked the first Marine.

'I don't know . . . it's not good.'

'Give me the phone. I need to cross,' Mark said again.

'Is there someone you can call?'

'Yes, but they won't help us. At least not yet. Not until I've got across the bay.'

Gomez looked like he was about to cry. 'We tried everything . . . after the radios broke . . . we left signs, smoke signals, everything.'

'They bombed us,' said the second Marine. 'Our own side, they bombed us.'

A shot rang out. Mark flinched but the Marines didn't move. 'We've got a couple of snipers guarding the perimeter,' said Gomez. 'That sounded like Corporal Marshall.' A second shot. 'He must have missed first time.'

'Who are you shooting at?'

'We're not sure any more.' In the corner the injured Marine started coughing again, a dreadful sound, as if he were trying to throw up his intestines. 'There's so much evil out there, so much chaos.' Gomez's eyes turned one way and another as he spoke, as though tracking targets in the trees. 'But we still have our duty, our honour, isn't that right, men?' The two others nodded. 'We're all that's left.' The soldier turned to him. 'So what are you doing here? What do you want?'

'I've been sent to kill Kalat.'

The sergeant twitched. 'You're just one man.'

'I've been told Kalat is sick. He probably doesn't have long to live. I think . . .' Mark rubbed his face. 'You and your men should get out of here. You don't need to stay.'

Gomez flinched. 'We have our orders.'

'So do I,' Mark pressed. 'But what do they really count for out here? Orders. Do they still make sense?' He paused for a moment, again surprised by what he was saying. He cleared his throat. 'Why bother holding this island? If the Marines want to take Miami, there is nothing to stop them. You should fall back.'

The sergeant blinked at him and licked his lips.

Mark tried a different approach. 'I've been travelling across the Zone. People talk about a new army coming from the west, a gang of Witch Hunters sent to make war on Kalat. What do you know about that?'

Gomez shook his head. 'Witch Hunters? Fuck that.' He looked disgusted. 'I don't know anything. Our radios don't work. Our commanding officers are dead – that or they ran away.' He shook his head. 'Fuck them. Sometimes I think they've forgotten us. Sometimes I think we've been left behind and that it's true, all the good men have been swept to heaven and it's just us and the anti-Christ to battle it through this great tribulation. I never used to believe.' He wiped his lips. 'The wind and the rains come and somehow we hold on. The sea washes everything away and we hide in the trees. We can't last much longer.'

'What the hell happened to you?' With a stern expression and a commanding tone, Mark addressed his comments to all the soldiers. 'You men look like you've been through the works. How did this happen?'

Gomez sat back, a shadow blocking his face. When Mark had worked with American Marines before, he had always been impressed by their determination and professionalism, but as Gomez spoke he could tell that the spirit of these men was broken, their morale as fractured as the city around them.

Initially Gomez's account seemed to chime with what Philip had told him. The attack had gone well, the sergeant confirmed, the Marines advancing rapidly into the central business district and achieving their immediate objectives, eliminating pockets of resistance and taking virtually no casualties. Then it seemed everything changed. Whereas Philip's account had been obscure in the hazy light of Kalat's magnificence, a different sort of ambiguity overwhelmed the sergeant's accounts. 'A great storm seemed to come from nowhere,' he said. 'The bright blue sky just flipped out with heavy clouds.'

'It was like the sea had been sucked upwards,' interjected his comrade. 'The sky and the sea changed places. The sky was black with water. Ain't never seen nothing like it. Never.'

'This wind came across the ocean like a demon,' Gomez continued. 'It slashed down the palm trees and threw them about like sticks, shards of glass and stones everywhere. It was a hail of shrapnel and we had to hide in ruined buildings or else get blown away. Then came a great tidal surge. Me and my men were lucky. We managed to shelter on the fifth floor of a Hilton hotel. It washed the rest of the men away. We spent three nights up there, buffeted by wind and rain.' He paused for a minute, almost unable to believe what he was saying. All around them heat and dull grey light, a dead wind whispering in the trees. As he continued his account became particularly confused, the sentences stumbling and dead-ending. Sometimes they exchanged fire with gunmen hidden in neighbouring buildings, he said, but they never got a clear sight of the enemy, and sometimes they became convinced they were shooting their own side. The storm did something to the radios and they lost touch with the rest of the battalion and it rained and rained and he said the sky went a strange colour, neither day nor night but some terrible in-between. They saw a helicopter, engulfed in flames, spiralling like a shooting star and crashing into the upper floors of a high tower, which some of the men interpreted as a sign, he said, the fire come down from heaven. For hours on end the screams of the dying, of Marines begging for mercy and other sounds unlike anything heard before. The sergeant shuddered. Something had walked across their soul and strung their nerves from a high wire and twisted their nightmares into solid forms and many men had gone mad, throwing themselves from windows into churning black waters to be pulled down by the weight of battle-suits and flak jackets and some even turned their guns on themselves rather than face another minute in that place. 'Eventually,' said Gomez, 'the rain stopped and the wind was gone and the sun turned the water into a sea of glass and fire and we withdrew to this island and here we stay, digging in, holding the line, waiting for orders.' Twice strange men had tried to attack their position. A wild mob rampaging across the bridge with machine guns and rocket launchers, seemingly impatient to die, cut down easily by their gunfire. Days later, he said, a second assault came at night, two dozen attackers racing across the water in speedboats. Some made it to the island and they had fought, vicious and close, with fragmentation bombs and bowie knives, bayonets and sub-machine guns. Maybe they were terrorists, maybe they were gangsters, maybe they were Kalat's people, but the bodies, in the morning light, had looked much younger than that, like pubescent boys and here the sergeant had seemed ashamed, covering his face as he said they buried the ones they could, deep in the mud. 'We tried to pray for deliverance but day after day it was the same.' He pointed to the sick Marine in the corner. 'Corporal Hines said a vial had been spilt over the sun and that it was all true, the end of times is upon us with poison in the water and badness in the blood.' His words trailed away. The chemical wind tugged across the camp, rippling dry palms and making the regimental flag flap back and forth. The sick Marine coughed again and again.

Mark left the sergeant sitting with his head in his hands mumbling incoherently. Carrying his rucksack, phone and weapons, he was escorted by the Marine who first confronted him back to the edge of the island. 'Kalat is over there, somewhere.' The soldier pointed to the final bridge and the city beyond. A thick tangle of barbed wire blocked the entrance, the ground around it littered with spent ammunition and bits of kit. Mark climbed carefully under. Nearby he saw two corpses, the air thick with their foulness, features unrecognisable with decay. Covering his mouth, he hurried forward.

. . .

Stars flickering in the wind like small candles delicate
     –   I'm cold.
as if a cold fire had been cast across the heavens
    thin black clouds stretched across the horizon
       black clouds like the flags of some
       undiscovered nation
    – Am I going to die?
in the grass her arms around me
he would meet her on the bustling station concourse or
the steps to the museum
    after driving all night in the suburbs of hell

*flicker*

# MIAMI

Mark advanced towards an impressive skyline of grey towers. In the giddy boom years shortly before Winthrop, when the reckless exigencies of the free market had propelled the world into a golden bubble of implausible and unsustainable prosperity, Miami witnessed an unprecedented expansion, scores of luxury condominiums built forty, fifty, sixty stories high. Most had still been unoccupied, many still unfinished, when Winthrop struck. Climate shock and global economic meltdown had left behind an almost unparalleled Xanadu of desolation.

Flocks of gulls and other, larger birds circled the fractured heights of the towers. Some of the buildings leaned precariously, bent by brutal winds and waves, and others had partially collapsed, sections folded down into rubble-choked streets. Windows and walls had been blasted out and the reinforced concrete cores and steel supports stood bare like the skeletons of a vanquished Titan race. Mark could also see signs of recent conflict, scorched black smears across the high façades, ugly blast holes from rockets and the smaller peppered spots of machine-gun fire. How many times, he wondered, was it possible to destroy a city? Water, fire, wind and war, all had left their mark.

Dehydration and lack of sleep must be getting to him. He paused, head swimming, took a quick sip of the warm water in his flask and picked up his rifle again. Everything felt so heavy. He knew he lacked a coherent strategy, knew that walking blindly forward like this was hardly the right way to approach such things, and as he looked at all the towers and wondered in which one, exactly, he might find Kalat, he felt a confusion so great he wondered if his spirit could persist. What choice was left? He could neither join the Apocalyptics on the beach waiting for the wind to sweep them away, nor the Marines on the island, trapped by orders that no longer existed. Nor had he been able to steal away in the night with Philip. Something else drove him onwards. It wasn't just the agency, not any more, nor was it his loyalty to Alisha. No, it was something else, something stronger and more mysterious.

*Kalat.*

Crossing the final bridge, Mark saw that the waters of the bay had retreated, leaving behind a floodplain of mud studded with the slime-encrusted silhouettes of sunken yachts and tugs and the hulls of much larger vessels, a great cruise liner upturned like the bloated corpse of an immense whale. Scattered among it all was shrapnel from wind-smashed houses and vehicles, even a passenger jet, wings thrust up out of the ground like an inverted gallows pole, as though land, sea and sky had traded places in a macabre game and he looked now upon the residue of a twice-fallen nature.

Miami.

The Everglades were taking back the city. Dry green moss covered the wide boulevards and pools of stagnant water gouged out of the tarmac by fists of wind boasted bulrushes and clumps of thick green algae. Strands of sawgrass sprouted from churned concrete and split macadam. He stopped for a while, waiting, looking and listening.

Ahead he saw a cracked road bridge, supports sprayed and resprayed with various images: eyes and pyramids, a handprint, open mouths, faces hidden by gas masks, a swastika, a peace sign, an American flag, slogans in Spanish and other less easily identifiable languages. Some of the graffiti was quite fresh, bright new colours replacing fainter images beneath. The structure was a palimpsest of claim and counterclaim, a monument to all the renegade cultures and fugitive regimes that had found sanctuary in the forlorn metropolis.

Another sudden bout of dizziness made him stop and he wiped the sweat from his face. A touch of the fever again, jungle in the bloodstream. He was far from well. Closer to Kalat and the more he felt as though he were slipping through time, stumbling to the ends of the earth, or the very beginnings – he could no longer tell. Was the burning pick-up ahead the result of one of their bombs, did the broken concrete buildings belong to some unnamed Shia suburb? He shook his head, trying to keep a fix on things.

*A burning pick-up.*

Where had it come from?

The fire was not fierce and as he drew closer he saw the vehicle was already a wreck, flames burning from boxes placed around and inside it.

Figures appeared behind a low concrete wall.

He heard a sharp cracking sound. Shells struck the ground around him. He turned, ducking, running fast.

Ahead a number of single-storey retail sheds and beyond – but too far to reach – numerous high-rise condominiums. No choice. He ran into the nearest shed.

Cocking his rifle he darted out firing two short bursts, left and right, and then ducked back undercover.

'Salga! Estas rodeado. No es bueno!' They were shouting at him.

Staying low, he peeked out, rifle raised.

A figure moved across his sights and he fired a quick burst.

'Eso estaba estupido – no queremos matarte!'

Glancing back and he realized that his choice of shelter was short-sighted. No way out, the chamber behind piled to the ceiling with rubble and plastic sheeting.

He picked up a brick and flung it outside. Another barrage of gunfire. He pressed himself to the floor. A second brick brought a sustained deluge of shots. His assailants lacked discipline. Much more of this, he calculated, and they would have to reload.

He took off his rucksack and tossed it into the back of the shed. Checking the M16 he dashed out of the doorway. He saw two figures on his left and a third on his right, rag-tag individuals in tatty fatigues, faces hidden by garish masks. One of the men was fumbling with an AK-47, the other raising a twelve-gauge.

He ran towards them, war-face fixed in a fierce scream, firing from the hip.

The man with the AK-47 took several hits and spun back.

The other was struggling to aim his shotgun. A second blast opened a red curtain across the man's stomach and he tumbled down.

He ran over their bodies, aware of more gunmen close around. Something punched his left arm and knocked him sideways. He dropped his rifle and stumbled to one knee.

He pulled out his pistol and fired several shots. A masked man to his right took a bullet and collapsed forward.

Something came bouncing towards him: a blinding flash, a cloud of scorching smoke, his ears ringing, he couldn't breathe, he was firing wildly, he couldn't see, the clip was empty and the ground was hard on his face and he realised he had fallen over. He tried to breathe but his lungs were full of fire and tears filled his scorched eyes.

They were all around him now, kicking and punching. A rifle butt struck his arm and his body shook with pain. Now they stood over him – Kermit, Goofy, Minnie Mouse, Ronald Reagan and Darth Vader.

Goofy and Ronald Reagan dragged him to a waiting jeep and flung him into the back. He landed on his injured arm and screamed. He did his best to roll over and held up his hand. The top of his shirt was red with blood and more blood was running over his fingers. Gunmen got into the flat back of the pick-up. Masked faces loomed over him and rough hands pulled him up.

One of the men he'd shot was also lifted into the back. His Bugs Bunny mask was removed to reveal a Cuban man in his early forties. He had blood on his lips and pressed his hands tight against the red hole in his belly. 'Jesus salvame,' he mumbled, gazing at Mark with hate-filled eyes.

They were travelling in a two-pick-up convoy, driving slowly towards the downtown. Battered skyscrapers loomed all around. Mark glanced about anxiously, the pain in his arm making him nauseous. Hard to know. He thought he saw faces staring out of broken windows, faces amid the scraps of plastic and wire, the disembowelled guts of business towers hanging loose, that and flags and banners, ominous symbols, premonitions of regimes even more brutal than those gone before. Gunmen stood at the back of the lead jeep, machine guns trained on the surrounding buildings. *Jesus salvame*. Darth Vader had recovered his rucksack and he watched as the bandits shifted through his belongings. Darth Vader took out the satellite phone and a ripple of delight passed among the men.

Kermit leaned close. 'Tendremos una recompensa muy buena para ti, el espía que jode!' Kermit turned to his friends and said something else. The injured man had closed his eyes now and Goofy was applying a bandage to his stomach. The pain from Mark's own injury was getting worse, like a trail of fire blazing through a tinder-dry forest, black spots wriggling over his eyes, blood leaking between his fingers pressed over the hole in his left bicep.

The air vibrated hot and white, the shockwave rippling off the canyon wall, punching out his ears, sucking the air from his lungs. He pitched forward onto the injured gunman. Kermit slumped over him. Others were shouting. Someone opened fire. Someone toppled out of the pick-up. Goofy was shooting at something above them, spent cartridges burning as they fell onto Mark's legs. Goofy dropped his AK-47 and clutched at his neck. A jet of blood spurted into the air. A huge hole opened up in his chest and he tumbled back.

Mark raised his head over the back of the truck. The lead pick-up had been knocked onto its side and was on fire. He could see no trace of the men who had been riding on the back only a moment before.

Darth Vader was running away. His body jerked like a fish caught on a hook and he sank to the floor.

A bloody fist grabbed his hair and yanked him back. Bugs Bunny reached around his neck, trying to choke him. With all his remaining strength, Mark fought back, thrusting his body against his injured opponent. The grip lessened a fraction and Mark rolled away. He pulled himself forward and dived out of the back of the pick-up. He landed on his injured arm and screamed. He lay on the ground. Ronald Reagan was next to him, limbs twitching, floundering in a growing pool of blood, tugging in vain at his mask with weak fingers, unable to remove it.

Using his good arm, Mark gripped the side of the vehicle and pulled himself up. More pain – a hot iron pressed against his flesh – and he heard himself scream, although his voice sounded far away. He stood. Sharp tang of burning gasoline, the air rippling and cracked like dry earth. A few feet away he saw Minnie Mouse flat on his back, his mask blasted into his face, an Uzi machine pistol by his side. More pain, blue and white shudders. He bent over and picked up the pistol. It occurred to him he hadn't yet been shot and there must be a reason for that and then he saw a figure hurrying from the darkness of a skyscraper lobby. He saw it but he wasn't sure what he thought. The figure – man or woman he could not tell – was moving like a drop of oil, clad ninja-like head to foot in flowing black robes, a black scarf wrapped around their face, a sniper rifle strapped to their back. He tried to raise the machine pistol but he seemed to have lost all feeling in his body. The black-cloaked figure slipped rapidly among the fallen gunmen. It jumped panther-like onto the pick-up and Mark heard Bugs Bunny scream. *Jesus salvame.* Another wave of pain and the last he saw was brown eyes flecked with gold and emerald peering at him, a black veil like clouds at midnight.

. . .

Open and shut

   – I'm cold

*flicker*

   – I said

Stars flickering in the wind like small candles delicate
in the cold breeze as if too much might extinguish them
and blot out all the light of the heavens . . .

   – I'm hurt. I'm hurt bad, aren't I?
Yes, yes you are.
   – Am I going to die?
. . .
   – I am, aren't I? I'm dying.
No, you're not. You'll be all right.
   – Are you sure?
Yes. Does it hurt?
   – Yes.
The morphine will help.
   – Okay. Jesus. What a fuck-up.
Can you fight?
   – I don't know. Where are you?
I'm here. I'm close.

– It's so dark.

It will be light soon.

– Have I been unconscious?

Not for long.

– We're in danger, aren't we?

We're not safe. We need to be quiet.

– They're out there?

Yes. But it's okay. We can fight.

*the wind*

The man behind the veil was sick. Mark could hear him coughing and struggling for breath. The veil hung from the ceiling, a delirious curtain flecked with specks of blood and mucus, the sickness made tangible. Sometimes the wind tugged at the veil and it would turn one way and then another while the man coughed and coughed and coughed – a terrible sound – like he were being pulled apart, bit by bloody bit. Mark saw only the shadow of the sick man. A shaven head, bare and irregular in form, like a football half deflated and the silhouette of a body ravaged and skinny the way a forest looks after a fire has blazed through it. But the talk was incessant. The voice, that high, tight whisper, layer upon layer of words, a gauze of words, a haze of words. A sick God locked in his high tower. He paused only to cough or catch his breath in brittle moments when his lungs rasped like a plastic bag dragged across stones and Mark watched as the silhouette raised a bowl to his face to drink or splash water across his brow. He was surprised by how much he remembered. Sometimes the wind blew sudden and fierce and the veil would flap vigorously, billowing around as though in a tent or caught under the corroded wings of a great moth.

*flicker*

–   We killed a lot of people, didn't we? I mean, I'm not surprised that they got us, that our luck ran out in the end.
Don't talk that way, don't give me that bullshit. Look inside and what do you see?
–   What do I see?
You should see a brave warrior who has made sacrifices for his country. A soldier. Someone has to get their hands dirty. Every dream has its nightmare, you know that. We do this so they keep on sleeping.

*the wind*

–   I don't know.
After what we've done.
–   We killed a lot of people.
It's true. Accept it. The blood is on our hands.
–   Why did you choose me? I don't understand.
You're like me.
–   Am I? I only ever wanted to be like other people, a face in the crowd, invisible, that's all.
You're like me.
–   I'm cold.

*the wind*

–   Do you think – after this?
There is no after.

*the eyes the stars*

After she was gone he would sit under the trees, his arm stiff with bandages. I wanted to tell you about the wind, he would think, the cold north wind with the promise of snow and the frost that would gather in the shady places, colours blazing up the twilight sky, shades of pink and orange like a strange celestial fire. He would think about that, the way the clouds would catch the shards of the evening light, so many colours like the soul of God . . .

–   The stars. You don't think the stars will go out?
No.
–   It's just that they keep flickering. I don't want the stars to go out.

*the wind*

Are you there?
–   Yes.
Not fading out on me, are you?
–   No . . . no, it hurts too much for that.
Good. You need to hold on to the pain, it will keep you alive as long as you can feel it.
–   It really hurts. It's not good, is it?
You've been shot.

They were high above the wasted city. The sun shone through the broken windows of the tower, gauzy beams illuminating the cracked white walls of the apartment. The penthouse had once been owned by a famous actor, the crowning glory of a glittering skyscraper bought for ten million dollars in the months before Winthrop struck. From up here Mark could see everything, the whole of Miami stretching off into the Everglades. Above them clouds churned the sky, vaporous archipelagos threatening rain. Behind the veil he could hear Kalat coughing and mumbling. He saw no army of fanatics or devotees ready to die for their leader, only a dark and lovely woman who attended to them both. She moved with measured steps, her neck held high, her braided hair coiled tight as a snake around her head. She wore innumerable necklaces of glass and silver, bizarre things, witchy charms and totems that glittered and trembled with every step. He was aware of Kalat's talking in the background, the constant sound of his voice if not always the words and sometimes she would also speak, an exotic amanuensis dabbing the sweat from his body while feeding him with images fantastical, her words wrought and elaborate as the façade of a baroque palace, a building far fetched and forgotten, beguiling as a golden cage or a pagoda set on an island and surrounded by treacherous waters. She spoke in an accent soft with Caribbean consonants, hints of Africa and North America, an identity dismantled and rebuilt in lilting musical sentences that overran and flowed from syllable to sibilant vowel like endless rivers mythical, Nile and Niger, Amazon and Mississippi, Ganges and Yangtze. He could not say where she had come from, this intoxication of the Occident and the Orient, stalking his delirium like a portent of the drowned world, an Ethiopian jewel washed upon smoggy ruins. With her gaze unflinching, her brown eyes flickering with gold and emerald, she bathed his brow and cleaned his wounds, bringing herbal tea and nourishing broth to his parched lips. In the far corner of the huge room, opposite the great panorama of devastation, he saw a radio transmitter with wires reaching up through cracks in the ceiling, a pile of CD-Rs and a laptop rigged to a portable solar generator. Scattered around were various books and magazines, pages fetid in the humidity. He lay sweating, listening to the voice. It was true. Ashe had stepped beyond his name. They had called him an overlord and a hierophant, an archon and a fallen angel with wings of dark fire but he was not sure if the man he saw now was any of these things. With tight whisper and rasping tongue he spoke through the veil, his voice gaunt with nostalgia for what they had lost, a pale remembrance of love amid the glaze of endless sunshine.

Kalat.

    –   If I die
You won't die.
    –   You'll tell Susanna, won't you? If I die . . . you'll
tell my sister, won't you?
You won't die.

*flicker*

    –   Can I ask you something?
Go ahead.
    –   It will help to take my mind off things . . . the
pain, you know.
Okay.
    –   When you met Susanna, did you know she was
the one? Did you know you'd marry her?
I was never sure. Not at first.
    –   You're sure now?
Funny, isn't it, love? The things you do.
    –   Talk to me about love.
I remember there was a children's playground opposite
the house where Susanna was living at the time we
started to see each other and I remember how once, late at
night, when neither of us felt like sleeping, we went in the
playground. She sat on the swing and I pushed her back
and forth, higher and higher.
    –   That's nice. Like children.
Yes. We felt so innocent. I think that's something. Can you
imagine? I felt innocent? True love makes you innocent

again. Like Adam and Eve in the garden, before it all went wrong. You can never stay in the garden for long though, can you? Something always happens.

– Yes.

The world takes over again.

– Yes.

You have to do things. You end up saying things.

– Yes.

My God, I remember how we lay in the grass with her arms around me and the stars bright above. It was a warm summer night and everything was hushed and the warm weight of her body was a joy indescribable . . .

– Yes.

When I least expect it she comes back to me. In my mind's eye she is present again.

– Is she with you now?

Now? No. She is far away.

– Oh.

It struck me in stages. I would think I knew her and then she would reveal another side of herself to me. I think that was how I knew it was love, this constant, gradual change, a sort of sharpening or refinement of feature and character. That was part of it. I remembered how we went walking in the park in the sun and then the rain, the rain in her hair, her smile moments before we kissed.

– My sister . . .

She was wonderful to me, Mark, someone too special, too beautiful for this world, too beautiful altogether. But now I feel like every new thing that starts means something has to end and all joy is bittersweet . . .

– So much blood. Look. The sand is red with blood.

Once each winter would contain the summer, each summer contain the winter, only now it's just the summer, isn't it? Month after month in this sour paradise, just one thing, the same thing, over and over again.

— Yes.

I had an ominous feeling, before we came out here.

— You did?

She comes to me in dreams, darling Susanna, and I keep saying goodbye, over and over again I keep saying goodbye. I miss her so much. When I think back to the last time, it's like her face is bathed in light, radiant with light but the room around is dark. I see her as an image pulled out of time and preserved for ever in this moment. All the light of the day concentrated on her brow and her fair hair falls around her face like an ashy halo and her dark eyes look at me and she stands alone in the front room of the house. A clock is ticking and she doesn't move and outside trees are blue in the rain.

— Yes.

She's thinking about us, you and me, her brother and her husband. She's waiting, far away.

— Yes.

Love.

— Yes.

The day before I left to come here, I had such an ominous feeling, I can't tell you.


*flicker*

In the midst of his fever the woman was there, dark and lovely, tending diligently to his ailments. Tireless, she nursed them both, gliding back and forth around the veil. Nights were worst, like he were being held in the mouth of a giant. The sickness was testing him, pulling him one way and another, dragging him through valleys of heat and sweat and leaving him stranded on plateaux cool and distant. In these moments he would dare to think that maybe it was over. She would stroke his forehead and gaze upon him with eyes neither kind nor judgemental, eyes filled with the indifferent light of stars flickering in a cold black sky.

'Alisha,' he asked, his tongue thick in his mouth.

'No,' she answered. 'Not her.'

Across the Zone, in all the fringes of the state, amid the sweltering housing projects and the prisons swimming with filth, in rusted ships moored off the gulf, the trailer parks and the shacks made from wood and metal strips jumbled one way and another in boggy groves and by the side of vast freeway junctions, they sat hunched around radios, listening in dark tugs loaded with contraband and in the camps of the Queer Liberation Army and the scattered settlements hidden behind defensive walls and razor wire, in trucks and vans powering through the night, with drivers peering at a green world luminous with night-vision goggles and machine guns resting on their laps . . . listening . . . *'Let me tell you what I remember of who I was, the ghost that haunts me still, the shadow that follows me, this way and another . . . Ten years ago I was in a helicopter in Kurdistan on the most secret of missions. Something hit the chopper and hurled us headlong flaming from the heavens like a meteorite. I awoke shackled to a lake of fire, trapped beneath a gasoline sky, the flames peeling away my skin . . . hear this now, the truth of my suffering . . . I was in a dark room, pain consuming my body . . . Abject and lost and far from that power that once made glory from my willing subjugation . . . I thought I had died and perhaps this world was the afterlife, a paradisal hell of sunshine eternal . . . I don't know . . . Women came to me, as I lay, women with faces hidden by veils, their beauty modestly focused in eyes full of care and attention, treating my scorched body with soothing creams and lotions. Many weeks I spent in this grey limbo, a floating world racked with ceaseless pain, a slow dance with death – always death – his face in the shadows whispering ceaseless, tempting, secretive things. When I returned to*

310

*some semblance of consciousness I thought perhaps these people intended to keep me, that I was a hostage to be ransomed to the highest bidder, my government or others. Later I understood these people had saved my life . . .'* On his pallet in the high tower he listened, the cracked voice from the radio blending with the whisper behind the veil. *'After a while the local imam came to see me. He spoke some English and I spoke some Arabic and between us we were able to converse. He seemed to believe I had a message for him, that I had been touched by God. The village was high in the mountains, a remote place, close to the essence of things, the high peak, the snowy rock, the sharp wind. Sky close enough to touch with your fingers. Sound of goats being led to the rocky pastures. The purity of nature. Fire and pain had been a cleansing force and when I returned to health I knew if nothing else that I was not the man I had been. My old self had been burned away by the baptism of those scouring fires. I was no longer a white man, no longer a child of the West. Thankful, I followed the imam's instruction and recited the shahadah and each day I went with the other men to the mosque at the edge of the village. My body was weak, my mind a shattered husk, but through these rituals I found strength again. Submission, obedience and faith, the law of God above all else . . . so I thought . . . You see, I tried, I tried so hard to believe . . . One morning Peshmerga fighters came down from the mountains. The Turkish army had been attacking positions south of the village. Until this point I had been forgetful of the greater struggles unfolding around me. The fighters came to see me. High in the mountains I showed them what I had been trained to do . . .'* Amid the ramblings of the voice Mark tried to rise but the woman put her finger to his lips and laid him down again. 'Why?' He tried to speak but with her finger she silenced him. Candles flickered in the ruined chamber. *'One day shepherd boys sighted something, a giant metal kite circling the summits around the village. There was a great commotion, rumours of soldiers advancing on the valley below. I went out with the fighters. I should have heeded the* warning. We heard the missiles, sudden thwacks reverberating across the valley, lightning bolts of an all-controlling Zeus. There was nothing left of the village when we returned, except black bile ruptured from the stricken earth and blood on the stones. These people had saved my life and this was my repayment. My masters had spied me with their electric eyes and they had taken revenge. I begged the forgiveness of the imam but what could he offer, simple, poor man stricken so savagely? He cursed God, cursed me, cursed the cruel face of heaven . . . And so my punishment began, nothing but ruin and misery and sad remembrance of what once had been . . .'

Mark found the satellite phone. With shaking fingers he dialled the number.

'Casement . . . this is Casement.'

'Yes.'

'Kalat.' He couldn't find his voice. 'We don't need to worry,' he whispered. 'I'm here. He's sick. He's no threat to us.'

'It's too late for that now.'

'What?'

'We've called it in.'

'But—'

'I said we've called it in. Your position has been disclosed to American forces.'

'There's no need . . .'

'Save yourself if you can.'

He lay on the pallet, shivering with sweat.

Quiet. Listen.

– What?

Do you hear something?

– Yes, I hear them.

How is your arm?

– Hurts pretty bad. But I can fight . . .

Check your weapon. Be ready.

The storm came, sudden and terrible, conjured from a salty sky of swollen bruises, a swift wind bringing rain lashing, lashing, lashing and behind the veil the man shrieked with wild delight, surrendering himself to the tempest as if the conflagration of elements was for him alone. Battered the skyscraper swayed, rain and wind channelled into howling banshees through broken windows, up stairwells, corridors and lift-shafts, the wind tugging away the veil and amid the brilliance of lightning flash Mark saw the man who had married his sister stand transfigured, his hairless head like a tribal trophy or pagan totem tilted back euphoric, burned flesh moulded and reformed, eyes pitiless hollows, a mouth open dangerously wide as though to devour the earth or swallow entire the storm, a body painfully thin, knots and joints and bony edges and webs of scar tissue standing illuminated like a pharaoh resurrected from his tomb in this terrible instant of flicker and flash, open and close, the aperture of a camera shooting into the underworld. Then darkness once more. Delirious, Mark wandered through the tower. Wind blowing strong enough to knock him over and sometimes he would have to crawl, his body bent against the gale, or pull himself along the wet floor clinging to broken tiles until finally he found a suite with windows intact where he could press his face to the splattered glass and peer over the torment, dirty water plunging unstoppable through sunken streets, the sky submerged, the sun drowning in the sea. When the eye passed over the city a great calm descended, God held his breath, the heavens a laundered crystal blue, darkness empyrean on the horizon shaken with stabs of lightning while above the atmosphere magically still, particles of the city high-flung and suspended like birds glued to some strange diorama, a moment out of time. He stood, pressing his face against the mossy glass. Then the eye passed and God turned his face from the world and the onslaught resumed.

Delicately the woman dabbed the sweat from his body.

'What is it?' he tried to ask her.

He remembered sitting in the garden, sunshine dappled through the trees, the shadow of leaves on the patio, watching the other patients in their white coats, waiting for the beautiful doctor to come. He had been awake all night and could almost believe . . . trees heavy with the scent of medication, beads of pollen floating on the balmy breeze, the air thick with tranquillisers, painkillers and anti-depressants . . . in the corner, still clutching her rucksack, he recognised Mary, paler than before. He said her name and she tilted her head towards the sound of his voice like a blind person. 'Mary?' 'The man in the high tower,' she said. 'Alisha?' he said. He saw them, leading the beautiful doctor away. As she left she gave him a strange look he struggled to interpret.

'Shhh.' The woman put her finger to his lips.

The storm had passed, the dawn battered with wispy trails of clouds scattered like torn pages. 'Where is he?' he said, looking around. 'We need to get out of here.'

Soldiers listening covertly through earpieces on lonesome guard duty or on illegally tuned radios in Humvees and transporters as they plough along glistening new highways . . . rumours circulating among wandering mobs dazed without purpose and desperate for miracles . . . on short-wave receivers held by crocodile-stalkers and bobcat-trappers amid the plastic relics of amusement parks . . . online with bored teenagers sheltering in air-conditioned bedrooms in the faded sprawl of Tallahassee and Tampa . . . *'Remember,'* said the voice. *'Those of you who can . . . those of you who are old enough, how that great man was elected in a surge of hope and optimism, a second American revolution . . . that fine President whose heritage encompassed three continents? You might remember how the world held its breath and dared to hope for better things. But the cracks were already so deep . . . Remember? What could one man have done against all that? Don't you remember? They have tried to efface his memory. They have submerged this history. Reality is bent by those with the power. The economic heart attack . . . the death throes of free-market capitalism . . . remember? And that was but the start. The warnings were already in place. The scientists knew. The wise economists knew. The clear-sighted citizens knew. The artists knew. The amnesia of catastrophe. Shocks to wipe clean the mental slate . . . Something broke then, did it not?'* For a long time the voice is silent. He calls out, 'Ashe', but no one answers. *'. . . I have crawled like an insect through the outer darkness, far from all hope, far from all human love and kindness, a shade haunting the Mesopotamian badlands, my faith shattered, my dark arts put in the service of whoever would pay. I had tried to believe, tried to find a faith in something higher. But no. We cannot evade responsibility for all that we are or what we do . . . Without discrimination I put my talents in the service of anyone who would pay, Sunni and Shia militia, the Iraqi and Iranian secret services, the CIA, Mossad and the SIS, al-Qaeda and the Taliban – yes, even them – all the nightmares of the West, all the forces that would destroy our values, everything we care about, democracy and those tender baubles, human rights, women's rights, free speech, the beautiful garlands that grace the trees flowering in the garden of our power. I served them all, those and other players more obscure and treacherous yet, pedlars of strategies infernal, manipulators of brutal fundamentalisms, people whose loyalties had been turned again and again. The intention always to spread mistrust and anxiety, to keep a people divided against themselves, to keep them willing to surrender the common interest, to turn against their brother and bow down before a power nebulous and pervasive. The illusion of omnipotence, the eye internalised and each of us kept locked in the cell of our own making. Hear this, children of the swamps, even amid this anarchy, blinded by my rage, blind to my own intention, still I served the forces of control. My heart had become an empty place, a sphere of hardness . . . Know their names, gentle people, the horrid kings besmeared with the blood of human sacrifice and watered by parents' tears, Moloch and Chemosh, Baal and Ashtaroth, Astarte with crescent horn, Marduk and Tammuz, Belial, Mammon and Azazel, the Crawling Chaos, Kutulu and Ishtar dancing at the gates of hell . . . Let it be said that certain people made contact. I met them in the Spanish Quarter of Naples, city of lust and corrupt beauty smouldering under clouds of burning garbage, votive offerings to pagan saints and ancestral skulls in the medieval lanes . . . We met in a crumbling palacio, walls adorned with frescos of Roman orgies and symbols divine, three young men, two white Europeans and an Arab. This is what it came to. They told me about a secret organisation, a power formed in the ashes of the Third Reich by old men dead long ago. Then, they said, their target had been Communism. Now their enemies were more diverse, threats fragmentary and fluid. We talked of many things – the old man in the mountains, the book of secret names locked in a vault in the Pentagon, agreements made many decades ago. Most of it was lies. I wore the mantle of a holy man or a beggar, matted hair, ragged beard, my clothes torn and stinking. After their departure the city was shaken by killings brutal even by Neapolitan standards . . .*

*the wind*

   —  Can't you tell me, Charlie, please . . . why did
you choose me?
Try not to talk.
   —  I need to know. I was nobody. I was nothing.
You were nobody.
   —  I was just a waster, a fuck-up . . .
That's right. You were a disgrace to your father's name,
to his reputation.
   —  So why me?
You must try and understand, Mark. You could have
been anybody. It was never so much what you had that
was important. It was what you didn't have.
   —  Those things I had to carry . . . the messages . . .
You were already serving your country.
   —  But . . .
Important information, Mark, vital intelligence.
   —  What was it?
I don't know. My role came later.
   —  Susanna, though . . . you married her. That I
don't understand . . .
I love your sister.
   —  It wasn't all a set-up?
I married your sister and then I met you. Understand?
A thread runs through all our lives. There are no
coincidences.

–    I feel as though my whole life has led up to this
moment.
In a sense it has, Mark. In a sense you're right.


*flicker*

'We're calling it in.'

'Wait! There's no need for that. Just give me a little more time.'

'We're very disappointed.'

'Please, just let me speak to Foxy.'

'Operation Casement has been terminated forthwith.'

'Ashe is no threat. Not any more. Just let me speak to Foxy.'

'These orders come from Foxy. We're calling it in. Get out while you still can.'

After travelling all night they reached the outskirts of hell. Tired drivers slumped at the wheel, eyes red searching for a dawn that never came . . . hinterland of pornographic film studios and weapons-testing facilities . . . churches hunched between liquor stores and ju-ju men with leashed wolves and alligator skins . . . waiting . . . Huddled languid postures on a barren, concrete beach, gathered around small fires roasting flesh and listening to the sluggish lap of water clotted as a clogged artery, thick with all the crap of the planet, great chains of waste straddling the oceans . . . and floating above it all the spectral airwave voice, a votive offering to the elements . . . *'We might think of Winthrop as the start, the event that went beyond all expectation, the storm that shattered our predictions and revealed to us how late it was, how far our planet had slipped beyond our models, our restraints and our reasons. We might. But it had already happened. It had happened and it was happening and it is happening still. Oh my children gathered on the melancholy shore, do you know about Cyclone Catarina? Not Katrina, not the fabled sinking of New Orleans, although that too was an augur of what was to follow, but Catarina, the first recorded cyclone in the South Atlantic. It struck Brazil years ago now, all the way back in 2004 when many still denied the truth of their own eyes, back when many thought we could still continue, as if all was well and all would be contained. Catarina was nothing when compared with what has followed . . . Catarina did not vanquish any city nor did it shatter an ecosystem but it was what the scientists call a threshold event, a dire portent signalling an abrupt change in our climate system . . .'* He lies on the pallet, sweating and shivering at the same time. His nurse, veiled in purple robes, sits by the transmitter, plumes of incense sweetening the air around them. '*Experts had always said that conditions in the South Atlantic meant it was impossible for hurricanes or cyclones to develop. They said sea temperatures were too low, the wind shear too strong. But they were wrong. Look at the forces that surround us. Everything that is known – mapped and monitored, assessed and evaluated – all the comforts of projection and control are intercut and overshadowed by qualities not amenable to such measures. Instability is built into every system. Chaos rules the heart of all things. More exists in this universe without our knowledge than with it and existence itself has an order no mind can compass. The clues are written in the history of our fragile planet. Look at the Younger Dryas event, thirteen thousand years ago, when a great ice dam collapsed into the Atlantic and vanquished the Gulf Stream and plunged Europe into an ice age that endured for a millennium. What can be said? Industrial capitalism, the excavation of the earth to unlock the power of the sun, the conversion of nature into disposable objects, the replacement of one system, organic and self-sufficient into another, an engine devoted to the production of waste . . . all of this has unlocked powers so powerful that our planet has been plunged into an unknown realm. We have crossed a certain threshold. We have transgressed every law of nature. The climate has humbled our powers. Technology and reason waste away in strong wind and endless sunshine. Raw power and super-stition bloom like poisonous flowers in the spaces left behind and we wander through the undergrowth, corrupt gardeners tending to our delirious blooms . . .*' The voice was fading . . . '*All this has come to pass . . .*'

Over there.
    –   You see them?
Yes.
    –   Shit.
Is your weapon ready?
    –   Yes.

     . . .

       . . .


Stay down.
                          There.
    You see them?

                            *flicker*

Hands were shaking him awake. He opened his eyes to see the woman crouching over him. The air was filled with the sound of helicopters.

'What have you done?' she hissed. 'Witch Hunters everywhere.' Wrapping a cloak around herself, she took her rifle and dashed out of the penthouse.

Behind the veil Kalat was silent.

Mark heaved himself to the window. He could hear two or three choppers circling their tower and he caught glimpses of their spidery shadows flashing past on the stark concrete of the surrounding high-rises.

It was happening. Foxy had called it in.

–   I'm cold.

*Flicker*


–   The stars, you don't think?
        The stars of heaven down to earth . . .

You see, before we left, I had an ominous feeling. I thought if I could just hold her one more time, you know, hold her like I used to and call her the silly loving names I used to call her, hold tight to the memory and make the memory eternal then if I had to die I would not be afraid . . .

    –   They ask so much of us.

The Black Hawk chopper had settled on the flat roof of the office block opposite Kalat's tower. Mark watched as a number of men clad in combat suits disembarked. The chopper rose, banking hard, rotors sounding loud in the still air of the city. The men remained on the rooftop, setting up equipment, pointing telescopes and sensors at Kalat's building. Instinctively Mark flinched back, ducking down. It wouldn't make any difference. They'd be able to see him. They'd be able to tell exactly how many people were in the building. He reached for the satellite phone, intending to beg Foxy to call off his men. If only it wasn't too late. But the phone was dead. Batteries void, signal cut off. He could hear noises in the street below and caught glimpses of figures hurrying towards the tower.

–   Can you?
        The radio.
–   Can you?
    Hello . . . this is . . .

He pulled back the veil.

Kalat looked up. Naked and cross-legged on a small mat, his worn skin glistening with snakes of sweat. A faint smile on his lips, as though he were remembering a joke long since told. In his arms he cradled a machine gun. Twists of wire and plastic littered the room around him.

'We need to leave,' said Mark. 'We don't have much time.'

'We ran out of time a long time ago.'

'They've come to kill you.'

'It was always going to happen this way.' Kalat's gaze was steady and flat as a highway across a great desert. 'Why don't you do it? Do it now. Do what they want. Kill me.'

'I tried to stop them,' he began. 'I said you were no threat. I said there was no need . . .'

'No threat? No need? Have you understood nothing?'

'At first . . . I thought . . .'

'You didn't think. You obeyed.'

'I obeyed.'

'But then they gave you no choice, did they?'

'No?'

'My very existence is a threat. They can never let us go. We know all their dirty secrets. We *are* their dirty secrets. They cannot tolerate anything to exist without their permission. Autonomous life is an insult to them. If they could, they would put all the birds of the world in a cage.'

'It's not just them. I was curious. I wondered what had happened to you.'

'Did you want to kill me?'

'I hoped it wouldn't come to that. I was thinking of Susanna. I thought . . .'

'Yes?'

'She might like to know . . .'

'What? That I was still alive?'

'Why did you never try and contact her?'

'How could I? I was dead. Better for her to live with the memory. Better for her to live with the dream of who she thought I was. She was always a true believer, full of faith and innocence. Better she never know the truth. That was my final present to her, the final token of my love.'

'But your son . . .'

Kalat frowned. 'My children are all who heed my words. My children are like spores and seeds scattered hither and thither. They are the little weeds growing through the asphalt.'

'Alisha is pregnant. I will be a father.' His voice faltered.

Kalat narrowed his eyes.

'Do you think I will ever see my child?'

Kalat exhaled softly. 'They are coming and they will kill you too. There is no turning back. Our fate was sealed a long time ago. Don't be sad, Mark. We have lived through many things. We are just a small part of the whole. Nothing is ever wholly lost. Listen.' He tilted his head. 'They come.'

   –   Twenty minutes according to headquarters.
They mean forty at least.
   –   Can we last that long?
Over there – watch out.
   –   I see them.

     . . .

        Open fire . . .
This is it.


        We're fucking surrounded.
   –   I need a fresh clip.
We're running low.
   –   We're surrounded.

Mark could hear them advancing up the tower, floor by floor. He was calm now. Calm and cool. The fever had swept through him like a storm but now everything felt clear and far away.

Scampering feet and raised voices. Then the door burst open. He fired twice, taking out the first two Witch Hunters. One struck in the heart tumbled backwards, the other jerking awkwardly, half his face blown away. Not easy to shoot with his arm so injured. A third entered the room whooping and hawing until a bullet removed his throat, and then the fourth and the fifth came rushing in, almost upon Mark as he fired, again and again, one falling back screaming and the other toppling over him. He kicked the body away, stood up and walked forward. Calm now. Calm and cool. He stood at the top of the stairwell, listening to their approach. He switched the rifle to automatic and let off a burst of fire, aiming down the stairs, the sound of the shots echoing loudly, rounds ricocheting off the concrete walls. Then he was out of ammunition, abandoning the rifle, pulling out the pistol and moving back into the penthouse.

Another Witch Hunter lunged into the room. Seemingly indifferent to death he was despatched with a single shot to the temple. Mark darted back out of the line of fire. Yet another, this one with his machine gun held high. The first shot hit the man's stomach, causing him to stumble, machine-gun fire ripping inaccurately around the penthouse. A second bullet stopped him. Mark kept his shots precise and to the point. The way he'd been trained.

He waited.

He could hear more of them, gathered on the landing, goading him.

He stepped over the dead Witch Hunters, his boots trailing bloody prints over the white floor. A casual glance outside and he could see the men watching from the building opposite, talking on radios, monitoring the assault, tracking the approach.

On the landing the mocking voices ceased. He prepared himself.

The door burst open.

The veil was torn asunder and Kalat stood, naked and terrible, an emaciated warrior with a skin of burnished steel, a machine gun in his wiry arms, a strange ululation uttered from his chapped lips. Kalat opened fire, clearing the room with two blasts. A third took out two more Witch Hunters waiting on the landing. 'Cheap fucking punks.' Kalat seized Mark, pulling him to the stairwell, in his hand a vial wrapped and bound with wires. They could hear more assailants approaching. Kalat threw the vial down the stairs and Mark remembered the explosions in the desert, the shockwaves that would ripple across the terrain. This time the blast knocked them both down, the tower shaking, a wall of smoke billowing upwards . . .

This is it.
Stars go out like candles.

# FOXY

Black flies whizzing in the heat-blistered haze. Two bodies stripped naked, unconscious on the grime-streaked tarmac.

A man with a sweep of silvery hair and a deep tan. Jaded as the most extravagant debauchee. Weary lines engraved around his eyes and forehead. A pervasive sense of ennui surrounding him. He wore a black combat suit, black boots, gloves and protective vest, a handgun and a radio dangling from his waist. Colleagues similarly attired. Tough, serious men with sunglasses and machine guns.

He stood over the bodies. 'A shame,' he sighed, waving the flies away from his face. 'A bloody rotten shame.'

Mark moaned, his eyes flickering open and shut.

'Mark,' he whispered, kneeling down and touching the injured man's hand. 'Hush . . . Best not to speak.' He put a hand over the man's lips. He could already picture himself at the funeral, offering kind words to Alisha and Susanna. What a peroration he would make, what noble sentiments he would utter, bouquets of rhetoric to grace the fallen soldier. Burrows: a hero, a noble warrior, a selfless servant of the state, tragically lost in action in enemy territory.

He turned to the other body. Ghost of a man. Wreck of a body. Bent and worn like driftwood or scrap metal. Faintest twitch of a pulse at his veiny throat. What to say about this one? Nothing. Better to say nothing at all.

He turned to the men who had brought the bodies. A dozen of them, battle-hardened warriors, their black trousers and white shirts stained with mud and sweat, black-brimmed hats torn by the exertions of war. A briefcase was handed over. 'Just make sure we never hear anything from these two again,' he said to the leader.

'A new order now reigns in the Zone,' one answered. 'God's will has been done.'

'Whatever,' he said, swatting at the flies.

The chopper circled the battered downtown summits before speeding northwards. Foxy watched the diminishing skyline. If sad, he gave no sign.

# SUNSHINE STATE

She moved from building to building, running up worn flights of stairs and jumping from flat roof to flat roof. Once she landed a little too hard, a jabbing pain in her left ankle reminding her of a previous injury when she stumbled during a skirmish with the Marines. She recovered quickly, squatting tight on her haunches, her palms pressed to the dusty tarmac, eyes peeping left and right, readying herself like a panther about to pounce. And then onwards, pirouetting through the ruins, a gymnast in a glittering leotard of dark silk and silver. On the high rooftop of an art deco block she perched behind a cluster of satellite dishes that bulged like monstrous fungi. The city had fallen and danger, never far, was now ever-present. Earlier a menacing black helicopter had circled the downtown, looking for something before disappearing northwards. Cautious, she scanned the sky, a blue fist of oblivion swimming around the blaze of a sun fat and swollen as a ball of gold. Wiping the sheen of sweat from her face she waited, her shadow stretched long and skinny across the white concrete. She did not need to wait long. A flock of birds rose from the western side of the city, the scraggy black scavengers announcing the approach of the army.

Plumes of dust swirling white and ashy and moments later

they appeared, riding one after another up the boulevard. She unslung the sniper rifle strapped across her back, set up the tripod and peered through the sights at the scene. With a whoop and a rebel yell they came galloping on pale steeds branded with crosses like crusaders of old reclaiming the Promised Land from Saracen and Moslem, their banners fluttering, dragons red and eagles fierce and the Confederate flag, totem of a South that would rise from the ruins of the old Union. At the front was a Grand Wizard perched like a bird on the jaws of a crocodile. He wore the pointed hood and long white cloak of his order, a spear clasped in one gloved hand and around his neck a garland of human ears severed from sodomites and heretics. She fixed him in the cross-hairs, her finger taut on the trigger. Behind him came the multitude. Warriors rode steeds limping with swamp rot, their white cloaks stained by the dust and blood of battle, wielding spears and swords, others wearing black cloaks and camouflage hoods, rifles and machine guns slung over their shoulders. Many were naked save for sunglasses, boots and leather thongs, their sweat-lathered bodies adorned with elaborate tattoos of the crucifixion, the word of God made flesh.

Now they came in sand buggies and stolen SUVs, pick-ups mounted with heavy machine guns, roaring motorbikes and monster trucks with tyres twice the size of a man, crushing juggernauts of Armageddon. Howl of engines, blue reeking fumes of diesel and petroleum, vehicles battered and besmeared, caked in dirt, caged with wraps of barbed wire and bull-bars and animal skulls set on bonnets and radiator grilles. She saw a truck with a human body strapped to the front, a weathered corpse of leathery skin and bones protruding and still they came, swollen with the rush of conquest. There were military Humvees, green hulls covered in stencilled quotes from the Bible, Witch Hunters riding shotgun wearing protective goggles and helmets looted from dead Marines and then a sixteen-wheeled truck, its open back packed with warriors brandishing antique cutlasses, sabres and pikes, and still they came, a convoy of vehicles loaded with supplies and weapons and others carrying cages full of prisoners, dazed Seminoles plucked from deep swamp settlements, survivors pillaged from fringe towns, criminals and runaways and members of secret gangs seized in the red. Through the rifle's sights she watched it all.

After the vehicles came others singing hallelujah and hosanna as they marched forwards. Festival macabre and antic, costumes bizarre and blasphemous: a man wearing a business suit and a Barack Obama mask roaming hand in hand with another dressed as Osama Bin Laden and then, skipping gamely forward, Hilary and Bill, he with a huge plastic phallus strapped to his waist, she with devil's tail, horns and pitchfork, and behind them minstrel Witch Hunters in blackface and others dressed as voodoo witch doctors, Catholic priests and Jewish rabbis, flamboyant transvestites with brightly coloured wigs, faces caked with foundation, crimson lipstick and blue eye shadow, wearing bikinis or long dresses and tottering in heels, and it was unclear, as she watched the gaudy procession, whether all was mockery or if the disordered spirit of carnival had consumed them, origins grown obscure and purposes forgotten in the feverish clime, many marching with open mouths slack-jawed drooling, bloodshot eyes roaming like uncut stones half-crazed with heat and sun and sleeplessness, immolated with passions perverse. Inflamed by conquest of the swamps, slaying, raping and burning until reasons blurred and intentions were forgotten and the Zone sucked them deeper into its mazy reaches, a labyrinth of thorns and bleeding briars with no way out. She saw a woman displayed on the back of a flatbed truck, arrayed in scarlet and adorned with precious stones, mincing and prancing and blowing kisses. She saw a dozen men pulling a trolley with a huge golden calf and sitting on it an obscenely fat man, his body slithery with oil, his eyes red and jaws gnashing, a lamb cradled in his arms.

Trailing after the army, a procession of exhausted refugees – downcast women and scrawny children with dirty bare feet, many pushing shopping trolleys laden with cans of food seized from flooded supermarkets or dragging heaps of bedding and belongings pulled from trailer homes and condo outposts or else religious icons, crosses and images of the Redeemer made of plastic and wood, tokens of faith manufactured in Mexican sweat-shops and pillaged from fireside churches and backstreet revivals. She watched them go until all that was left were a few stragglers, the sick and lame, people with deformed legs propelling themselves with their hands on wheeled platforms, blind men in filthy rags leaning on sticks and deranged women, bare thighs and breasts smeared with menstrual blood, and lost children with reptilian diseases, their lumpy skin like burned plastic and bubble-wrap.

Finally she saw what she had been waiting for – a small posse of Witch Hunters moving on foot. They walked with weary purposefulness, many with torn clothes and bloody injuries freshly bandaged, absent from their manner the indulgence of those before them. Carried aloft on the shoulders of several fighters were two men lashed to heavy wooden crosses. One was older than the other but his skinny body was shrunken and bent, his eyes and mouth sealed shut. The other man was stretched like metal wire, a bloody bandage covering one shoulder, his face not so easily remembered. His eyes flickered open and shut and his head lolled insensible with heat, pain and exhaustion. Tight ropes around his wrists and ankles turned the flesh purple and blue.

She had nursed both men. The first, her close companion, had fallen ill after the great battle with the Marines. As anticipated, the second had been sent after the soldiers, come to steal her man and send him back to the sun. The first she had loved, drawn to him in a dance of servitude and mastery, mesmerised by his cold charm. He represented the end of something and in his way, with all his sadness and strange words of regret and longing, he had been as beautiful and enthralling as the most melancholy twilight. The other man was a traitor and a fool.

Eventually the woman stood and turned her ebony face to the south, her skin gleaming blue-gold like freshly spilled oil, the beads and amulets that adorned her body rattling as she gathered herself, wrapping a shawl tight around her face until only her eyes were visible – brown eyes flecked gold and green – the small mirrors and silvery buckles on her belt and boots glinting light kaleidoscopic as she darted forward, fast now, a moving mosaic jumping from roof to wall to floor and running through overgrown streets, conflations of swamp and concrete, jungle and tarmac.

She found the two men set up on crucifixes in an empty precinct. The nails went in and then a crown of barbed wire. A third man was hammered to a cross beside them, a lunatic the Witch Hunters had found masturbating in a cemetery. Still conscious and seemingly oblivious to the pain, the madman railed at his tormentors until his voice became hoarse. Eventually all was silent, nothing but blood dripping on to cracked earth, the low crack of black birds ominously circling and the sun sinking in the west, shards of light blazing through the gaps between the palms, the broken windows and the gaping, empty spaces.

The woman stood for a little while, looking at the three crucified men. Perhaps the sight stirred in her some distant memory of things she had witnessed as a child, in another country, a long time ago. She watched for a while longer but she ventured no closer. Then she too was gone.

# ACKNOWLEDGEMENTS

I wish to thank my parents, Kevin and Roxanna Miller, and my grandmother Brenda Rawlinson: they have given my writing their unfailing support for so many years now – without them this book would not have been possible.

I would also like to thank John Saddler, Richard Beswick and everybody at Little, Brown for all their advice and hard work.